One Mississippi

One Mississippi

A NOVEL

MARK CHILDRESS

Little, Brown and Company
NEW YORK   BOSTON

Little, Brown and Company
Hachette Book Group USA
1271 Avenue of the Americas, New York, NY 10020
Visit our Web site at www.HachetteBookGroupUSA.com

First Edition: July 2006

Library of Congress Cataloging-in-Publication Data

Childress, Mark.
  One Mississippi : a novel / Childress—1st ed.
    p. cm.
  ISBN-13: 978-0-316-01211-9 (hardcover)
  ISBN-10: 0-316-01211-4 (hardcover)
  1. High school students—Fiction.   2. Male friendship—Fiction.   3. Mississippi—
Fiction.   1. Title.
PS3553.H486O54 2006
813'.54—dc22   2006002337

10 9 8 7 6 5 4 3 2 1

Q-MART

Book designed by Brooke Koven

Printed in the United States of America

For Kirby

One Mississippi

I

"You feel anything?"

"Nope."

"Maybe you're supposed to hold it in longer."

It was summer in Indiana, the week before I turned sixteen. All afternoon my friends and I had been on our bikes, following the mosquito truck through the streets, breathing the sweet-smelling clouds of DDT because we'd heard it would get you high.

One glimpse of Dad's steel-blue Oldsmobile Delta 88 in our driveway on a Thursday was enough to bring all the fun screeching to a halt. I waved the boys to go on without me.

My father was a good man — I can say that now, after all these years and everything that happened — but on a day-to-day basis, he was about as fun as Hitler. Dimly I remembered a time when he picked us up in his arms, hugged us, played with us like any other dad. As we got older, though, he turned against us. He had to be hard, he said, to keep us from turning out soft.

His name was Lee Ray Musgrove. He came from a poor Alabama family of Musgroves who went all the way broke in the Depression. Dad never got over how poor they used to be. The Depression always loomed over our family like a dark thundercloud, a certain promise of doom just beyond the horizon.

Every Monday at four a.m. Dad would arise to eat his lonely bowl of Wheat Chex, check his list of sales calls, and head out to keep that thundercloud at bay for one more week. Monday to Friday he was a traveling salesman, the jolliest most hardworking devoted salesman in the history of TriDex, District Salesmanager of the Year three years in a row, a good smile, a nice word for everybody. All week he saved up his anger, all the slights and disappointments and frustrations of a salesman's life, and on Friday nights he brought it all home to us.

But now he was home on a Thursday. This was different. At our house, different was never good.

I managed to stow my bike in the garage without making a sound. The back door squealed and gave me away. His growl from the family room: "Get in here. Where have you been?"

When Dad used that voice, he didn't want an answer. I crept into the room. The whole family was gathered around the TV but the set was turned off. This must be some really bad news.

I eased myself down between Bud and Janie on the sofa. They all looked so somber I thought someone must have died.

"All present and accounted for," Dad said. "Okay, here's the big announcement. I got a transfer. We're moving again."

I tingled all over, as if my body had gone to sleep for an instant. *A transfer.* TriDex transferred its salesmen every year or two, to keep them on their toes. Indiana was our sixth transfer in ten years. TriDex did not know or care that this was my favorite of all the places we had lived. Lately I'd been hoping we might get to stay here. I loved Indiana. I had lots of friends. It was flat, you could ride your bike everywhere. In the winter it froze hard and snowed a lot, so you could stay inside and watch TV all the time.

I waded into the rising silence: "Moving where?"

"Mississippi," said Dad, "and I don't want any lip out of you."

"Aw now, Lee, don't say it that way." Mom interposed herself between Dad by the sliding glass door and us on the sofa. "Y'all, this is big news for Daddy — for all of us, really. You know how bad I been wanting to get closer to Granny and Jacko . . . and you know how I hate the winters up here."

That was true. Mom was a flower of the South. Her feet had been cold since the first time Dad moved her away from Alabama.

"Are you nuts?" Bud said. "We can't move now, Mom. I just made varsity." Bud was a wrestler. Dad was proud of the fact that Bud wrestled so hard he puked after every match.

"Aw now, Bud, come on, it's a better territory for Daddy," said Mom, "and anyway we haven't got a choice, so let's just go on and be happy about it."

"You all can go, I don't care, I'm staying," said Bud. "I'm a senior this fall, Mom, we can't move to — where did you say? Mississippi? That's the dumbest thing I ever heard!"

Bud took my breath away saying things like that, things that would have got me backhanded and sent to my room. Dad darkened and loomed in his corner, but stayed silent. Bud looked like Dad, and Dad respected him for that.

"Okay Bud, you stay here," Mom said with a desperate smile. "Who's gonna cook your supper and wash your dirty clothes?"

"If Buddy's staying I wanna stay," Janie said.

"Nobody's staying," said Mom. "We know how to move, we've done it plenty of times. The movers will be here Monday morning bright and early to start packing."

Bud got up and slammed down the hall to his room *BANG!*

"I'll be dog," said my father. "I'll be god dog, that boy . . ."

"Now Lee," Mom said, "don't start."

"Start what? Don't *you* start."

"I told you they'll need some time, honey. Of course they're not gonna be happy at first — having to go off from all their little friends." She turned anxious eyes on Janie and me. "I promise, you'll like it down there. You'll make new friends. Daddy's found us a beautiful house in the country. The schools are supposed to be great."

I mustered up a sneer. "Yeah, I bet. Mississippi?" I'd never been there, but I knew all about it from the evening news. Mississippi was last in everything you could measure. There was nothing down there but redneck sheriffs and protesting Negroes and civil rights workers buried in earthen dams.

"There's nothing wrong with Mississippi," Mom said. "It's nice and warm, for one thing, and at least the people will understand me when I talk."

"What if we don't want to go?" I said. "Why do we have to?"

"Daddy's got a new territory." She fingered a sheaf of honey-gold hair from her eyes. "A smaller territory, so he won't have to be gone so much." She turned smiling, but Dad's eyes were narrowed down, fixed on me, waiting for one word that would give him the right to come over there and strangle me.

"Mississippi is the Magnolia State," Janie read from the *World Book*. "The capital is Jackson. The products are cotton, lumber, poultry, and cattle."

"Good, Janie," said Mom. "I told you those books would come in handy."

Mom was trying to sell this as a big promotion for Dad, but I knew better. I was almost sixteen, I knew everything. I read their mail, I went through their filing cabinet. I read the life insurance policy and thrilled at how rich we kids would be if they died. Many nights I had heard my father god-dogging the name of Larry Semple, his district manager. I knew that a smaller territory in Mississippi had to be a comedown from a three-state sales district based in Indiana. I knew just where to stick in the knife. "Why does he have a smaller territory?"

A subterranean vibration from Dad's side of the room, a trembling of air.

Janie preened for the invisible camera that always followed her around. "Well, I'm *glad* we're moving," she announced. "I hate this place too, Mama. It's cold. And I want to live closer to Granny."

"Attagirl," Mom said. "The power of positive thinking."

I coughed the word "suck-up" into my hand.

"Mom! He called me a suck-up!"

"I did not. I coughed. Can't a person even cough?"

On Monday we watched the movers load our things onto a giant orange tractor-trailer from Allied Van Lines.

On Tuesday we set out down the brand-new interstate highway toward our future. We drove all day, into the late afternoon. South of Memphis we hit a bump that banged my cheek against the glass. The four-lane highway had become a broken two-lane. A sign said

WELCOME TO MISSISSIPPI

The land flattened out and got wide. At first glance it looked like Indiana again: green flat fields running off to the horizon, fence lines and grain elevators in the blue distance. But instead of neat Midwestern farmhouses I saw tarpaper shacks, poor black folks on the porches: skinny kids in rags, stooped old men in straw hats. Occasionally a mansion peeked out of a huge grove of oaks — a Greek temple with columns, white and impressively hidden.

Mom said, "Can you imagine living in a house like that? I would feel just like Scarlett."

"Mama," said Janie, "that girl hasn't got on a shirt."

"Don't stare, Jane. People can't help it if they're not as well off as us."

"Hmp." My father scratched his neck. "Anybody's willing to work can get along these days. Not like we had it in the Depression."

"They let her just run around without a shirt?" Janie threw herself against the seat to watch the girl receding in the rear window. "She's as old as me."

"Well, it's hot down here, honey," said Mom. "I'm sure she has a nice shirt she wears all the time."

In our air-conditioned car we were almost chilly, but beyond the glass you could see waves of heat rising up from the road and the fields. Even flashing by at sixty-five miles an hour, you could see sweat on people's faces.

"Oh heavenly days," Mom said, "it's so good to be home. Let's just open up and see how she feels." She cranked down her window. In an instant, every ounce of cool air was sucked out and replaced with this blast of summer air — a hot, wet slap in the face. We hollered and moaned until Mom rolled the window back up.

She grinned. "Hot! Just like I like it." Now that we were back in the South, Mom's accent had kicked in — the thickest sweetest south-Alabama accent you ever heard. *Just lack I lack it!*

"I am never going outside again — never," said Bud. "This house better have dang good air-conditioning."

"Oh, you'll be seeing plenty of outside," Dad assured him. "You boys got a world of grass to cut."

"It's a country place, y'all," Mom said. "It's out from town, so it's got all the peace and quiet you'd ever want, and a great big old yard. I can't wait to put in some azaleas. They'll be blooming when Indiana is still up to their eyeballs in snow."

"Nobody knows if the stupid school even has a wrestling team," Bud said.

"I'm sure if they don't, they have something just as good," said Mom. "They practically invented football down here."

"I hate football," said Bud.

"Don't let anybody down here hear you say that," Dad said. "I mean it, Bud."

"Mommy, I'm hungry," said Janie.

"Well you weren't twenty minutes ago, when we had lunch." Mom rattled the Kroger sack. "What you want, honey? Peanut butter, or there's still one ham and cheese."

"Peanut butter but take off the crust."

"The crust is the best part," said Dad.

Dad was not just saying this to make Janie eat the crust. This was the thing about Dad: not only was the crust good enough for Dad, he considered it the *best part*. He liked the neck of the chicken on Sunday. He liked leftover corn pone with cracklins, served cold, with turnip greens, for breakfast. He liked food that tasted like when he was poor.

He squinted into the distance at the long line of cars backed up in our lane — a traffic jam in the middle of nowhere, stretching around the next curve. "Would you look at this?" He blew out a sigh as if all these cars had stopped way out here just to get on his nerves. He folded his hands behind his neck, cracked his shoulder joints. "Come on, people," he said, drumming his fingers on the wheel. "We got miles to go."

We idled behind an old station wagon from Kentucky, overflowing with kids who stuck out their tongues at us and smeared their dirty feet on the windows. You could just smell the misery rolling off that car. The parents were shrunk down in the front seat, ignoring everything to the best of their ability.

"Thank God we had just the three," said Dad.

Mom smiled. "Amen to that."

"You guys," Bud said. "Thanks a lot."

"Take a look at that car, boy," said Dad. "That right there is as good an argument for birth control as you'll ever see."

"Lee."

Janie said, "What's birth control?"

"Now see what you started?"

"It's a way of making sure you don't take on more than you can handle." Dad laid his hand on the horn to join the chorus.

Across a flat field I saw a column of black smoke rising behind a wall of pines. "Hey Dad, something's burning."

He looked where I was pointing. "You know you may be right, it's a durn house afire, and all these people are just rubbernecking." He pounded the horn. "Get a move on! Didn't you ever see a fire before?" The guy with all the children honked too, and waved his fist out the window.

That was something large and on fire, sending up rolling clouds of black smoke and flashes of flame. The people in front of us began three-point-turning their cars, driving past us.

Mom said, "Everybody's going the other way."

Dad coasted forward one car length. "It would take you twice as long, time you went around." He fiddled with the radio, settling on an old flat-voiced man giving a farm report.

"Your soybeans is headed up again, and your cotton holding steady as she goes," the man said. "All you boys out spraying today, this report is brought to you by the good people of TriDex Chemical, We Know What Bugs You."

My father said, "Hey hey!" and turned up the volume. "Listen to that. Just got here and already talking about us on the radio."

"That's a good sign," said Mom. "It's like a welcome. I tell you, Lee, this is all going to work out for the best."

More people were giving up, turning around, heading the other way.

We crept around the bend. Now we could see it was not a house burning but something in the road, hidden by the rise just ahead. State trooper cars flashed blue lights. Troopers in wide-brimmed hats waved traffic off the highway.

"Heck of an accident," Dad said. "Must be a tanker truck, way it's burning."

"That's cool," said Bud.

"It's not 'cool,' Bud," Mom said. "Someone might be hurt."

"No, but I mean look at it burn," Bud said.

"Don't get too close, Daddy. I don't want to see any burned people."

"Don't worry, Janie. Neither do I."

Now we could see it was a tractor-trailer jackknifed, sprawled on its side across both lanes. A crowd of firemen and state troopers stood at a healthy distance, watching the fire — a huge orange toy, broken and burning, pouring fire from the cab and the split-open trailer.

Two men in gray uniforms stood off to one side. One of them bent over with his hands on his knees, as if he was about to throw up.

It took me a moment to think, Hey I know that guy, and to flash a picture of where I'd seen him: yesterday, closing the doors of the Allied Van Lines truck at our house in Indiana.

"Hey Dad," I said, "that's the guy who put our stuff on the truck."

"What?"

"That guy, there! Isn't he the guy from Allied?"

And then it dawned on me why our driver was standing there

with those state troopers beside the burning wreck. The wreck was his truck. Our truck.

Dad steered the Oldsmobile onto the grassy bank. He switched off the engine, rolled down his window, folded his hands on the wheel. Hot acrid air filled the car. We heard the popping and crackling, the rifle-shot of aerosol cans exploding, a deep monstrous underneath sound, like a beast sucking air.

Janie said, "Why did we stop?"

"You idiot!" I cried. "Don't you get it? That's our stuff!"

"What do you mean our *stuff.*"

"Children." I shiver to remember the silvery calm of Mom's voice. "I don't want to hear another word."

A trooper came bowlegging down the hill toward us. "Folks," he said, "I'm gone have to ask you-all to just move on along."

My father's neck turned very red, as if he'd been sunburned suddenly. I could not see his face, but the sight of it was enough to back the trooper up a step.

"Come on now," he said. "Y'all had your look, let's move on along now."

My father did not speak. He just stared at the man.

"Sir? Maybe you didn't hear what I said."

My mother leaned across the seat. "Officer, that truck is from Allied Van Lines, isn't it?"

"Why, yes ma'am, it is."

"Well see, I'm Peggy Musgrove, and this is my husband Lee? And the thing is, I do believe those are our belongings on that truck."

"Hm." The man's face didn't change. "Y'all movin' down this way?"

"Yes, sir, we were," Mom said, in a voice that probably sounded chipper to him, but seemed to me one note short of a scream.

"Well, I hate to be the one to tell you, ma'am, but I don't think you're gone be able to save too much out of that." He indicated the conflagration with a little wave of his hand, as if maybe we hadn't noticed it. "Could you ask your husband to come up here and talk to us a minute?"

"I don't think he is able, right now," Mom said. "Would it be all right if I came in his place?"

Bud opened his door. "I'll go with you, Mom."

"Me too," I said.

"Bud, you come. Daniel, you and Janie stay here with Daddy." She glanced at her hair in the mirror and got out, smoothing her skirt.

I had often seen our mother rise to one occasion or the other, but I've never seen her rise as she rose that afternoon. She marched with Bud up among all those troopers and stood answering their questions as if she had practiced for just such an occasion.

We watched the truck burn. Dad squeezed the steering wheel.

The Allied driver sat under a tree with his head on his knees. The other man crouched beside him, whispering in his ear.

In the roaring innards of the split-open trailer I saw Mom's antique hall tree ablaze, all the wardrobe boxes, the jumble of the dinette set, chrome legs drooping like wilted flowers. Our possessions made a hot fire. The firemen stood watching with excited eyes. I guess they had decided to let it burn awhile before turning on their hoses. I heard a great crackle-cracking and a *BOOM* as our television shot straight up from the inferno, sailed through the air, and smashed facedown on the pavement in front of me.

A fresh cloud of fire billowed up from the wreck. Some of the passing cars honked their horns, cheering this display.

After a long time, Bud and Mom got back in the car. Dad started the engine and gunned onto the highway, spraying gravel.

We rode at least a mile before the first sound — the *scritch!* of Mom's Zippo. "Lee," she said carefully, around a mouthful of smoke, "I understand if you're too upset to talk. Probably just as well. But we're all here, honey, we're all together and safe, and it doesn't matter if we lost those things. Just things, Lee. The insurance will replace it. It's none of our fault — not yours, and not mine. It was that driver. The son of a bitch was drunk."

"Mama, you cussed!" Janie cried.

"Shut up, Janie. He was drunk, Lee, I could smell the whiskey from ten feet away, and the troopers, they smelled it too."

"I didn't take the insurance," Dad said.

Mom cocked her head to one side. "What was that?"

"Homeowners don't cover stuff while it's on the truck. The movers wanted extra for it, and TriDex won't reimburse it. So I declined. I had to sign a paper saying I declined."

"You did that?" Mom said.

"You know how much they wanted for insurance that only lasts three days?" he said.

"Well!" She let out the breath she'd been holding. "Isn't that interesting." In our house the only thing worse than "different" was "interesting."

How long do you think five people can ride in a car without talking? Let me tell you, it's longer than you think. We kept driving, long after dark. I would bet we drove for three hours without anyone saying another word.

At last Mom gave a tentative cough. "Lee, shouldn't we be close to Jackson by now?"

My father never even glanced away from the road.

Mom said, "Honey, that sign said twelve miles to Hattiesburg. Isn't Hattiesburg south of Jackson? You know, I believe it is. I believe we have done rode right past Jackson. Bud, would you please hand me that map?"

My father kept driving. Even when Mom turned on the dome light and confirmed that we were seventy miles southeast of Jackson and getting farther away every second, my father had nothing to contribute to the conversation.

As we entered the outskirts of Hattiesburg, Mom said, "Lee, now, you're scaring me, honey. Let's just stop for the night at one of these motels. I'm sure we'll all feel much better after a good night's sleep."

Dad didn't answer. When we drew abreast of the Rebel Yell Motor Lodge, he suddenly turned the car in and jerked to a stop at the office. He left the motor running. He went in and came back with a key.

I don't know why I felt moved to speak. It was like when I was little, playing hide-and-seek — I could find a good place to hide, but I couldn't stand staying hidden. I always gave myself away.

I got up on my knees in the backseat to peer out the window. "Dad," I said, "are you crazy? We can't stay here. The pool doesn't even have a *slide*."

It's a good thing there are laws against killing your kids. What I will never know is how he managed to hit me all the way from the car to the room without making a sound of his own.

2

THE OLD SCHOOL bus labored up the hill toward us, belching and groaning, flashing its one working headlight as a warning. The bus was so dilapidated I had to laugh — it looked hilarious, ridiculous, like a cartoon of a hillbilly school bus in *Mad* magazine. We had only been in Mississippi for two weeks. So far everything about it struck me as pretty damn funny.

"Last bus to Hooterville," I announced.

Bud didn't even smile. He was still half asleep. Janie hopped up and down on one foot and ignored me.

The bus squealed to a halt and flapped open its door. "Hurry up!" said the red-faced man at the wheel.

I climbed on after Janie and Bud. The bus lurched ahead, sending the three of us stumbling, free-falling down the aisle, crashing in a heap to the floor.

The other kids roared with laughter. Apparently this was a trick the driver liked to play on newcomers who didn't have the sense to hold on.

I untangled myself from Bud. We helped Janie up from the floor and tucked ourselves into the nearest empty seats. I saw the driver's grin in the overhead mirror. The air on the bus smelled like sour milk. The green vinyl seat covers were so worn you could see cheesecloth showing through the gaps.

Janie said, "I think I hurt my arm."

"This is all a bad dream," muttered Bud. "I just want to wake up."

"Too late," I said. "We should have run away while we had the chance."

"I'm working on it," Bud said. "I didn't get to be seventeen and a half just to get dragged down to this stupid hellhole for the rest of my life."

A red-haired boy turned all the way around in his seat to gawp at us. "Y'all!" he cried. "Listen at 'em talk! Go on! Say somethin' else!"

"Excuse me?" said Janie. "Are you speaking to us?"

Her Yankee accent brought a titter from both ends of the bus. The black kids leaned up in their seats to hear better.

We'd had a lecture from Dad about keeping our heads down, staying out of trouble. Our first day of school also happened to be the first day of court-ordered integration in the public schools of Mississippi. Everyone was half expecting knife fights and riots.

The red-haired boy couldn't get enough of us. "Where y'all fum?"

"Indiana," I said. "But our parents come from Alabama originally. Are you guys all from Mississippi?"

Everybody laughed. Nobody from Mississippi pronounces the middle syllable, as I would come to know. They say "Mis'sippi," as if it's too hot down here and too exhausting to say the whole word. Another boy repeated what I'd said exactly, "Mis-sis-sippi" and "originally" and "you gize" in this high-pitched nasal imitation of me that brought a big laugh from his friends.

I felt my face redden. I was used to being the one doing the laughing.

"Make the girl talk again," someone called from up front.

I pressed my face to the window and let my mind wander outside. The bus stopped at every kind of house, down to the shackiest tar-paper shack. Some of these places were so poor you couldn't tell which of the fallen-down structures were for people and which for the animals. The kids from the poorest houses were white — skinny, sickly-looking kids with faces like wild kittens. They clustered at the front of the bus, three and four to a seat.

The black kids walked past us to the back of the bus and sat together. Everyone knew they didn't have to do that, not since Rosa Parks in Montgomery, but they seemed to prefer it that way.

In Indiana you never saw people like this. In Indiana everyone was white, we were all the same. We lived in neat ranch houses and bought our clothes at Sears, Roebuck. On this bus, we three Musgroves stuck out like dressed-up Sears mannequins. We were nothing like these unsmiling black kids, or the tough redneck boys and their sisters, or the bus driver who barked at every last kid to hurry up, even the ones who were already hurrying.

Janie was almost thirteen, a whiz kid at math, a significant pain in my butt. Just now she looked like a little child on the verge of tears. "Why are they laughing at us?"

"Oh, you'll be okay," I said. "Just ignore 'em. Pretend we're still in Indiana but everybody talks weird. That's what I plan to do."

"How come y'all ain't going over to the Council?" said our red-headed friend. "You look like you oughta be going over there."

"Our dad is too cheap to send us," Bud said.

Council schools were springing up all over Mississippi, the White Citizens' Council's answer to desegregation. Dad said he didn't care how bad the public schools were, he wasn't about to pay to send us to a private school operated by the Ku Klux Klan.

Instead he made sure to buy a house in one of the "consolidated" school districts springing up around Jackson — integrated enough to be legal, white enough to be comfortable. Our new house was in the country eleven miles outside Minor, which was ten miles outside Jackson. The sign at the Minor city limits meant to call it One of Mississippi's Nicest Towns, but someone had changed it with spray paint:

ONE OF MISSISSIPPI'S   TOWNS

From the outside, Minor High looked like a regular school: low and long, with tan brick, a flat roof, and one modernistic touch, a round glass-walled library nestled like a flying saucer in the front courtyard. The halls smelled of chalk dust and disinfectant, lunch-room spaghetti, Brut, Charlie, Right Guard. I heard lockers banging, gym shoes squeaking on a floor, a trumpet section rehearsing a fight song.

I was relieved to see other kids in clothes that might have come from Sears. Not everyone looked as rawboned and poor as the kids on our bus. Maybe it was because our house was so far out from town. Those were country kids on the Hooterville route.

In my shiny new Florsheims I clopped down the hall to Miss Anderson's homeroom. All the black students sat together at the back. I sat in front with others of my kind. Miss Anderson was a pleasant black lady who called roll, then sat quietly painting her fingernails until, half an hour later, the bell rang.

Every class was like that, all day. After all the uproar in the news-papers about integration, nobody even mentioned it. It was hard for us whites to feel threatened, since we outnumbered them four to one and they sat in the back.

Nobody tried to teach us anything. The teachers took roll, handed out textbooks, then spent the hour gossiping in the doorway with other teachers while the students fired spitballs and caught up on their summers.

Fourth-period English was Mrs. Thomas, a big black lady who got our attention by smacking the blackboard with her open hand. "Listen up! Y'all gonna learn one thing in my class, and that is the writings of Mister William Shatespeare. He just about the best writer they ever was." She wrote his name on the board, *Shakespeare.* We would be reading a "whole mess" of his plays, she said, including "Julius Seizure," "Hamblit," and "Henry V-8."

I looked around to see if anyone else found this amusing. I saw a smirk lighting up the face of a pale, lanky kid with a shock of black hair falling into his eyes. He was struggling to keep from laughing out loud.

After Mrs. Thomas went to chat in the hallway he swung into the desk beside mine, darkly muttering, "Henry V-8!"

That cracked me up.

He said he was Tim. I told him I was Daniel. We shook hands on it. I was pleased to find they used the same cool-guy handshake down here as in Indiana — hook thumbs, then wrap your hands together to make a mutual fist.

"What if I told you Mrs. Thomas is one of the best teachers?" he said. "Wait till you see her act out the parts. She does an incredible Romeo."

"I thought there weren't any black teachers last year," I said.

"Hey, what are you saying?" Tim looked shocked. "You mean — Miz Thomas is black?"

It took me a second to be sure he was kidding.

He winked to confirm it. "Minor's always had a few Negro teachers," he said, "to show we're not prejudiced."

"But no black students, right?"

"Not till today."

I followed him up the hall. "So I guess the whole integration thing turns out to be not such a big deal after all, huh?"

"Oh, it's a big deal, all right. Everybody's killing themselves trying to act like it's not, but it is. Don't worry, you'll catch on to how things work down here. The one thing you're never supposed to do is talk about it."

"Oh. Sorry."

Tim smiled. "I mean to other people. You can talk to me about anything. I can translate for you. I have been trained to speak and understand most forms of Yankee."

All you need is one friend who makes you laugh, who laughs at the same things you do. Almost at once I knew Tim Cousins would be my friend. We had three classes together. He enjoyed making fun of everything as much as I did. Right there on the first day of school, we formed a team, just the two of us.

Tim said Minor High was perhaps the best school in the greater Minor metropolitan area. I said my lousy first impression probably stemmed from the fact that I was a Yankee snob from Yankeeland.

The teachers seemed to be fresh out of junior college, or else they were cranky old women teaching out their time until retirement. In retrospect my teachers in Indiana seemed witty, dynamic.

"You should have stayed up there," Tim said. "If I'd known you were coming, I could have warned you."

"It wasn't my choice," I told him. "My parents kidnapped me and brought me here by force."

I explained how we had lost all our worldly goods on the trip south, so we were having to furnish our new home one garage sale at a time.

"Your family sounds almost as weird as mine," Tim said. "How long are you in for?"

"Twenty to life."

He grinned, and clapped me on the back. "Me too! We can be lifers together!"

After lunch the day slowed to a crawl. I made elaborate doodles in my notebook with my new felt-tip pen. It seemed forever until the three o'clock bell.

Bud plopped beside me on the bus. "How'd it go?"

"Okay, I guess. I met one guy that's cool."

"That's one more than me," he said. "Are all your teachers complete morons?"

"Seems like it."

"Mine are, definitely." He cast a disparaging eye at the kids getting on the bus. "We gotta tell Dad. We can't go to this school. We'll be as dumb as these people in a month."

"Are you crazy, Bud? Don't you dare say a word. Think about it — guaranteed straight A's from now on, and we never have to crack a book. I mean, I'm a junior, and they're just now reading 'Julius Seizure.' We read it in ninth."

"I swear our history teacher was drunk," Bud said.

I told him everything I'd learned about the school from Tim Cousins. Mrs. Passworth, the algebra teacher, was rumored to have spent time in a mental institution. Miss Williford's French I and II classes were legendary; she spent two-thirds of every class period

showing slides of her three trips to Paris. Mr. Mapes, in social stud-
ies, would write the answers on the board the day before a test, and
he never gave below a C. Every day in fifth-period chemistry, Mrs.
Deavers put her head on her desk and took a nap. You were welcome
to nap too, do whatever you liked, as long as you didn't disturb Mrs.
Deavers.

Janie got on the bus with this smirky grin.

"You okay, Idjit? How'd you make out?"

"Daniel, this school is so easy!"

"Shhh . . . that's gonna be our little secret."

Mom and Dad never asked how we became straight-A students
overnight. At school I quickly learned to modify my Yankee ways. I
rolled up my sleeves and let my shirttail hang out at the back, in
keeping with the fashion down here. After enduring dozens of sarcastic remarks about my Indiana accent I began saying "y'all" for "you
guys," "Co-Cola" instead of "pop," and "seb'm" for the number after
six. I learned to say "ain't" and "cain't" and "hale, yeah," and of course,
"Mis'sippi."

Bud did not try to adapt. He lived in his room with his portable
TV, except for the daylight hours, when we were mostly outside cutting grass. Our new house was a brick rancher, with four dinky white
columns holding up the front porch roof, but it was set on a rolling
lawn so huge that Mom said it made her feel like Scarlett O'Hara. I
pointed out that Scarlett had slaves to take care of her yard. "And I
have you boys," she said with a smile.

Three acres of grass in Mississippi was a job that never ended. By
the time you mowed down the last patch of V-headed stalks, new V's
had sprung up where you started. If you missed a couple of days,
the lawn turned into a jungle of high green uncuttable Mississippi
piano wire, teeming with biting flies, no-see-ums, yellow jackets, and
fire ants.

Dad bought us a huge Yazoo mower with a thirty-inch blade and
bike-sized rear wheels for leverage — a real Rottweiler of a mower
that made our old Indiana Lawn Boy look like a poodle by compar-
ison. It took strength just to push the Yazoo across the flat part of the

yard. Great gouts of grass spewed up from the chute, bathing me in a swirl of green dust.

Bud and I took turns at the helm of this monster. This was our welcome to Mississippi: incredible heat that started early and cranked hot all day and stayed sweltering long after dark, August all the way through September and straight on into October without any letup, muggy heat and mosquitoes and the roaring Yazoo and the tang of cut grass and Dad coming out to point out the spots we had missed. I grew to hate every inch of that yard, every fire-ant hill and rock poking up, every patch of gravel spitting back at me like shrapnel. I prayed for a hard freeze to come sweeping down from the north.

On his birthday, November 11, Bud stood up at the supper table to announce that he had joined the Marines.

Mom and Dad were appalled — Vietnam was on Cronkite every night — but there was nothing they could do to stop him. Bud was eighteen. He had signed the papers.

"Basic's hard, but then it gets better," he told me that night. We were up late eating big bowls of vanilla ice milk drowned in Hershey's syrup, and watching Johnny Carson. "You get to pick your specialty. I could learn to fly a helicopter, or electronics. All kind of things."

"Buddy, you can't leave me to cut all this grass by myself!"

"Sorry, brother. You knew I was never gonna make it down here."

"I could go with you," I said. "I could say I'm eighteen too."

"First off, who would believe that, and anyway, Dad would come after you and kill you. No Danny, you gotta stick it out like I did."

"You've only been here a couple of months. I've got two whole *years* until I graduate."

"Think about poor Janie. She's got, what, five years in this dump? If Dad doesn't get transferred again." Bud licked his spoon. "You'll both turn into total rednecks, you watch. You're already starting to talk like them."

"No I ain't." I grinned. "Dadgummit!"

Three days later it was time for Bud to go to Parris Island. Dad didn't want any scenes at the bus station, so we had our scene in the driveway at home. Mom cried. Janie ran wailing into the house. I swallowed my grief and stared at the new seed heads poking up from the grass we had mowed just the day before. "Come back soon, Buddy," I said.

He turned my hug into a handshake and finished it off with a slap on the back. "Take care, brother. And stay out of my room. Mom? Make sure he stays out."

No need to worry: that room would become a shrine to Bud the Departed. Only Mom would be allowed in that room, to dust and to weep over his wrestling trophies. A perfectly good TV would sit in there going to waste, on the chance that someday Bud might come back and want to watch it.

Bud had always been my best friend. We grew up together. He learned how to do everything first, then taught me how. I would miss him so much, but I wasn't going to be such a baby as to cry about it.

Anyway I had another friend now. Tim Cousins. All you really need is one.

3

Every Saturday night Tim and I watched *The Sonny and Cher Comedy Hour* over the phone, Tim in his house in town, me sprawled in our family room out on Buena Vista Drive.

"Sonny Bono is so grotesque," Tim said. "Why do you think she ever married him? He's not handsome, not funny, he can't carry a tune. He pretends to be making fun of himself, but actually he thinks he's so smart for marrying a meal ticket like Cher. Look at that smirk."

"Maybe he's got a big wingwang," I said.

"But God, he's so queer! Would you look at that nasty mustache . . . it's like one of those vacuum cleaner attachments you use to clean upholstery. I bet he gets food and stuff caught in it all the time. I bet it gets all sopping with Cher's vulvular juices."

"God, Tim, gross me out why don't you?"

"Wait wait wait," he said, fumbling the phone. "Here comes her solo."

At some point in every show, Cher would emerge in an outrageous Bob Mackie costume to sing a torchy ballad. Cher was skinny with no boobs to speak of, but Bob Mackie cut her gowns on dramatic angles to create the illusion of boobs. Each week we waited to see how Bob would surpass the previous week's spectacular — a blinding curtain of red sparkles, a beaded lime-green wraparound thing with a skullcap, a thatch of springy wires with little balls on the end. This week Cher was the center of an explosion of white feathers, perched on a swing in a giant birdcage, a stuffed Dove of Peace mounted in her hair. She looked fabulous and absurd on her birdswing, singing a throaty ballad, "Your Love Is Like a Golden Cage."

Tim's laugh was sharp and startling, like a terrier's bark. "Ha! Look at that! Incredible!"

"I must say, I am speechless."

"Looks like that dove is about to crap on her head."

"That's *just* what I was thinking!"

Tim said, "So listen, have you given any thought to the prom?"

My heart tugged downward in my chest. Tim had a way of lobbing in these big hand-grenade questions as casually as if he were tossing flowers. "No," I lied, "I haven't even thought about it." The Junior-Senior Prom was early this year — the first week of April, less than four weeks away.

"Better start thinking. Gotta buy the tickets by Monday. Unless of course you don't want to go."

"What do you mean? We *have* to go, don't we? I mean, everybody's going. Wouldn't it be weird if we just didn't go?"

Tim persisted. "So who were you thinking of asking?"

A flutter of panic in my chest. "I have no idea. You?"

"I asked you first."

"Okay, you're right, this is serious. Let's see. What if I ask Terri Cawthon, and you ask Mary Jo Parks."

"Mary Jo is so stuck up."

"Yeah, but she likes you. I bet she would go with you."

"Not a chance. She'll go with Bill Munger," said Tim. "You really think Terri Cawthon would go with you?"

"I don't know. Maybe not. Why not?"

"Who else could we ask?" he said.

"Uhm . . . Lisa and Molly?"

"Are you nuts? Lisa's practically going steady with Randy Felts, he's gonna ask her any minute. And Molly will go with Gary Brantley, won't she? I mean, I just assumed."

"I guess you're right." Lisa and Molly were cheerleaders: cute, glamorous, popular. Tim and I were buddies of theirs. We were fine for kidding around in the lunch line, but for dating they had real boyfriends — big handsome football players at the top of the Minor High popularity pyramid. You wouldn't find Lisa and Molly sitting home on a Saturday night watching *Sonny and Cher*.

"How about the McLemores? They crack me up."

"They're going with Kirby and what's-his-name," said Tim. "But I did have an idea. Just an idea, now, don't get all . . . you know."

"Who?"

"Debbie and Dianne."

"Oh please. Are you joking?"

"Think about it. They're nice. We'd have fun. And besides, you know they'd say yes."

"But Tim. They're such —"

"Don't," he said. "Don't say it. Nice girls, Durwood. They're *nice*. They have great personalities."

It was true. Everybody liked the Frillinger sisters. They were fraternal twins. Neither one had been treated kindly by the looks department. They wore chunky eyeglasses, steel-wire-and-rubber-band appliances on their teeth, and plain shapeless dresses sewn by their mother. Their family belonged to some Full Gospel Pentecostal church in which dowdiness was part of the religion. They belonged to the Glee Club, the band, Christian Youth Fellowship, 4-H, Campus Life, Math Club, Science Club, and the Future Homemakers of America. They were very nice girls. Girls you asked for the algebra notes, not to the prom.

Not that Tim and I were exactly prime prom material ourselves. We weren't all that ugly, but we were brain/loser, musical, intellectual, verbal, nonathletic geeks. We ran with the brain/loser/choir/band/geek underground. My favorite subject was band; Tim's was art. The only sport we were good at was making withering jokes about the popular kids.

Tim was tall and skinny and pale, with that thatch of forward-falling dark hair. Handsome but frail, anemic-looking, as if he'd never finished a meal in his life. I was five inches shorter, on the "husky" side, having never gotten up from a plate with food on it. Aside from my huskiness there was nothing special about me, except a certain hawklike intensity in the eyes (Mom called it my "mean look") and my bristly whitish-blond crew cut. Dad said long hair was for sissies. He saw to it that I had the last remaining crew cut in the eleventh grade. These were the days of Johnny Winter, remember, and Led Zeppelin, the Moody Blues; you had to grow your hair at least below the collar.

Despite my crew cut and Tim's general oddness, we believed we were cooler and smarter and funnier than anybody at Minor High. We were so cool that nobody even knew we were cool. We loved Sonny and Cher, so square-trying-to-be-hip, so aggressively uncool. Like us! At this moment, Sonny wore a forty-gallon cowboy hat and fringed chaps, and Cher was done up as an Old West saloon madam, all curly blond wig and fake tits. The jokes were lame, Cher rolled her eyes delivering them, but she did look fantastic in that wig with those big bazooms.

"There's nothing wrong with the Frillingers," Tim was saying. "Don't be such a snob."

"Come on, for God's sake, Debbie and Dianne? Couldn't we at least try for a couple of non-eyesores, like Terri and Mary Jo? And keep the Frillingers in reserve just in case?"

"They'll hear about it and get all hurt," he said. "Whereas if we go ahead and ask 'em, everybody will know we did it from the goodness of our hearts, so they could go to the prom. Nobody will think they're, like, our *real* dates or girlfriends or anything. See?"

I saw. We could shoot for the moon, in the form of Terri and Mary Jo, risking a humiliating rejection which would become schoolwide knowledge, or we could go for a guaranteed yes from the Frillinger sisters and become the gracious benefactors of two nice girls with good personalities. We'd be reaching down from our heights, instead of reaching up from our depths. We would arrive at the prom enhanced by a glow of charity that might help us trade up once we got there. I said, "Maybe you're right."

"Not maybe. I *am* right. I've thought a lot about this."

"Just, I was hoping we could do a little better. That sounds more like a backup plan." Cher swept her arm down the bar, sending a torrent of glasses to the floor. "Is this skit supposed to be funny?"

"It's surrealism. Like Salvador Dalí."

"Like you and me and the Frillingers."

"You got any better ideas? Be realistic."

I chewed my toothpick. "I see the advantages. I do. I'm just trying to picture us walking into the prom with them."

"It's not like we would have to kiss them or anything."

"What? Of course you would. It's the prom, for God's sake. What are you gonna do, take 'em and not kiss 'em? That's cruel."

"Which one would you want to ask?" said Tim. "Theoretically, I mean."

"Theoretically, I would like to ask Cher," I replied. "Would you look at her? Why can't we take her? Or somebody just the tiniest bit good-looking, Tim, please? Pretty please?"

Cher had put on a sparkly white gown and two pounds of eye shadow for the closing rendition of "I Got You, Babe." She cuddled little Chastity in her arms.

"Attention, Durwood," he said. "We don't know any good-looking girls who would go with us."

"No, well maybe not like completely gorgeous, but at least not —"

"Don't say it —"

"At least not a pair of howling, barking dogs!"

"Stop it!" He roared with laughter. "You shut *up!*"

"Daniel. Do you know what time it is?" Mom's voice up the hall. In our house, ten o'clock was the middle of the night.

"Gotta go, Timmy. Let me sleep on it."

"Poor little Chastity. Look how unhappy she is," he mused. Sonny Bono lifted the child's pudgy hand to wave night-night. "All those bright lights in her eyes. Shouldn't she be home in her crib?"

"She's the most famous baby in America," I said. "She has a job to do."

"Betcha Sonny nuzzles her all the time with that mustache."

"That is so revolting! I'm hanging up. Later —"

"Gator." He beat me to the click. We always raced to see who could hang up first.

The next night on the phone we refined our Frillinger prom-asking strategy. Tim insisted we had to choose individual Frillingers and ask them separately. Girls were weird about stuff like that, he said, especially twins, who always got treated like two halves of the same person.

We tossed a coin. Heads — I won. I chose Dianne.

"No fair, you got the pretty one," Tim said with an evil laugh. There wasn't a pretty one.

God, how mean we were. We told ourselves we were funny, but really we were cruel.

Mom's sleepy voice up the hall: "Daniel, hang up that phone. You've been on there for hours."

"It's a local call, Mom. It doesn't cost anything."

She said, "Did you ever think somebody else might want to call us?"

"Jesus, she sounds *exactly* like my mom," Tim said in my ear. "Are you sure they're not the same person? Have you ever seen them in the same room?"

"Timmy, gotta go. Later —"

"Gator." He beat me again.

We finally settled the Frillinger question with a plan for simultaneous hallway invitations after Mississippi History. Juniors all across Mississippi were required by law to take a yearlong class in the subject of our state's glorious past. Our current assignment was to memorize the names of all the counties. Coach Atkins spent the last ten minutes of each class intoning the list in his narcotic monotone: "Neshoba, Newton, Noxubee, Oktibbeha . . ."

At the bell Tim walked straight over to Debbie Frillinger. That left me no choice but to sidle up to Dianne, mumbling, "Hey can I talk to you a minute? In the hall?"

She must have thought I had gossip. She leaned against a locker, ready to listen. I blurted it out — "Listen, you want to go to the junior-senior with me?"

Her mouth fell open, actually fell open for a moment, her eyes lit up behind the glasses — then she decided it must be a joke. Her eyes hooded over. I saw the wounded little creature behind her eyes. I never told Tim or anybody, but just then I was so glad I had asked this particular girl.

"No, I'm serious." I smiled. "You wanna go?"

Her eyes melted. "Oh Daniel, really? That is *so* sweet. But I can't."

An alarm horn went off in my mind — oh God, NO! she's already got a date, I'm about to be turned down by Dianne Frillinger! The shame! Oh, the infamy! I kicked at the floor. "What, somebody already asked you?"

"No, no, are you kidding? Even if they did I'd rather go with you. No, it's Debbie. Nobody's asked her. How can I go if she doesn't get to?"

I felt faint with relief. "Tim's asking her, even as we speak."

"Really! My gosh, are you — Daniel, you guys are so wonderful!" She flung her arms around me and brushed my cheek with her lips, a moist little kiss.

I glanced down the hall to make sure no one had seen it. The girl thing had been an uncomfortable mystery since the sixth grade, when most of the boys got their first real crushes. I didn't really understand all the fuss, but dutifully I got a crush on a girl called Lucy Meagher, a blond slender thing who could do long division in her head.

I remember a rainy day, the smell of wet children just in from recess. I labored over my love note, copying it out twice to improve the handwriting. I folded it four times and watched it make its way, hand to hand, down the line of desks to Lucy. She read it. She made a mark with her pencil, refolded the note, and started it back up the line.

Miss Kamen spotted the surreptitious movement. She pivoted at the blackboard, her cat-eyes brightening. She clacked over on high heels, seized the note, and brandished it before the class.

"Look, children, one of us can't wait for the bell to share a secret. I think we should all find out what's so important, don't you?" A strange groan rose from the class, half in favor, half against. Miss Kamen smiled as she unfolded the note. "Now let's see . . . 'Dear Lucy, I like you do you like me.' Missing a comma there, and a question mark. 'Yes, no. Please put a check by the answer and send back. Love, Daniel.'" She looked up. "Daniel Musgrove?"

The only Daniel in the room. I died a few times.

"Your penmanship is improving, Daniel," she said, "but I'm afraid Lucy has checked 'No.'"

Miss Kamen ripped the note in two, dropped the pieces in the trash, and went back to the blackboard.

I never cast another glance at Lucy, or wrote another love note, or showed any glimmer of feeling for any girl until all these years later in the hall after Mississippi History when I asked Dianne Frillinger to the prom.

She said yes! She kissed my cheek! I felt sophisticated, a man of the world. There's no mystery to it. You just pick the right girl, walk up to her, and ask.

"Okay great, it's a deal, then," I said. "We'll be calling you with the details."

"My goodness, there's not much time! We have to get our dresses, get our hair appointments, and everything!"

"Yeah. And we gotta rent tuxedos."

"Oh, you'll be so handsome!" She looked so excited I thought she might kiss me again. I fended her off with a friendly bop on the shoulder and strutted off to chemistry.

Tim said Debbie was equally thrilled. Our news got all the right reaction in the halls, our generosity was noted and admired. People understood that we could have done better. Girls, especially, liked us for making sure two nice girls got to go to the prom.

Stepping into the Brant & Church Tuxedo Company we were greeted by a loud industrial buzzer like prisoners entering a cellblock. Tim hastened back to shut the door. A beefy little man popped up among the jackets. "Gentlemen! In the market for formal wear?" I noted the sweat circles under his arms. "So what's the occasion — let me guess. School dance?"

"Not just a dance," Tim said. "The Junior-Senior Prom."

"Absolutely. So what sort of look did you fellas have in mind?"

On all sides stood bronze-colored mannequin guys with molded hair and wrists tilted just so, wearing tuxes in a rainbow of colors. "I thought tuxedos were black," I said. Tim murmured agreement.

"Oh no, gentlemen, welcome to 1973!" the man said. "Black is more or less only worn by old fogeys like myself these days. The young fellas today like to put a little more pizzazz in their act, like for instance this beauty, the Colonial Gent in Rich Burgundy. Isn't that just tremendous?" It put me in mind of a bellhop. "Or the more adventurous guys are going for the Sophisticated Squire in Sky Blue or Forest Green, both extremely popular this year."

"You don't have any black tuxes?" I said.

The man smiled. "Tell me your name again?"

"His name is Durwood," said Tim.

"Okay, Durwood, let's try it from another angle. What color will the lady be wearing?"

I shrugged. "How should I know?"

"Pink." Tim spoke with authority. "Dianne's wearing pink and Debbie's wearing cream."

I gaped at him. "How do you know that?"

"I asked."

Who knew to ask the color of their dresses? Was there a Prom Manual they'd handed out to everyone but me?

"Definitely blue is the way to go alongside either pink or cream," the salesman said. "Can't go wrong with blue, either the Sky Blue or the Royal Blue. I would go with the Sky Blue, myself. Much more pizzazz."

"I think the Royal Blue," Tim said. "The other one is too bright."

"But see, you're viewing this fabric under showroom lighting conditions. It'll be ten times darker than this at your dance. That blue will look just elegant. Trust me. I've been in this business thirty-two years."

He measured us. We picked out patent-leather shoes and frilly-front shirts and bat-wing bow ties, suspenders, cuff links, spats, wrist corsages for "the ladies." It was all wildly expensive, all the money our parents had given us and some of our own, but we paid it and got out of there as fast as we could.

On prom day when we came to collect our tuxedos, they were a good deal lighter blue than we expected. We distinctly remembered asking for the Royal Blue, whereas these tuxedos were . . . Sky Blue is what they were. Sky Blue with swirly decorations on the lapels, black satin stripes down the pantslegs. The salesman was nowhere in sight, and the crabby woman at the register said take it or leave it, if you leave it we keep your deposit, come on boys I ain't got all day.

We carried our Sky Blue tuxes in their plastic shrouds to the car. Tim had convinced his father to loan us his gleaming new Buick Riviera for the evening, with injunctions of murder if we put a single scratch on it. We hung the tuxedos carefully on the coat hooks in back.

Tim eased into the driver's seat. "That color is making me ill."

"Oh come on, they're not that bad. The guy said Sky Blue is very popular this year."

"The guy was a goddamn idiot." Tim groaned. "We're gonna look like . . . like two O'Jays! Like a couple of Pips!"

"Maybe people will think we're trying to be funny."

"Oh sure. Ha ha. Great joke." He scowled. "This is gonna be a hell of a night. I'm not going."

"You sure as hell are," I said. "You dragged me into this. I've already spent forty-eight dollars! Now snap out of it and let's get this car cleaned up."

For an hour we scrubbed and vacuumed and polished and waxed and sprayed Mr. Cousins's Riviera full of Glade Summer Meadow, a scent so realistic it made me sneeze like cut grass.

Tim drove me out to Buena Vista and waited in our driveway while I went in to shower and put on my tux. Mom asked why Tim didn't come in. I didn't want to tell her that he was creeped out by the sight of old Uncle Jacko. I just said he was nervous about leaving his dad's new car alone for two minutes.

"Well, that's strange. He's a strange boy. The car is perfectly safe in the driveway." Mom craned to see out the window. "Are y'all taking these girls out to dinner beforehand?"

"We thought we'd go to the HoJo. It's not that far from the Holiday Inn, and it's not too expensive." For weeks the junior and senior girls had been amassing crepe paper and ribbon to transform the Holiday Inn Medical Center ballroom into "A Night of a Thousand and One Stars." Some of our classmates had made reservations at ritzy restaurants like Primo's and La Parisienne, but Tim and I had decided, why waste a lot of money on food when the dance was the big deal anyway?

"Don't you think you'll be a little dressy for Howard Johnson's?" Mom said. "Is that your tuxedo? Let me see! Oh honey, look! It's so *blue*."

"You think it's too blue?"

"Oh no. You know I like blue. Just, I don't think I've ever seen one quite that blue."

"It's called the Sophisticated Squire. It's supposed to be real popular this year."

"I'm sure it is," she said. "Timmy's waiting, now. Run put it on. I'll put the film in the camera."

I snapped and suspendered myself into the tux, and crept back out to the family room. I felt like a frilly Sky Blue Popsicle. "Don't you look fancy!" Mom snapped six pictures, pow pow pow, filling the room with white stars. "My little baby all grown up and going to his big dance! Let's go show Jacko, he'll love seeing you all duded up."

Janie ran through the room, took one look at me, and burst out laughing.

"Mom, I gotta go," I said.

"Just one minute. It will mean so much to Jacko."

She hurried out past the kitchen. I heard the drum of wheels as she rolled Jacko by the shoulders through the kitchen.

Jacko was my great-uncle, Mom's uncle. Her mother's brother. He was seventy years old and bald and scary-looking, with crooked white hairs sprouting from a Snuffy Smith nose. His legs were useless, a child's legs, shriveled and folded beneath him from polio when he was a baby. He had never walked a step, never been to school. All his friends back in Alabama were country black people, and he talked just like them. He wore denim shirtdresses because there were no pants to fit those legs. He got around our house by pushing himself on his "stroller," a little padded platform with roller skate wheels.

When I was little and someone plunked me on the floor beside him, Jacko liked to sneak out his hand and pinch my leg to see me cry.

Mom had wanted to move to Mississippi so she could be closer to Granny and Jacko in Alabama. The first December after we moved, Granny died, and Jacko came to live with us.

"Look at ol' Danums!" he crowed. "Where you gwine off to, boy?"

"Hey, Jacko. Big dance for our school tonight."

He cackled. "Like a big ol' fat bluebird."

Mom beamed. "Danny's got a date with a girl, Jacko. Don't he look handsome?"

"Biggest fat old bluebird I ever saw," said Jacko.

"Mom, let me go."

"Go on then. Be careful. Don't stay out too late. Oh, and Daniel —" I let her give me one more hug. "You be nice to that girl. Be a gentleman, you hear me?"

"Don't be try and kiss 'em," Jacko said. "She slap you upside the head."

I fled outside to find Tim pacing the driveway. "Jesus, I thought you would never —" He stopped to take in the sight of me.

"Well?" I braced myself.

"Honest opinion?" He studied me. "Not as bad as I thought. No, really. It's okay."

"Jacko says I look like a big fat bluebird."

"What did your mom say?"

"She said I was handsome."

"You know what?" Tim cocked open his door. "I believe she is right, you ol' dawg."

I grinned and got in the car. We rode fast into town with the windows down, the Carpenters on the radio, "Calling Occupants of

Interplanetary Craft." It was sweet to be alive and sixteen and going to the prom. Who cared if my tux was Sky Blue? The world seemed to stretch out before the long, long hood of Tim's father's Buick. Every hill and molehill of Mississippi was glowing in the soft light of an April evening.

Maybe my time as a brain/loser was ending and my new life was about to start. I was only a junior. There was still time to become popular, go on dates with real girls, rise above the brain/loser crowd, start having the kind of fun you're supposed to have in high school.

Going over to Tim's always reminded me that his folks had more money than mine. Their house was on the best street in Lake Forest. It was a little nicer and so much cleaner than other houses. His mother was spooky that way — you never saw her cleaning, but her house was so clean it made your teeth hurt. And Patsy Cousins was just as cheerful and sparkly as her kitchen. While Tim went to shower, she offered me a Coke and a seat at the bar with a view of that immaculate kitchen.

"You kids are going to have a *grand* time. I'll never forget my own prom. That's the night I first fell in love with Timmy's father. Just like in the movies."

"Mr. Cousins was your date for the prom?"

"Oh no, I went with some other boy — I forget his name." Mrs. Cousins batted her eyes. "Just a boy who asked me. But then I saw Timmy's father dancing with another girl, and our eyes met across a crowded room . . . it was so romantic. They were playing 'Que Será, Será.' Doris Day. That song still makes me all mushy."

I wished Tim would hurry.

Mrs. Cousins leaned across the bar with a confidential air. "Tell me something, Danny. Are you and Dianne going steady?"

"Oh, no ma'am. Nuh-uh."

"I wish Tim would find his special someone," she said. "He's so shy around girls! I'm delighted you finally talked him into going tonight. I tried and tried to get him interested in the prom, but he wouldn't hear of it."

"He's the one who talked *me* into it," I said.

She wrinkled her brow. "He did?"

And here he came, a tall awkward Sky Blue Sophisticated Squire with curlicues on his lapels, just like me. I told him how great he looked. He let his mom do her hugging and picture-taking. She followed us out to the car with her bright happy chatter and stood snapping photos as we pulled away.

"What did she say to you?" Tim said as soon as we were clear of the driveway.

"What do you mean?"

"Did she talk about me?"

"She said you're shy around girls, and she's glad I talked you into going to the prom."

"She should keep her fucking mouth shut," Tim said.

I'd never heard him use the word "fucking" that way. Especially referring to his mom. "She didn't mean anything, Tim. She was just making conversation."

"Don't tell me what she meant," he snapped. "She's my mother."

"Okay," I said. "Jesus."

"I hate her," he said. "She's the whole reason I had to repeat the stupid ninth grade. My grades were fine, but she called them up and suggested they should keep me back! Can you believe that? She said I wasn't 'socially mature.' Whatever the hell that means."

"It's okay," I said. "I'm glad. That way we got to be juniors together."

"Yeah, it worked out great for you." He slung the Buick out onto Old Vicksburg Road. "You know, I really am not in the mood for this stupid-ass dance."

"Fine. Let's just skip it," I said. "Is the real reason you're pissed off because we look like dorks, and we're taking the two skaggiest girls in the whole school to the prom, and everybody's gonna laugh at us for the rest of our lives?"

"There are skaggier girls," Tim said. "And anyway, seriously, didn't you hear me say to the guy, 'Royal Blue'?"

"We can hang a sign around our necks that says 'We Told the Guy Royal Blue.' Hey, slow down. Don't kill us on prom night, okay? Talk about a cliché."

"Where the hell is their stupid-ass house, anyway?" Tim said. "I'm all turned around."

"Make a right on Dorothy and supposedly it's the third house on the left."

All the Minor subdivisions had curving streets named for the children of developers: Bethany Drive, Ronnie Lane, Mary Ellen Way. The Frillingers lived on Dorothy Drive in a house like Tim's house, like our house — two-car garage on the right, bedrooms on the left, living room, family room, and kitchen in the middle. On the garage door, a bedsheet strung up as a banner:

HAPPY PROM NITE DEBBIE AND DIANNE!!! WELCOME TIM & DANIEL!!!!

And besides all the smiley faces, they had drawn little Jesus-fishes everywhere, and IXOYE, and flowers, and hearts. It looked like something a crazy person might do.

Tim stopped the car with his headlights trained on the sheet. "Do you see this? Do you see how they spelled 'nite'?"

"I see."

"Dagwood, these people are crazy. What should we do? Should we leave?"

"We can't."

"Dagwood, they've got our names on their *garage door*."

"Oh God, I know. I know."

He switched off the engine. We grabbed the corsage boxes and slunk past the banner.

The front door swung open and there stood Mr. Frillinger, white-haired and beaming like an overfriendly preacher, welcoming us in. "What handsome young gentlemen we have here tonight!" he boomed as if he wanted the neighbors to hear. "All decked out for a night on the town!" He ushered us back through the house to his private den.

The house smelled of cigarettes and Pine-Sol. Down the hall we heard a girly getting-ready commotion.

Mr. Frillinger's den was crammed with Ole Miss plaques, pennants, and trophies. He waved us to a sofa draped with a Rebel flag. He asked our full names, ages, what our fathers did, and whether we liked Ole Miss football.

Oh yes sir, we said. We sure did.

His unnerving green eyes settled on me. "Well let me ask you this then, son, have you accepted the Lord Jesus Christ as your personal savior?"

For a moment I was speechless. Then I managed to say, "Yes sir, I sure have."

"Good." He turned on Tim. "And you?"

"Oh yes sir, praise the Lord."

"Well since you boys are believers, you'll know what I'm about to say is just between us men, and in keeping with the spirit of the Lord."

"Yes sir."

"My daughters," he said, "are blessed vessels of the purest virginity. And I mean to see they make it straight through to marriage with their purity intact. Now don't think I don't know what can happen between young people — believe me, I know! Something touches something. Something *rubs up* against something. Next thing you know the Devil has you by the hand and he's taking you straight to *HELL!*" The bang of his fist made a ceramic Rebel Colonel hop an inch off the coffee table. He steadied it with his other hand. "Now, I'm not threatening you boys, but I am *deadly* serious when I say that if either of my girls comes home tonight with one hair out of place — wellsir," he said, laughing sadly, shaking his head, "I wouldn't want to be you. Daniel Musgrove? What do you say?"

My voice came out a chirp. "You don't have to worry, sir."

"Good," he said. "Tim Cousins?"

"Your daughters are safe with us," Tim said, twitching under the force of a postponed explosion.

Thank God here came Debbie, Dianne, and their mother swirling up the hall all a-chatter, and Mr. Frillinger was forced to let us go. The girls squealed in pleasure at the sight of us, they said our tuxes were *cool,* we were *sooo incredibly handsome,* who on earth except Tim and me would be *avant-garde* and *hip* enough to wear Sky Blue tuxedos! That was our cue to praise their dresses. They had made every effort to look different from each other. Debbie's dress was a prim ivory-lacy thing with a high lace collar. Dianne's was a pink shimmery gown that made her look something like a candle. They weren't wearing makeup, but their faces radiated excitement. They'd even taken the rubber bands off their braces.

I couldn't tell if their mother had made these dresses for them. Probably best not to ask.

The mother was a plain-scrubbed, slightly hysterical woman with a ponytail. She fell all over Tim and me, hugging us, thanking us a touch too fervently for taking her girls to the prom. It almost seemed as if she wanted to go herself — as if she might fall to her knees and beg us to take her — and considering the way Mr. Frillinger lurked in the doorway scanning with his cold green eyes, I wouldn't blame her.

"Did you see the banner we put up for you?" she cried, breathless from talking so fast. "The girls and I made it ourselves!"

"Mommy's so excited," Dianne said. "We hoped it wouldn't embarrass you."

No, we said, it was cool, we loved it. "I hope you didn't have to mess up a good bedsheet," said Tim.

Everyone tried to ignore the connotations of that remark.

Mrs. Frillinger bustled around in search of flashbulbs for the Polaroid. "Now where are they, where are they," she muttered, "they were here just a minute ago, what am I thinking, everybody so dressed up and pretty, and silly me can't even find a box of stupid flashbulbs! In a minute they're gonna get sick of waiting and leave, and I won't have a single picture!" I think she was even weeping a little. I couldn't wait to get the hell out of there.

At last she found the flashbulbs — "Right here in the drawer! The whole time! Oh how stupid, how stupid can one person be!" She lined us up in a row and blinded us with repeated flashing attacks, then led us blinking from the house to the garage. We reenacted the presentation of the corsages in front of the banner for her camera.

"Now look into each other's eyes like little sweethearts," she said. "A little closer."

"Come on, Mommy," Debbie pleaded, "take the picture."

"Deborah Ann," Mr. Frillinger said. "Cooperate."

"Daddy — please? We don't want to be late."

"Oh honey, I just can't let you go!" Mrs. Frillinger wailed, dragging Debbie in for yet another hug. "Don't leave me like this — whatever you do just don't *please* don't leave me alone in this house! Please not! Please not!"

"Deirdre, for God's sake let's don't have a scene now. The neighbors are watching." Mr. Frillinger tugged her arm, pulling her back toward the house. "Boys, drive safe and get 'em home before twelve."

Debbie and Dianne ignored the spectacle of their father dragging their mother up the sidewalk. Their faces went carefully neutral, like the female crew of the space station in *2001*.

"Wow, is she gonna be okay?" I said.

"Oh, yeah," Dianne said. "She's just a little nervous around people. Can we go?"

For a moment I felt a twinge of pity, *God how embarrassing,* and then I remembered the monster in my own house. I guess lots of families have monsters. To me it was normal to have a crippled half-man rolling around our house on a padded scooter. If these girls saw Jacko, they'd be giving me the same look of pity I was giving them now.

Tim and Debbie took the front seat. I got in back with Dianne.

Now, the backseat of a Riviera is a very roomy place. I don't know if it felt too roomy for me back there, if I thought we might flop around loosely and bump into each other or something — I don't know what, exactly, led me to buckle my seat belt, but I did, and I told Dianne to buckle hers too. "Tim drives like a maniac," I said. "We don't want any casualties."

"That's so thoughtful of you, Daniel." Dianne giggled and smoothed her dress. "Drive careful, Tim. I don't feel like buckling in. I'm living dangerously tonight."

Debbie turned in her seat. "Did you guys hear? I mean, did you hear?"

"What."

"You're going to die," she said. "Guess who thinks she's gonna be Queen of the Prom."

"Molly Manning," said Tim.

"Not Molly, of course Molly's got a chance. An excellent chance."

"Lisa Simmons?" I said.

"Oh be serious, Daniel! Lisa *ought* to be queen. Cute as she is, and hard as she's worked this year? She organized that whole bake sale by herself. Nobody lifted a finger to help."

Debbie said, "I'll give you a hint. Who is the *last* girl in the eleventh grade you think would ever get elected Queen of the Prom?"

Tim pulled into a 7-Eleven just inside the Jackson city limits.

"Rachel Bostick," I said. Poor Rachel weighed about two seventy-five and had fur on her arms.

The girls made sympathetic little cries at the sound of her name. "Be serious," Debbie said. "This girl is going around telling everybody that when they see her prom dress, they'll have to vote for her. They won't be *able* to vote for anybody else."

"Can you imagine?" said Dianne. "So conceited."

Debbie got up on her knees on the seat. "Give up? Brace yourselves. Arnita Beecham."

"Arnita?" Tim said. "Yeah, I can see that." He got out of the car.

Debbie looked peeved by this mild response. She whirled on me. "Daniel?"

"Well, Arnita is really pretty, you have to admit."

"Oh come on, Daniel."

"What?"

"Well, she's black."

"Yeah, I noticed." Nobody had ever seen a black girl like Arnita.

Her father, Lincoln Beecham, had been the janitor at Minor High forever. Arnita was pretty but studious-looking, with wire-rimmed glasses and old-fashioned ironed hair. She played first-chair flute in the band. She belonged to all the clubs and organizations and was every teacher's pet. She was not meek like the other black girls, who tended to clump together, speaking in private black-girl code. Arnita sat in front, raised her hand, argued fiercely with the teachers. Last fall she caused a commotion in Canzoneri's government class with a speech entitled "Why Castro Is Right." She had a 4.0 average and a full scholarship to Ole Miss a year before graduation. I'd never thought of her as the beauty-queen type, but I was sure she could do it if she made up her mind.

"There's only like twenty percent black in our school," Debbie said. "You don't really think she has a chance to be Queen?"

"Why not? She's a great girl." I knew why not, but I wanted to make Debbie say it.

"Of course she's great," Debbie said, her voice rising. "Nobody's saying she isn't *great*, it's just — oh, never mind."

Dianne spoke up: "Come on, Daniel, it's pretty unrealistic to think Arnita could win."

"Why?"

"Well silly, to win she'd have to get not just all the black votes but a whole lot of white ones too."

"I'd vote for her," I said.

"Daniel's a Yankee, he doesn't understand," Debbie said. "Listen, we're perfectly fine with them going to our school, but they can't just walk in and expect to win everything their first year. They have to earn it like everybody else."

How had I wandered into this danger zone? Every so often I got a sharp jab of the elbow to remind me that I was not from around here.

"Well," I said, "you can always pray for her to lose."

Here came Tim not a moment too soon, carrying a brown paper sack.

"Timmy, what did you buy?" Dianne called.

Tim reached one hand in the bag and whisked out a six-pack of Champale.

The girls gasped. "Oh my *gosh!*" Debbie shrieked. "That's — is that *alcohol?*"

"They didn't have champagne," Tim said. "The guy said this was the closest thing they had."

Dianne was scandalized. "How on earth did you buy it?"

"Fake ID. Y'all ready to party?"

"Oh no, Daddy would kill us," said Dianne.

"Daddy's not here, Dianne," her sister said. "Couldn't we have one tiny taste?"

This was a new frontier for all of us. Our parents were teetotalers, and so were all the kids we ran with. Those Champale bottles glistened like two rows of bullets in the light from the 7-Eleven. Tim popped off the caps and passed us each a bottle. "A toast," Tim said. "To our big night." We clinked.

I braced myself and took a slug. I choked it down, grinned, and said it was tasty. That's the word I used, "tasty." In fact it was foul. Everybody took a sip and pretended to like it, but we were all thinking, *Why would anyone drink this?*

"Now don't get too drunk, Tim," said Debbie.

Tim said, "I wonder if this is even close to champagne."

"I tasted a beer once," Dianne said.

"You did not!" her sister exclaimed.

"Yes I did, at Uncle Sibley's funeral. That man from the power company had a beer and I had some when nobody was looking. It tasted different than this."

"Oh my God, the demon rum has loosened her tongue!" Tim said. "It's true confession time! Drink up, ladies!" The girls giggled and took timid sips. We felt naughty and grown-up — dressed up, drinking and driving a big car fast, as the night sky fell over Jackson.

The downtown huddle of buildings looked rather handsome from the interstate. One or two more tall buildings and it would be a skyline. The tallest old building had the words STANDARD LIFE lit up in red letters on top. ("Truer words were never spoken," Tim liked to say.) There were four or five tallish office buildings and two capitol domes, Old and New. On the plain below the city was the brand-new Mississippi Coliseum, a yellow-sided futuristic building shaped like a merry-go-round, with a white pleated roof. The interstate swept a wide loop around it and shot us off to the north.

We took the exit for Fortification Avenue, which I pronounced "Fornication" to general merriment. The Champale got better as you drank it, and brought on a giddy sensation I found myself enjoying. Soon we were pulling off the frontage road into the parking lot of Howard Johnson's.

I trotted around to open Dianne's door. She said, "Thynk you, suh," attempting an English accent. Tim shot me a look that I managed to ignore.

It was only when we were inside, waiting by the sign that said PLEASE WAIT HERE, that I realized what a sight we presented in our Sky Blue tuxes and their long fancy dresses. The HoJo was full of truckers, salesmen, families with squabbling children. The most dressed-up people were the waitresses in turquoise and orange. One of them approached us with sympathetic eyes.

"Good evening," she said. "Don't you ladies look lovely tonight, and the gentlemen too. Will we have the pleasure of serving you dinner this evening?"

We nodded.

"Right this way, if you please," she said. I will always be grateful to Myrna (her name tag) for the effortless grace with which she swept us across that room and seated us in the corner booth. Everyone cast admiring glances as we passed. We sat in splendor at the best table in the house and ordered cheeseburgers, french fries, chocolate shakes.

Myrna treated us like celebrities, even brought us two slices of strawberry pie on the house. I thought Dianne might burst into tears. "Oh boys, this was the perfect place to bring us," she said. "I'll never forget this night as long as I live."

"Dianne is tipsy," said Tim.

"I am not!" she cried, welling up again.

Once more I buckled up in the backseat. Once more Dianne said she was living dangerously. We rolled off toward the Holiday Inn with the radio cranked so we could all sing along with Elton, "Rocket Man."

Maybe it started with the singing.

More likely it was the girls' perfumes mixed with the Glade Summer Meadow in the confines of the car that caused me to sneeze. And again. And again. Everyone laughed. I rooted around in the floorboard for a Kleenex box, grabbed a tissue. I blew my nose and sneezed again. Every time I sneezed, Tim made a funny noise, "Ow!" or "Oof!" Each one of these sent the girls off in a fresh gale of hilarity. I couldn't stop sneezing. I rolled down my window and asked them to roll theirs down, but oh no God forbid they should mess up their hairdos. I sneezed all the way down Fornication Avenue while everyone had a good laugh about it.

I didn't find it amusing. I was already nervous about the Sky Blue tux and the whole prom thing and Mr. Frillinger's lecture and Mrs. Frillinger's frenzy of desperate need, and how the people at the HoJo stared at us, and now I could not stop sneezing. I mashed my nose with the wad of Kleenex.

My nose started buzzing. A sneeze exploded, and another —

"Daniel!" Tim yelled. "Get a grip on yourself!"

"If you could just roll down your — *Gachoo!*" I saw stars.

Dianne looked alarmed. "Are you okay?" She pressed the button, dropping her window. "You're not getting the flu, are you?"

"It's got to be psychosomatic," said Tim. "He's allergic to the prom."

"Oh go to hell," I said. "I can't help it if I — Gaachoo!" A fierce twinge in my nose — my ears popped — my nose started to run. I mopped it with Kleenex.

"Daniel — you're — oh no!" Dianne squealed. "Y'all, he's *bleeding!*"

And so I was: that was blood running over my lip, into my mouth. I stared in cross-eyed horror at the sticky stuff coursing over the back of my hand. I tilted my head back, groping for Kleenex. The warm tang ran down my throat.

Debbie said, "My gosh, are you okay?"

"Yeah, yeah — it's just — subtimes I get dosebleeds," I said into the tissue.

Dianne shrank back; I might bleed on her dress. "Oh you guys, he's bleeding a lot!"

"Put a tourniquet on his neck, why don't you," Tim said.

That last sneeze had popped something loose, some vital point in my head. My second-to-last Kleenex was sopping with blood. Debbie got up on her knees to get a better look.

"Just relax," I said. "It'll stop in a biddit."

"At least you quit sneezing," Tim said. "I prefer the bleeding. It's much quieter."

We rolled past the vast pile of University Medical Center. Dianne said, "Y'all, he's bleeding a lot. Maybe we should go to the emergency room."

"Doe!" I cried. "Let's just go to the *prob!* I'll be *fide!* Just — would you talk about subthing else please? Iddything!" The river ran out the hole in my head, pumping out a steady warm stream. What if the bleeding never stopped and this was my life draining out of me? I didn't want to die in the backseat of Tim's father's Buick.

"Don't get blood on the seat," Tim said.

Dianne scolded, "Tim! Please!"

Any minute now I would stop bleeding and this would become a great big hardee-har-har. We swung into the Holiday Inn parking lot, cruised slowly through a herd of promgoers. Tim found a spot under a tree. I kept my head back, resting on the shelf under the window. I saw girls in shiny prom dresses passing by, upside down.

My fingers scrabbled in the bottom of the box. "Tib, you got any more Kleedex?"

"Wait." I heard Dianne rummaging in her purse. She pressed something soft and white into my hand, some kind of cottony pillow. I laid it against my face and smelled faint perfume, like toilet paper.

I realized what it was. I thought I might die.

I bled into it anyway. After a while the river slowed to a trickle, and stopped.

Gingerly I sat up. "I think I'm okay." The dam seemed to be forming, and holding. "Yep, I think it's good. Let's go in."

"You sure?" said Tim. "We don't want to walk in there and your head explodes."

That's when I went to unfasten my seat belt and found that it would not open. The button was stuck. I pressed harder.

It would not open.

Everybody else got out of the car. I pressed with all my strength against the center button of the buckle. I engraved the Buick emblem in the flesh of my thumb. That little steel bastard was frozen in place as if it had been welded shut.

Tim leaned through the window. "You bleeding again?"

"No." I tried to keep my voice calm. "Tim."

"What."

"The seat belt, Tim. It's stuck."

"*What?*" His face lit up, pure joy — what a perfect fool I was! This was total humiliation, the kind you can hang on to and lord over a friend for the rest of your lives. Tim laughed, oh my how he did laugh. He had to step back from the car, he was laughing so hard. I would have laughed too, if it had been anyone other than me.

Debbie and Dianne crowded around. From their fussing and clucking you would think I had planned the whole thing, the nosebleed, the seat belt. I invited any of them to take a crack at the buckle. They all took a turn. No one could make it budge.

Tim had stopped laughing. "Why the hell did you buckle it in the first place?"

"I don't know. I'm an idiot. What can I say?"

"Say it again," Tim said. "Say 'I'm an idiot.'"

"Tim, be nice," Dianne said. "He didn't mean to."

Tim found a screwdriver in the trunk. We pried and scraped, trying to wedge it open. Suddenly Tim got all squirrelly about damaging the seat belt of his father's fine car.

"Get back in the car," he said. The girls obeyed. We drove through the stream of promgoers, two blocks up Mortification Avenue into the unholy glare of a Texaco station. The bellcord went *ding!* A greasy man in a gray shirt came out. The name-patch said Doug.

"We don't need gas," Tim said. "My friend has managed to get himself stuck in the seat belt back there. Do you think you can help get him out?"

Doug turned to see me in my frilly Sky Blue tux with the seat belt forever locked around my waist. His face lit up. His shout carried to the far garage bay. "Hey Raymond! Come get a loada this!"

Raymond came, carrying his big belly before him. He joined in with guffaws and clever remarks. He called the other fellows from the garage to have a look.

I groaned, and leaned back in the seat. Somehow that insignificant movement tore a hole in the dam in my nose. The spectators gasped as a rivulet of blood spilled across my lip. I flung back my head and groped for the sanitary napkin.

The Frillingers sat quietly, their eyes averted as from a terrible accident. I cursed myself. WHY in the HELL did you have to fasten the damn SEAT BELT you damn stupid MORON. Every molecule of my stupidity danced before me in midair. Why had I buckled up? Not for safety. What was I afraid of? That Dianne might try to snuggle up to me? Was that it?

Never has there been a bigger fool.

The sight of blood ran off all the spectators except Raymond and Doug, who squatted to examine the buckle. "Yessir," Raymond announced, "that thing is flat stuck. What you thank, Doug?"

Doug nodded. "Have to cut it."

"What do you mean?" Tim said.

"Cut the belt."

"No way! That'll ruin it!" Tim came around the car. "Can't you pry it open? Don't you have some kind of special tool for when this happens?"

"No," said Raymond. "It's stuck."

"That's what I've been trying to tell him," I said. "It's not my fault, Tim. It's stuck."

"Well I can't let 'em cut the seat belt! My father will freak out! This car is brand-new! It's his baby!"

"Well excuse bee," I said. "I didn't do it on purpose."

Doug said, "I'll get some shears."

"NO!" Tim pounded the roof of the car. "You cannot cut the seat belt!"

I lifted the napkin. "Tim, for God's sake. What am I supposed to do, sit here all night?"

"Fine with me," he said.

"I can stay with you," Dianne said.

"No," I said. "No, we're gonna cut the durn seat belt and we're all gonna go to the prom, and I'll buy your father a new seat belt, okay? So you can just shut up about it. Okay?" I felt light-headed. Watch me faint, like a girl in a novel — just keel over from loss of blood.

"I'll never get to drive this car again," Tim moaned.

"Look — it's not my fault the precious seat belt is stuck!"

"Why the hell did you buckle it in the first place?"

We were skidding toward a collision. "Tim, one more word about the damn seat belt and I'm not gonna be the only one bleeding."

Doug returned with a pair of shears. He looked at Tim. "You want me to cut it, or you want to do it yourself?"

Tim stepped back. He raised his hands in a posture of defeat. "You do it."

Doug knelt beside me. Snip, snip, in one second I was free. He said no charge, but I handed him five dollars. (I'd have given him a hundred if I had it.) Doug crammed the bills in his pocket and said, "Y'all go on now, have fun at your party."

"See there, everything turned out fine," Dianne said. "Are you still bleeding?"

I checked. "Not much."

Tim climbed back in the driver's seat. "Okay, *nobody* fasten their seat belts, all right?" We rode in silence to the Holiday Inn. We could hear music throbbing from inside the building. Tim let his breath out slowly — like Dad when he was trying to keep from hitting us. "You ready now, Durwood?"

"You guys go ahead. I'll just sit here till I'm sure the bleeding's really stopped, then I'll come in."

Dianne said she would wait with me. I said sometimes it takes a while to stop all the way. "Y'all go on. I'll be in soon."

"You think it might stop faster if we leave you alone?" Tim said.

"Yeah."

He popped open his door. "Come on, girls."

"Okay, well . . . you hurry in, Daniel," Dianne said.

The minute they left, the pounding of my heart began to slow, the flow of blood easing. I stared up through the window at the stars poking through the haze over Jackson. It could have been worse, I kept telling myself. It could have happened in front of everybody, instead of just Tim and the girls and some gas-station guys.

Maybe one day it would be funny, but not yet. It was still too humiliating. Also I'd seen a side of Tim I didn't really want to see. No doubt we would go on being best friends, but I didn't enjoy how ready he was to leave me strapped in his father's backseat.

The pulse of "Back Stabbers" vibrated the air in the lobby. I went to the men's room to dab at the bloody crust on my nostril. By some miracle I had managed to lose all that blood without getting a drop on my Sky Blue tuxedo.

The bathroom door banged open and there stood Larry McWhorter and Red Martin, star linebackers of the varsity team. Their bow ties were off, their faces flushed from dancing and probably drinking. Red hooted at the sight of me. "Jesus Gawd, would you look at ol' Daniel Musk Ox?" he cried. "Howdy, Musk Ox! Where'd you get that tux at, Nigger Mart?"

I tossed the bloody napkin in the trash. "Brant and Church."

"Nigger Mart!" Larry snickered. "Good one, Red! Hey, Musgrove, who's your date tonight — Arnita Beecham?"

"In his dreams," Red said. "No, he's already got a little wifey at home. Tim Cousins."

I combed my crew cut and pretended to ignore them. They took up positions at the urinals and jacked their feet apart in manly fashion.

"Man," Red said, "did you get a load of her titties in that god-damn dress?"

"Mm, mm," Larry said, "sweet li'l ol' Hershey kisses."

I could have just slipped out the door, but with bullies it was important to show you were not intimidated. "I never noticed Arnita's tits till she put on that dress," I said, in the spirit of good fun between guys.

"You wouldn't notice tits on a bull," Red said, "cause you got your head stuck up your ass, jackass."

Larry haw-hawed at that. I grinned in a good-natured way. "Jeez, Red, with your talent for repartee you oughta go on Johnny Carson!" I got out the door before he could work up an answer.

Beside the double doors was a folding table manned by Coach Rainey and Mrs. Passworth, my algebra teacher. It was strange to see the coach in sport coat and necktie, even stranger to see Mrs. Passworth in a purplish satiny evening dress with pleats and bows and a generous view of her freckled bosom. "Well hello, Daniel, don't we look handsome tonight!" she exclaimed. "Ticket?"

"Tim Cousins has it. They already went in."

"Oh, right. He said you were having the most awful nosebleed! You poor thing, are you okay?" She put a kindly hand on my arm.

"I'm fine. Can I go in?"

"I'm sure you were just nervous," she said. "Go right in, have a wonderful time!"

A blast of warm air and music blew through the doors with a herd of chattering girls. I straightened my shoulders and walked into the prom.

My first instinct was I was in the wrong place, who were all these people? My classmates had been transformed — the girls glowy and fancy in their formals, hair piled to unnatural heights or teased and sprayed into clouds of curls. The boys looked handsome and grave in their tuxes. The spatter of light from the huge disco ball made every-one glamorous. To my relief I spotted several bright pastel tuxes — Mike Patterson wore a creamy yellow one, Greg Ptacek a Sophisti-cated Squire in Lime Green.

Crepe paper twirled with glitter-painted stars in the streams of colored light. The room was crowded, warm, thrilling, like I imagined a glamorous nightclub might be. A disc jockey was spinning records beside the dance floor jammed with couples swaying to Seals and Crofts, "We May Never Pass This Way Again." A sprinkling of teachers stood by, ready to break up any sexy dancing.

"There you are!" Dianne seized my arm. "How's your nose?"

"Fine. Cool decorations, huh?"

"Listen, if you need it, I've got another — thing in my purse. Just in case."

It was too dark for her to see me blush. "Thanks. I'm okay now. Where's Debbie and Tim?"

"Dancing! You wanna dance?"

The past two Saturdays I had watched *American Bandstand* and imitated those kids, the cool sweep of the arm and the juking thing with the feet. Janie came in and caught me in the act, and laughed so hard I had to quit. Now Dianne tugged me by the hand to the dance floor.

It was jammed, everybody shuffling in place. In that crowd no one looked significantly more ridiculous than anyone else. You can do this, I told myself. You can. I tapped my feet, snapped my fingers, grinned at Dianne. The beat was easy to follow. I found myself almost enjoying it. *You can get through this, try not to think how spastic you look.*

The lights made a shine on Dianne's face. She'd taken off her glasses, so her eyes looked naked and puffy, but they were nice eyes, the eyes of a girl having fun on her first date with me. A lot of steel in her smile. I gave her a smile in return. This was not so bad.

We did three fast dances in a row. I pulled her off the floor when the deejay put on "So Very Hard to Go" by Tower of Power, a slow dance any way you cut it.

"That was great!" she cried. "Let's go get some punch!" She was so excited that everything came out a little scream. She kept squeezing my arm as if to make sure I was real. We pushed through the crowd to a table laden with punch bowls and cookies, cocktail weenies, chips and dip. Dianne squealed and hugged everybody, how gorgeous how fabulous oh my gosh Brenda that dress is out of this *world!* We were in full prom mode, all right, we were here and doing the total Prom Thing. Dianne spotted Debbie at the end of the table. They ran into each other's arms shrieking as if they hadn't seen each other in months.

Tim tossed me a pig in a blanket. "How's your nose?"

"Never better."

"I saw you dancing. You been taking lessons at Arthur Murray, don't deny it."

"It wasn't as hideous as I thought it would be," I said. "Oh and thanks for telling Passworth all about my nosebleed, she's notifying all ticket holders as they come through the door. I'd hate it if everybody didn't find out immediately."

"I had to tell her, Skippy. I had to give her the ticket for you to get in."

"I'll do the same for you sometime."

He ignored my sarcasm. "Did you get a load of that?"

I followed his outstretched finger to an incredible vision: Arnita Beecham in a glimmering white gown, a very thin, stretchy, translucent, revealing gown. The lights behind Arnita outlined her figure in that dress in a very particular way. All the boys were gathering on this side of the ballroom to take advantage of the effect.

The dress was a white goblet containing the upsweep of Arnita's long legs and tiny waist, swelling outward to her bosom and naked shoulders. The midi skirts and prim white blouses of Studious Arnita had vanished, along with the eyeglasses, the vocabulary words, and the opinions. In their place stood this astonishing lovely strapless creature — star-glamorous, like Diana Ross or Leslie Uggams. A rim of light outlined the gleaming sheaf of hair curved around her face. She wore long spiky fake eyelashes, gold lipstick, a gorgeous wide smile.

"Good God," I said. "She is *beautiful.*"

"Unbelievable," said Tim.

"She's amazing. There ought to be a law against that dress."

"Apparently she's got an aunt that works in some store in New Orleans."

I turned on him. "You were such an asshole to me before. Do you realize that?"

He shrugged. "What do you want me to say?"

"Try 'I'm sorry.'"

"I'm sorry, okay?" He didn't mean it. "Jesus, Dullwood, you're weird tonight! First all that sneezing, and all the bleeding, and buckling in, and now you're all — what happened, did you get drunk off that one Champale?"

"Aw, forget it." I pushed his hand away.

Mrs. Passworth came through handing out ballots and tiny pencils like the ones at the Putt-Putt. I nominated myself for Best Personality (Boy), so I'd be sure to get one vote. I put Dianne down for Best Personality (Girl) so I could tell her I did. Cutest Couple was easy — Tim and Debbie. I looked around for King of the Prom and settled on Greg Ptacek since he had the pizzazz to wear Lime Green.

Tonight the plain girls were much prettier than normal, and the pretty girls were beautiful, but there was only one Queen: Arnita Beecham, hands down, nobody even close. Tim tried to see my ballot but I said, "Secret ballot." He asked who I put for King. I said Greg Ptacek. He rolled his eyes. Greg was a brain/geek like us and didn't stand a chance.

Mrs. Passworth came through collecting pencils and ballots.

"Did y'all put Lisa Simmons for Queen?" Debbie said.

"Secret ballot," I said.

"*Y'all!* Lisa needs our votes!"

Her sister said, "Debbie, they can vote for whoever they want."

"Well, Daniel probably voted for Arnita just to make me mad! Look at her! She looks like a, like some kind of prostitute!"

"Oh come on," said Dianne. "She looks pretty."

Her sister looked horrified. "Pretty? I bet she's not wearing any underwear!"

"You can say that again," Tim said. "Have you ever seen anybody who looked less like their normal selves?"

"Oh Tim, you didn't vote for her too? Y'all! You're gonna make Lisa lose! After all her hard work!"

I glanced at Lisa Simmons, laughing in the arms of Randy Felts. She was too much the springy little cheerleader to be Queen of the Prom. The Queen should be someone who makes your jaw drop. Like Arnita Beecham. Nobody could stop looking at her. I wondered if her fabulous new self was a statement on behalf of the few other black girls who had dared to come to the prom in their Simplicity-pattern homemade ball gowns. They hung out at the back of the room with their boyfriends, who had puffed-up Afros and dark sport coats, not tuxes. Arnita was all over the room, dancing with black boys and some white boys too. She enjoyed the stir her dress was creating. I'd never seen a black girl acting sexy and proud like that, not keeping her eyes down, not staying within her group. It was shocking, a bit revolutionary. I found myself hoping she'd win.

Dianne dragged me back to the dance floor. We bobbed through "Jungle Boogie" and "Crocodile Rock" and "Midnight Train to Georgia" (whoo whoo!). I was surprised to find I enjoyed dancing. Nothing to it, just bop around and act goofy. I was so glad to have escaped the backseat of that Buick, I would have danced the whole night had not the deejay put on Maureen McGovern singing "The Morning After."

"More punch?" I proposed.

Dianne followed me off with a wistful glance at the couples slumping into each other's arms.

I didn't want any part of a slow dance. Tim and I had worked up a plan to kiss the girls at the end of the evening — I'd even practiced on my forearm — but wrapping my arms around Dianne Frillinger in public was more than I could ask of myself.

I found Tim lurking at the punch bowl.

"This song makes me think of Shelley Winters trying to swim through a porthole," he said.

"Swim, Shelley, swim!" I said. "Swim sideways! Come on, you can make it!"

Tim's sharp little laugh. "Look, she's teaching the whales to sing!"

"You boys are so awful!" Dianne said. The song was over and Coach Rainey was helping Mrs. Passworth onto the stage.

"Okay now," the coach boomed over the PA, "all you kids shut the hell up and pay attention!"

Mrs. Passworth shot him a look for the profanity. "Good evening boys and girls," she said — the mike howled — "or should I say *ladies and gentlemen!* On behalf of the faculty of Minor High, I welcome you all to the Night of a Thousand and One Stars! Isn't this just a magical evening!"

This statement would have provoked jeers and catcalls in Thursday assembly, but here we were in formal clothes in a crepe-papered ballroom with nice twinkly lights, and the evening *was* somehow magical, even if it was corny. We applauded in spite of ourselves.

"We'll get back to dancing in a minute, but first a big thanks to the junior girls for these fantastic decorations! Didn't they do a great job? Let's hear a big round of applause!"

The junior girls clapped the loudest for themselves. Coach Rainey bent down to rummage in a box of bouquets and tiaras.

"And now without further ado," Mrs. Passworth said, "let's meet our Royal Court!" From her hand fluttered a long piece of paper. "Okay, I had to add these up myself, bear with me — you see, boys and girls, math *can* come in handy —" Scattered boos. "Anyway, first off for Best Personality, Boy, come on up here when I call your name, the winner is . . . Jeff Wilcox! Congratulations Jeff!"

Jeff was a football player with all the personality of a loaf of Sunbeam bread. Mrs. Passworth hung a medal around his neck. Jeff clenched his fists together and raised them like a victorious boxer.

"Next, the girl voted Best Personality, let's hear a big hand for — Lisa Simmons!"

A violent shriek. Lisa jumped up and down, screaming and crying as if she'd just become Miss America. Her friends had to help her onto the stage, she was crying so hard.

"Oh that's awful!" Debbie cried. "That means she won't be Queen."

"Arnita Beecham," I said smugly.

"Shut *up!*"

"Now we have Cutest Couple — and let me say this vote was nearly unanimous — come on up here, Molly Manning and Gary Brantley!"

Another shriek. Molly tore through the crowd, jumped onstage, and hugged Lisa. They cried, hanging on to each other. Gary shuffled his feet as if this whole thing would be too stupid, except Jeff Wilcox was up there too. They poked at each other, exchanging sheepish grins.

"Isn't this exciting?" Passworth exclaimed. "Now here we go — ladies and gentlemen, this year's King of the Prom — Red Martin!"

Oh my God. Who would vote for that big dumb bully? A lot of people, apparently, from the rousing cheer that went up. Okay, so he did pick up three fumbles for touchdowns in the Warren Central game. He was MVP, for God's sake, why did he get to be Prom King too? He was still a junior! Wasn't the King supposed to be a senior? Why did the same two or three people always have to win everything?

Red tilted down his big head to receive his sash and gold-plated crown. He pumped his fist in the air to show that being crowned King feels just like scoring a winning touchdown.

"And now — okay Red, settle down — allow me the pleasure of presenting your Queen. Ladies and gentlemen, Miss —"

I didn't even hear her name for the shout that went up. Arnita Beecham threw her hands in the air and strode across the room with a huge smile of victory. She seemed to see fine without her glasses — she walked a straight line toward that tiara.

The opening cheer quickly died away to a hush of amazement. My God, she won! A black girl is Queen of the Prom!

Dianne and Debbie looked stunned. Of course Arnita had gotten the black vote — the kids on that side were going crazy, bellowing their delight into the general hush. I could see that lots of white boys had voted for her too. The white-boy vote put her over the top. All the white boys took one look at Arnita in that dress and couldn't help writing her name in the blank. We had voted for that dress and how naked she looked in it.

But nobody had imagined she would actually win, except Arnita.

She hopped onstage for her sash and tiara, a dozen red roses, hugs and squeals from Molly and Lisa, cheers from the back of the room. She took the mike from Mrs. Passworth. "Oh my God! Y'all! This is truly the most amazing thing. Do you know what you've done? An incredible thing. I'll never forget it, as long as I live. Thank you so much. Thank you!" She performed a little curtsy, steadying the crown with her hand.

Debbie Frillinger rolled her eyes. "I guess people just wanted to show how liberal they are. I bet you think that's great, huh Daniel?"

"Oh come on, she looks fantastic."

"For pity's sake, it's not a *beauty* contest!" Debbie snapped.

"Yes it is! That's what it is. What else could it be?"

"Don't you think effort ought to count for something?" said Dianne. "Or school spirit? Lisa Simmons worked her heart out! She worked harder than anybody!"

"Come on, girls," Tim said. "You're just mad because Arnita won and she's black."

"We're not *mad*," Debbie said furiously. "I just can't imagine that many white people voting for her, that's all."

"I bet they didn't," Dianne said. "Mrs. Passworth probably gave her extra votes so we'd end up with a black prom queen."

"Poor Red," said Debbie. "He has to be in the pictures with her. Can you imagine?"

Red Martin did look uncomfortable with Arnita on his arm and that silly crown on his head, while Bruce Davenport squatted before them snapping yearbook photos.

Suddenly I wanted the whole stupid prom to be over. I wanted to be stretched out on the family room floor watching Sonny and Cher with Tim over the phone.

The deejay was playing the Hollies' "Long Cool Woman." I said, "So, are you guys about ready to go?"

Tim and Debbie stared as if I was speaking in tongues.

"*Go?*" Tim said. "Are you joking?"

Dianne said, "Gosh, Daniel, am I really making you that miserable?"

"No, I just thought — I don't want us to be the last ones to leave. Never mind. Wanna dance?"

We went back to the floor. The deejay seemed to be playing four fast songs for every slow one.

I felt a little sorry for Arnita, the discussions taking place all over the room. She didn't seem to realize that the verdict was not unanimous. She floated through the crowd, cradling her roses, pausing every few feet to let herself be hugged.

Eventually Coach Rainey got back up onstage to tell us good night, get the hell out of here, and drive careful going home. The lights came up, turning us into a bunch of blinking kids in rented clothes.

We poured through the double doors to the lobby, the parking lot. Some of the boys were drunk — Randy Seavers, Doug Pine. Red Martin still wore his lopsided crown, and carried his tiny date, Margaret Lipset, in the crook of his arm like a football.

The girls and Tim took turns warning me not to buckle up. Ha ha, I said. We joined the line of cars heading for the interstate, a flotilla of promgoers in our parents' Buicks and Oldsmobiles, shooting out west, toward Minor.

"Oh, don't take us home yet, Timmy," Debbie said, snuggling close. "I don't want this night to ever end."

Dianne said, "Deb, it is getting close to midnight."

"Yeah, I know." Debbie stretched her arms. "I'm not ready to turn back into a pumpkin yet."

The plan was for Tim to stop the car in the Jitney Jungle parking lot, we would kiss them and take them straight home. We wouldn't have to kiss them very long. Mostly we were concerned about those braces. Tim said it would be like kissing a motorcycle, I said an Erector set. He turned that into a vulgar remark. As we took the Minor exit I was thinking how much easier it would be to kiss a pretty girl — like Cher, like Arnita Beecham — but I had to stop thinking that way or I'd never go through with it.

I fought off the memory of my one and only kiss, outside the emergency room in Pigeon Creek, Alabama. The one that turned me off the whole idea of kissing. I would kiss Dianne tonight as an antidote to that. Dianne Frillinger was a nice girl with a great personality. We'd had fun dancing, she'd been sweet to me all night. If there's one thing she deserved, it was a kiss on Prom Night. I could do that much. I knew I could.

I thought, *Here goes nothing*, and folded my hand around hers. Her hand was clammy. When she smiled, her braces caught a glint of light from the street.

Tim was telling some pointless story about Anne Marie Davis not dancing with Russell Briscoe as he steered the car into the parking lot.

"Timmy, why are you bringing us here?" said Debbie. "The Jitney Jungle is closed."

Tim put the car in park but left the motor running. "I'll show you why." He took her face in his hands.

That was my cue. Dianne's eyes flickered up to the front seat then back to me, yes yes please kiss me now. I closed my eyes and moved my face forward until it touched hers. I kissed. It felt odd. I opened my eyes. I was kissing her nose. Her face was upturned, her eyes closed in anticipation. I kissed her nose again as if that was what I'd meant to do, then moved to her lips. They were dry and strangely cool. I pressed my mouth against hers. We stayed that way for a while, mouths pressed together.

There had to be some part of it I was not doing right. This could not be all there was to it. I know you're supposed to open your mouth, but I was afraid my tongue would touch metal. I held the kiss as long as I could without breathing or moving, then pulled back.

Dianne opened her eyes. "Oh, Daniel, that was sooo nice. You've kissed girls before, huh?"

I coughed. "Yeah. A few times."

"I thought so. That was my first time. I'll never forget it."

Debbie and Tim were really going at it, mouths open, as if trying to swallow each other. Dianne looked shyly at me: *Should we try it like that?* I hesitated. She patted my hand, consoling me, as if she were my mommy.

I cleared my throat. "Hey you two, break it up! Jeez!"

Debbie pulled away, laughing. Tim said, "Sorry. We got carried away." He put the car in gear. The radio was playing "Nights in White Satin" and it all seemed suddenly romantic, the bad parts of this night adding up to one good part. I squeezed Dianne's hand. She put her head on my shoulder.

As we swung onto Dorothy Drive she untangled her fingers and moved over by the door.

"What's the matter?" I said — then I saw Mr. Frillinger outlined in the porch light. In his hands he twisted the banner from the garage door, like a rope he meant to wrap around somebody's neck.

"Oh God," Debbie said, "he looks mad."

I felt a flash of reflex panic before remembering we hadn't done anything wrong.

"What time is it?" Dianne held her watch to the light. "It's only a quarter to twelve!"

Mr. Frillinger stalked to the car shouting, "Get out! Get out of the car!"

"Daddy, what's wrong?"

"Get out and go in the house!"

"Daddy?"

"Deborah Ann! Do as I say!"

"You better go," I said. "We'll see you at school."

The girls scrambled out of the car.

Mr. Frillinger filled the driver's window. "You boys know what time it is?"

"Yes sir," Tim said. "A quarter to twelve."

"You were s'posed to have them back here by eleven. Where the Sam Hill have you been?"

While Tim had his attention I slipped out of the backseat, up front into shotgun position.

"I'm sorry sir, but you told us midnight," said Tim. "The prom's just now gotten over. We brought 'em straight home."

I leaned over the seat. "He's right, sir. You did say midnight."

"That's the last time you take out my daughters, either one of you," he said. "I've a good mind to call up your daddies."

"Go ahead," Tim said, starting the car. "I think maybe you're confused about what time you said."

"Don't tell *me* I'm confused." The man leaned close to the window. "Did you kiss them? Did you touch 'em?"

"No sir, no way," Tim said. "Let me tell you something, Mr. Frillinger, you've got yourself a couple of barking dogs there. I mean *barking*. I wouldn't touch either one of 'em if you paid me. We took 'em to the prom out of sympathy, okay? No one is ever gonna want to kiss 'em. You're safe."

The man's mouth made an O. Tim gunned the car backward, slammed it in drive, and screeched off down the street.

"My God, Tim, did you — I can't believe you said that!"

"Did you see his face? Did you see?" he howled. "That old bastard. 'You kiss 'em? You touch 'em?' Jeesus H. Christ!"

"But I mean, one minute you're like making out with her, then you tell her father she's a —"

"Dogwood, relax! It's over. We don't have to ask 'em out or even talk to 'em, ever ever again. He's gonna call up our *daddies!* I don't know who's crazier, him or the mother."

"Yeah, I know, but . . . oh damn. Never mind." I pictured Mr. Frillinger with his mouth open and I couldn't help it — a snort, a giggle. In five seconds, we were helpless with laughter. We rode around, hooting, past the darkened school, onto Barnett Street, laughing all the way.

Taillights ahead. Tim touched the brakes. "Is that a cop?" We weren't drunk, but as hard as we were laughing we might seem that way to a cop.

"No, Blindy, it's a car and . . ." I squinted through the windshield. Barnett Street was raised above its sidewalks. The houses along here had deep lawns and long driveways. In the distance I made out — was it one person on a bicycle, or two people riding together? Cruising beside the bike, slowly weaving back and forth between the lanes, a jacked-up fastback sports car — GTO? Mustang? Cherry red, with yellow flame decals licking down the sides, around the fender.

The car's irregular motion made the bike wobble. The rider veered off the pavement and fell off the bike.

The car hesitated a moment then roared off with a blast of exhaust.

When we got there she was picking herself up, a brown girl in a green sweatshirt and khaki shorts, bent over, pulling on one of her shoes. Riding a bike in high heels! The second rider was actually her infamous white dress, now in dry-cleaner plastic, crumpled on the ground beside her. A tiara and a dozen red roses had spilled out on the grass.

I stuck out my head. "Arnita? You okay?"

She peered into our headlights. "Who is that?"

"Daniel Musgrove," I said, "and Tim Cousins. You need help?"

"No, no I'm fine." Arnita gathered the dress.

Tim leaned over from the driver's side. "Someone bothering you, Arnita?"

"That damn Red," she said, "he's just *too* drunk."

"Red Martin?"

"Yeah, he's the King, y'know, the big bad Kang, thinks the Queen just automatically belongs to him for the night."

Tim said, "What are you doing out here?"

"Riding home from Charlene's, man, she's having a biiiig party!" She took a deep breath. "I went with Tommy Johnson but he got mad at Red and took off. I hope to God I didn't mess up this dress. It's not mine. I gotta give it back to my aunt."

"Arnita, where are your glasses?"

"I . . . I don't know, I think I lost 'em. It's okay, I can see."

"Why don't you let us give you a ride?"

"No, y'all, thanks, I'll be fine."

"I'm glad you won," I said. "I voted for you."

"Oh, aren't you sweet." She had no idea who I was. She climbed on the bike and wound the dress around herself to keep from tangling it in the wheels. "Thanks, y'all, I'm just gonna go home now."

"Aw come on, Arnita," Tim said, "you've had a little bit to drink. Let us throw that bike in the trunk and drive you home. It's late. You coulda got hurt."

"My house is just over the bridge," she said, pushing off with her foot. "I'll be fine."

Tim coasted along beside her. "Let us ride along with you to make sure."

"No, I'll be fine." Her voice took on an edge. "Thank y'all so much. Good night!"

"Come on, Tim, she says she's okay."

He pulled a few feet ahead. "I don't like it." He kept one eye on the rearview. "Red's an asshole, he was drunk, and he might come back. God knows what he was trying to pull."

When he said "pull," he turned around in his seat to look at her. His hand slipped off the wheel. The Buick drifted wide to the left. Another car coming —

I grabbed the wheel, jerked it right just as Tim slammed on the brakes. A mild little *flonk!* from the back of the car — as if Arnita had slapped the trunk with her hand.

"Shit!" Tim yelped.

I turned. I didn't see her.

"Where is she?"

I looked down. The grass sloped to the sidewalk, where Arnita lay sprawled on her back, her arms flung out, the dress wrapped around her like a flag.

"Arnita?" My voice sounded small. "You okay?"

Her head rested against the edge of the sidewalk. She looked up at the dark sky.

"Oh God," Tim said, "oh my God." He tromped the gas, throwing me back in my seat. We flew away faster than the speed of light.

4

"WHAT ARE YOU DOING? She's hurt! Turn around and go back!"

Tim tromped the accelerator. "Shit shit *shit!*"

"Tim! We gotta go back and help her!"

"We can't do that," he said in a strangled voice.

"Well you can't just leave her there, are you crazy? She's hurt!" The big Buick flew over the railroad tracks — I swear all four wheels left the ground. "Tim, I mean it, we have to go back!"

He turned, his eyes cold and gleaming — the eyes of somebody I didn't recognize. "Would you shut your damn mouth?"

"All right — stop the car. Let me out!"

"We're going to get help, okay?" he yelled. "We're gonna get her some help. I'm *thinking!* Would you shut up and let me think?"

"It was an accident, an *accident!* It is not our fault, please turn around and go back."

"You jerked the wheel!" he cried. "Why the hell did you do that?"

"Stop the car. Stop it now!"

After everything that happened, "Nights in White Satin" was *still* playing on the radio — or was it playing again? The guy was reciting the portentous spoken-word part, "breathe deep the colors of the night" or whatever it was. I kept seeing Arnita with the dress wrapped around her. Her head resting against the concrete edge. The rear wheel of the bicycle lazily spinning.

Tim said, "Okay. We'll find a phone and call somebody."

"Good. Good idea. Where's a phone?" We zoomed past Buddy's Bait and the Gibson's Discount. I pointed to a phone booth glowing at the edge of the road by the Pic-N-Pay. "Who do we call, the police, the hospital, what?"

The Buick's tires crunched on gravel. "Nights in White Satin" was rising to its pounding conclusion. He switched off the engine.

"I'll do it," he said. "You're hysterical. Stay in the car."

"Would you *hurry!*" I cried.

He walked around the back of his father's car and squatted by the bumper to check for damage.

I ran to the phone booth, picked up the receiver, and dialed 0. It rang twice. I heard Tim running behind me and then he was on me, wrestling the phone away. "Yes operator, hello?" he said. "I, uhm, listen, we're here in Minor, we need to report an accident. A black girl's been hurt. She fell off her bike. An accident, yeah, can you send an ambulance — Sorry? Uhm, sure — Barnett Street, like three blocks to the, to the west of Minor High School. What's that?" He paused. "Uhm, I don't know." He hung up.

His eyes came around to me. "Think they can trace that call?"

"How should I know?"

"Get back in the car."

"Where are we going?"

"I'll take you home, and then I'm going home. We have to forget this ever happened."

"Tim. We have to go back. Or it looks like we did something really wrong."

"We left the scene," he said, checking the rearview.

"Look, we go back right now," I proposed, "we tell the truth. She ran into us, she fell off her bike, you freaked out and drove off, we called an ambulance and came back. There's nothing wrong with that."

"What do you mean *I* freaked out? You're the one who grabbed the damn wheel."

Terrible, what fear can do to a boy. Fear can take a perfectly good boy like my best friend Tim Cousins and turn him into this shaky pale guy, unnerved but weirdly composed, his eyes spinning.

I was scared too. Oh yes. I knew I should march back to that pay phone, call the police, and tell them the truth. I thought about doing that, but instead I got back in the car.

Tim started the engine. "There's not a scratch on that bumper," he said. "Now listen to me. I can't explain it right now, but I can*not* get involved with the police, okay? Don't ask why. Just trust me." He started the engine. "We called for the ambulance. They'll know what to do. We've done everything we can."

"She saw us, Tim. Aren't you forgetting that?"

"Who?"

"Arnita! We talked to her! She knows who we are."

"Oh shit. You're right."

"We have to go back," I said.

"You saw her. Did she look dead?"

"You drove off so fast I couldn't — Jesus, Tim, what if she *is.* What if we . . . ?"

"It's not our fault. She ran into *us,* remember? We stopped to help her. . . ." His voice trailed away.

"What?"

He straightened in his seat. "You're right. We don't have to stop, necessarily, but we have to go back. At least ride by and see. If she's awake and talking, then we'll stop." He drove slowly. "She fell, we stopped to help her, then went to call an ambulance. What's wrong with that? We're not drunk. We didn't do anything wrong."

The Jitney Jungle lot was deserted. It seemed like a year ago I was steeling myself to kiss Dianne Frillinger under this sickly yellow light.

We sat at the stoplight by the Dairy Dog, left blinker clicking. Just as the light changed, a car blasted through the intersection, flashing headlights and blowing its horn.

Tim said, "Jesus!"

"Police," I said. "Minor Police."

We crept over the railroad tracks, onto Barnett Street. Ahead I saw the blue winking lights of cop cars parked at angles, their headlights trained on one place.

Tim said, "Easy, now. We're just riding through, we haven't got a care in the world."

Two police cruisers sat nose to nose, an ambulance between them. As we passed I saw two men lifting Arnita on a stretcher into the ambulance.

Her bike lay where it fell.

Just beyond the police car was a jacked-up Mustang Fastback, cherry red with yellow flames. The trunk and doors were wide open. There were cops in the backseat, digging around. Another cop held Red Martin spread-eagled on the hood.

We glided by, taking it in. The cop pressed Red's cheek against the hood.

I held my breath to the end of the block. I didn't dare look at Tim. I knew what he was thinking. I was thinking it too.

Finally Tim said, "Did he see us?"

"I don't think so. There was a lot going on."

"Red Martin," he said.

"Yep."

"Arnita said he was drunk."

"Yeah, she did."

"Could you see her?"

"Just, she was on the stretcher, I . . . no."

"They didn't seem to be in a hurry, did they?" he said. "I don't think that's a good sign."

"Yeah, I know. Jesus, Tim. We gotta go back."

"Red knocked her off that bike, Skippy. He did. Before we did. You saw it happen. It's the truth. He drove off and left her on the ground, right? You saw it. She could have got hurt then." His voice was growing calmer every second. "I mean, we were trying to help her. Red is the one who was bothering her."

"What are you saying?"

He looked sideways at me. "Red did this. Not us. Okay, it's not exactly the way it happened, but in a way it is, see? Red's the one who's drunk. Not us. He was hassling her. We stopped to help her. You see what I mean?"

"So what do you want us to do?"

"Nothing. We go home and wait. See what happens. Maybe she'll be okay. Maybe they'll let Red go. I don't know. We just have to see."

We circled around on Larry Lane. Tim took a roundabout route through the backstreets of the subdivisions, away from the busy streets.

"What happens when Arnita tells them it was us?"

He shrugged. "She hit her head, right? She's probably confused. We stopped to help her, that's when she saw us. We went to call for help. Who do they think called the ambulance? We even drove by a second time, to make sure the ambulance came. And it did."

I peered at him. "Wow, you're good at this."

"It's all new to me," he said.

"Take me home, Tim," I said.

"That's where we're going. Right now." He switched on the radio, a loud used car commercial. He switched it off again. We drove out into the country, where the roads were fast and the Buick's high beams pushed back the darkness. "It's gonna be fine, Skippy."

"I don't know. I have a bad feeling about this."

He tried the radio again. The Spirit 99 deejay was sending late-night dedications to Bunny in Yazoo City from a secret admirer, to Randy from Tina with a love that will never die, to T.J. in Vicksburg love you always from Carol, "and a very special Prom Night dedication from the twins to Daniel and Tim," he said. "Whoa, twins on Prom Night! Is anybody having fuuuuun?"

"Oh my God," Tim said. "They called the radio station. I don't believe it. It wasn't enough for them to put our names on the garage door."

I leaned my face against the cool glass. "I just hope we didn't kill Arnita."

"Well, so do I."

"Really? Is that what you hope?"

"Of course! What do you think?"

"It's hard to tell with you tonight," I said. "You're full of surprises."

"What's that supposed to mean?"

I turned on him. "What is it, Tim? Why are you so scared of the cops? You've been in trouble before, right?"

"Once." His eyes never left the road.

"For what?"

He blew out a breath. "It was last Thanksgiving. Reckless driving. I never told you or anybody. I spent the night in jail. I used my one phone call to tell my folks I was spending the night at your house. Thank God you didn't call me that night."

"Reckless driving, what is that? That's not so bad," I said, although it did sound serious.

"It was bad enough. They suspended my license for six months. Nobody knows that either."

"Well damn, Tim. And you're still driving?"

"Not after tonight. Believe me, I'm taking this car home and I'm never driving again. Just get me home tonight, Jesus. I swear I'll ride my bike from now on." He snatched off his bow tie, flung it out the window.

"You're gonna have to pay for that."

"That is the least of my problems," he said.

Buena Vista Drive led up a low hill. A split rail fence marked the beginning of our yard. Normally I hated that yard and every blade of grass on it, but tonight it looked like home and I was glad to see it. Mom had left the porch light on for me.

"We can't leave it like this, Tim. It's not right."

"Call me tomorrow," he said. "For now, just don't tell anybody. For God's sake don't tell your folks."

"You think I'm crazy?"

He turned into our driveway, setting up a howl from Mrs. Grissom's beagle across the street.

"Call me first thing," Tim said. "No. I'll call you. You'll be home?"

"Yeah, I always stay with Jacko while they go to church."

"You okay, Durwood?"

"No, I am not okay."

He squeezed my arm — an invitation to join in, play along, stick together, help him tell a very big Lie.

I slammed the door. He waved and drove off. I stood breathing the piney air of Buena Vista Drive as Mrs. Grissom's dog howled at me.

If we hadn't stopped to kiss those girls at the Jitney Jungle, Arnita would be home in bed now, with her roses and her crown on the nightstand beside her.

If I hadn't grabbed the wheel . . .

We ran over the Queen of the Prom. We didn't mean to do it. But leaving the scene — leaving her lying on the ground — that we did on purpose.

I was amazed by Tim's coolness under fire, his ability to calculate his next move while the situation was unraveling. He was figuring out our alibi while I was still in the first shock of seeing Arnita on the ground.

"Shut up, dog," I yelled. The beagle obeyed. Poor dumb dog, it was just waiting for someone to say shut up.

Our house was asleep. I tugged off my bow tie and went in as quietly as I could. As I reached in the fridge for orange juice Mom appeared, heavy-eyed, in her flannel robe. "Hey honey, how was your prom?"

"Good, Mom. Go back to bed."

"What time is it?" She pushed hair from her eyes.

"Almost one," I whispered. "Go back to sleep."

"No, I want to hear all about it. Pour me a glass of milk."

"It's late. We can talk about it tomorrow. We don't want to wake him up." I jerked my head in the direction of Dad.

"How was Dianne? Did y'all have fun? Did she look pretty in her prom dress?"

"Yeah," I said. "On the way there I got a bloody nose."

"Oh honey, no." She patted my arm. When I was a kid I had

bloody noses all the time, and Mom was always the one who sat up with me until it stopped.

"It wasn't so bad. Just a little one."

"Did it spoil your whole evening?"

"No. We had fun. We danced and everything."

When she blinked, her eyes wanted to stay closed. "Oh sweetie, I was hoping you'd have a perfect night."

"We did, don't worry. It was fine." I felt so much older than my mother just then. Lying to her, to keep her from worrying. Mom was prettier than Doris Day, with long wavy hair, light gold like an ice-cream cone. At the moment she looked like a sleepy little girl. I took a slug of juice from the carton. "Go to bed, Mom. I'll tell you all about it in the morning."

"Don't put that carton back after you've drunk from it." She leaned up to kiss me. "Look at my little baby, all grown up."

"I guess so."

"Night, honey. Turn off the lights, okay?"

"Night, Mom."

Half a carton of orange juice didn't begin to slake my thirst. I moved on to ginger ale. I gulped it down so fast it sent a big gingery belch ripping up through my nose.

I went in from the kitchen to find Jacko hunched on the floor beside my bed. "Damn, Jacko! You scared me!"

His eyes gleamed. "Somebody dead," he announced.

"What are you doing up? It's late."

"Somebody dead," he said. "What you know about it?"

"What are you talking about, old man? You having another one of your bad dreams?"

"Ain't no dream," he said.

"Well then, you must be crazy," I said. "But that's not exactly news." I was polite to Jacko only within earshot of Mom. He lived in the room next to mine, in the converted garage I had named the Freak Annex. If I didn't snap back at him, he would drive me nuts with all his creepy muttering and cackling. His latest notion was that he had buried bags of gold all over our yard and our neighbor Mrs. Wagner across the street was sneaking in at night with a shovel, digging it up while we slept.

I rolled him back to his room. "Go on to bed, Jacko. I ain't putting up with your mess tonight." I heaved the sliding door shut behind me.

I flopped on my bed. I stared at my Beatles poster, and *Hair*, and Roger Daltrey looking blind on the album cover of *Tommy*.

I heard Jacko laughing in there.

I felt so lost, so alone. It was just me, and the memory of Arnita stretched on the ground with her head resting against the sidewalk.

5

BY THE TIME I got up, Jacko was puttering in his tackle boxes and Janie and Mom were already off at church. The burnt-toast smell of the kitchen put me in a dark mood. I wandered into the family room, kicking the stupid ottoman, flinging myself onto the stupid sofa. I hated this half-empty house, the cheap furniture we'd picked up at garage sales, thrift shops, along the side of the road. Mississippi had brought us nothing but bad luck from the very first day.

We should have stayed in Indiana. Bud and I tried to tell them, but did they ever listen to us? Did any parents ever listen to their kids?

The phone jangled me out of my chair.

"Arnita's alive," Tim said.

Oh God, thank you God. I pressed the phone to my mouth. All morning I'd been staring at the phone, waiting for it to ring. Trying to pretend Prom Night was a bad dream.

"She's at Baptist Hospital," Tim said. "Intensive care, but they wouldn't tell me her condition. You have to be a member of the family. . . . Dagwood? You there?"

My voice came out a croak. "How did you find her?"

"I called every hospital in town."

"You didn't tell them our names, did you? I mean — should we even be talking about this on the phone?" These were Watergate days. You never knew who might be listening.

"Wait, that's not all I found out. They arrested Red Martin on a DWI. He spent the night in jail. His daddy bailed him out this morning."

I turned to find Jacko in the doorway, watching me with his blue beady eyes. I stretched the phone cord into the living room, shut the door on the cord, and dropped my voice. "Look, we can't just sit back and let Red get in all this trouble."

"Since when are you concerned about Red? Are you forgetting he's like the world's biggest asshole?"

"So what? That's no reason to let him take all the blame for this."

"Sure it is. Name me a better reason." Tim's tone was precise. "I told you, I cannot be involved with this accident, Durwood. I've got too much at stake."

"Look, what if we call the police," I proposed. "Anonymously. We don't give 'em our names. We just tell 'em we are certain Red didn't do it. Tell 'em we can't get involved, but he's definitely innocent." I knew it was a bad idea before I got through describing it.

Tim said, "Yeah, that is too brilliant."

"Well? We have to do something."

He made a skeptical grunt. "March down to the jailhouse and turn ourselves in?"

"Maybe so."

"Well then do it! Go ahead! Fuck up your life — and my life too."

I said, "We did a pretty good job fucking up *her* life, huh?"

"For the thousandth time, goddammit, it was an accident!"

"Not the part where you drove off and left her," I whispered furiously. "That was you. Your decision. You were the one driving. Not me." There, I said it. No more of this "we." Lay it on the table, just who did what.

"Hey. What do you want me to say? I freaked out, so did you."

"No, I was yelling at you to go back the whole time. And you didn't freak out, Tim. That's what was so weird. You were cool, you were just so cool."

"In a situation like that you gotta think fast," he said, "or you're completely screwed."

I thought, Yeah? And where has your fast thinking gotten us?

"Listen, Skippy, call me if you hear something. Otherwise, see you at school mañana. Okay?"

"Yeah."

"Later —"

I hung up. I was not in the mood for the game.

I found Jacko in the family room watching our Sunday-morning favorite, Channel Four, the Reverend Alfred L. Poole live from the Faith Holiness Tabernacle Church in Vicksburg. Reverend Poole was a plump, shiny man, with pink skin and a lofty black pompadour. "Jaheezus, our Lowered, is looking down upawn us right now," he intoned. "Those of you with crippuling injuries, place your hands atop your television consoles at home, and receive the holy healing power of the Lowered."

Jacko liked the man's curdly voice and the way he smote the cripples on the forehead to heal them. He said maybe someday I could drive him to Vicksburg and get Reverend Poole to heal his legs.

Janie came clacking through the door in church shoes, then Mom, overflowing with news of Arnita Beecham. The whole town was talking about the poor girl, skull fracture, brain injury, coma, hit-and-run, the Martin boy arrested on the spot.

I put on my most neutral expression. "Yeah, Tim called. It's terrible. You heard she was elected Prom Queen last night? She was so happy."

"Those poor people, her mama and daddy," Mom said. "You know her, Daniel?"

"Oh sure, I even voted for her. She's in the band, and two of my classes. She's super smart. Pretty too."

When I told her that Arnita's father was the school janitor, I thought Mom might cry. "This is the saddest thing I've ever heard. We have to do something for them."

"I'm not that good a friend, Mom. I just know her from school."

"She needs all the friends she can get. I'll bake a cake one day next week. We'll take it over there, and you can cut their grass for them or something."

I caught Jacko squinting at me with one blue eye. I stuck out my tongue.

Jacko went into a coughing fit. Mom reached down to hammer his back. "Okay now, honey, tell me everything. What did the girls wear? Did you dance?"

"Yeah, we danced. They wore these long dresses." I eased up from the sofa. "I got grass to cut, Mom. I better get to it." That's how desperate I was — I would rather cut grass than sit there and be interrogated one more second. The next innocent question might lead me to break down and tell her everything. I couldn't stand Jacko's blue eye on me.

Next morning the school bus hummed with rumors. Arnita was in serious condition, possibly critical. Red Martin knocked her off her bike on purpose. Or by accident. He was drunk. Or maybe he had nothing to do with it, just happened to drive by with an open beer and the cops pulled him over.

The black kids huddled at the back of the bus, more silent than ever.

When we turned onto Barnett Street everybody hurried to the left side of the bus to see where it happened. Nobody could figure out which driveway exactly. I kept my eyes fixed on the jumble of equations in my algebra book.

Dianne Frillinger was waiting when I got off the bus. In the light of day, in her shapeless plaid jumper, she had resumed her old identity. I felt a little queasy at the memory of the Jitney Jungle parking lot.

"Oh my gosh," she said, "it's so awful about Arnita, did you hear?"

I nodded. "But she's gonna be okay, right?"

"It sounds real bad. Oh Daniel, I just feel so guilty, you know? Like it's all my fault!"

"Your fault?"

"Well — we were so horrible about her when she won! When I think of the things I said about her . . . of course I had no idea that was going to happen. Let me tell you, I almost wish I was a" — she dropped to a whisper — "a *Catholic* so I could go to confession. You were right, Daniel, I was just awful."

"Listen, Dianne —"

"And Debbie feels terrible too. Please, *please* don't think we meant anything about Arnita. I had the nicest time at the prom, truly I did, and I'd hate it if you thought I was prejudiced or anything. Especially after her accident."

"Forget it." I tried to escape, but she had my arm in a vise.

"But I did have the nicest time the other night," she said.

"Yeah, except for that damn seat belt," I said.

Her braces sparkled. "That made it memorable. Mama says thirty years from now that's the part we'll remember the most."

"Great, I'm glad you told her all about it." I made a subtle move to detach my arm from her grip. "You think Red ran over Arnita on purpose?"

"They say it was an accident, but who knows? We saw him leaving the Holiday Inn, remember? He was definitely intoxicated."

"They must not think he's too guilty, right? If they let him out of jail."

"He plays football. He'll be fine." She made a face. "Anyway, a bunch of the girls are going to the hospital tonight to see Arnita. They're working on a special song for her."

I wanted a report on Arnita's condition. "You going?"

"Oh I don't think so . . . wouldn't it be kind of hypocritical? After the things I said?"

"It might make you feel better," I said.

"Our pastor offered a special prayer for her yesterday. They've never prayed for a black before. Not in our church. Oh Daniel, it's just too unbelievable."

The bell rang, thank you bell.

"Call me if you hear anything else," I said. I hurried into homeroom.

Tim's desk was right next to mine. It was still empty when Miss Anderson called roll.

"Cousins," she said, and was met by silence. "Tim Cousins?" She made a mark and went on with the roll.

Chicken! Deserter! Playing hooky to keep from showing his face! I doodled an elaborate maze on the back of my notebook. Didn't Tim know how guilty it looked for him to cut school, the Monday after what happened on Saturday night?

The loudspeaker squealed. Although Mr. Hamm had been principal at Minor since dinosaurs roamed the earth, he was still learning to use the PA system. He warmed up with a couple puffs of air, then set the speaker buzzing with his rotund syllables. "Good morning, boys and girls, few announcements here, first to say we're all just real sorry to hear about the accident this weekend. I know we'll all say a special prayer for the speedy recovery of Arlene Beecham."

Arlene?

A hum of static. Click click went the microphone key. "Scuse me," Mr. Hamm said, above the background whisper of the office secretary, Miss Pitts. "I seem to have misspoke. *Arnita* is her name, of course. We all know her, she's the daughter of Mr. Beecham, our — maintenance engineer, and she's a real special girl. So anyway let's send a kind thought to her family, if we can. Sergeant Magill of the sheriff's department is handling the case, and I'm sure they'll find whoever injured the girl. Next, we've had a problem with people leaving their sweaty gym clothes all over the locker room, so from now on we'll have a new policy. . . ."

That was it? That was all he had to say? If I got run over and almost killed, I would want Mr. Hamm to say a few more words about me before moving on to the sweaty gym clothes.

The bell rang. I shuffled into the noisy jam of slamming lockers. In high school it's all about how you walk down the hall — whether you stroll through the flow or dart along the edges, whether you hold the stack of books on your hip with one hand (guys) or press them two-handed to your chest (sissies and girls). Notes are scribbled and passed, rumors fanned and blown down the hall. This morning, the word in the air was *Arnita.*

I kept my head down, books propped on my hip, and plowed straight down the middle.

The bell shrilled, draining all this excitement into the classrooms, where it was swiftly killed off. Eight-thirty algebra, first class of the day. When she wasn't crowning the Prom Queen, Mrs. Passworth could be found at her overhead projector, beaming a square of light onto a pull-down screen at the blackboard. She sat in the upward-thrown glare of the projector, lit up like the Bride of Frankenstein, drawing spidery equations on the acetate sheet with a wax pencil. The shadow of her hand swooped and fluttered batlike around the screen.

"Today we're going to learn something new," she said. "Who can tell me how to determine if a number is natural, integer, rational, irrational, or real?"

No one volunteered. We slumped in our seats. Dutifully I copied the squiggles and numbers into my notebook, but all I could think was Arnita — what would she remember when she woke up? What if she didn't wake up? How does it feel in a coma — is it a massive wave of confusion, like algebra, or is it like being asleep, or lost in another world? Was her family gathered around her bed? A bouncing green dot keeping track of her heart?

"Can anyone tell me why we need to reverse the relative positions of these two factors?" said Mrs. Passworth. No one breathed, for fear she might call on them. At first algebra had appeared to be just a complicated form of arithmetic, dense but eventually understandable. After Christmas, though, Mrs. Passworth had wandered off into a fantasy world of linear relations and functions, polynomials and radical expressions. For weeks now, none of us had known what the hell she was talking about.

Normally Tim and I spent this period passing hilarious notes across the aisle. All our teachers were laughable in some way, but Passworth's starchy exactitude, her prim posture at the projector, the upward sweep of her beehive, combined to give us a full fifty-five minutes of fun every day. She wore a plain white blouse and no-nonsense gray skirt, and so much mascara that you wondered how she could keep her eyes open.

"Class," she said, "class. We're not focusing. We need to focus our minds, or we'll never catch on! These are important concepts!"

"Mrs. Passworth," Sandie Williams said, "I just don't get it. Why did you put that thing under that other thing?"

"What thing, Sandie?"

"The thing with the V on it. You know, the little checkmarky thing that goes across. Why did you move it down there?"

Mrs. Passworth snapped off the projector. The room fell into darkness, a hush. "My God, this is hopeless," she said in a quiet, dangerous voice. "Do you people know or even care that I have a master's degree? Do you realize I could be teaching on the college level instead of to a bunch of —" She left unsaid what we were. She stood abruptly and walked to the front of the room. "I don't know why I even try. I sit there and explain it all perfectly clearly to you, and you're not even listening!"

I shifted in my seat. Sandie Williams looked ready to cry. Passworth was just getting started. She marched back and forth railing about how, if you don't know the names of the basic building blocks, how do you ever expect to learn the blah blah blah, year after year teaching these rooms full of small-town dullards without the least imagination, on and on for long minutes until it got a little weird, trapped in that dim room with her saying, "Doesn't anyone care about anything? I can't take much more of this. I tell you, I can't!"

It seemed to me that we were no more stupid than on any other day. But Mrs. Passworth had become suddenly unable to tune out our stupidity. We had no hope of understanding what she was trying to teach us, and it was really getting to her.

Jimmy Yelverton spoke up: "Miz Passworth?"

"What?!"

"Can I go to the bathroom?"

She flung the laminated pass at him. Jimmy picked it up from the floor and ambled out.

Mrs. Passworth burst into tears.

We all looked at each other. You don't often see a non-substitute teacher break down and cry.

She went to her desk, turned her chair to the wall, and made little mewling sounds. When at last she turned to face us, her eyes were all smudged. "Y'all will just have to excuse me," she sniffed. "Things have been very strange lately."

"We'll try harder, Miz Passworth." Mindy Maples was a cheerleader in every sense of the word.

"No, it's not you. You're children. What do you know? You can't help it if you're ignorant — no, and it's not just this terrible thing with the Beecham girl. Let's face it, it's me."

"Ma'am?" Mindy cocked her head to one side.

"There are lights, you know, in the nighttime. Very bright lights around my house," Mrs. Passworth said.

"Do you think you're having a nervous breakdown?" asked Mindy. A couple of boys tittered but the rest of the class sat dead quiet. This was no joke. Mrs. Passworth was rumored to have spent time in an actual loony bin, some years back.

"No, Mindy, I don't think I am," she said, "but thank you for asking. I've been under a lot of pressure but so what? We're all under pressure." She folded her hands on the desk. "Labor Day weekend, I decided I would make myself a little barbecue, you know, it being the holiday, and there I was thinking, Oh how sad, all alone on Labor Day, cooking up my little hamburger patty in the backyard, when all of a sudden — let me stop here and ask, has anybody in this class ever been attacked by a blue jay?"

To judge from the stillness in the room, no one had.

"Well you see there, how unusual it is. How astonished I was when the first one came down from a tree and struck me on the head. Right here." She touched her brunette pouf. "And then another one. And a third. Three separate blue jays came from out of nowhere to attack me."

"Like in that movie," said Kevin Donohue.

"*The Birds*," I offered.

"Exactly," said Mrs. Passworth. "I had to leave my patty on the grill and run for cover! It wasn't like I was disturbing them — I was minding my own business! Can anybody think of a reason why three blue jays would suddenly decide to attack an innocent person?"

"Maybe they wanted your burger," said Kevin Mayhew.

Our laughter exploded down the hall and died away. Every eye went to the clock: eighteen minutes to go and the second hand crawling so painfully slow.

"Miz Passworth?" That was Beverly DeShields, a plump Christian girl, a total brainiac. "Is any of this gonna be on the test?"

"No, Beverly. None of it."

"Cause I had a question about last night's homework. The binomials?"

"Save it, Beverly," she snapped. "I am done for one day. Class dismissed."

We bounded out of our desks. By lunchtime, the whole school knew Mrs. Passworth had flipped out in first period and gone home. Mr. Hamm took over her classes and showed filmstrips of the national parks. I couldn't wait to tell Tim — chicken bastard that he was, hiding at home.

I went to the pay phone in the courtyard. Tim let it ring twelve times before picking up. "'Lo."

"What the hell are you doing at home?" I said.

"I'm sick."

"Oh yeah, I'll bet. Don't you think it looks a little strange, you going AWOL today of all days?"

"Yes, Mother. Quit worrying. Everything's fine. What's the news?"

"Apparently, that person is still in intensive care." Other kids were filtering past from the cafeteria. "Look, I can't talk here. I'm coming over to your house after band. You better be there."

"I will. Jeez. Calm down, Skippy. Everything's fine. Okay?"

I let out a breath. "Okay."

"Stop worrying, you'll give yourself a heart attack."

"I thought I would have one in algebra this morning," I said. "You won't believe what she did."

"What?"

"No. I'm not telling. You don't deserve to hear, you stay-at-home traitor!"

"Fine. Be that way. I'll see you after school. Later —"

"Gator." I hung up first.

Dropped in another fifteen cents and called Mom to tell her I'd be home late.

"Honey, remember Daddy's coming home tomorrow. You've still got to finish the grass."

"I'll get up early and cut it."

"That's what you always say. You be sweet at Miz Cousins's house, you hear?"

Be sweet. What would Mom say if she knew the truth of what we'd done? She would march me straight to the cops to confess the whole thing. If Tim wouldn't go with me, I'd still have to tell the whole story. Including him. That's what Mom would say.

It would be big trouble, oh yes, the worst of my life, but in time you could get beyond trouble. Even trouble that bad. Trying to hang on to a secret like this, on the other hand, was the kind of mistake that could mess up the rest of your life.

Tim was not my master. He was not in charge of me. I would tell him straight out — either he went with me to the police or I'd go alone. He wouldn't like it, but that's how it was going to be. Take it or leave it.

Once I made up my mind, I felt better. Anxious but better. I saw a glimmer of possibility in the darkness.

"Take it or leave it," I said. "I am not going into my senior year with this thing hanging over my head."

"I understand how you feel," he said. We sat cross-legged in his mystic cave of a room, with its thick maroon shag, the lava lamp, the twirly lantern scattering silvery light across the bed. Tim's art-class drawings covered the walls. He specialized in elaborate renderings of fairy-tale castles, fortresses, ruined temples, a few tiny people here and there on the ramparts.

"We'll go to the police together," I said. "Right now. Before we lose our nerve."

"That's a really noble impulse, Dogwood. Do you think Red Martin would do the same for you? If the situation were reversed?"

"I don't care what Red would do. This is what *we* have to do."

"I just want you to think through the logic of what you're proposing."

"It's really simple, Tim. We tell the truth. We don't have to hide anymore, or cut school to sit around wondering when we'll get caught."

He propped up on his elbows, studying me. "They charged Red with drunk driving, right? Not with hurting Arnita, or anything to do with her. Think about it. He *was* drunk. He *was* driving. He got busted. Case closed. How is that our fault?"

"Everyone in school thinks he's the one who ran her over."

"Who cares? The police must not think that, they haven't charged him with it. So your big confession won't change a thing for Red — or for Arnita."

"But Tim. It's just not right."

He jumped up to pace the floor. "Look. If I thought the cops would believe us? I might go along with you. But Skippy, why should they? If we tell, we end up doing a few months each in the juvy home. Where, you know, we will get fucked, because that's what they do to the new boys out there. If I ever get out, my father won't let me back in the house. I won't get to go to college. I'll end up working in some auto parts store. All because you had this bizarre urge to help Red Martin." He put his head down and kept talking. "Meanwhile Arnita still got hurt, Red still got his DWI, and we've got a felony record for the rest of our lives."

"That's not necessarily how it would go," I said.

"That's the *best* it could go. The best possible outcome. You think the cops are going to give you a prize for honesty? Believe me, they won't."

"If you won't go with me," I said, "I have to go by myself."

"Look Skippy — you want me to admire your principles? Okay, I admire 'em. But don't ask me to confess to something I didn't do. I didn't hurt Arnita. She ran into our car. I never laid a finger on her. And if we happen to be the only two people who know Red had nothing to do with it, I can live with that. Really."

I shook my head. "I don't think I can."

"Fine. Just wait. Don't do anything now. Let's see what happens. Maybe she'll be okay."

Tim knew me so well. I didn't really want to go to the cops. I didn't want to confess. I came over here so he could talk me out of it. He only had to persuade me a little. I did not want to hear my mother's voice when I called her from jail.

"Arnita is gonna nail us," I said.

"If that happens, we'll deal with it," Tim said. "Now tell me about Passworth. Don't leave out a single detail."

That was my last chance to put everything right. I walked right on by.

6

Every couple of days Mr. Hamm read a hopeful report from the hospital: Arnita had moved her toes. She drank from a straw. She recognized her name.

The Frillinger twins went to the hospital with a group of girls bearing flowers, teddy bears, and balloons. Arnita's mother intercepted them in the waiting room. "She was kind of standoffish," Dianne reported. "We'd practiced a song for Arnita, but the mother wouldn't let us anywhere near her."

"What song was it?"

"'We've Only Just Begun,'" Dianne said.

"My God, were you trying to kill her? Don't you know the Carpenters can be fatal?"

"It's not a joke, Daniel. It's so sad. They say she might have permanent brain damage."

"She's gonna be fine," I said. "Don't ask me why, but I have this feeling she is." That was pure wishful thinking, of course. If I kept wishing hard enough, I might help it come true.

Red Martin came strutting into physics on Thursday sporting a brand-new crew cut and a tight yellow T-shirt that showed off his muscly chest. It was his first time at school since Prom Night. He was cracking gum, grinning, enjoying the stir he had provoked just by showing up. "Watch out, ladies, steer clear of the jailbird!" he crowed. His buddies laughed. Red faked a pass with his chemistry book, did a graceful linebacker pirouette, and swung into his desk.

The black kids in back put out a silence so cold you could feel it. Gradually the rest of the room fell quiet. It wasn't all that smart of Red to come in cutting up, cracking gum, just after Mr. Hamm had read out the latest medical report on Arnita.

"What?" he said. "What did I do?"

"Just shut up, Red," said Emily Pickens, a do-gooder in barrettes and a pink sweater. "You've done enough."

When Red realized she was speaking for most of the room, the light went out of his smile. This was Red Martin, remember, in his third big year atop the Minor High jock-popularity pyramid, and now suddenly he was the jerk who ran over the Queen of the Prom.

His face slowly turned the color of meat. "Well hell, people. Y'all got it all wrong. I didn't hit her."

I felt almost sorry for him.

He whirled on me sharply, as if he had detected it. "What the hell are you looking at, Five Spot?"

I glanced to both sides. "Me?"

"You're the only Five Spot I see. You like my new haircut? I got it so I could look more like you."

His buddies snickered. It took a moment for Five Spot to register, then I understood, with a flood of shame, that he meant the five tiny patches on the back of my head where hair stubbornly refused to grow. Mom said with my blond hair no one noticed, but I begged the barber to leave it longer back there.

I said, "Why'd you really have to cut it, Red? Can't get rid of those pesky head lice?" It wasn't the greatest comeback ever, but a few kids gave me a laugh.

The rest of that day, wherever I went, there was Red. "Hey, Five Spot, how's it going?" "Five Spot, lookin' goood." He and his henchmen called me Five Spot so loudly and often, kids I didn't even know began saying, "Hey, Five Spot!"

I thought back over my Prom Night encounter with Red and

Larry in the men's room off the lobby at the Holiday Inn, searching for something that might account for this sudden, all-out campaign of harassment. I couldn't come up with anything.

"Red hardly ever noticed me before, and suddenly he's my worst enemy," I told Tim. "I don't get it. Maybe he did see us that night. Maybe he knows what we did."

"Look, he's in deep trouble," said Tim. "Twisting slowly in the wind. Everybody turns against him, he starts looking around for a target, and the first person he sees is you. Tomorrow, you watch — it'll be somebody else."

He was right. The next day, it was Tim. Red decided Tim should be known as Stinky in honor of his fondness for English Leather cologne. All morning Red made comments about Stinky's hair, Stinky's dorky black high-tops, Stinky's embarrassing wide-wale bell-bottom corduroys. He made kissy sounds when Stinky got called to the blackboard in chemistry. By lunchtime all of Red's cronies were crooning "Hey, Stink-ayyy" when Tim walked by.

"Maybe he does know," Tim said. "Why else would he go after the two of us?"

"We've gone from being nobodies to the world-famous Five Spot and Stinky."

"Yeah, what is he talking about, anyway — Five Spot?"

"These little places on my head," I said.

"What? Let me see —"

I turned my head so he could see.

"Look at that." He touched one spot with his finger. "What happened?"

"Nothing. My hair won't grow there anymore. No reason."

But there was a reason.

Last December in Alabama, our first visit to Granny and Jacko since we moved to Mississippi. Granny asked me to ride along in her old Rambler wagon to buy worms for an afternoon of fishing.

We were driving to town, talking. From nowhere a huge truck roared up behind us, blasting its horn, whipping around in a storm of flying gravel. Granny cried, "Whoo, honey! Where did he come from?"

The truck dwindled quickly in our windshield, flinging rocks that pecked at our glass.

Granny's fingers fluttered around the rim of the wheel. "Daniel, if it's all right with you, I think I'll pull over for a minute."

"You okay, Granny?"

"Oh yes, I'm just . . . a little shaky, I reckon. That truck was going so fast!" She eased the Rambler to the shoulder and switched off the engine.

All the color left her face. Her hand came over her mouth.

"Granny? What is it?"

A mysterious flicker in her expression — a wince. Or a smile. "Oh my!" she said, then slumped against her door and died.

Just like that. That's how fast she died in the seat beside me, with cars whizzing past. The sweep-second hand on the dashboard clock ticked off the seconds. Traffic rushed by *whoom whoom* like the Indy 500. Oh God, Granny, please!

I opened the door. A string of blackbirds flew up from the field by the highway. The word Help rose in my throat. Somebody Help.

I started waving my arms at oncoming traffic. Many cars flashed by before a white pickup slowed and crunched onto the gravel shoulder. I ran up as he was getting out, a tall slender man in a cowboy hat, a glint of gold in his smile. "What's the trouble?"

"It's my — my grandmother, she's — sick or something!" I couldn't bring myself to say *dead.* "You gotta help us, please! Hurry!"

The man peered into the Rambler. I hung back, squeezing my arms to my sides, fighting the urge to take off into that field of weeds and keep running.

He pushed Granny out of the driver's seat, started the engine, and barked at me to get in back. He drove the Rambler faster than I knew it could go. In a few minutes Granny lay on a stretcher in the emergency room in Pigeon Creek, with a doctor pounding her chest.

I waited in the hallway with the tall man, and listened to her dying all over again.

"It's my fault," I said.

"Don't go blaming yourself. Wasn't for you, she'da been out there all alone with nobody to help her. She's lucky to have you." He ruffled my hair. "Poor kid."

And then he did something I still can't believe, something so swift and unexpected that it was over almost before I knew he was doing it. His hand slid around, cupping the back of my head. He bent down and pressed his mouth to mine, kissing me hard on the lips, gripping my head to hold me there.

I shoved him hard with both hands. "Get *away* from me!"

He leaped back as if I'd bitten him. "Sorry," he said, with a strange, painful smile. He lunged for the door, nearly running over a pair of nurses.

I never told anybody what he did. The only sign of it was those five little spots on the back of my head where his fingertips touched me. Where the hair wouldn't grow.

And now Red Martin had pointed them out to the world.

Tim said, "Listen Dumwood, I'm getting really sick of being tortured by him. We need to start up a counterinsurgency." He aimed his index finger and squeezed off a shot. "Hey, isn't that your mother's car?"

Indeed it was. "That's strange," I said. "I'll give you a call — later, gator." I loped over to the green Country Squire wagon. "Hey Mom, what's up?"

"Hey honey, get in but don't put your feet on the cake."

I breathed in the warm sugar smell. "Who's it for?"

"I'm taking you to the Beechams' house, remember?"

"What? Mom. No."

"I managed to get that mower in the back of the car all by myself, so you can unload it. Mrs. Beecham said she'd be delighted for you to cut their grass."

"You called her?"

"Just as nice as she could be. She and her husband have been at the hospital day and night, they've had to just let their yard go. I told her how much you wanted to help."

"Mom, I didn't say that."

"Well, I said it for you." She turned right on Bridge Street. "So you might as well smile and be gracious about it."

"Mom —"

"No backtalk. I'm dropping you off and taking Janie to the doctor. We'll pick you up around five."

Our tires roared crossing the iron bridge above the Yatchee, a sluggish little river with steep weedy banks. A passel of East Minor kids hung out at the railing, throwing rocks in the water.

I said, "Where'd you get the idea I'm this big friend of Arnita's? I barely know her."

"Doesn't matter. You can still do her mother a favor," said Mom. "I'm surprised at you, Daniel. I thought you'd be eager to help."

"Okay! Sheesh!" I glared at the falling-down houses and house trailers of East Minor, the barbecue sheds, mangy dogs, half-naked kids running through sprinklers.

"Your brother finally called this morning. He broke his foot a second time, so at least they can't send him . . . overseas. I told him he's a fool to keep riding that motorcycle, but he won't listen to his old mother." She glanced at the paper in her hand. "Help me look for it. Three twenty-two Forrest Street. Why can't they get some street signs on this side of town?"

I spotted an aging frame house, peeling paint, a large weedy yard, and a chain-link fence. "There's 322," I said. "Nobody home. Can we go, please?"

"She said let ourselves in the gate if they're not there."

"Mom, if they're not home I don't wanna —"

"Daniel?" Her sharp gaze pinned me in place. "Take this cake to the porch before you get your hands all greasy taking the mower out of the back. Ring the bell. She's home. I'm sure they don't have a car."

I carried the plastic-wrapped cake, still warm from the oven, across the yard and up two steps to the porch. I placed it on a little table beside the front door. There was no doorbell. I knocked.

The porch floor shifted under approaching footsteps. A large brown woman peered out.

"Mrs. Beecham?"

"Mm-hmm."

"I'm Daniel Musgrove. I think my mom called you. To come cut your grass?"

"Hullo, Musgrove. I been waiting for you." Mrs. Beecham must have been beautiful like her daughter once, the same delicate line to her face. Time and a lot of food appeared to have widened her out. She filled the doorway in her crisp white uniform.

"My mom baked you a cake," I said.

"Well here, give it to me." She opened the door with her elbow, reaching for the platter as she squinted past me. "Does she want to come in?"

"She's gotta take my sister to the doctor," I said, but Mrs. Beecham was already waving to Mom to crank down her window.

"Don't you want to come in?" she called. "I can make coffee."

"Oh, no, thank you so much, I've got a million things to do," Mom said. "Daniel, come get this mower." She was glad to bring me over, but she couldn't wait to get out of there.

After she was gone, Mrs. Beecham stayed on the porch to watch me gas up the mower. "So this is the famous Musgrove," she said. "How do you know my Arnita?"

"We're in the band. And we've got a couple classes together."

"Because after your mother called, I asked Arnita about you," she said. "She's never even heard of you."

"She's awake? That's great! I mean, the last I knew she was in a coma."

"No." Her eyes never left my face. "So if she doesn't know you, what are you doing over here wanting to cut my grass for me?"

"It was my mom's idea. When she heard about the accident, she wanted to make you a cake. And she thought I could give you a hand with the yard."

"You look like somebody who knows something, Musgrove. Like

maybe you know what happened to her that night. She has a hard time recalling exactly."

"Oh, no ma'am," I said, "I don't know anything about it."

"Maybe you had something to do with it," she went on, gently mocking. "You got to feeling guilty, came around here thinking you could do me a favor, that would help you feel better about the whole thing."

I had expected Arnita might nail us. I was not prepared for her mother. "I'm sorry. That's not how it is. I just came to help. If you want me to go, I will."

"Aw Musgrove, try and look a little bit indignant when you are wrongly accused. Unless you just want everybody to *know* you're guilty."

"But I'm not!"

"Tell you what." She swept an arm across her unruly yard. "You cut all that grass. Rake up what you cut and put it in them bags yonder — see that roll of yard bags where I'm pointing? Don't be leaving grass clippings all over my yard."

"Yes ma'am."

"And then I'll let you know what else." She opened the door and went in.

"Yes ma'am!" I held off saluting until she shut the door.

I yanked the mower to life. The big Yazoo roar drowned out everything.

I threw myself into cutting that yard, sending up a green fog of pulverized grass. My heart pounded, not just from the effort of pushing the mower. Mrs. Beecham was onto me even before I set foot on her porch. More psychic than Jacko! Jumps to conclusions faster than a speeding jackrabbit!

But the news was wonderful: Arnita was not in a coma. She was not going to die. She didn't know who I was, had never even heard of me. She wouldn't accuse me or Tim. Our Lie would not be found out. I felt a great selfish flood of relief. I could already hear Tim saying *I told you so.*

Mrs. Beecham stepped outside as I mowed the last slice of grass. She had changed from her maid uniform to a blue flowered house-dress and flip-flops.

She held a beautiful glass of lemonade with sweat-beads rolling down the side. I wondered if this might be evidence that she was softening to my presence. I killed the engine.

"Hot day," she said. She put her lips to the glass and drank deeply.

"Yes ma'am."

"If you're thirsty, there's a hose out there by the shed. I'd offer you some lemonade, but this is the last of it." She eased herself to the porch swing.

"Thanks. I'm not thirsty." I started raking. The cut grass was quickly whitening in the afternoon heat. I thought I might die of thirst watching Mrs. Beecham sip from her tall, frosty glass, but I refused to drink a drop from the garden hose while she sat there with her lemonade.

It took a long time to fill a dozen large bags with cut grass and stack them at the curb.

A beat-up orange taxi pulled up. Mrs. Beecham stepped back in the house for her purse and keys. "I'm going to spell Beecham at the hospital," she said, locking the door. "He's been there since last night. Is your mother coming back for you?"

"I hope so."

"All right then, I'll see you tomorrow at four-thirty."

"Ma'am?"

"You get out of band practice at four, correct? So you can be here by four-thirty. Don't be late. Do you have a ladder at your house?"

"Yes, but —"

"Bring it. We've got work to do." She climbed in the taxi and rode away.

She might have said thanks, Daniel, nice job, thank you for mowing the yard from the goodness of your heart — but no! Come back tomorrow! Bring a ladder!

I carried the last rakeful of grass clippings to the garbage can by the back door. I lifted the lid to find my mother's lemon pound cake, still in its plastic wrapping, sitting atop the smelly garbage.

I put the lid back on the can and dumped the clippings on the ground beside the can.

Mom and Janie drove up soon after. "Oh look how nice it looks!" Mom said. "You did a good job, sweetie. I bet Miz Beecham was thrilled."

"Not exactly. She says I'm supposed to come back tomorrow."

"Get in, Danny," said Janie. "We're gonna go buy the stuff to make a volcano."

I hoisted the mower onto the tailgate. "Mom, I cut her whole yard for free. Do I really have to come back and do more tomorrow?"

"She must really need you," she said. "I think it would be very sweet of you to do that."

"For free?"

"Of course for free," Mom said. "Look at their house, you think she can afford to pay you? Imagine their hospital bills, that child has already been in there a long time."

"But Mom —"

"Did she say anything about the cake?"

I looked out the window. "She said she loved it."

"I knew she would. Everybody loves that cake."

The next day after band I trudged across the Yatchee bridge, past the usual gang of boys throwing rocks into the river, up the long hill to the stoop where Mrs. Beecham sat waiting for me. "Hullo, Musgrove."

"How's Arnita today?"

"Better. They've got her using a walker. Beecham said she made it down the hall and back by herself this morning."

"Mrs. Beecham, how bad is she hurt? I mean, is she getting better?"

"Sure she is. She's not exactly her old self yet, but every day a little more. Hey now, didn't I tell you to bring a ladder?"

"Yeah, but how am I supposed to carry a ladder? I take the bus to school, then I have to walk all the way over here."

"Well, we'll just have to borrow you one," she said. "How you expect to paint the house without a ladder?"

"I'm not painting the house," I said.

"Sure you are! Look at that house! Don't you think it needs painting? Who do you think is gonna do it?"

"You expect me to paint this whole house by myself? I've never painted anything."

"Let me tell you, the best painter who ever lived had to start somewhere. And I bought you the good kind of paint too, look here. Not the kind that comes flaking off in the first rain. Got you a big scrub brush and some Clorox so you can get off all that mildew before you go putting good paint on there."

"Mrs. Beecham, listen."

She folded her arms. "What?"

"I've got homework, you know. And I'm in the band . . . and we have this huge yard I have to cut by myself since my brother went off to — Vietnam." With my luck Bud would now be sent to Vietnam and that would be my fault too. "I don't have time to paint your house."

"I don't expect you to finish it this week," she said. "You just work on it nice and steady, couple hours a day. You'll be done before you know it."

"Mrs. Beecham. We live eleven miles out in the country. I ride the bus to school. How am I supposed to get home from here?"

"You got a bike?" she said.

I nodded.

"Ride it. You could stand to lose a few. That's how Arnita stays so slender, she rides that bike of hers everywhere. Or she did, before this happened."

I heard the message: Arnita is not riding her bike now.

I believed that I understood what she was offering me: a chance to work off my guilt without having to confess. Instead of trying to explain anything, I could come here every afternoon and pay down the balance of what I owed.

Tim got mad on the phone. "Why are you getting mixed up with those people? Are you trying to get us caught?"

It was my mom's big idea, I explained. I was trapped. "This Beecham woman has got our number, Timmy. She had us all figured out before I even got there."

"That's impossible," Tim said. "I think you just look naturally guilty. You go around *radiating* guilt. To me, what looks the most suspicious is you showing up wanting to do favors for her, while Arnita's still in the hospital."

"Tim. The woman knows."

"Oh come on. You're so paranoid you're gonna get us caught. Cut it out, Skippy. Quit thinking about it."

"I can't, Tim. I'm not like you. I can't just forget what we did."

"You could at least try," he said.

Every morning I got up an hour early to ride my bike to town, so I could spend the afternoons painting the Beecham house a soft minty green with white trim. At first it was hard waking up to my lonely bowl of Rice Krispies, pedaling off down the road at dawn, but actually I began to enjoy it. Dad was around the house more these days, with his smaller territory, so it was good to be out of there before he got up. The open road was better than the smelly old school bus anyway — bugs humming in the weeds, the whir of my skinny tires on pavement. I learned every wrinkle in the road between our house and town. I whizzed along fast enough to startle quail from the weeds.

But once I got to school, I was the quarry. Each day began with homeroom torture from Red and his gang. Somehow Tim and I had become the answer to the bully's prayers. He used all the time-honored methods — a fart sound when I sat at my desk, an elbow to topple my books to the floor, a chorus of boys chirping "Five Spot!" in cartoon falsetto. Red was a genius at slow torture of the drip, drip, drip variety. Once you made it onto his list, you could never feel safe. Two days or a week might pass without incident, you'd begin to breathe a little easier — then a foot shoots out to trip you, a hand slams open your bathroom stall, an elbow sends your lunch tray flying.

It went on week after week. I wished to God I could be an anonymous brain/loser again. I hadn't realized how good I'd had it when nobody knew me at all. Now everyone in the whole school was either torturing me or feeling sorry for me — poor Five Spot, the object of Red's relentless attention. Now and then some kid shot me a furtive glance of sympathy, but once you're singled out for the full bully treatment, no one sticks his neck out to help you.

I had pitied and avoided other kids in this fix, like Rachel Bostick, the obese girl with hair on her arms, and poor Cissy Chappell, whose nose and receding chin provoked whinnies wherever she went. Never had I imagined myself as one of them: a pariah, an object of pity and contempt.

It bothered Tim even more than me. He got a little quieter and madder each day. Something had spilled over inside him, some kind of corrosive liquid.

Every morning, a new round of public humiliation. The other kids watched it happening and looked away; it was only one of many such campaigns under way in our school at all times. Torture was a time-honored Minor High tradition, along with gossip, flirtation, school spirit, and seniors cutting class on Friday afternoons in the spring.

Red Martin was an excellent linebacker. No one would stop him from doing anything he wanted to do. The only way it would ever stop was if Red got tired of us and moved on.

In the meantime I refused to let him ruin my life. I did my best to ignore him.

Tim wasn't able to do that. He took every sideways glance from Red as a frontal assault. I could never convince him that his furious reaction only encouraged the bully. He fumed, he seethed. His face flushed every time Red came within forty feet of us.

We talked about it at night on the phone. Tim wanted only one thing: revenge. He wanted to do something awful to Red. Blow his car up. Burn down his house. Fill his locker with dead animals. Tie him up, shoot him in the eyes. Drag his body down a dirt road. "County Road 43 is real long and bumpy," he said. "I think that would do fine."

We moved through school like a pair of shadows, trying to be invisible. The worst day was Thursday, mandatory assembly in the auditorium. With no seating chart, Red and his friends were free to sit where they wanted, which meant they sat directly behind us.

We started sitting up front under the watchful eye of Mr. Hamm.

Tim hunched over his sketch pad, shading in the bricks of a turreted castle. I studied the shapely legs of the Red Cross lady onstage as she stood before the easel with the half-red thermometer showing how much blood they'd collected so far. Something wet touched my ear —

I turned. That was Red's spitty finger. His pals started up snorting.

"Cut it out, Red," I said, loud enough to draw a look from Mr. Hamm.

A minute went by, then I felt Red's fingertips touching the bare spots on the back of my head.

"A perfect fit," he whispered. "Oh, honey, come home with me after school!"

His gang tittered.

I knocked his hand away. "Stop it, Red!"

"Boys!" Mr. Hamm said. "Can we try to act like adults, please? Even if we're just little children? Miz Prentice, please continue."

Something poked me in the butt.

I reached back to wrest it away. A rolled-up newspaper. A tee-hee from Red's gang of Munchkins.

Tim stared straight ahead, his mouth set in a grim line. If Red wanted to poke at me like a fourth-grade bully, I could slap his hand away and go on with my life. Tim couldn't do that.

"County Road 43," he said softly.

Mr. Hamm aimed a quizzical expression over my head. I turned to see a man in a Smokey hat and uniform, and another man in civilian clothes, strolling down the aisle of the auditorium toward us.

Cold sweat sprang from my pores.

Red said, "What's the matter, Five Spot, see a ghost?" Then he turned in his seat and saw something worse than a ghost: a Hinds County sheriff's deputy.

"Sorry to interrupt, Mr. Hamm," said the man in shirtsleeves. "We've got a warrant for a Dudley Ronald Martin. Is he here? Dudley Martin?"

Oh my God. Dudley was Red. Red was Dudley. Dudley! Ol' Five Spot could make good use of this information. *Oh well hello, Dudley, lookin' swell, Dudley. . . .*

Currently Dudley looked terrified. He rose halfway out of his seat. For a second I thought he was going to try to dash out of there, but his shoulders slumped. He sank back down in his seat.

"Come on, son," said the tall cop.

"What's the charge?" Red said.

"Assault with a deadly weapon," said the cop, "leaving the scene of an accident with injuries . . . you want to hear the rest?"

"I didn't assault nobody," Red said. "This is fucked up."

"*Don't* use that language with me!" The cop jerked Red's arm behind his back.

"Red," Mr. Hamm said, "go with these men. I'll call your daddy. Go on, son. We'll get this straightened out."

Red's friends shrank back to let them by. He tried to wave off the handcuffs. "You don't need those, man! I said I'll go with you."

"Procedure," the cop said. "Turn around, put your hands behind your back." He snapped Red's wrists together and walked him up the aisle.

"I didn't hit her," Red said, loud, so everyone could hear. "I didn't do anything wrong."

Tim was the first one to put his hands together. He began clapping slowly, deliberately. Others joined in. A swell of applause rose as the cops led Red out of the auditorium.

Mr. Hamm said, "Stop! Boys and girls, everyone be quiet!" The clapping broke into pockets of derisive laughter. "I just want to say, Red is a fine young man as well as an excellent football player, and I'm sure this is all a mistake. He didn't hurt anyone."

"Bullshit!" came a shout from the back. One of the black boys.

Now it was the white kids' turn to grow quiet.

"Mr. Hamm, why you stick up for him?" That was J. T. Lewis, a black stringbean basketball player. "I didn't hear you sticking up for Arnita Beecham when he run her over!"

"Yeah!"

"Red's been walking around free all this time," said Leon Barber. "Arnita still in the hospital! You think he'd be walking around free if she was white?"

"Wait a minute," said Mr. Hamm. "This is not the place to have that kind of discussion."

J.T. cried, "You say Red didn't hurt nobody. How you know that? Was you there?"

"Sit down and be quiet, J.T.," said Hamm. "Miss Prentice has come all the way from Vicksburg to share her important information with us."

The Red Cross lady looked terrified, what with cops and handcuffs and shouting, but she tried plowing ahead with her presentation. She didn't get far. The muttering grew to a chant: *Arnita. Arnita.* Shoes tapped the floor in time to her name.

"Isn't this fun?" Tim said in my ear. "Did you see Red's face?"

"Dudley's face, you mean."

He laughed. "God, don't you love that?"

"I've got a bad feeling about this," I said.

"Aw, Eeyore, you've always got a bad feeling. Lighten up!"

Miss Prentice fled the stage. Hamm called for order, too late. Black kids were up out of their seats, yelling. Nervous white kids were streaming out of the auditorium. It was one kind of shock to see the star linebacker handcuffed and taken away, quite another to find that our black students — the well-behaved twenty percent of our school who stayed quiet and kept to the back of the auditorium, the classrooms, the bus — were not so quiet now. They were angry and loud. This was new.

That afternoon I rode over the river to find Mrs. Beecham in her yard, whacking a rug with a broomstick. She wore her hair bound up in a polka-dot kerchief, like Mammy in *Gone With the Wind*. "Musgrove! You're late!"

"Assembly went long today. The police came in and arrested Red Martin."

"Is that right." Her stick went *smack!* on the rug.

"Yep. They put handcuffs on him." I dragged the latest gallon of paint from under the steps.

Mrs. Beecham said, "Did they say what the charge is?"

"Assault with a deadly weapon. I don't understand it. Are they saying he had a gun?"

"No. If you run over somebody, your car is considered a deadly weapon."

I spilled a pool of pale green paint into the tray. "Also leaving the scene of an accident, and something else. I forget."

"They wish it was an accident," she said. "They'd like to cover it up. They didn't want to arrest him. But there was one problem with that. Arnita remembers."

My heart started banging against my ribs. "She does?"

"That's why they came and got him today," she said. "They said they couldn't do anything without a witness — well, now they've got one. She remembers. Don't sit there and tell me you can't make a case against him! Hell, you had him in jail the night it happened — and let him go! But he plays football, his daddy's some kind of a deal at the Baptist college. You watch — they make a show of arresting him, then a month or two from now they will very quietly drop the charges."

"Did Arnita say he ran into her?"

"Ah, Musgrove." She grinned. "How you coming along on that wall in back? You nearly done with that first coat?"

"First and only coat," I said. "I'm just counting the days till I'm done. Do you know I have to spend my whole weekend cutting grass at our house so I can come over here all week and paint your house?"

"Good for you," she said. "Keep your mind off the girls."

The only girl on my mind was Arnita. I'd stretched out the painting job, taking longer than was really necessary on the eaves and trim, knowing she'd be home from the hospital any day. I balanced the paint tray up the ladder.

Mrs. Beecham said, "Red Martin tried to follow her home

from Charlene's. He was drunk. He was trying to get her to go with him. When she wouldn't, he knocked her off her bike. And took off."

"That's what she says?"

"Why, Musgrove? Did you see different? I always thought you might have been there that night. For sure you know more than you're telling."

I flung down my paintbrush. "I've told you a million times, I was not there! I'm painting your stupid house for free — what else do you want?"

"Okay, watch out!" She harrumphed. "Ol' Musgrove gettin' *pissed off* now. Watch out!"

"Well? Stop accusing me of stuff!" I picked twigs off the brush.

"Musgrove, I got good instincts," she said. "Some folks are just not born to be liars. If you could see yourself. Your poor ears go just as red . . . it's like the truth is just a burden weighing on you."

"Why are you so hateful to me?" I said. "What the heck did I ever do to you?"

"Hateful, how?"

"Even to my mom — she went to all that trouble to make you a cake, and you threw it in the garbage!"

She peered at me. "Ahhh, you been carrying that? You could have just asked. That was a lemon cake, Musgrove. I'm deadly allergic to lemons. I swell up if I even touch one. I had to get it out of the house."

I didn't dignify this with an answer. I'd seen her drink plenty of lemonade. I hammered the lid back on the paint can. I didn't need any of this. I would get on my bike and ride the hell out of here.

"You know, Musgrove, I think you are a good boy, I surely do. A hard worker too, especially when you're scared. And you are scared. Every minute of the day."

"No I'm not."

"Something working on you," she said. "You're even scared of me."

"Not scared. But you do make me mad."

She made a face, me being mad. "How's that?"

"You're always testing me. Always."

"I thought we might do a bit of digging and put in some flower beds," she said. "Wouldn't that look good, a whole bunch of zinnias going all the way around the house? Plenty of good sun for it. Zinnias like the sun."

"Miz Beecham, I offered to do you one favor. You're starting to take advantage of me."

"Starting?" She laughed. "I been taking advantage for a while now. But you just keep showing up, don't you? You surely do. What power I got over you? I'm just some old cullid woman, yassuh I jes' works cleanin' de house for de nice white folk like yo mama and daddy. My husband, he the janitor in yo white chillun school. Now how come is a white boy like you over here doing these favors for us?"

I thought it over. "I guess I like painting the house. Nobody ever asked me to do anything this big by myself."

"What did I tell you? Stick with me, we'll get you straightened out. You want some lemonade?"

"No thanks. I'm allergic to lemons."

She grinned. "Too bad for you."

Mom said how odd that I would do all this work for Mrs. Beecham, when at home I wouldn't put a plate in the sink without being nagged for an hour. I reminded her the whole thing was her idea. If she didn't want me mixed up with the Beechams she should never have taken me over there. "I don't know how she does it," I said, "but the second she starts ordering me around, I forget how to say no."

"You never had any trouble with that word in my house," said Mom. "Just explain to her you have other things to do. Twice now Daddy has come home and found the yard uncut when he specifically told you to cut it. I'm tired of being caught in the middle of you two. It was my idea to help these people out, but my goodness, there is a limit. If I have to call her, I will."

"No. Don't. I'll tell her."

Walking out of English the next day I found Lincoln Beecham waiting for me. I was used to seeing him in his blue jumpsuit, pushing a dust mop down the hall, or sitting in his janitor's closet with the door open, listening to his radio. It was Mr. Beecham's job to clean up after eight hundred kids. His face was solemn, his hair silvered from many years of this work. He was never home in the afternoons when I was painting his house. He always went straight from school to the hospital. "Young Musgrove."

"Yes sir."

"Understand you been doing the work at our place," he said. "Like to thank you for that." He looked uncomfortable saying that many words in a row.

"It's okay, Mr. Beecham."

"We bringing her home tomorrow. If you was to come around four, you might hep us take her out of the car. She ain't walking all that good yet."

"Sure. I can do that."

"Wife said you might." He nodded, and let me go.

7

DISORDERLY NOISE FLOODED out of the band hall, drums rat-a-tat-tatting like machine guns, horns and saxes blatting, flutes shrilling, Jimmye Brashier honking away on her bassoon.

The band hall didn't look magical, but it was the only place in school where actual magic was made. The first time I heard these wild jumbled noodling sounds pouring out the doors, I wanted to be a part of it. I was the Mighty Marching Titans' mallet-instrument specialist, a talent I brought with me from Indiana. In concert band I played xylophone, vibraphone, bells, chimes. In the marching show at football halftime, I carried the glockenspiel, the lyre-shaped arrangement of chrome bars — the easiest instrument in the band, except for cymbals.

I didn't care about playing an instrument. I just wanted to be in the band. If you weren't jock-popular, which I never would be, band was the coolest thing to do in high school. While everyone else had to suffer in the classroom, you got to go outside and march around and make a big noise. You got to perform at all football games, home and away, which made for interesting bus rides on Friday nights in the fall.

The best part was that sometimes within the concrete-block walls of the band hall our noise came together into actual music, and left us all flushed with pleasure.

Bernie Waxman was probably the only Jew in Minor, except for his wife. To us his Jewishness made him exotic. He was the only teacher who let us call him by his last name without the "mister." (I had found a few teachers at Minor who really knew their subjects, but none of them cared as much as Waxman.) Band was his obsession: he walked, drank, slept, ate, and breathed Band. He had a big head of curly black hair, dark eyes, big trumpet ears that scooped up every sound in the room. If a third-chair clarinet missed a note, Waxman heard it. He would wave us to a stop, chewing the tip of his baton while he figured out what was wrong. By this time in the band year, that baton was nibbled halfway to the quick.

The first chair in the flute section was still empty, in honor of Arnita.

Waxman charged out of his office tap-tapping a nervous rhythm in his palm, and stepped up on the carpeted box supporting his podium. "Okay, germs and germies, let's go! Places, places. 'King Cotton.'" *Whack!* His baton cracked against the rim of the music stand.

We were heading for the climax of the band year — our journey to Vicksburg in May for All-State Band Competition, which we referred to as Contest. Contest was a huge deal to Waxman, and by constant wheedling and rehearsing he had turned it into a huge deal for us. Band practice grew more intense by the day. We marched our marching show until we could have done it backward. We played our concert pieces dozens of times, refining them phrase by phrase. A jaunty Sousa march, the moody "Incantation and Dance" by John Barnes Chance, and "A Tribute to Stephen Foster" — we played them in our sleep, we heard them in our dreams.

The Sousa got off to a ragged start, and Waxman looked disappointed. "No, sloppy, sloppy, the brass — are you guys asleep back there? Wake up and try it again. Drummers, come right in, nice and crisp. Ready?" He counted off. He was quickly displeased by something in the reeds. "Band. In Vicksburg we can't stop and start over. If we don't have a nice crisp attack, we're sunk. Do you want to bring home straight Twos again?"

Bad bands got Fours at Contest, and great bands got Ones. Year after year, the Mighty Titans had earned solid Twos in all four categories: performance, musicality, presentation, marching band. Only once in history had Minor brought home a One, for musicality, back in 1968. That certificate hung on the wall behind Waxman, to goad us on toward our most elusive goal: another One.

The closer we got to Contest, the more Waxman snapped at us. He was hearing only the mistakes. Everyone could play their parts blindfolded, but to blend them into a unified sound was harder than it looked. As the mallet-instrument specialist, I had exactly one moment of solo glory, one place where all you heard was me — a xylophone run in the Stephen Foster medley. I had practiced that run till my wrists ached.

Today I staggered in a beat late, and missed half the notes in the run.

Waxman rolled his eyes and waved the band to a halt. "Daniel Musgrove? Anybody home?"

I knocked the mallets against my head. "Sorry, Mr. Waxman."

"You've only got that one run, but if you let us down, it's like Jim missing every note on first trumpet. Pay attention, would you?"

Oh the ignominy! Waxman never had to stop the band to correct me. The mallet parts were so unimportant that he let me bang away back there as I pleased.

One day I was alone at the piano in the band hall, feeling out the melody to "Color My World" by Chicago, when Waxman came out of his office. "Musgrove, that's pretty good. I was under the impression you didn't have a musical bone in your body."

"I'm just fooling around," I said.

"Seriously, all this time I thought you had zero talent. I could have been teaching you a real instrument. Why didn't you tell me you could play?"

I smiled. "I didn't want to mess up a good thing."

"Okay," he said. "It'll be our little secret."

Now he backed the whole band up to measure 128, taking aim at my four-second gap. I lifted my arms and struck out blindly with my mallets, a blizzard of notes. The band hall echoed with the tinkling excellence of that run — sharp, sprightly, every note in place.

Waxman gave a nearly imperceptible nod and moved on to "Oh, Susannah."

When he stopped to work on the trumpets, Debbie Frillinger leaned back from the row of clarinets with gossip. "They're letting Red Martin come back to school for one week so he'll be eligible to play football next year."

"Oh, is he out of jail yet?" I tried to sound nonchalant. "I can't keep up."

"His parents paid ten thousand dollars to bail him out," she said.

"I'm sure it was worth every penny."

"He really should transfer to some other school," Debbie said. "They'll make it impossible for him to have a normal life here."

"Who will?"

"The blacks. They've got it in for him now — well, you were at that assembly, you heard them. They'll make his life miserable."

"I hope so," I said. "Just like he does me and Tim."

"Daniel Musgrove!" Oh Jesus: Waxman glaring at me again! "Is this why you miss your one solo, cause you're too busy flirting with the clarinets?"

I had no defense. I shrugged, guilty.

"You're a junior, supposed to be an example of Pride in this outfit, and there you sit flapping your jaw. What is it, people? I can feel it — y'all are not here! Half of you are off in the clouds somewhere. I can't have that in Vicksburg. I won't have it in my band hall, you hear?"

"Sorry, Mr. Waxman."

"Sorry doesn't cut it. Back to 148. Flutes? I want to hear that daaaa, da-dee dum — let that sing out, you carry the melody here. Oboes, give it everything you've got on the rise. And Daniel, let me really hear that chime."

"Way Down Upon the Swanee River" reached its pensive denouement. I lifted my felt hammer and struck the domes of the long gold tubes with all the art I could muster.

Something went wrong — not my fault! Somebody talking? In the brass section, somebody talking out loud. Waxman flung down his baton. "What is going on here?"

"I said, do you even know what this song says?" said Shanice James, one of the French horns. "Because I looked it up, Mr. Waxman. I looked up the words. I don't think you ought to be making us play it. It's insulting."

Waxman gaped. "Shanice, what are you talking about?"

Shanice James was big and round as the bell of her horn, as round as her Afro and the rims of her horn-rimmed glasses. The whole horn section was black, including all three tuba players — something about the big brass appealed to the kids from East Minor. Shanice lifted up her sheet music. "Here's what the words say — 'All de world am sad and dreary, ebrywhere I roam. Oh, Darkies, how my heart grows weary . . .'"

"Shanice, this is an instrumental," said Waxman. "We're not using the words. And anyway the song is a hundred years old. What is the problem?"

"I just don't think we ought to be playing a song about darkies," said Shanice. "I'm an Afro-American. I am not a darkie. That's all."

"I ain't a darkie either," said Brian Fairchild on tuba. Every black member of the band muttered assent.

Waxman bristled. "Are you telling me you don't want to play this *melody* because you don't like the *lyrics?*"

"Well, yeah," Shanice said. "That's right. I don't."

"For gosh sakes," said Waxman, "I picked this piece myself, and I'm Jewish."

She crossed her arms. "So?"

"Are you trying to say that I, as a Jewish person, would intentionally pick music that I thought would offend a black person? Look, Stephen Foster was an old-time composer working in the tradition of minstrel music. He wrote beautiful melodies. You can't just not play his tunes because you don't happen to like the social conventions of his time."

"Did he write any songs about Jews? We could play one of those."

Shanice's friends laughed, but she was dead serious.

Waxman said, "Look, Shanice, I'd love to debate you on this. You may even have a point. But Contest is two weeks from tomorrow. We don't have time to put aside the Stephen Foster and learn some entirely new piece. You understand that, don't you?"

She turned her nose up. "I still think it's insulting."

Waxman ran a hand through his unruly hair. "Look, it shows great initiative that you went to the trouble to look up the lyrics. And now let me apologize on behalf of Stephen Foster that he was so old-fashioned on the subject of race. But that doesn't mean we can't play his music ever again. Don't you see the difference? The man is dead, he died a long time ago. His music lives on."

"If you had some music Hitler wrote," said Shanice, "would you play it?"

Waxman cracked an unexpected smile. "Depends if it was any good."

His little joke saved the moment. Shanice had to be a good sport. Once again I had witnessed something new from the black students, this new style of interruption and confrontation. A willingness to argue, to talk back.

They seemed to be making new rules for themselves.

"Okay," Waxman said. "We will stipulate that the lyrics are racist and reprehensible. Shall we pick it up from 148? Shanice, if you don't want to play, just hum along."

THE FAMILIAR ORANGE taxi crept to a stop by the mailbox. It wasn't really a taxi, just an old beat-up orange Plymouth driven by a man called Jimmy for the East Minor folks who needed a ride to the doctor, et cetera. He charged them a dollar each and loaded his car up with older folks. Today his passengers were the Beechams. Lincoln Beecham got out and hurried around the car.

"Hullo, Musgrove," Mrs. Beecham said. "Look baby, your first visitor!"

Arnita smiled up at me from the backseat. She was even lovelier than I remembered, bright brown eyes, a luminous smile that lit her whole face. Her hair was cropped close to her head, like a boy's. She wore her wire-rimmed glasses, and a plaid lumberjack shirt over pink flannel pajamas. "Hello," she said. "Who are you?"

"I'm Daniel. We're in the band together, remember?"

Her eyes flickered past me. "Is this your house?"

"No, it's your house."

"Mr. Musgrove," said Lincoln Beecham, "if you'll take that arm, we'll just stand her up and see can she walk to the house. You can walk that far, can't you, Arnita?" We stood her on her feet. "Don't let her drop."

Arnita swayed in place, regarding the house with a dreamy smile. "Why are we here? I'd rather keep riding around."

"Now, now," said her father.

"Arnita? Stand up and walk now," said Mrs. Beecham. "Like at the hospital. Come on, baby." She led the way to the door, bearing a suitcase and three paper sacks.

"If you could remind me where it is we're going?" Arnita said.

"Home," Mrs. Beecham said. "This is our home."

"Are you sure? This really doesn't ring a bell."

"Maybe because I painted it," I offered. "See how it's green now, remember it used to be yellow? And those flower beds, those are all new."

She shook her head. "This is not my house. I've never been here before."

"Bring her on up the steps." Mrs. Beecham opened the door. "Baby, you're gonna have to take my word on it. This is home. We're home."

We eased her over the threshold. In all my time working around the place, I'd never been invited inside the house. White walls and pine furniture, a rich smell of food and old rugs, pictures of ancestors and babies and Jesus and Martin Luther King on the walls.

"Tell me your name again?" Arnita's breath smelled like strawberry candy.

"Daniel. Daniel Musgrove."

"I know you told me, but I forgot."

"That's all right."

"Honey, where you want to be?" said Lincoln Beecham. "You want to sit by the TV?"

"Are you sure this is the right house?" said Arnita. "You'd think something about it would look familiar."

"We'll put her right here in this chair, Mr. Musgrove." Beecham guided her with his large hands.

"It's so good to be out of that hospital." Arnita drew her legs up under her, and gave me that glorious Prom Queen smile. "Maybe you can explain it to me, Daniel. I don't quite understand why these people have brought me here."

Mrs. Beecham was fishing around in one of the sacks. "Arnita, we're all home now, I'm your mama and that's Daddy and we're home."

"What's that?" Lincoln Beecham turned, cupping a hand at his ear.

"Talking to Arnita," his wife said loudly.

"Well," Arnita said, "I guess I should thank you for everything you've done."

"You're just confused," Mrs. Beecham said. "It's your injury. The doctor says it's getting better every day."

Arnita clutched my arm. "Do you know these people? I keep telling them I've never seen them before, but they don't believe me. They keep insisting they're my parents. Don't you think that's kind of ridiculous?"

"Not really," I said. "I mean — I don't know —"

My confusion made her laugh. "Oh, come on. Don't get me wrong, they're nice as can be, but I certainly can't be related to them. I mean, look at me! I'm not black!"

I glanced to Mrs. Beecham for some hint that she was in on this joke. She was giving her daughter the same cool, appraising stare she'd been giving me all these weeks.

"I really hate to make an issue of it," Arnita said. "I don't have anything against black people, but I'm sorry, you cannot be my mother and father."

"Arnita," her mother said, "baby, remember you had an accident, you hurt your head. The doctors say no two brain injuries are the same. I am your mother, and this here's your father. He's been sitting beside you the whole time, remember?"

Arnita said, "Daniel, what do you think?"

I swallowed. "She's right."

"It's a matter of opinion, I suppose," she said, with a trace of irritation. "What time is it?"

I glanced at my watch. "Five-thirty."

"*Gomer Pyle* is on." She sank back in the chair.

Mr. Beecham switched on the TV and walked me out to the porch. "It's a serious thing, Mr. Musgrove."

"She thinks — she said —"

Beecham said, "Sometimes she knows us, and other times not. She thinks she's a white girl. Called Linda."

"Linda?"

He nodded. "Ever since she woke up."

Mrs. Beecham came out. "Musgrove, those doctors told me things I could hardly believe. Did you know there's a place inside your brain where you keep just your name, and a picture of what you look like in the mirror? If that one particular part gets damaged, you don't know your own name. You can't recognize your own face. That's what's happened to Arnita. When she looks in a mirror, she can't see who she really is. She sees this other girl."

"That is weird," I said, because it was.

"She thinks Arnita is somebody else. A girl she went to school with. She remembers things that happened to Arnita. She says Arnita had an accident. But she's convinced she's this Linda."

Mr. Beecham touched my elbow. "We was hoping you might come around, help her catch up with her lessons. She 'posed to get a scholarship if she can keep up her grades."

His wife looked me in the eye. "You don't have to do it, Musgrove. You've done a lot already. I ain't gonna make you do anything this time."

A blue jay pelted the air with its cries.

I peered through the screen door to where Arnita sat quietly watching *Gomer Pyle*. "Do they think she'll always be like this?"

"Oh, no, she's already so much better. If she keeps on making progress, she'll be going back to school in the fall."

"She likes you," Mr. Beecham said. "She talks to you. She hardly talks to anybody. Not to us, anyway."

I squared my shoulders. "I guess I could talk to her teachers."

"I done that already." Mr. Beecham drew a much-folded paper from his pocket. "If you see Mr. Hamm on Monday, he'll have her work ready for you."

Lincoln Beecham had arranged it all in advance. His wife must have told him I would do whatever they told me to do.

"You a fine young man," he was saying.

"Don't tell him that, he's already got the big head," his wife said. "Do you see now, Musgrove? See why Red has to pay for what he did? He took my baby from me. My beautiful baby don't even know who she is anymore. I can't let him just walk away scot-free, can I?"

Her husband said, "Now Ella, leave it be." That was the first time I'd heard her name. Ella Beecham, with tears running down her face.

I could have said Wait, you've got it all wrong, Red didn't do it, it was an accident, yes we did drive off and leave her, yes we let Red take the blame. I tasted those words on the back of my tongue.

I climbed on my bike and rode away.

8

TIM ORDERED A BANANA split. I got a cherry Big Slushee that froze my brain on the third slurp. I staggered to a booth and sat down, gripping my skull in my hands.

"Oh my God Durwood, don't look up — don't!"

I looked. Mrs. Passworth was studying the Dairy Dog menu with her Jackie O sunglasses pushed up on her forehead. She spotted me looking. "Hey, boys!"

Tim waved hello, *don't come over don't come over.* The minute she had her chocolate swirl cone in hand, she came right over. "Mind if I join you? This place is filled to the gills!" She eased down beside me on the bench. "I just had to have a little something cool before I got in that car. My A/C's on the blink. Good gravy, is it ever hot!"

"Of course it's hot," I said. "It's Mississippi. When is it ever not hot?"

"Daniel, I wanted to thank you for helping Arnita with her homework." She spoke around a mouthful of ice cream. "That's very admirable. Poor girl, how's she coming along?"

"Pretty good," I said. "I just hope she doesn't need any help in algebra. I'm useless."

"Oh, you're fine," she said. "At least you pay attention in class, instead of just giggling and cutting up." Plainly she had me confused with some other guy.

It felt bizarre to be sitting with a teacher in a public place, away from school. That was breaking an unwritten law. And there was this aura of loneliness around Mrs. Passworth, even in a crowded place. You never heard anything about a Mr. Passworth. She licked her cone and asked what our plans were for the summer. When we said we didn't have any plans, she got all excited.

"Really? Oh, that's great! It's a miracle! There's a project at our church you'd be perfect for," she said. "You're both musicians, aren't you?"

Not really, we said — I played xylophone, glockenspiel, a little self-taught piano, and Tim played a bit of guitar. "Perfect!" she cried. "Piano and guitar are exactly what we need! I'm in charge of this fantastic new Christian rock musical our youth group is putting on. Two boys from the combo up and quit on me yesterday, the rats. Y'all are a gift straight from heaven!"

"You don't even know if we can play," Tim said.

"I'm sure you'll do fine. The music's easy. The next rehearsal is Sunday. You'd be absolutely saving my life. Plus you'd make good money. Oh, am I glad I ran into you."

Something about the word "combo" appealed to me. I got a mind-picture of Tim and me dressed up as Yardbirds, as Monkees.

"How much money?" I said.

"Twenty dollars a rehearsal," she said, "and thirty for each performance."

Wow, that was better than good money. Way more than I ever made cutting grass. "Thirty dollars for both of us?"

"Each, honey. We're Baptists — what do you think? Just come to one rehearsal, see if you like it. It's a very hip show, it's like *Godspell* without all the cursing. We're having a great time with it." She lifted an eyebrow. "Lots of cute girls too."

"That does it, I'm in." I elbowed Tim. "Come on, Timmy, what do you say?"

"I've never been in a *combo*," he said, with an evil smile.

"Great! It's all settled. Full Flower Baptist Church, on Van Winkle Road in West Jackson. Five o'clock Sunday."

"If we don't like it, we can quit, right?" Tim said. "You won't get mad and flunk us out of Algebra Two?"

She smiled. "Of course I will."

She chattered on awhile, then took off. *Oh God what have we done?* On the face of it, a Christian youth rock musical sounded embarrassing, but we were counting on big laughs, especially with Passworth involved. If it wasn't one hundred percent hilarious, we would quit.

"Let me get this straight," Mom said. "Now you're going off every night to some church? To do what exactly?"

"They need musicians for a combo. They're paying twenty bucks a rehearsal!"

"Well, if it's a church, I guess I can't say no," she said. "When did you learn to play piano?"

"Fooling around in the band hall," I said. "I'm not very good, but Miz Passworth thinks I'm good enough. Come on, Mom."

She took off her apron. "Honestly, Daniel, I wish you'd stay home more and help me with Jacko. Instead of just leaving me to do everything. No. I'm sorry. I'll have to ask Daddy about this when he comes home."

"Mom, please? You know he'll say no. You *know* he will. Come on, this is not something you have to ask him."

"What does Timmy's mother say about it?"

Patsy Cousins said we were fools to get mixed up with those Jackson Baptists — they would work our fannies off and never pay us a dime. I paraphrased: "She says it's a great idea."

Jacko said, "What you gwine do, boy?"

"Gonna play the piano in a church."

He cawed. "Nah, you been seeing that nigger gal, ain't you?"

"Don't call her that, Jacko."

"Gone sweet on her! You tell yo mama?"

"Be quiet!"

"You got it bad," he said. "Boy like him a taste of the dark meat! Mm-hmm!"

Mom was scandalized. "Jacko, you hush!"

"That's right, old man, and we're gonna get married. We're gonna name our first baby after you!"

That sent him into a fit of laughing and coughing.

Mom regarded me gravely as she pounded his back. "You be nice to that girl. Girls are tricky. I know you don't believe it, but I used to be one myself."

"Mom, please."

I RODE MY BIKE across the Yatchee bridge to find Mrs. Beecham watering the new flower beds. "Hey Musgrove, you need to start coming on time or we'll have to get somebody else." She made as if to squirt me. "You thirsty?"

I dodged the stream. "Lemonade, please."

"Yeah, I'll show you lemonade. What you got in the box?"

"Arnita's homework. They said we should start at the top and work down."

"Don't you be showing her that big old box! You'll scare her to death."

"They want me to take her assignments on Fridays. After school lets out, the summer-school teachers will grade them for her."

"She's not well yet," Mrs. Beecham said. "Don't you be pushing too hard."

I placed the box on the porch. "Hey, whatever you say. It was your big idea. We can skip the whole thing as far as I'm concerned."

"Maybe y'all could just go for a walk today. Lord knows she needs to get out — I'd like to throw that TV out the window. All she does is sit there watching that trash. See can you get her to come outside."

I knocked, eased the door open. "Arnita?"

"Arnita's not here," she sang from the upholstered chair. I heard the *Green Acres* theme. Arnita peered around the back of the chair. "Oh, hey!"

"Hey. I'm Daniel, remember?"

"I know! I've been waiting all day for you! Are you ready to go?"

"Go where?"

"She said you could take me for a walk." Damn, she was cute in her dainty white T-shirt, Big Smith overalls, bare ankles, flip-flops. "Can we go, please? Come on!" She tugged me by the hand to the door. Her touch sent a thrill through me, a shot of electricity. I smelled strawberry candy.

She broke away and danced off the porch, tipping her face to the sun. The lenses of her glasses became dazzling white disks. "God, it's so hot out here!"

Mrs. Beecham waved the hose at the zinnias. "Look how good our girl is walking!"

"Terrific," I said. "Big improvement since the last time." I stayed close, in case she wanted to grab my hand again. That was the first time a truly beautiful girl had ever touched me. It made the air of East Minor seem golden, heavy with light.

"Y'all have fun, now, don't go too far," Mrs. Beecham said.

"See you later, thanks for everything," Arnita called, pulling me down the walk. "Come on, Daniel. Let's go to the other side of the world."

I suggested the little park on the riverbank, just over the bridge. The Yatchee wasn't much of a river, but that was a pretty spot.

"I'll go anywhere to get out of that house," she said. "Those people are driving me crazy. They keep going on and on about my 'injury.' I'm sick of it."

"That must be weird," I said.

"See, I went in the hospital to get my nose fixed — then everything got all mixed up. Obviously for some reason they think I'm their daughter. Do you like my new nose?" She traced the center line with a finger.

"It's great," I said. "I mean, it's the same as before. It's always been a nice nose."

"The mark of great plastic surgery is, you can't even tell it's been done."

"I don't know exactly what I'm supposed to do here, Arnita."

"What do you mean? We're taking a walk."

"But I mean this stuff you're saying — it's not true. Am I supposed to tell you that, will it make you mad, or am I supposed to pretend . . . ?"

"God, you are so polite." She tugged down her glasses. "Are you always this polite? Feel free to tell me if I say something stupid."

"Okay, like, for instance — you did have an injury. A brain injury, not a nose job. And the Beechams are your parents, I swear."

"No, my father's name is Steve, and my mom is Eydie," she said. "We live in a split-level ranch house with a big oak tree in the front yard."

I shrugged. "See? Now that's just something you made up. Steve and Eydie are those singers on TV."

We stopped to peer over the side of the bridge, down into the slow-moving river. I noticed a little hoard of rocks piled in a hiding place on one of the bridge stanchions. I remembered the gang of kids that always hung out here, throwing rocks. "Arnita, you want to throw a rock?"

"Please don't call me that. I understand why *they* call me that, but couldn't you please call me Linda?"

"Sure, okay . . . Linda."

"Arnita's not me. And I am not she." She dropped the rock, waited for the *plonk!*

I hurled one a long way upriver.

We took turns dropping and throwing rocks until we'd used up most of the boys' stash.

We crossed the bridge and descended a little slope to a rusted swing set. Blue jays screamed in the trees. A tinge of leaf-smoke hung in the air.

Arnita sat in the swing. "You knew Arnita before it happened. Was she different than me?"

"Not that much. And you're getting better, you're already a lot better than you were. Pretty soon you'll be good as new."

"Well you can't fight City Hall," she said. "Everyone in the world can't be crazy, so I suppose it's got to be me."

"It's not your fault you got hurt." *It's my fault* was on the tip of my tongue, where it remained.

"I try to be Arnita when everyone is looking," she said. "I don't know where my real family is."

"Steve and Eydie?"

"I guess they forgot all about me." She glanced up at me. The look in her eyes just melted my heart. I placed my hands on her shoulders and nudged the swing.

"Do you remember Prom Night?" I said.

"Arnita was elected the Queen of the Prom," she said.

"I mean after that. The accident."

"Oh. No. I don't want to talk about that."

"Red Martin," I said. "I'm not like his best friend or anything, but are you sure he's the one that hurt you?"

"He knocked her off her bike. She fell and hit her head."

"But it was an accident. Wasn't it? I don't think he meant to knock you down."

"Yes he did," she said. "Red is not a nice guy. He was mad cause Arnita wouldn't kiss him at Charlene's party."

I edged out onto thin ice. "Okay. But I mean later, when you were riding home on your bike."

"Red was drunk," she said.

I gave another gentle push. "Nobody else bothered you?"

She shook her head. "Do you think she looked pretty in her prom dress?"

"You were beautiful. Unbelievable. I couldn't stop looking at you. Nobody could. What a dress. I mean . . . That was a dress."

She dug her toes in the sand to stop swinging. I memorized the warmth of her shoulders under my hands.

"It didn't belong to Arnita," she said. "Her Aunt Sarah works in this very expensive shop just off Canal Street. She was supposed to send it back. But they said she got blood on it."

"You think we should be getting back?" I said. "Your mother will skin me alive if I keep you out here too long." It hadn't been long at all, really, but I was slightly afraid of this girl. The places her mind seemed to wander. The flashes of static electricity crackling from her.

"She is not my mother," Arnita said. "I wish you could remember that."

"Doesn't matter, she's back there waiting for us."

We stopped to throw the last rock into the river — I let her do the honors. We walked up the hill to Forrest Street.

Arnita hesitated. "We can be friends, okay? You can keep track of all the really dumb things I say. That'll be your job."

"I'll do what I can," I said.

"I don't really want to go back to that house, Daniel. It just feels wrong to be with those people."

"Where else could you go?"

"Is there room at your house? I could come stay with you."

"You wouldn't want to do that," I said.

"Why, is it bad?"

"Not that bad, just . . . my dad's real strict. And we have this great-uncle living with us. Things are weird at the moment."

"Didn't you say you have a brother?"

"Bud. He's in the Marines. And Janie, my sister, she's twelve. I'm the middle."

"If he's in the Marines couldn't I stay in his room?" she said. "Is your house far from here?"

"Eleven miles. All the way out the Old Raymond Road. I ride my bike to town every day just to see you."

"Maybe I could come over to your house sometime." She touched my shoulder. Her fingers felt like a kiss. She ran to the porch.

I pedaled away with the sun in my eyes. It was silly to imagine anything with Arnita — but what a pleasant jolt when she touched me. I loved walking next to her, drinking her in. I liked how she peered over her glasses to mock me with her eyes.

I pictured Steve and Eydie in a split-level house with an oak tree out front. I imagined them standing at a window, looking out, waiting for their Linda to come home.

9

M OM'S WAGON BLEW a head gasket, so Dad had to drive me to Full Flower Baptist Church in the company Oldsmobile. He only got one day off, he said, one day a week with nothing to do but go to church and watch a little TV, and here he was spending half the afternoon driving me to the other side of the world. "What is this thing you're doing, anyway?"

"A church musical."

"Oh, that is sweet. Do you think you might ever get a real job? Fellow I work with has a boy same age as you, he'll be rolling pipe in a pipe yard this summer."

"Wow, lucky him," I said.

"Don't you sass me. That boy will be making real money while you're goofing around doing your ballet dancing or whatever."

"I play the piano, and I'm getting twenty bucks a rehearsal," I said. "If you'd let me borrow the car, I would drive myself."

"Not in this car. You want to drive? Save your money and buy a car."

I considered how much more pleasant life would be if I just bought a parrot and taught it all of Dad's lines.

"How am I supposed to get a job when we live in the middle of nowhere and you won't let me drive?"

"You figure it out," he said.

The truth was, Dad didn't like me all that much. I made him uncomfortable, and vice versa. He had pretty much given up on all father-type activities, except for the Sunday-morning funnies with Janie. It was their tradition, the two of them on the sofa poring over *Beetle Bailey* and *The Family Circus*.

Dad and I had our own tradition: he assumed everything I did or said was designed to piss him off, and I did my best to oblige. Every time I opened my mouth, he was there to point out whatever was stupid, rebellious, or wrong about what I said. Sometimes I wondered what other dads said to their sons — if they weren't yelling at each other, what on earth did they talk about? I would have to ask Tim. Although I remember him saying he and his dad didn't talk much either.

"I give you one job to do," Dad was saying, "one little job, in return for which you get a roof over your head and all you can eat. And you can't show me even that little bit of respect."

"What job?"

"The yard. In back, that place I pointed out to you yesterday. Did you finish that? No. You intentionally forgot. You laid around on your butt all weekend, and now you're off to play with your little ballet-dancing friends."

"All I do is cut the grass." My voice started shaking. "Okay? That's all I do. I come home, I cut grass. I get up before school and cut grass. I cut grass all weekend. Twelve months a year. The yard is three acres, okay? It will never stop growing. I am never gonna be through cutting it, do you understand? It is never gonna be *finished.*"

His hand shot out fast and smacked my face. "Don't you smart-mouth me!" I saw white stars dancing in the air. The echo of the slap resounded in the car. "Wait'll you have a real job," he said. "You will pine for something as easy as pushing a lawnmower."

"I can't wait, Dad," I said, rubbing my jaw. "I mean it. I wish I had the money, I would pave that yard over for you right now. Today. Just asphalt it over. You'd never have to see another blade of grass as long as you live."

"This is Van Winkle Road," Dad said. "What did you say this place is called?"

"Full Flower Baptist Church." It had been a few months since the last time he hit me. When we were younger he used to hit Bud and me all the time, usually for some infraction he considered serious enough. But in the past few years it always happened like this, out of nowhere, no warning. For no reason at all. Like something he couldn't control.

"Full Flower?" he was saying. "That sounds Chinese or something."

"It's Baptist," I said.

Dad said, "All the real nut cases are Baptist. Your mother's whole family, for starters. Crazy bunch of idiots and alcoholics and cripples, and every one of 'em a hard-shell Baptist."

"There it is — Dad, slow down! Oh, you passed it."

He heaved a sigh at the massive inconvenience of having to turn around.

For me the name Full Flower had conjured up an image of a quaint little church, but this place was huge, like a shopping mall with a steeple. You could fit two or three Minor High Schools inside the main building, and there were other sections branching off, and a big high-ceilinged part in the middle.

"Look at this," Dad said. "Jesus H. — look at that — four, five, that's eight Cadillacs in a row! How much are these people paying you?"

"Twenty dollars."

"Ask for more. These people are rich."

I climbed out. "Thanks for the smack in the face, Dad. I'll get a ride home with Tim."

He drove off shaking his head at how I could continue to smart-mouth him with my face still burning from his hand. I'm sure he thought my persistence was ridiculous.

The heat shimmered the air above the asphalt. Tim came loping over, his guitar case bumping his knees. "Hiya, Skippy!"

"Apparently Jesus drives a Cadillac," I said, wondering if one side of my face looked redder. Tim didn't appear to notice.

We walked up the covered passageway into the blissful chill of the sanctuary. The dark vastness of the place stopped us in our tracks. "Whoa. . . ."

This had to be the swankiest church in Mississippi. Stained-glass windows admitted thickly colored light that gave everything a deep yellowish cast. Ranks of pews marched to a rocket-shaped pulpit, an altar table of sleek polished granite. Suspended above the altar was a silver cross, hanging swordlike in midair above a stage full of chattering teenagers.

I spotted Mrs. Passworth beside the drum set. She was delighted to see that we'd actually shown up, and immediately presented us to the Combo: Ben, the skinny bass player; Byron, on drums, with a frizzy blond Afro; Mickey, the long-haired guitarist. They showed Tim where to plug in. I sat down at the piano. They handed me a spiral-bound book of sheet music. The cover featured an elaborate hand-written script:

CHRIST!
A Musical of the Lord
Words and music by Edwin B. Smock

Tim thumbed through the score with an expression of rising joy. Mrs. Passworth waved over the young choir director, a skinny guy with goofy glasses, a droopy bow tie, and a goatee. "Boys, this is Eddie, our Minister of Music. You'll be in his hands from now on. Eddie, these are some of my best students from school — this is Tim, and that's Daniel."

"Boys, welcome!" Instantly I knew that Eddie's nasal honk was enough to make this whole enterprise worthwhile. You could summon geese with that voice. His handshake was moist and sincere. "Welcome aboard, deelighted to have you. You've met the rest of our Combo?" Ah, so: that word must have come from him. "It's pretty simple musical structure on the surface, three or four chords in most of the songs." He turned the pages over my shoulder. "I didn't write a piano part, so you can just play arpeggios, whatever you think. I've got my work cut out for me with the chorus. Basically all I need from you guys is to keep the beat and stay out of my way, okay?"

Sure, we could do that.

It dawned on me that Eddie must be Edwin B. Smock, composer and lyricist of *Christ!* "Hey Eddie, did you write this whole thing?"

"You bet I did," he said, grinning, "and don't give me any you-know-what about it!" He went off to gather the choir.

Tim wore a big doofus smile. "Deeelighted," he said. "Did you get a look at these songs, Skippy?"

"Not yet," I said. "But I have a feeling we're going to be very happy here."

This was one great-looking bunch of Christians. Not a pimple in sight — why do Christians always have such great skin? Also these Jackson girls wore clothes you didn't see in Minor. Every one of them was showing off a spring tan with a skimpy blouse or sleeveless top, short-shorts, miniskirt. The boys looked sporty too — plaid pants were in that year, and Van Heusen velour pullovers in colors called "mustard" and "rust."

I recognized a few kids from Minor: Celia Karn and her brother Greg, John Henry Ward and his sister Mary Virginia, Kirby Cook, Beth McDonald, Cathy Sessums, Tammy Lyall, Erin O'Bryen.

I flipped to the first page of the book.

> ACT I
> "Christ!" (Jesus, Chorus)
> "Hey Mary, Guess What?" (God)
> "Joseph, You've Got to Believe Me" (Mary)

Tim strummed the opening chords. "Oh Dagwood, this is better than I ever dreamed. Did you get a load of our Minister of Music?"

I smiled. "I surely did."

Byron the drummer overheard us. "Eddie's cool," he said. "He's only twenty-three, and he wrote the whole show himself. He's amazing. You'll see."

Mickey twanged a note on his electric guitar. "What's the matter, these guys don't like Eddie?"

"I'm sure he's great," Tim said. "We just met him."

"He's a professional," Mickey said. "He's been to New York to see real live plays on Broadway. What shows have you seen?"

"This is my first," I said. "I was hoping you guys could show us the ropes."

"Jesus loves you," said Ben the bass player. "That's all the ropes you need."

"Right on," said Byron. "You guys are saved, right? I mean, why else would you be here?"

I recalled Dianne Frillinger's scary dad asking the same question. I thought these guys must be joking, but Tim knew they weren't. "Yeah," he said, "we got saved about a year ago."

Mickey frowned at me. "You don't look all that saved to me."

"Oh yeah," I assured him. "One hundred percent."

Tim said, "J.C. is my man."

"Okay folks, listen up!" Eddie clapped his hands. "Is everyone excited?"

The girls applauded and went "*Whoo!*"

"Cause I know I am," Eddie said. "Y'all chorus have been working so hard all spring. Now we're ready to put this baby together, and take her on the road. Are you prepared to stride forth and make musical theater history?"

Everybody shouted *YES!* like at a pep rally.

"Like to introduce two new members of our Combo," said Eddie. "That's Tim on guitar and Dan on piano, everybody give 'em a big Full Flower welcome!" They clapped for us. We waved hello.

"Now listen up, people," said Eddie. "There were those who predicted we'd never even get this far. And yet — here we are. On our way. This is the fulfillment of a dream for me personally. And before it's over, I think this experience will touch each of us in ways we never expected."

"Praise the Lord," said a girl with lovely red hair.

"Praise the Lord," Eddie said. "Now we're headed into the

homestretch. We have to make it great — not just good. This will be our first full-length run-through. Y'all know I'm a tough taskmaster, but you need to remember, when I'm being tough, it's for you. With all the love in my heart. So just keep that in mind when I get on your nerves, which I plan to, a lot."

Everybody chuckled.

"We're with you, Eddie!" Mickey gave his guitar string a comical twang.

"Way to go! Way to go! I love it!" Eddie cried. "Now, the opening number is our grabber, folks — we gotta seize the audience by the throats and never let go. I want snappy, excited, bouncy . . . I want *bounce*. Combo? Kick us off."

The chorus spread in three ranks across the stage. Byron rapped his drumstick on the rim, a peppy two-four rhythm. The choir sang:

> *Christ!*
> *La la la la la, la la la*
> *Christ!*
> *La la la la la, la la la*
> *If you're feeling sad and blue*
> *Who's got real good news for you?*
> *Who died on the cross for you?*
> *Christ!*
> *La la la laaaaaaa!*

"Okay that's good," said Eddie, "but I really want to feel that punch when you say it — *Chrrrrist!* Like that! Okay? I don't hear my baritones. Boys, sing out."

Up With People, the New Christy Minstrels, the Fifth Dimension, the Pepsi Generation — Eddie Smock drew inspiration from all over. Tim and I kept our heads down and played softly. We dared not look at each other.

> *He was born in Bethlehem*
> *No room at the inn for him*

Pilate wanted death for him
Christ!
La la la laaaaaaa!

"Okay, well, that harmony's still pretty rough," Eddie said, "but hey, doesn't our new and improved Combo sound great? Fantastic! You guys add a whole new dimension! Now, I want to just plunge on ahead."

The second song featured a tall, good-looking boy, Ted Herring, as God, singing to the Virgin Mary, a beautiful brunette named Alicia Duchamp.

Hey Mary, guess what?
You're gonna have a baby!
Yeah, ready or not —
I know you don't believe it!
Of all the gals in Galilee
You're the only gal for me
Hey May-rayy, guess what?!
Ya gonna have a Savior boy!

The songs were not rock and roll, but they were authentically snappy, lively show tunes. Eddie was a guy with a dream. He was also the most excited, cheerful guy in the room. He laughed and poked fun at our mistakes without hurting any feelings. He was not much older than we were, though he tried to look older with that goatee. I'd never seen anyone so comfortable in charge of other people.

From the sunny faces of the choir I could see that they'd all been saved, and Eddie was a hero to them.

I doubted I would ever fit in here. Everybody seemed a little too happy.

Eddie called a ten-minute break while he worked out the dance moves for the second big production number, "Third Manger on the Right." Byron and Mickey said, "Hey, guys, come with us." We went out of the sanctuary, down a maze of long twisting hallways.

Tim said, "Where are we going?"

"To hell if you don't change your ways!" Byron said with a grin.

Mickey stopped before a tiny elevator, punched the button with his elbow. "They just installed this thing for the rich old ladies who can't hack the stairs," he told us. "Gotta keep those big offerings coming in."

We crowded in. I didn't really like being jammed in this tiny space with all the other boys. A steel gate slid shut. The elevator rose slowly.

Between the second and third floors Byron pulled out the STOP button, jolting us to a halt.

I said, "Hey, what are you doing?"

"Be cool." Byron brought from his wallet a skinny hand-rolled cigarette and a book of matches. His eyes came up to mine. "Are you cool?"

"No!" I cried. "I mean yes!" Jesus, what was I doing here? Be cool, Daniel. At least act like you are. "I mean sure, go ahead. Not for me. What is that? Is that pot?"

"Tim? Are you cool?"

Tim said, "Fire it up."

I said, "I thought all you guys were, like, Jesus freaks."

"We are," Mickey said.

"Praise the Lord and don't Bogart that joint," said Byron, striking a match. He touched it to the end of the cigarette, sucked in the smoke, and handed it to Mickey. Mickey inhaled and twisted up his face, and blew out the smoke laughing. The elevator filled with acrid perfume.

"What about Ben?" I said.

"Ben doesn't partake," Mickey said. "Ben is naturally stoned."

"Stoned on Jesus," said Byron.

I was shocked to see Tim take a puff. We had talked about pot, and decided it was stupid. Go to jail for smoking a weed? No thanks! Besides, the smoke made a terrible stink. I thought of that Three Dog Night song, "Mama Told Me Not to Come." I put myself in the role of the guy who wants the hell out of the creepy party. If somebody caught us in here . . .

"I bet Jesus got high," Mickey said. "There must have been dope growing everywhere in the Bible times. There was no law against it back then."

"I can't really picture Jesus using that stuff," I said.

"You don't think Jesus was cool?" Byron sucked in a chestful of smoke.

"I'm sure he was," I said.

"But he couldn't have smoked weed, Mickey, they were out in the desert! I bet they had hash or something."

"Man, did you see Alicia Duchamp?" Mickey said. "In that little stripey thing? Wouldn't you love to take that thing off with your teeth?"

"I hear you, man." Byron offered the burning thing to me. I waved it away and watched Tim take another sip of smoke. I was impressed and appalled at how sophisticated he was pretending to be.

Byron said, "I'm done. Tim?"

"No more for me!" Tim's grin was stupid. "You guys make a hell of a *Combo*."

Byron spat on his fingers, pinched out the tiny cigarette. Then he pulled out a tiny spray can and squirted mint deodorizer over our heads. Mickey pushed in the STOP button. The elevator jerked back to life.

The three of them tittered all the way down the hall. We passed a couple necking just inside the double doors to the sanctuary.

This was not like any church I'd ever seen.

My favorite part of *Christ!* so far was a plaintive Act II ballad by the teenage Jesus, played by earnest, red-haired Matt Smith.

> *I'm just a boy with two dads*
> *One is a carpenter, he's so sad*
> *One is a Father I never see*
> *He's up in heaven, waiting for me*

I watched Eddie Smock huddling with Carol Nason, the tall silky blonde in the role of Mary Magdalene. Eddie sang a scrap of melody, and Carol sang it back. "Give it everything you've got," he said. "This is your Ethel Merman showstopper."

People said I was a girl of the streets
I wasn't worthy to sit at his feet
Can't they see that I'm not that kind of girl?
He fills the world with his beautiful song
He feeds the hungry, he rights the wrong
I'd like to help, but I'm not that kind of girl

Not that kind of girl, no!
I'm just clay in God's hands to play with
Not that kind of girl, no!
I've only got two hands to pray with

This time she belted it out, really let it all go. We whistled and clapped. "Carol!" cried Eddie. "That was heart-stopping! Oh folks, I don't want to jinx us, but — is anybody else beginning to think we've got something really special here?" His enthusiasm roused the chorus for the remaining songs, of which there were many. Edwin B. Smock the songwriter was extremely prolific. It was way late in the night by the time we reached the chorus of "Find a Way to Believe," the Invitation, the closing anthem intended to rouse people from their seats and bring them down front to accept Jesus Christ as their personal savior.

We played the last bars and collapsed in the pews.

"Of course it could use a trim here and there," Eddie said, "but I think it's just great, don't y'all?" He was up on the balls of his feet, smacking gum, bursting with energy from hearing his masterpiece for the first time.

We all tried to swallow our yawns. Mrs. Passworth rose up from the pew where she'd been snoozing. "Kids, you were wonderful! Eddie, we need to cut it."

"Yes, I was just saying that, Irene!" he said in a tight voice. "While you were sleeping! But did you have any opinion of the parts you managed to stay awake for?"

"Wonderful," she said, "really, it's wonderful, but look at the time! My Lord, it's half-past eleven!"

Eddie's smile froze. "Okay! Well! I'm just the composer and lyricist and director, so maybe that's why I thought it went great for a first run-through!"

"Of course it did, Eddie, we're all exhausted," she said. "Can we talk about this tomorrow?"

He stalked up the aisle, waving goodbye over his shoulder.

"Beautiful," Tim said as we climbed into his dad's Buick. (I had tried to pay for the new seat belt in back, but Patsy Cousins wouldn't hear of it.) "Start to finish, every moment a memory that will last us a lifetime. Do you agree, Skippy?"

"Oh yeah."

"Edwin B. Smock will go down in history," he went on. "Centuries from now they'll be building monuments to Edwin B. Smock."

"And you wanna know the weird thing? I *like* him," I said. "I mean, yes he is a total goofball, but also — he really believes in this stuff. He means it. You can tell."

"Yeah, my bones hurt from trying not to laugh," Tim said. "What a massive fruitcake!"

"Tim — how did it feel, getting high? I can't believe you did that."

"I didn't really feel it, but I didn't want to say anything. Apparently there's all kinds of wild action going on at this church. Byron said last year some of them got drunk and stole the preacher's car and drove to Biloxi. They didn't even get in trouble."

"You think all the kids are that wild, or just Byron and Mickey?"

"I don't know, but we're gonna have fun finding out," he said. "And the great thing is — it's church! Church! Who's gonna question us? Did you see those girls sneaking out to smoke? Some of them were making out, too."

"With each other? Gross!"

"No, Dumwood, with guys. Mickey said all these Christian girls are super horny."

I reached for the seat belt, thought better of it. "He said that?"

"Their daddies are Christian, so they never get to go on dates or anything. The more Christian they are, the hornier they get. By the time they get old enough for youth group, they're on fire."

"Do you think — wow."

"And no chaperones. Telling you, son, bad boys have all the fun. We shoulda known, the place to find the wild bunch was church."

"You should be careful," I said. "I don't think you oughta be smoking that stuff."

"Was that not crazy? Right in the elevator! I couldn't believe it."

"I mean, seriously. With your police record and all."

He braked for the first stoplight of Minor. "Are you gonna keep throwing that up to me from now on? Damn, I'm sorry I ever told you."

"You didn't tell me. I forced it out of you."

"Oh forget it," he said.

"You said reckless driving? They put you in jail?"

"You ready to go home now, Skippy?"

"Tim, what the hell is so bad that you still can't talk about it?"

He turned east. "My God, you love to drag stuff up! It was nothing, okay? A stupid speeding ticket. They put me in jail for one night, to scare me."

"But they suspended your license. And you're still driving around without it."

He shook his head. "I don't know, son. You're not as much fun as you used to be."

I couldn't argue with that. We rode in silence down the Old Raymond Road.

Tim said, "Look, truce. Okay?"

"Sure. I don't care."

"What can I say?" He grinned and started singing. "I'm just a boy with two daaaaaads . . ."

I couldn't help joining in: "One is a carpenter, he's so sad!"

10

I WAS UP LATE, skimming *Great Expectations* for the final. Three more exams, then Contest in Vicksburg, and school would be out for the summer. Outside I heard a car horn — *shave and a hair-cut, two bits!* — answered by the howl of Mrs. Grissom's beagle.

Jacko snored on the other side of the Freak Annex. I hurried out, flapping my flip-flops down the driveway.

Tim spoke from the darkness. "Check it *out!*"

"You're waking up the whole neighborhood!" I hissed.

"Would you shut up and check out my wheels?" He slapped the roof of a gleaming dark blue Ford Pinto, spotless and sleek-looking, with pinstripes and the dealer sticker in the window.

"Wow. Timmy — this is yours?"

"Bet your ass, Skippy! Mine, all mine! Happy birthday to me . . ."

"My God, they gave you a car? I didn't even know it was your birthday."

"Actually it's not till tomorrow so you still have time to get me something." He patted the hood. "Pretty damn fantastic, huh?"

Maybe twenty kids at Minor High owned their own cars. "They gave you a new car *plus* they let you drive it around at one in the morning?"

"I snuck out. It was too late to call your house, but I couldn't go to bed without you seeing it. Mom and Dad haven't even told me yet — I had this sneaking suspicion and I went to the carport and — ta-daa! There it was, with the keys in it!"

"Anytime you're ready to swap parents, just let me know," I said. "Man! And brand-new! Hardly anybody in the whole school ever got a *new* car."

"Red got that Mustang. And Sandie Baxter got that orange Maverick last year, but that was so ugly it doesn't count," he said. "You ready for a test drive?"

"I have to go back in. This is the time of night Jacko tends to get weird. The other night he woke me up to tell me Dad was beating Mom over the head with a skillet."

"Well, was he?"

"No. But I gotta admit, I did go back there to make sure."

"Aw come on, Durwood, live a little! We'll drive around for five minutes, I'll bring you right back."

"Really I can't. I just hope all the honking didn't wake up old Hitler."

He snorted. "Great, okay, we'll wait till the *next* time I get a brand-new car for my eighteenth birthday."

"Let me sit in it, anyway." I opened the passenger door and eased in. "Aw, man. Smell that smell. Nothing like it in the world."

"It's the GT, the sport edition — see the stripes, and AM-FM, eight-track tape deck, tuned sport suspension, custom floor mats . . . don't you love it? The color is Starlite Blue."

"Starlite Blue is definitely a better color than Sky Blue." I stroked the woodgrained plastic dashboard. "They didn't give you any clue?"

"None. They were so good. I never even suspected until yesterday morning, I heard them whispering and rattling keys."

I tried to imagine my parents conspiring to give me a surprise like this. "You know what this means," I said. "You have to be nice to them for the rest of your life. You can't complain about anything, ever."

He grinned. "It sure makes up for a lot of god-awful sweaters through the years."

"You better be careful, though, driving around without a license. When are you supposed to get it back?"

"I already got it, no problem," he said.

"That was fast. I thought you said —"

"Put your leg in, Durwood. Shut the door. We'll just run her down the street and right back."

"I told you, I can't."

"We won't even leave your stupid street," he said. "We'll just ride right down to the circle, turn around, and come back."

I stepped all the way out. "Sorry. Not tonight." Why was his new car making me angry? It meant freedom for me too. Tim would drive me anywhere I wanted to go. It wasn't the car I coveted, it was the size of the gift. My parents would never love me that much. They loved me the price of a bicycle, maybe. Never as much as a car. If Bud hadn't joined the Marines, I bet they would have bought him a car.

"Congratulations." I patted the doorsill. "Great car, Tim. And I love Starlite Blue. Pick me up after band? — no, wait, I promised Arnita."

Tim's smile was a little off-center. "You go over to her house every day now, huh?"

"Not every day."

"Yes, you do. What do y'all do all that time?"

"Her homework. Sometimes we go for a walk or something. We hang out by the river. Nothing much."

"You like her, don't you, Skippy."

"She's nice."

"No, I mean, you *like* her." He raised an eyebrow.

I scoffed. "Don't be stupid."

"Why, because she's black?"

I made a face. "You think I want to get in her pants?"

"Well, don't you? She's so fine, that's what any red-blooded American boy would want."

"Knock it off, Tim. She got hurt, remember? She's still not okay. You and I had something to do with that."

His smile dwindled. "But your face gets this gooey look when you talk about her."

"I'm just trying to help her. You can believe me or not. I don't care."

"Well if the big moment does arrive, son," he said, wagging his finger, "be sure and use some protection. We don't want any little coffee-colored babies running around."

"Would you shut up?"

He sang out in a throaty voice: "Half-bree-eed! That's all I ever hearr-rd!" His Cher imitation was getting better. "Get in, Durwood. Let's go to Jackson." He revved the engine.

I backed away. "I can't."

"Aw Durwood, you're always so scared." He pitied me for a moment with his eyes, then put the car in gear and hummed off down Buena Vista Drive.

He was right — what would have happened if I'd gone for a ride? Nothing. I was scared. Even Ella Beecham had pointed it out. I walked around every day with this chronic low-grade free-floating fear of everything. It started with life under Dad. I'd spent most of my life being scared of him, trying to stay out of his way. It was hard to get out of the habit.

I went back to the house. At the door to the Freak Annex I stepped around Jacko. "What you doing still awake, old man?"

He peered up. "Where you been at, boy?"

"You're the mind reader. You tell me."

"Talkin that Tim," he said. "Got him a new car, huh."

The skin on my neck prickled up. "Jesus, how do you *do* that?"

He laughed.

ARNITA JUMPED OFF the porch when I rode up. "You're late!" she sang in a teasing tone.

I laid my bike against a bush. "You're worse than your mother," I snapped. "I'm not punching a clock here, you know. Sometimes I have other things to do."

The irritation in my voice rocked her back on her heels as if I'd slapped her. In all the time we'd spent together, I had never been anything other than extremely nice to Arnita. "Wow, are you in a bad mood. What's wrong?"

"Nothing." Tim's accusations were bothering me. I needed to prove to myself that I was not getting carried away with my thoughts about this girl.

"Come on, Daniel, you're always happy. You're *never* like this. What is it?"

I turned my face away. "What should we do? Walk? Homework first? You decide. I'm tired of being the one who always has to decide."

"Hey," she said. "Whatever it is, don't take it out on me. I didn't mean to."

"Sorry," I sulked. "I don't mind coming over here, you know. I'm glad to help you. But I don't like getting yelled at if I happen to be five minutes late."

"Did I yell?" She searched my eyes. "I'm sorry. I guess I was anxious. I get so scared you won't show up."

My tactic wasn't working. She was supposed to be mad at me by now. Instead she was sweeter than ever.

"Didn't you notice I'm always out here waiting for you?" she said. "I wait every day. I don't let myself come outside 'til quarter to three. Because you've never gotten here before three, except that one time when school let out early. I'm sorry, Daniel, I can't help it. You're the high point of my day."

She was so lovely in her white cotton summer dress, scratching the back of her leg with a bare toe.

I frowned. "Don't try being nice to me. I'm not in the mood."

"Let's go to the river." She reached for her shoes. "You definitely need to throw rocks."

I headed straight for the hiding place in the bridge stanchion. One by one I hurled all the rocks, the whole collection, into the river, one satisfying splash after another.

Arnita stood watching. She knew better than to talk to me.

Tim had set all the alarm bells ringing in my head. Was I falling in love with this girl? I'd never been in love, so I didn't know the symptoms. At first I thought I was only going over to her house to make up for what happened on Prom Night. But now I couldn't help going over there. I had to be with her. I felt sick if I had to miss a day. I felt rattled and short of breath whenever she stood anywhere near me.

Theoretically it would be great to fall in love with a smart, beautiful girl like Arnita. Theoretically. But she was black, I was white, it was impossible at this time in Mississippi. Maybe in Indiana, or New York, or Europe. Not here, not now. No use even thinking about it.

Also: Arnita was too pretty for me. She was the Prom Queen, I was a brain/loser nobody Five Spot pariah. The idea of us together was laughable. I was the perfect buddy for her, a babysitter, bringer of homework, taker of walks. Also I satisfied her mother's need to have a white boy she could boss. Anything beyond that was just my own overheated imagination, or Tim trying to get on my nerves.

I threw myself on the grass, yanked up a dandelion, and began scraping out the yellow heart of the flower with my thumbnail.

Arnita knelt beside me. "You were throwing those rocks at me, weren't you?"

I shook my head.

"That's how it felt. Don't be like this, Daniel. Everybody else in the world can be in a bad mood, but you're not allowed. You're the only fun I get to have."

"That's because you never see anybody else." I tried not to sound mad. "You had friends before the accident, lots of 'em. What happened? I think you depend on me too much."

"They don't come to see me," she said.

"Have you called them? No. You don't go out. You just stay in your house and don't see anybody."

She smiled. "I see you every day."

"You can't blame people for thinking something's wrong with you. You haven't been back to school once. They all think you're damaged." I saw her wince at that word. "Why don't you come next week?" I suggested. "Finals are over. Come for one day. Let every-body see you're okay."

"They'll expect me to be Arnita," she said. "And that's just not who I am."

I put the stem of the ruined flower in my pocket. "You can pre-tend, can't you? I think that's what you're gonna have to do. What choice do you have, really? You can't go around telling people you're Linda the white girl. They know you're Arnita. They'll all think you're nuts."

"You can help me," she said. "You can tell me about her. What was she like?"

"It was you," I said. "She was you. You know that. You were real popular. The smartest, prettiest girl in the whole school. Why do you think we all voted for you?"

"You like me, don't you?"

I frowned. "Sure."

"You don't look at me and think, Oh, poor her, she's so damaged?"

"No." But she was damaged, and "poor her" is exactly what I thought sometimes.

"Because I think I'm getting a little crush on you," she said. "I'm not sure if I really am, or it's just something going on inside my messed-up head."

It had to be her injury. What I really thought was, She'd have to be brain-damaged to have a crush on me.

But who cares why? I could take the hand she was offering, fol-low her down that path. I could stroke the skin of her shoulder, trail-ing down . . .

"Honestly?" I said. "I think it's all in your head. You're lonely, and I'm the only one here. I mean, we used to have classes together, and you never even noticed me at all."

She leaned back against the tree. "How awful. Such a sweet boy and I never noticed?"

"Nope."

I heard a noise, above. A gang of boys stared down from the bridge with accusing eyes. I waved, trying not to look like the guy who had just cleaned out their whole stash of rocks for the second time. They muttered among themselves but kept walking.

The moment they were gone Arnita grabbed my gawky hot hand and pressed it between her cool brown hands: a hand sandwich. Our eyes met. I started skidding down an incline toward the vast darkness that seemed to be opening beneath my feet.

I stood up and put both hands in my pockets. "This is not a good idea."

She reached for my hand.

I wouldn't let her have it. "Don't, okay? Let's go back to your house. Your mom's waiting."

"She's not my mom." She locked my wrist in her fingers, tugging me closer. "Kiss me, Daniel."

"I don't want to."

"Yeah, you do. It's easy. Like this."

Oh it was soft, flowing warm honey straight from her lips. She closed her eyes and urged her mouth against mine. I didn't want to kiss her, then I didn't want to stop.

It went on a good long time.

At last we came up for air.

Man. That was nothing like kissing Dianne. The urgency, the heat, the tongues, the way the whole world seemed to shut down while it lasted — the way we twined around each other — it felt more powerful, like that terrible kiss outside the emergency room in Alabama. But sweet.

"Did you like that?" she said.

I grinned. "You're trying to get me in trouble."

She flashed a glittery smile. "Yes I am."

"Listen — you're the prettiest girl in the world. One of these days you're gonna remember that, and you'll forget all about me."

"Just be my friend, okay Daniel? And kiss me once in a while." She placed her hands on my shoulders and pulled me in again.

I closed my eyes. My whole self narrowed down to the warm softness of her mouth. Her sighing was like music.

This kiss was just as much mine as hers. We kissed all the way, like lovers in a story.

My head turned backflips. Young Love, First Love ... is this how it feels? A little dizzy, out of breath? A little sick to my stomach?

One voice in my head said, Relax! Enjoy it! Have fun! Kiss her again! Be in love! Another voice was saying, Whoa, Daniel, slow down.

But I sure did like that kiss.

THE BAND BUSES ROLLED through the green heat of a Mississippi morning, first week of May and hot summer already. On our bus Bernie Waxman had to shout to be heard over the rush of air through the windows, whipping the hair of the long-straight-haired girls.

"Band, let me tell you about Vicksburg," he said. "Once upon a time this little town was the most fought-over spot in the world. As long as the Rebels held this town, they controlled the entire Mississippi. And they knew whoever owned the river was gonna win the war."

This was old news. We knew all about the battle of Vicksburg, after three weeks of the subject in Mississippi History plus the annual class field trip to the battlefield. We'd all been to the visitor center many times to see the dioramas of Vicksburg under siege — mannequins posed in a cave tunneled into the hillside to escape the rain of artillery.

The park ranger explained that although the starving towns-people had been reduced to eating rats, they served them on their heirloom china, with their best silverware. The lesson seemed to be that a true Southerner retains his superior manners, even when faced with unfamiliar food.

"That's us, band," Waxman was saying. "Surrounded and out-numbered. This is not some piddly district competition, okay? This is All-State. The big time. Every big-school band in Mississippi is headed in with their heavy artillery . . . Columbus, Starkville, Warren Central . . . rich kids from rich schools. We're a bunch of stubborn cave dwellers, poor but proud. We don't have much, but we do have each other. And our instruments. And our Pride. What do you think, can you do it? Can you bring home a One?"

We roared, *YEAH, YEAH we can DO it!*

"What is the word?"

"Pride!"

"What is it?"

"PRIDE!"

We poured off the bus in a frenzy of pride, One-lust, ambition, exhilaration, and onto the oak-shaded campus of Vicksburg Bible College.

Debbie Frillinger rushed up, eyes welling, clasping her clarinet to her breast. "Oh Daniel, do you really think it's possible we could get a One?"

"It's possible," I said. "But if we want to do it, we gotta really burn down the house!"

"Yeah! Burn it down!" That was Brian Fairchild, lugging his tuba.

"It's a good thing we're doing the marching show first," I said, "cause we're too pumped up to play concert right now!"

Brian laughed. "Ol' Musk Ox gettin' worked *up!*"

Somehow we had passed through Vicksburg without getting a glimpse of the mighty Mississippi, but you could smell it, moist and muddy, in the air. Walking triple file through the trees toward the stadium, we heard the thunder of drums.

Waxman watched us pass in review with his family, who'd followed the band bus in their car — his tiny wife, Candy, their pudgy little boy and baby girl. Of course he had brought them. This was the biggest day of his year.

Waxman was so committed to the band that I never pictured him anywhere other than the band hall. I thought of that nibbled stub of a baton, the light in his office burning at all hours, the splotches that came out on his cheeks when we played the same wrong note for the twenty-third time. I bet his wife got sick of hearing about us.

We rounded the corner to Nebuchadnezzar Stadium. A thrilling blast of brass rose to meet us.

Contest was two parts: marching in the stadium in the morning, concert band in the afternoon. On the field, a vast band in navy and white executed precise diagonals. Large squadrons of flag girls twirled flags, rifle girls tossed weapons in the air, three drum majors twirled their maces in glittering arcs.

"Columbus High," Waxman called over our heads. "They're big, but we're better."

Good God what a sound! We could never produce such a fat brassy sound. The gust of trumpets on "Also Sprach Zarathustra" was enough to slick back the fur on our hats.

"Keep moving, keep moving," Waxman shouted.

Wait — we were going on immediately after Columbus High? Everybody knew they were the best high school band in Mississippi. Straight Ones at Contest, many years in a row. The hardest act to follow in the entire state.

Waxman knew better than to tell us this news in advance. He let it sink in while we stood there watching Columbus finish their show. He didn't look worried. He lifted his little boy to his shoulders and waved us to our starting position, behind the end-zone line.

Lionel Wooten pranced down the line with sharp chirps of his whistle. Lionel was lanky, skinny, black, a bit of a priss, with a shiny gold tooth and pneumatic pistons for legs. He danced, cavorted, bounded to his starting position. In his big bearskin hat Lionel looked twelve feet tall. He swung his tasseled gold-headed mace around his shoulder, tossing it high in the air, then hurled it like a thunderbolt so the sharp end stuck *sproinnng* in the mud of the field.

"Band!" Lionel boomed. "Atteennn-*hut!*"

We snapped to attention. The drummers clicked sticks on the rims, marching us forward at Parade Walk.

We were alone in the stadium except for a little crowd of Band

Booster parents and the judges peering down from the press box. "Ladeeees and gentlemen . . . please welcome, under the direction of Bernard Waxman and the field leadership of Drum Major Lionel Wooten, the Mighty Marching Titans of Minor High!"

At football games this raised a gratifying roar from the stands.

"Band!" Lionel screamed into the silence. "Haaaaaaaawns *up!*"

The trumpeters opened up on the fanfare. When the piercing high C broke into a chord, we picked up our feet and marched.

We opened up into "Hands Across the Sea," and things got complicated in a hurry. We spread into trapezoids and triangles, a three-masted schooner sailing across the field, an eagle with its wings spread. We marched the eagle downfield while the drummers banged a beat for the twirlers' routine. I had a moment to think, *Hey, we're doing great!*

The march dissolved into "Bad, Bad Leroy Brown." In quick succession we formed a steam engine, a Star of David, a pair of dice, old King Kong, and a junkyard dog. This called for a frenetic series of pivots and turns, our curving lines anchored on constantly shifting targets.

Then the thump of "Go Titans," our fight song, a quickstep to the sideline, where we formed lines like rays radiating from the frolicking sun of Lionel Wooten.

We aimed our instruments at the judges and gave them a last shot of noise. Snapping down our instruments we shouted in cadence: *"We are the Mighty Marching Titans — of Mi-i-nor High!"* A rim click took us off the field.

I felt a thrill rising. *This* is how it feels to do something better than you've ever done! Once we reached open air we hollered and hugged and pounded on each other. Jon Crisler said, "If that ain't a One, the goddamn judges are blind!"

"Jon!" cried Janice Lipscomb. "Don't take the Lord's name in vain, you'll jinx us!" She hugged me. "Daniel, you were great! I always get scared when we have to make that pivot, but there you were, like the Rock of Gibraltar."

Waxman wore a big smile. "Excellent marching. Find some shade, eat your lunch, focus on concert. It's make-or-break time."

We retrieved our sack lunches. Mine was a baloney sandwich and an apple with a note Scotch-taped to the stem: *Daniel, Best of luck today. Dad and I are proud of you! Love, Mom.*

I struck my mallets in thin air, working through the memorized motions. My gravest fear was that my arms would seize up on that xylophone run in the Stephen Foster. I could blow the band's chance for a One, all by myself.

All around me were band members thinking the same — eyes scrunched shut, lips brushing mouthpieces, fingers twiddling keys.

Waxman dandled his baby on a blanket under a tree.

Dianne Frillinger came up to me. "You okay, Daniel? You look so serious."

"I'm fine. I'm just thinking about my part." I had managed to mostly avoid her since Prom Night.

"It's nerve-wracking, isn't it?" she said. "Contest is so important."

"Yeah, it is."

She peered up through thick oval lenses. "Daniel, can I ask you something? Are you still mad at me?"

Uh-oh. Here we go. "When was I mad at you?"

"Well — I don't know, ever since the prom, you pretty much stopped talking to me."

"No I didn't." I examined my shoes. "I've been busy, that's all."

"Because I thought when you kissed me that night, it meant — something! But we were better friends before the prom than we are now."

This is why I stayed away from girls. "Aw come on, Dianne —"

"It's true." Her eyes flashed. "You never call me."

"I never called you before."

"I know, but you never kissed me, either. Then after you did, and you didn't even call — oh, this sounds so stupid. Stupid! Would you please tell me to shut up?"

"Look," I said, "it's just that I help Arnita after school. Then I have to ride my bike all the way home, and I've got all this grass to cut . . ."

She frowned. "What do you mean, help her?"

"With her homework. So she can keep up with her classes."

"That's so admirable it makes me want to throw up," said Dianne. "But what does it have to do with us?"

"Us?"

"Just tell me if you like me even a little, okay?" she pleaded. "Or if you don't. Either way, would you please just tell me and get it over with?"

"Look, Dianne, you heard Waxman. Today is important. We don't need to get distracted."

She blinked, took a step back. "You're right. I'm selfish and stupid. I apologize."

"That's not what I said."

She backed away. I saw tears in her eyes. I didn't stop her from going.

WE MARCHED SINGLE file across a dazzling white concrete plaza, up wide steps to a covered portico. The Clinton High band burst through the far doors, racing one another down the steps. They were done, their fate sealed. I envied their freedom and their joyful commotion.

I couldn't wait to tell Tim that we had played Weener Auditorium. Except for its name, the building was unremarkable, plain as a Bible. Gloomy light fell through the tall narrow windows, onto simple wooden pews and a proscenium stage. We entered quietly, with solemn purpose.

I walked past the woodwinds to the table where my toys were laid out — concert bells, xylophone, vibraphone, chimes, crotales, triangle, tambourine, wood block, ratchet, slapstick. In the concert band, I was Incidental Percussion. My job was to bring a sparkle to the edges of our sound.

I squinted past the lights to the judges in midbalcony. I thought I saw them frowning at us.

Waxman spread his score on the stand. "All right, band. Let's tune."

Cecilia Karn rose to play a vibrato-free E. Cecilia was first-chair clarinet, a serious student and musician who would probably go on to become secretary-general of the UN someday. She took invisible breaths and kept playing E until her face turned as crimson as her uniform jacket.

Waxman studied us for a long minute over his half-glasses, then lifted his baton.

"King Cotton" started off like a circus parade, jaunty and cheerful until a few minor notes introduced a shadow. Then came sounds of war, resolving in the steady rising crunch of soldiers marching and firing, every cymbal going *clash!* The "King Cotton" march is a delicate thing for its size. We played it well enough to raise Waxman's left eyebrow in pleasure. He even smiled.

We plunged into "Incantation and Dance," a moody modern piece with frequent rhythm shifts, tons of Incidental Percussion. The opening was as somber as the leper music in *Ben-Hur.* Then a noisy jumping chaos got me scurrying among the timbales, wood blocks, and chimes, *bong! chok-chok-chok,* and *ka-ching!* Luckily the piece was so disorderly that no one could tell when I missed.

Everything in "Incantation" came down to one crucial duet between oboe and bassoon. Deirdre Adams and Jimmye Brashier performed this beautiful exchange of phrases, ladling the melody back and forth. Amazement rippled through the band — did we really sound that good?

A great shiny gold-plated One appeared in the air above our heads, floating, sparkling. All we had to do was reach up and grab it.

Waxman raised his baton. Cecilia played the opening solo of the Stephen Foster, the melody of "Camptown Races" in plaintive A minor, to a counterpoint from Tommy Wilson on cornet with a hat mute.

The full band came in for the first big wash of sound —

But something was missing. The sound was thin, lacking a bottom. Big brass.

I glanced across the stage to see Brian Fairchild and the other tuba boys placing their horns, bell down, gently on the stage beside them.

Shanice James did the same with her French horn. All the other horns followed their lead.

Every black member of the band stopped playing, placed his instrument on the floor beside him, and sat quietly with folded hands.

They were one-third of our band. Almost all the brass. Their silence ripped a great ragged hole in our sound.

In Contest there was no starting over, nothing to do but flounder on through the piece as the melody tailed off in embarrassing gaps, off-balance and wrong.

It took a long time to be over. The black students stared grimly at the floor. The rest of us strained, wild-eyed, playing louder, trying to make up for what was missing.

Waxman's eyes burned. His hands measured a beat in the air, but his hands seemed disconnected from the fire in his eyes.

Who cared that I hit my xylophone run perfectly? We struggled on, begging, Please God let it end.

Eventually we stopped. Not all at once. A sickening silence descended.

Waxman's mouth twitched. He appeared calm except for that twitch. I couldn't bear to look at him. "Band dismissed," he said.

We filed off the stage, too stunned to make a sound. The black kids coalesced in a mass toward the back. Their normal voices sounded like shouting. "We tried to tell y'all," Shanice was saying. "Nobody would listen."

"Ain't gonna play no slave songs," said Brian Fairchild. "There's a million other songs we coulda played, and he knows it."

"Shut the hell up, Fairchild," said Jeff Lehorn, big red-haired baritone sax, "unless you want me to come over there and kick your black ass."

Several white guys made a move to help Lehorn do that. The groups drew apart, everybody slapping at pants pockets. I edged away, thinking, Uh-oh, here comes the knife fight at last!

Waxman charged into the middle. "Stop it! Keep walking. Move your butts!" He actually swatted Jeff Lehorn to get him moving.

Jeff hurled his mouthpiece. It bounced off the pavement with a *ching!* and rolled into the gutter.

We split into two bands, facing off across the courtyard. We muttered at each other and paced back and forth, awaiting the judgment of the loudspeaker on the wall.

The Frillingers sobbed as if someone had died. Most of the girls on the white side of the plaza were crying, the boys cussing. The boys on the black side were having their own loud discussion with some of the girls. Everyone knew we had been on the verge of winning Ones, possibly the first straight Ones in Minor history, when they put down their horns.

I stood with the angry white kids — hell, I was one of them, wasn't I? Admit it! I was trembling mad. What gave them the right to do that — just to prove their stupid point? Okay, maybe not a totally stupid point about Stephen Foster and his minstrel music being demeaning, if you happen to be black. Maybe Waxman did brush off their objections too lightly. We all did. Did that give them the right to plot against us? To lie in wait, and ambush us at Contest? It was their sneakiness that shocked me — they caught us off guard, they betrayed us at the moment when we were all trying so hard, for once in our lives, to be excellent.

Couldn't they have made the same point at the final rehearsal?

No. Because that wouldn't have hurt us. They wanted to hurt us.

We glared at them like they were traitors. They glared back at us like we were oppressors.

Just for that moment, I hated them. Not because they were black, oh no — I was a Yankee, remember, I couldn't be prejudiced. I hated them for blowing our big chance. And for splitting our one big happy band into two bands that stood hating each other across this plaza.

I saw Brian Fairchild standing over there with that other band. This morning he had teased me when we were getting off the bus.

Now our eyes met. He gave a tiny shrug. Apology? Not really. More like: I'm over here. You're over there. Different sides, nothing personal. Just the way things divide up in Mississippi.

The speaker squealed. A woman's voice said, "Following are the results of competition for Minor High School. The judges' decisions are final. Performance, four. Musicality, four. Presentation, four. Marching band, one. Thank you, and travel home safely."

A shout went up from the black side of the band. They hugged and hammered on each other and did little dances of joy.

The scores proved their point perfectly. Without their participation, we were nothing. Straight Fours. With them, in marching band, we had scored the near-impossible One.

Suddenly I didn't hate them. They had simply stopped being good sports who went to the back of the bus without being asked. No matter how cruel it seemed for them to spoil our big day — just to prove their point! — they had taught me a lesson I would not have learned otherwise.

Waxman stepped onto the stretch of concrete between us.

Shanice James said, "Mr. Waxman? Excuse me?"

He turned. "What?"

"Are you gonna tell us again how we need to be like the Confederate Army? Cause we heard enough about that on the way over here."

"You shut up, Shanice." Waxman's voice was soft, deadly. "You're out of the band, okay? We don't need you or your attitude. You haven't got any Pride. Go get on the bus."

"But Mr. Waxman —"

"I said shut up! You've lost your right of free speech, okay? This is my band. I'm the one who says who can be in this band. Now you go!"

Her eyes flashed, but she went.

Waxman expelled a chestful of air. "Now, the rest of you on this side, listen good, cause I'm only gonna say this once. What you did to me today — hell, I guess I had it coming, didn't I? Didn't pay enough attention to your extremely important objections, isn't that right? I plead guilty to that."

"Mr. Waxman," tried Lionel Wooten.

"Be quiet," Waxman said. "So yeah, maybe I had it coming. But your friends over there, on that side, what did they do to you? What kind of spite would lead you to throw away a whole year of their hard work? Just because I didn't pay enough lip service to your ideas of what music we should or shouldn't play? Why not come to me and try to talk to me seriously, instead of —"

Lionel tried to answer.

"Don't!" Waxman cried. "I'm talking now. Y'all think I'm some kind of bigot? You are so wrong. I'm a Jew, for God's sake, I'm the best friend you will ever have in this town. And you tricked me. But I'm older than you, and I happen to have the power here. And I'm sure as hell not afraid to use it just because I'm white!"

Blacks would ride on one bus, he declared, whites on the other. "I always thought color-blind was the way to go. Obviously I was wrong. You want separate but equal? You got it. Move out!"

We moved unwillingly, both sides still aching to fight. The only thing that kept us apart was the hot righteous glow of Waxman's anger. I had a dull toothache sensation that I should do something to stop this happening — but let's face it, I was not that kind of boy.

We crept onto the buses. Waxman rode in the car with his wife. The silence on our bus came as a relief. I can't imagine any words that would have made that trip better.

12

WHEN I TOLD ARNITA what happened in Vicksburg, she laughed. "Wow, a revolution! That sounds like fun."

"Fun? It was terrible, don't you get it? We got Fours. We should have had Ones. And now everybody hates each other." Evening was descending on the river bend. Lightning bugs winked in the trees. We sat in our favorite spot, propped in the crook of the log.

"It's just a contest," she said. "Not the end of the world."

"Not to Waxman. You should have seen his face. The black kids said, 'Either you let Shanice back in the band or we all quit.' He said, 'Okay fine, you just quit.'"

"All of them?"

"Yup. Suddenly we're the All-Whitey Mighty Marching Titans."

"Can he do that?"

"He didn't do anything," I said. "They're the ones who quit."

"But he said, 'Okay, fine.'"

"They hit his sore spot. He has this idea that he can't be prejudiced because he's Jewish."

"Everybody's prejudiced," Arnita said. "Everybody looks down on somebody else."

"Who do you look down on?"

"Everybody," she said. "That's why it's so great to be white. We have so many different kinds of people to look down on."

"Aw come on, stop fooling. You're not white, and you know it." Wrapping my arms around her, I nudged her forward until we were leaning out over the water. "Look there. Who do you see?"

She squinted at the reflection. "Linda and Daniel."

"No. Your face." I nudged her with my head. "Tell me what you see."

She tried to wiggle free. "I hate this game. Let me go!"

"Not till you tell. And you have to be honest." I mashed my face into her shoulder, breathing her sweet pink sweater.

"A blonde," she said softly. "See? I'm a honey blonde. My eyes are set a little too far apart. But I have good skin, and I like my new nose. Don't you? Little turned-up Barbie nose . . ."

Her nose was not new, of course, nor was it little, or turned up. Her skin was a lovely dusky chocolate milk. Her smile was spectacular. She'd kept her hair cropped short since the hospital.

"Okay if I kiss you?" I said.

"Sure."

"You like the way I kiss you," I said.

She nodded.

We kissed for hours every day. Now that school was out, we had even more time for kissing. Generally I took her into the shadows under the bridge, but now it was getting dark, nobody around, so we kissed and kissed in the open, in front of the trees, the river, God, and everybody. You learn to kiss by doing and doing it. She puts her whole mouth into you, you put your mouth into her, the world narrows down to this hot jumping junction of mouths, the maximum sloppy sensation of feeling each other up with your tongues.

If sex is a whole lot better than this, I thought, I will die.

When Arnita touched me, I got hard as a big rock candy mountain — sometimes she brushed my leg and I thought my skull might explode. When we made out, she pretended not to notice that big old thing rambling against her thigh, but a few times I could have sworn she pushed back against it.

So here was I, weeks later, still standing there by the river kissing the hell out of her. She liked the way I did it. By that time I was the virgin of a thousand handjobs, the readiest, horniest virgin on earth, a walking throbbing pillar of unquenchable readiness. But the idea of actually doing it with a real girl — my delicious strawberry candy–tasting girl as opposed to the parade of gorgeous fevered girls in my head — that still scared me. As much as I was dying to try it. I had to watch out or the next kiss might spin out of control, getting hotter and wilder each second, a little whimper —

I broke it off. "God! Cut that out!"

She chuckled. "You are kinda sparky today. Can I call you Sparky?"

She was crazy. Not just brain-damaged, but pure sexy crazy. She had caused me to lose all interest in normal girls. Dianne Frillinger had been like kissing a refrigerator. Give me hot-blooded crazy Arnita any day, confusing my lips, driving my fingers to the brink of insanity.

We were not getting much homework done.

"Whoa, slow down," she said, coming up for air.

"Mm, that feels good."

"Take your hand off there, mister!"

That made me laugh. "Mister?"

"Mister Bad Guy, that's you." She tried to slide her arm through mine.

I pulled away and walked out in front to let my problem subside.

Headlights flashed over us. My neck hairs stood up — you didn't see many fastback Mustangs in this park after sunset.

Red Martin parked by the swing sets. He got out and walked a straight line toward us.

He wore his Titan jersey, number 42. A fresh crew cut made his head appear even pinker in the gloom. "Hello Five Spot, how you doin', ol' pal?"

I ducked the hand snaking out toward my face. "Well, if it ain't Dudley Ronald Martin."

He smirked at my boldness. "Arnita, looking good. I dig the short hair."

"My name is Linda," she said.

"Yeah? Since when?"

She caught my warning glance. "No, you're right, I am Arnita," she said. "Sometimes I get it mixed up. Do I know you?"

"I sure as hell think so. You've only got me arrested twice now," said Red. "We heard you might be a little bit —" He drew a circle around his ear with one finger. "More than a little, I'd say. I can't wait to tell my lawyer you didn't even recognize me. Five Spot, you're a witness to that."

"You're Red Martin," she said. "I know who you are. But you shaved off all your hair."

I stood up straighter. "What are you doing here, Red?"

"Hey, if y'all gonna do the interracial love thang in a public park, you can't act surprised when word gets out. Or did you forget you're still in Mis'sippi?"

"Oh so you've joined the Klan?"

"Ha ha, so funny. I came to talk to her."

"What about?" said Arnita.

He glanced over his shoulder, then back to her. "Look, this is serious shit you started. The district attorney would like to drop the charges, but your mother won't let him. She calls him two or three times a week. It's bullshit, Arnita, and you know it. I didn't hurt you. It wasn't me. No matter what the hell you think you remember."

"Sure it was." She eyed him. "You knocked me off my bike and drove off."

"When I drove off, you were okay," said Red. "You were mad, you were cussing me, remember? I came back around the block to see if you were all right — that's when I saw you laid out on the ground. And the cops pulled me over."

"That's not how it happened," she said.

"But you don't remember exactly? You don't know for sure." His voice was dead calm. "Look at me. Do I seem dangerous to you?"

Arnita looked him over. "Not at the moment."

I edged between them. I wasn't exactly helpless, but Red was big enough to toss me in the river if he wanted to.

"Look, Arnita, you're gonna mess up my life and yours too," he said. "You were kinda drunk that night, you mighta fell off that bike on your own. If you press charges, it'll all have to come out. Understand? The drinking, the white boyfriends, the pot you were smoking at Charlene's that night — everything would have to come out in court. Is that what you want?"

I saw a glimmer of fear in Arnita's eyes.

Red said, "That brain damage must be worse than I heard, you down here making out with ol' Five Spot. I mean, come on, if you want a white boy, you can have me. I am offering you a chance to be smart here."

"Don't listen to him," I told her. "He's not supposed to even talk to you, much less threaten you. They can put him in jail just for that."

"Down, Spot," he said. "I ain't threatening anybody."

Arnita blinked her deep brown eyes at me. "You don't believe anything he says, do you?"

"No. And neither should you."

She glanced at Red, then me. "Do you think — is it possible I could be wrong about that night?"

Red's eyes lit up. "Damn right it's possible."

"What?" I cried. "No!"

"Red knocked me down. He drove off and left me. But I do remember yelling at him as he left. Does that mean something happened after that?"

"No!" I seized her hands. "Don't do this. He's trying to confuse you."

She blinked. "You know the whole thing has always been real hazy for me."

"Don't let him put ideas in your head." I clasped her shoulders. "Come on, let's go. I'll take you home."

"Oh, that's fair," Red said. "Just when she decides to start telling the truth?"

"Fair, Red?" I lashed out. "Did you just use the word *fair?*"

"Aw come on, Five Spot, you know all that other was kid stuff. Okay? That was all in good fun. Arnita's right. This whole thing is just a big misunderstanding."

"That's not what I said." Arnita crossed her arms. "Don't put words in my mouth."

He loomed over her. "Drop the charges. All you have to do is tell your mother you're not sure, and the whole thing goes away. Just like that. Everything goes back like it was."

"Not me," she said, with an unhappy smile. "I don't go back like I was."

"I guess not." Red squared his shoulders. "Look, whatever happened, it was an accident. I didn't mean to hurt you. Don't send me to jail."

"You don't have to listen to this," I said softly. "He's just trying to save his own hide."

She turned to study me. "Why are you so suspicious of him?"

"Why do you think? He's devoted his life to making Tim and me miserable."

"Aw come on, that was playing around," Red said. "I was just having fun. You play ball with me, I guarantee I will leave you alone."

"I think it was brave of him to come here and talk," Arnita said.

Red preened at the word "brave." I didn't like the way this was headed. "He's not brave, he's scared," I said. "And desperate. He'll say anything to get you to drop those charges." Of course scared and desperate applied even more directly to me. I would say anything to keep Arnita from knowing that my hand grabbed the wheel of that car.

I had to protect her, even from myself. "Don't listen to him," I said. "Don't listen to me either. You have to do what's right."

"All I'm asking," Red said, "is for you to think it over. I've got your number, I'll call you."

"Oh, no." I felt my blood heating up. "If you try to call her, or come anywhere near her again, I swear I will call the police."

"Woooo. Five Spot, why so uptight? You need to get a hobby or something."

Arnita glanced between us. "Why do you call him that?"

"Tell me you never noticed?" Red's smirk widened into a grin. "You been spending too much time on the front of his head. Take a look around the back sometime." He hiked up his jeans, strolled off to his Mustang.

The roar of his unmuffled engine trembled the ground. His tires shrieked as he fishtailed out of the park.

To me Red seemed ridiculous, even a little pitiful, but I could tell he had made an impression on Arnita.

"I never noticed there were five of them." She spread her fingers to touch all the spots. "Why does he tease you like that?"

"Why don't you ask him? You guys are so chummy. Which I really do not understand, considering he ran over you and left you for dead." I meant this to sound casual and ironic but it came out childish, sullen.

"Daniel, are you jealous of him?"

"No. I'm worried about you. Your mother won't be all that thrilled to hear you're hanging out with Red Martin."

"You are! You're jealous!"

"Red's dangerous. I don't want you talking to him."

"Hush," she said, touching my lips. "Don't tell me who I can talk to. Okay?"

"Okay. Wow. Excuse me," I said.

We walked home in silence. I tried to make it light again, but her mood had changed. Maybe my sarcasm, or the subject of Prom Night. It felt like our first fight.

Mrs. Beecham sang from the porch: "Musgrove, you're late! Where have y'all been?"

Arnita walked up the steps and threw herself down in the swing. I followed her up on the porch and stood with my arms folded, looking down at her.

"Uh-huh," said Mrs. Beecham. "I see." Her slow blink evolved into a stare that settled on me.

I coughed. Was I supposed to say something?

"Musgrove?" she said.

"What?"

"What is going on here?"

"Nothing!"

"Yes there is." She drilled new holes in me with those eyes.

"Okay," I said. "Maybe there is."

Arnita got up and went into the house. She slammed the door behind her.

Her mother lowered her voice. "What the hell is the matter with you? She's not all right and you know it. Does she seem all right to you? Does she seem to have control of her mental faculties to you? No. But here you come, taking advantage of her. I thought you were better than that."

"I love her, Mrs. Beecham." I said it loud enough for Arnita to hear.

Ella Beecham winced. "Aw, shit. No you don't, crazy boy! You might think you do, but you don't."

"She loves me too, I'm pretty sure."

"Are you out of your mind? You think you can go with a colored girl? Well, just forget it. You can't. Not with *my* girl."

"I didn't mean for it to happen. But now I'm just . . . I can't stop thinking about her."

"No, now, I ain't having that kind of mess. Not from you." Ella shooed me off her porch. "If that's how it is, don't be coming around here. *No* sir. You stay away."

Panic laid a cold finger against my neck. Stay away? Was she joking? I couldn't stay away from Arnita. Nothing could keep me away. If Ella Beecham locked the door I would climb through a window. If she locked the window I'd break it. If she boarded it up, I would go find an ax.

When I was with Arnita I was vibrating, every atom of me whizzing, sending off sparks. Riding my bike to her house, knowing I would soon taste her lips . . . it made the pedals fly under my feet.

"Go on home now," her mother was saying.

I climbed onto my bike. "Tell her I'll call her tonight."

"Don't call," she said. "She don't need to hear from you."

"I will call," I said, "and I'll be here tomorrow, like always."

A furrow opened in her brow. "Musgrove, try to hang on to whatever little shred of dignity you have left. Don't you get it? We don't need you around here. We got no more jobs for you. You just ride on home."

I pretended to take her advice. I rode away knowing that tomorrow I would come back and try again.

13

TIM HAD BEEN BURNING some kind of fruit incense, grape or blackberry, and he had Elton cued up on the eight-track singing "Daniel" in my honor as we drove off to *Christ!* rehearsal. He smacked my knee. "How's it going with your little girlfriend?"

"You know what they say. Love is strange." I laid my arm down the side of the car and told him about our visit from Red. I told him that Arnita was examining her memories of Prom Night, and our Lie was beginning to outgrow the original crime. "Any day now she's gonna remember. Only now she'll truly hate me. With good reason."

Tim said, "Oh Skippy, don't tell me you're still feeling the urge to confess? I thought you had gotten over that."

I shrugged. "Sometimes when I'm with her I think, Why not just tell her? It was an accident. She'll forgive you. But it's too late. I've been lying to her from the very beginning."

Tim said, "For her own good, Skippy. Don't forget that. Just keep doing what you're doing. Stay close to her. You've done great so far. Don't screw it up."

"I have this feeling she's gonna break up with me," I said. "Maybe I should wait and tell her when she already hates me."

Tim said, "You don't think you're actually in love with her, do you?"

I shrugged. I couldn't lie, not about this. "Yeah, I am. Or at least I think I am. I don't know how I feel. Did you ever feel like that?"

"You're the one that goes around *feeling* everything all the time," he said. "I'm just trying to figure out how to get rid of Red."

"School's out," I said. "You mean he's still bothering you?"

"He never stopped! He drives by our house all the time with that super-duper muffler of his, it shakes the glass in the windows. The other night he took these sacks of garbage and tore 'em open and scattered 'em all over our yard! Can you imagine how crazy that made my mother? You know what a clean freak she is!"

"You saw him do that?"

"No, but I know it was him."

"I think you're being paranoid," I said. "What if it was some dogs that got ahold of your garbage? And anyway, doesn't Red have to drive past your house to get to school? They live up on Bluff Park Drive."

"I should have known you'd take his side," Tim said. "Just forget it." He put the Pinto onto I-20, heading east.

"Why do you let him get to you so bad?" I said. "He can't do anything to us. He's the one in trouble. I called him Dudley to his face the other day, and there wasn't a thing he could do about it."

"He's not human," Tim said. "He doesn't deserve to be called a human being. If you wiped him out you would be doing the rest of mankind a favor. Like killing a mosquito, or a poisonous snake."

"But his mama loves him," I said, "and he's kind to the furry little creatures of the woodlands."

"I'm not joking," said Tim. "I don't joke about Red. He's the enemy. The spawn of Satan."

"Well he's not exactly my best friend," I said, "but I don't think I'm quite as obsessed as you. He leaves me alone more, because I tend to ignore him."

Tim frowned in disgust. "You're like my mother. You think the solution to any problem is to ignore it."

"Thanks. I always did want to be more like your mother."

"Your lips are all chapped from making out with that girl," he said. "You ought to get a ChapStick. They only cost like fifty cents."

I rubbed my lip, thinking, What a weird thing to say.

"Wait, shut up, what was that?" He lunged for the volume knob.

". . . to the capital city for a very special concert," the deejay said, "Saturday, August the eighteenth — by special arrangement with Ruffino-Vaughn Promotions — tickets on sale today — it's our great privilege here at WDSU, Today's Hottest Hits —"

"Come on, asshole!" Tim smacked the dashboard. "Who?"

"— live and in person, one night only, at the Mississippi Coliseum . . . Sonny and Cher!"

Tim veered off the road and back on. "Oh my God. Oh my God."

"Hey, don't get us killed."

He jammed on the gas. "We're going to the Coliseum."

"Now?"

"Hell yes! You got cash?"

"Like, four bucks."

"I think I can cover both of us, as long as they're not more than twenty apiece."

"What about *Christ!*?"

"Skippy, think! What if it sells out and we can't get tickets? Can you even imagine? We would have to die. We'd have to kill each other in some sort of ritualistic fashion."

We sang along with Cher on her latest hit, "I Saw a Man (And He Danced With His Wife)," and before it was over we were taking the exit for the Mississippi Coliseum. Ours was the only car crossing the vast parking lot. "Obviously we're their only real fans in this whole stupid town," I said.

"This is truly pathetic," Tim said. "Let's face it, we are trapped in a time and place where we do not belong."

I had to agree.

One box-office window was open, occupied by a lady with bee-hive hair, filing her nails.

Tim said, "You have tickets for Sonny and Cher?"

"Sure. How many?"

"Two, I guess. Two, Durwood? Or should we get four and take somebody?"

"Who, the Frillingers?"

He laughed. "Purest vessels of the most holy virginity? No thank you, there's got to be somebody we actually like. Who do we like?"

"You don't like anybody," I said. "You mean girls?"

"Of course girls. Don't look so alarmed." He bent to the window. "How much are they?"

The beehive lady sawed away with her emery board. "Eight-fifty, general admission."

"If we're taking girls, I'm taking Arnita," I said, "but I'm not sure that's such a good idea."

Tim lifted an eyebrow. "Oh, right, I forgot. You can make out with her every afternoon, but you can't be seen in public with her. I knew that complexion of hers was gonna get you in trouble sooner or later."

"Her complexion has nothing to do with it."

"What is it, then, the fact that she's a little whacked in the head?"

"Are you trying to piss me off?" I snapped. "Cause right now you are doing a really great job."

"Let me get this straight," he said. "Arnita is black but that has nothing to do with why the two of you are the biggest secret since the atomic bomb?"

He had me. I talked a great game of equality, I looked down on Mississippi's backward ways with my good superior Indiana Yankee attitude — but had I ever treated Arnita like a real girlfriend? No. I hid her. I took her up under the bridge to kiss her. I made her swear not to tell anybody. Every time I kissed her, I found myself thinking — All this and she's black too! Beautiful, smart, damaged, and also exotic, forbidden, makes me want to kiss her even more!

I doubt that any interracial couple had ever walked the streets of Minor. Call me a coward. I did not want to go first.

"It's obvious. You have to take her." Miss Beehive peered at me through her tortoiseshell glasses.

"Beg your pardon?"

"Take the girl to the show. It's your business. Who's gonna care?"

Tim cocked an eyebrow. "What are you, Dear Abby?"

"No, but I'm from Chicaago just like Dear Abby," she said, "so take my advice. I'm a great believer in doing what you want to do. Down here that makes me like a Commie subversive. Take the girl to the show."

"Chicaago," I said with a smile. "Come aan, let's go drink a paap."

Her face lit up. "Oh my Gaad, where you fraam?"

"Indiana."

She beamed. "I haven't heard 'paap' since we got down here!"

We bought four tickets and went to the car. "So who are you gonna take?" Tim said.

"Arnita, I guess."

"Uhm . . . are you sure about that, Skippy? I mean, forget what the Yankee woman says."

"She was right, who's gonna care?"

"Somebody will," Tim said. "There's still people around here who care about that stuff, believe me."

"Nobody will even notice us," I said. "Some friends going to a show, so what? It's no big deal. Unless you turn it into one."

"You know what this means, don't you," Tim said. "I gotta find a girl who will agree to double-date with a *Negress*. Imagine what a howling barking dog *that* will have to be."

CHRIST! WAS REALLY coming together, thanks to radical surgery performed by Eddie at Mrs. Passworth's insistence. He howled every time she made him cut another song. It took plenty of howling to get the show under three hours, then under two. Eddie insisted at each step that every song was crucial to his Overall Vision.

He kept putting in (and having to take out) a swinging gospel-style number called "Bless the Devil." The idea of the lyric was, it's a good thing the devil is around to tempt us, since the temptations remind us how much we love Jesus. It was a risky song for church —

what if somebody came in late and just heard the chorus? — but Eddie pleaded for it long after it was obvious it would never go in.

"Take a deep breath, Eddie," Mrs. Passworth said. "The show's getting better. I do think we should make the rest of these cuts now — painful as they are. Then we can concentrate on the songs we'll actually be performing."

"Oh, here we go again." He rolled his eyes. "What do you want to cut now?"

Mrs. Passworth glanced at her clipboard. "'Fishes and Loaves.' I'm sorry, but that dancing part seems to go on forever. If we cut that, and 'Flowers in the Rain,' we'll be close."

"'Flowers in the *Rain?*'" Eddie squealed as if she'd stomped on his toe. "You want to cut the Crucifixion?"

"Well it's so depressing," said Passworth. "Do we really need it? If you go straight from 'Not That Kind of Girl' to 'When He Wakes Up,' you keep it on a positive note. I mean, just go straight to the Resurrection. That's the happiest part of the show, and believe me, by this point we are really ready for a little bit of happy."

"This is crazy," Eddie said. "Don't you understand the concept? Each song expresses a chapter in his journey — I can't believe I'm having to *explain* this! You can't just drop songs left and right and expect people to be able to follow the story!"

"People *know* the story, Eddie. You're not the first one to tell it, okay?" That was Passworth near the end of her rope, a voice I remembered from the outer reaches of post-Christmas algebra.

Eddie would not be moved. "You cannot skip the Crucifixion! That's like saying Jesus lived happily ever after. Next you'll have him dancing off down the yellow brick road."

"Don't be so dramatic," she said. "He still arises from the dead. You're just cutting the one song."

"I don't want to cut that song," he said, "or any other song. You cut any more, it's not my show. And while it still is my show, this is my decision and it's final."

"Not exactly," said Mrs. Passworth. "Eddie, I don't want to hurt your feelings — the songs are wonderful, there's just too many. Let me see a show of hands, how many of you kids think there's too many songs?"

Every hand in the chorus went up. Some people raised both hands. Even Matt Smith voted yes, and it was his song she was trying to cut.

"Eddie, we love you." That was Carol Nason / Mary Magdalene trying to soften the blow.

"Yes, Carol, I see that, you can put your hand down now," he said bitterly. "Apparently you love me thirty-five to zero. I'm just *drowning* in love up here. I mean, call me insane — I happen to like the show as it is." He whirled on Mrs. Passworth. "You want to cut it? Go ahead. I don't want to stick around for any more of that." He swept himself up in an invisible cloak and strode from the room.

Everybody groaned, *Eddie, wait!*

We glared at Mrs. Passworth, though we'd all just raised our hands to vote against Eddie. We loved him in spite of his crankiness and his tendency to quit in a huff whenever he got upset. We had learned to send a couple of kids after him, beg him to come back, give him a big round of applause when he returned — as he always did, after a decent interval. The welcoming cheer always seemed to take him by surprise.

He clasped his hands together like a victorious boxer. An odd smile played on his face. "Okay, let's get on with the show. Irene, how about I give you the dancing, and you let me keep the Crucifixion."

"Deal," Mrs. Passworth said. "Children, see how mature people behave? Eddie and I disagreed, he offered a compromise, and we worked it out."

"And now since we have all this extra time to play with," he said, "we can put 'Bless the Devil' back in."

"Don't push it, buster." Passworth wasn't smiling.

Eddie was determined to show her a thing or two about pacing. He whipped us through *Christ!* in eighty-two minutes, shaving twelve minutes off the previous land-speed record. "Short enough for you, Irene?" he cried at the end.

"Getting there!" she sang, handing out permission slips for our first performance, an overnight bus trip to Harold P. Wayne Bible College in Itta Bena, up in the Delta. "Now you people get these signed and back to me by the end of this week or you're not getting on that bus, understand?"

14

FIVE O'CLOCK SATURDAY afternoon. I was snoozing under *Jonathan Livingston Seagull* when Janie banged on my door and said phone for me. I hadn't even heard it ring. I shambled out in my undershirt and jeans, my hair all bent and stupid-looking. I didn't come all the way awake until I was holding the phone, saying "Hey Tim" to a dial tone. "Janie, was that Tim? He hung up."

"Not the phone, you idiot!" she yelled from the kitchen. "The door!"

"Right here," said a soft voice. My God! — it was my girl, my very own Arnita in our carport. A gorgeous smile. A blue suitcase in her hand.

I slipped out the door, shushed her all the way around to the front of the house. I set the suitcase on the porch and kissed her a good one, a straight-up electrical thrill — oh man it felt powerful kissing this girl!

I broke it off. "What are you doing here?"

"I should have called first, but I thought you might be mad at me." She did that pouty thing with her lip. "I was afraid you'd tell me not to come."

"You were the one acting mad. I've been trying to call you all week."

She wrapped her arms around me. "She doesn't tell me when you call. It's impossible, Daniel — I can't live with those people anymore. I'm going to stay here with you, okay? You said I could."

"Are you kidding? No!" I had to laugh. "I mean — of course I would love it, but my folks? I don't think so."

She squeezed my arm. "They'll learn to like me, if we give them time. I'll fit in so much better here. Let me talk to your mother. I'll help with the housework, otherwise she'll barely know I'm around."

I stroked her arm. "When did you decide all this?"

"The other night. When Ella hung up on you. You don't know how horrible she is. She hates you. She says I can't ever see you again."

"She's your mother," I said. "She really cares about you. Your dad too."

"No. You care about me. All they care about is Arnita."

"Same thing," I said.

She nibbled on the side of her index finger. "Logically, yes. But inside, I just don't feel it. I'm the only one who can see it through my eyes, you know?"

I made my voice as gentle as possible. "It's the injury that makes you think that way. It makes you confused about that one thing. I explain it to you fifty times, and you never remember. It's like the tape keeps getting erased."

"Don't you want to kiss me?" she said.

How did she know? I couldn't stand it. I grabbed her and kissed her.

Things sprang up, blood started rushing, new enormities began to develop. I cleared my throat and moved back. All I needed was Mom and Janie to come out and find me with Arnita and a raging boner.

I said, "How did you get here?"

"Jimmy brought me in his taxi. Why'd you tell Ella you were in love with me?"

I thought about it. I wanted to be really honest. "She gave me one of those looks, and it just came out. I think she already knew. She's good at that stuff."

"Yeah," said Arnita. "So *are* you? In love?"

"I guess so." I sighed. "It doesn't make me very happy, okay?"

Her smile grew into a wide shining river, the kind you could fall in and drown. "Let's run away, Daniel. I have a hundred dollars. I took it out of Ella's purse."

"You little thief! Be serious. Where would we go?"

"Anywhere. We can go a long way before anybody knows we're gone. Just pack a bag. I've got mine packed, see?"

"I can't just go off and leave Mom here, and Janie," I heard myself saying.

"Why not?"

"Dad would be hard on them if he didn't have me to pick on." This wasn't anything I'd ever thought before, but it felt true when I said it.

Arnita touched my face. "If we don't go now, you know what will happen. They'll find a way to keep us apart."

"Look, we can't run away," I said. "We're gonna be seniors, we have to finish school. And you've got that great scholarship —"

Her fingers stopped my lips. "From Jackson you can go anywhere on a bus. You can go to New York for thirty-four dollars." In her eyes I saw skyscrapers, high-kicking Rockettes. I saw Arnita dancing down a crowded sidewalk in high heels and a translucent dress with spotlights behind her. The vision was so strong I leaned in and kissed her again.

The flash in the trees was the sun winking off a windshield. The car passed out of the screen of trees and materialized in our driveway, Dad's steel-blue Oldsmobile Delta 88.

I pulled Arnita deeper into the shadows of the porch.

Dad drove almost to the carport, switched off the engine. He got out and walked straight over to us without shutting the car door.

I stepped into the sun. "Hey Dad. This is Arnita."

"Go in the house," he said.

I didn't move.

His eye fell on Arnita's suitcase. "What the heck is that?"

"I'm gonna be staying with y'all for a while, Mr. Musgrove," she said. "I hope you don't mind."

Dad's face knotted in anger. "Drive up to my house after I've been gone all week, to find you out here half undressed, with *her*, doing that in my front yard for the world to see? You get your hind end in that house!"

He had seen us kissing. This was all my fault.

Arnita turned on the full wattage of her Prom Queen smile. "Mr. Musgrove, maybe we could start over? I'm Linda. It's very nice to meet you."

"You be quiet!" he snapped.

That was my oldest fear coming true: Dad breaking the family code, which required that this side of him never be seen by an outsider.

"Whoa," said Arnita. "Don't yell at me."

I shrugged. "This is what I was trying to tell you."

"Go in the house!" he roared.

"No, Dad!" I cried. "*You* go in. You're the one being rude!"

He wanted to hit me — his right hand jerked up — but he didn't want to do it in front of her. He started to turn away, but then he couldn't help himself — his hand shot out *smack!* — a quick slap off the side of my head. Just hard enough to embarrass me in front of her. "Don't you *ever* talk to me like that." He stalked back to his car.

As always when he hit me, I had to talk back, to demonstrate that he hadn't really hurt me. My face stung a little, that's all. A roar in one ear. "Nice one, Dad," I said.

He took his suitcase and his briefcase from the trunk, and carried them to the house. The door slammed behind him.

"It's my fault," I said. "I made him mad. I wish you didn't have to see that."

"Don't apologize," Arnita said. "You didn't do anything."

"He's in a bad mood. I guess we should call the taxi to come take you home."

"Daniel. I'm not going back there."

I touched her shoulder. "It won't work. I'm sorry, but you can't stay here. You see how he is. My family is too weird for words, I tried to tell you."

"I don't care about that," she said. "I'm going in to talk to your mother."

"You're going in there by yourself?"

"It'll be better that way. You stay here. I'll be fine." With a cryptic smile she walked across the carport, opened the screen door, and stepped through.

I stood frozen in wonder, waiting for her to be blown back through the door like Wile E. Coyote in a cartoon explosion.

For the longest time, nothing happened. It was too quiet in there. I was afraid to go find out why.

Then I couldn't stand it. I went to peer through the glass of the storm door. Things looked oddly normal in the family room. *I'm just a boy with two dads . . .* Dad in his recliner with his feet up, a glass of iced tea on the end table. Local news on the Admiral. On the sofa across from him, Arnita stretched out with her bare feet tucked beside her, as if she lived here.

I could hear Mom in the kitchen, a slew of pans clattering to the floor. Whatever she was cooking smelled vaguely toxic, a hint of electrical fire.

I didn't want to do anything to disturb this arrangement. I went around to the front door, straight down the hall, to the Freak Annex. I took a shower, put on a clean shirt and jeans, and returned to the family room. "What are y'all doing?"

"What's it look like?" Dad said. "We're watching the news."

I perched on the arm of the sofa beside Arnita. "So what's the news?"

"Sonny and Cher are coming to the Coliseum," she said.

"Yeah, I know! Timmy and me already have tickets. I was gonna ask if you wanted to go."

"Whoa, hold on, you didn't clear that with me," Dad said. He winked at Arnita as if to poke fun at his reputation for strictness. He was trying to play the role of Jocular Dad. He wanted us to forget the fact that he had hit me a few minutes before.

Mom came out wearing an apron, a dusting of flour in her hair. I wondered what had brought on this sudden fit of cooking. She said,

"Linda, I talked to your mom and she says it's okay if you spend the one night."

Arnita begged me with her eyes, Please play along, let me be Linda!

Mom said, "You can sleep in the other bed in Janie's room, she'll be thrilled to have you. But remember what I said."

"Yes ma'am. Just the one night."

Mom smiled at me. "Linda's such a nice young lady, so well mannered. Why haven't we met her before?"

It had never occurred to me that Mom might actually like Arnita — but of course she did, who wouldn't? Arnita was so sweet, and oddly sure of herself. So changeable, quick as a smile. And here she was working her magic on the two least susceptible people in the world.

I'd never seen my family try to make any impression on a friend of mine, so I was surprised to see Mom bustling into the dining room, setting out cloth napkins and the Sunday china. Dad sat in his recliner talking to Arnita, tossing out witticisms, going to the trouble to pronounce the "g" on "talking" and "waiting" as he made conversation.

"More big-name entertainment coming to the State Fair in Jackson," the newscaster said, "but first, a civil rights protest in Jackson enters its second peaceful week."

"Aw great," said Dad, "just what we need, another civil rights protest." He cut his eyes over to see Arnita's reaction.

She smiled. "I bet you think I'm black, don't you, Mr. Musgrove?"

He peered at her, instantly suspicious. "You saying you're not?"

"What if I'm as white as you?" She turned on her sparkly-tiara smile. "Never mind what you think you see. Let's just say for the moment that the whole business of me being black turns out to be a big mix-up."

Dad folded his arms. "Uh-huh."

"Don't get me wrong, I have nothing against black people," she said. "In a lot of ways I think they're superior to white people."

"I wouldn't go that far," said Dad.

"But I can't fit in with them," she said. "I've tried. I can't do it. I seem to be the only one who understands that I'm white. Nobody sees who I really am."

Dad said, "I don't know what kind of nonsense you're trying to pull. And I don't care how light-skinned you are. From where I'm sitting you're still black as the ace of spades."

"Lee," Mom said.

"Well? She's got a smart mouth on her. I'm just giving it back."

Mom cleared her throat. "Linda, your mother told us you might say some strange things, and for us just to pretend you're making sense. So that's what we're doing. I hope you don't mind. Now y'all need to run wash up for dinner."

I showed Arnita the way to the bathroom — she dragged me face-first through the door, gave me a good wet open-mouthed *pop!* on the lips, then shoved me out again, mocking me with silent laughter as she shut the door in my face.

I pressed against it, scratching and whimpering like a dog.

"You two cut the clowning and come on," called Jovial Dad from the dining room. "Janie, honey! Dinner is served!"

"One more page till the end of this chapter," yelled Janie.

"I said move it! Your mother has worked her fanny off here!"

It felt odd and too fancy to dine in the dining room, on a day that was neither Thanksgiving nor Christmas. Mom had lit candles and loaded the table with her specialties: celery sticks stuffed with pimiento cheese, Shake 'n Bake pork chops, Tater Tots, home-doctored baked beans, tiny green peas.

"Would you look at this feed!" Dad said, beaming at Arnita. "Everybody eat up, or we're gonna have to pitch it to the pigs!"

I wanted to shout at him, *Quit acting jolly! Goddamn it, you are not jolly!* But I just kept eating and tried not to stare at Arnita's nipples in her sweater.

"Unbelievably delicious," she said. "Miz Musgrove, Daniel never told me you were a gourmet cook."

Mom fluttered fingers in the air. "Oh goodness, Lee, you hear that? Gourmet cook! No, this is just our normal everyday food. But thank you so much." She muttered almost scornfully, "Gourmet cook!"

"If it don't come out of a can, she don't cook it," Dad said. "Does that make you a gourmet?"

Mom shot him a scalding look, and actually turned her chair to face away from him. "I'd be happy to share my recipes with you, Linda. Daniel told me how much y'all liked that lemon pound cake I sent you."

Arnita looked puzzled. I changed the subject. I could see Janie thinking Arnita was the most beautiful glamorous thing ever to appear in our house, and she was. She brought life to the table; usually we just looked at each other and chewed our food. Janie kept asking how it felt to be Prom Queen, how heavy is the tiara, do the other girls hate you? Arnita acted as if all her questions were incredibly intelligent. "You can be a queen someday too, Janie, if you start preparing now. You're definitely going to be pretty enough."

That was when Janie's little crush melted into total devotion. Even Mom and Dad were being nice to Arnita, pretending to like her. What more could I ask? If I invited her over more often, maybe they could get used to her. Maybe, in time, her blackness would come to seem like no big deal. And then . . . who knows?

No. Who are you kidding? Mom and Dad? In Mississippi? Never happen.

Arnita yelped and skidded back in her chair.

A weird cackle came from down around her knees. "Whoa there, nigger gal!"

I jumped up. "Jacko, don't sneak up on people like that! This is Linda."

"Naw ain't no Linda, I know who it is," he said. "That's ol' nigger gal! Bout time you show up! Danum and me, we been waitin! We knowed you would come."

Arnita's smile froze on her face. "Why is he calling me that?"

"I'm sorry, you have to excuse Jacko," I said. "He had polio when he was little. He lives with us now, he's kinda —" I made my eyes do a jiggly thing to indicate a loose screw.

"Well if he keeps on calling me nigger gal," Arnita said, "he's gonna be missing more than his legs."

I laughed. Even Dad had to resist a smile. Mom looked shocked. "Excuse me, Linda, Jacko is an elderly man," she said fiercely. "He's from out in the country. They have a different way of speaking out there. As you can see he's very old and also he is crippled, so maybe you could be a little bit more forgiving."

"Jacko, huh?" Arnita said. "How'd you know I was coming, Jacko?"

"Been waitin, Danum and me," he said.

Arnita took in Jacko's denim dress, his shriveled legs, his cowhide-covered scooter. "Are you some kind of witch? You got magic powers or something?"

He laughed. "Maybe I is."

"I think so," she said. "I've known some before, and you remind me of them."

"Ol' Danum just been a-pining for his nigger gal."

"Jacko, stop saying that! God!"

Arnita said, "He's just doing it to get me. He knows I'm as white as he is."

"Yassum, you sho is," said Jacko. "Snow White."

"And he's black, ain't you, Jacko?"

He laughed. "Yes ma'am, I is."

Mom said, "That's enough! Linda, would you help me clear the dishes!" She grabbed up plates. The door to the kitchen flapped in her wake.

Mom let Arnita and me wash the dishes. Dad went to bed, worn out by the strain of being nice for that long a stretch. Janie took Arnita to her room and soon they were giggling like sisters. Mom put Jacko to bed and kissed me good night.

"She's a very nice — she's very nice," Mom said. "But I'm afraid she's not the right girl for you, Danny."

"I know, Mom." I didn't know that at all, but I was not about to argue this question with her.

"The sooner you let her down easy, the better it will be."

"Night, Mom."

She went to her room.

I watched a few minutes of the *Tonight Show*, hoping Arnita would find a way to sneak out of Janie's room. It didn't take long to remember that Johnny Carson wasn't as funny as he used to be. I turned off the TV and wandered yawning to the Freak Annex.

I stripped to my underwear. Being close to Arnita all evening without being able to touch her had made for a general throbbing condition, all that juice saved up for now. I snapped off my bedside lamp and slid under the covers to see about getting a handle on the problem.

A linoleum squeak from the kitchen.

Jacko was snoring in his room, beyond the partition. That was someone else in the kitchen, sidling up to my door.

Her shorty nightgown rose to reveal a flash of panties in the moonlight. My heart welled. I was hard, she was here, my God those are her panties, were we going to do IT? Were we going straight for the actual thing?

God help me. I'd never even been past second base.

Like any boy with a randy brain, I had lived for this moment and prayed that somehow I'd know what to do, my body would know how to do it, I wouldn't make a fool of myself. I knew you were supposed to save it for marriage but I couldn't imagine anyone wanting to marry me so if I was ever going to do it, better DO IT NOW while I had the chance here in my own skinny bed with my kissing girl, my most beautiful girl in the whole world — never mind Jacko on the other side of the wall, Mom and Dad sleeping forty feet away — oh I hope they're all asleep —

"Daniel?" Her whisper was lighter than moonlight. "Are you awake?"

"Shhhh. What are you doing?"

"Janie fell asleep. I got lonesome."

I mean, I had the basic idea, I knew what went into what and what to do once it was in, but who knew if everything would function as I had imagined?

When she eased down to the edge of my mattress, the heat of her hip against my leg worked all the fear up into my spine. She leaned in and kissed me. I went *sproing*, all the way up, springy-hard as a surfboard.

"Shhh, Jacko's there. He can hear through the wall."

She laid her lips on the smooth place behind my ear. "Then we won't make a sound."

"What do you want?" I said.

I felt her smile against my cheek. "I want to sleep with you."

"You mean — sleep?"

"No."

I grazed her arm with my fingers. "Now? Are you sure?"

"Yes." She kissed my ear.

"Don't you think we should wait?"

"For what?"

"Well . . . until we get married?"

"What if I won't marry you," she said, "or you never ask me? What if we die young, and this was our only chance to do it?"

Oh God oh God she said IT the word came from her not just my imagination. Oh she wanted it too!

I shushed her again. The word IT was strong enough to carry through that flimsy wall. I wanted no sudden appearances from the other side of that wall.

"Maybe I should go back to Janie's room," she said.

"Wait. Come here." I lifted the sheet. She slid underneath, into the warmth. I curled my arm around her.

I had enough of a bone on to make a definite impression, diagonally across the back of her thigh. She giggled and pulled away. I snuggled up to her, pressing it hard up against her so she could feel what she was asking for. What she was bringing on herself by coming to my bed in such a brazen manner.

I kissed her. Again. We kissed and kissed until our tongues felt like one animal.

She had that dusky strawberry taste, I mean this was a girl who smelled fleshy and alive like ripe fruit when you were licking her neck. Her skin was hot. She scratched her ankle with the ball of her foot. That motion brought her leg firmly up into my hot swollen crotch yes BAM we have contact, Houston we have contact! There is the white cotton of my Sears Best underwear and her white cotton panties, flimsy fabric. I am just seventeen. Overflowing with terror jubilation embarrassment pure horny goatish eagerness and this sudden fierce tenderness — this hot desire to make her pay for her boldness by treating her like the bad girl she is.

Is seventeen too young to have sex? Has Arnita ever seen a hard dick?

The sight of it didn't seem to frighten her.

There's a moment when your soul just floats up out of your body, up into the air over the bed looking down at yourself. I looked upon myself curled on that girl, tugging at the cotton that kept us apart, snuggling hard against her on the narrow bed, fully intending to insinuate myself into her gently because I knew it would hurt her the first time, I read that the man has to do it quick and hard to get past the barrier — but then it was so easy OH I slid in there I think I am in there, nothing stopped me — in the grip of the most marvelous velvet hand squeezing me OH man OH OH man BAM and it's over.

That fast. I shot like a big old hot quivery cannon. Hey, I was seventeen. I managed to do IT about five seconds and then BANG BANG BANG!

I kissed her neck. We lay there sticky, breathing hard into each other's mouth.

"Sorry," I said. "Kinda fast, huh."

"No — stay there, wait!"

"Shhh . . . what?"

She said, "That's not all. We're just getting started."

"But I already — you know —"

"No. You can't quit now. It's not over yet."

"How do you know?"

"Believe me on this," she said.

Oh my God. She has done this before. I hadn't considered that possibility.

Her eyes widened. "You mean — you never have? Oh Daniel, I just assumed, I mean you're a boy —"

I slid out of her, startling myself with my wetness. Suddenly I was ashamed.

"I'm sorry," I said. "We shouldn't do this."

"What do you mean? We just did."

"I'm serious, Arnita, it's wrong. We're too young. What if you — what if you —"

"I won't." Her eyes brightened with the beginnings of tears. "Damn."

I was supposed to be seeing lightning flashes, hearing thunder and bells, glorying in the moment of losing my VIRGINITY, which is something you don't even know you've had until it's gone — now it was gone, and Arnita didn't even have hers to lose. What was the big deal?

She groped at the foot of the bed for her panties. I felt sorry for her but I did not move.

I didn't know what to do. The kid I used to be was gone, blown away, in his place a full-grown boy who has just learned the difference between jerking off and real sex, which is the difference between gazing up at the moon and going to the moon on an actual rocket.

"What are you guys doing?"

How long had Janie been in the doorway? — in her pajamas, outlined in the light spilling in from the kitchen, across Arnita's bare leg and my naked condition, which I emphasized by yanking the sheet over myself. "Janie, you idiot! Go back to bed!"

She looked at us, awestruck. "What are you doing?"

Arnita tugged down her nightie as she stepped out of bed, crossed the room in a flash to put her arms around Janie. "I couldn't sleep, sweetie. Daniel was rubbing my back."

"God, you let him touch you?" Janie inspected me. "Don't you know he has terminal cooties?"

"I had my cootie shot," Arnita said. "Besides, you were no fun. We were supposed to stay up all night telling stories, but you went out like a light. Come on, let's go back to your room."

She was so smooth getting out of there. She didn't even glance back at me.

I couldn't wait to get her alone, so we could do that again.

I would do better next time. I had the hang of it now. It was easy, really. Like falling off a log. Now I'd done it, now I was a man.

Going to sleep I felt electric stars sparking out to the very ends of my fingers. I pretended not to hear Jacko chuckling behind his flimsy wall.

That delicious long moment of falling asleep was my last moment of being young. I felt a little older the next morning when I woke up, and every morning since.

15

I WORE THE MIRRORED Foster Grants that made me feel like I was Burt Reynolds in a souped-up Camaro, instead of riding shotgun to Tim in his Starlite Blue Pinto. I reached for the volume knob to crank up Billy Paul wailing "Me and Mrs. Jones."

The song had a different flavor. Everything tasted different today — the cool-edged warmth of the air, the vanilla perfume of Tim's dashboard air freshener. As much as it pained me to admit that Mississippi could be beautiful, the roadside was especially vivid and green today. Spanish moss picturesquely bearded the trees along the Old Raymond Road. It felt like someone had polished the window glass on the world.

"What the hell are you so happy about?" said Tim.

"What? I'm not happy."

"Yeah, you look real miserable."

"I like this song," I said.

"It's not the song, Durwood. Where is Li'l Miss Cullid Gal this morning? Did she really spend the night at your house?"

"Yup. She and Mom went to town before I got up." One taste of my family and me, and she'd fled back to the Beechams. She hadn't even left a note.

"So you two did the fucky-fucky last night?"

Can he smell her on me? I didn't have time for a shower. "Oh sure, yes indeed," I scoffed. "Right there in the house under Dad's nose! We did it like bunny rabbits, all night long."

"Seriously," he said. "You and her have done the dirty deed, haven't you, Skip?"

"None of your business," I said. "And anyway, no."

"You lie. Come on, Skippy. I see your face."

"You don't see squat," I said.

"Come on. You can tell me. Did she suck your dick?"

"Tim!"

"You get a finger up in her? Ever get that stinky finger up in her pussy?"

"Would you shut up! Jesus! You are so bizarre!"

He had this strange look on his face — his ironic smile bent into a smirk, something panicky behind the eyes. "If it was me that did it," he said, "you'd be begging for all the intimate details, and I would gladly tell you."

"Too bad! I don't want to talk about it."

"Come on, Dagwood, we talk about everything. That's what best friends do."

"Forget it! Jesus Christ! Sometimes you are such a pervert!"

We rode in silence for a while.

"Meeeee aaaaand Missa — Missa Jones!" he sang, a weak attempt to rally the troops.

I would not be rallied. I gave him the cold shoulder all the way to the Full Flower parking lot.

The company of *Christ!* was assembled in front of a big silver Greyhound bus, along with a few parents going along as chaperones for the overnight trip. We were off to a college in Itta Bena, way up in the Delta, to put on the world premiere of Eddie's show. I loved settling into the great Scenicruiser with its rumbling diesels, free-flowing A/C, and the steely Greyhound aroma of the upholstery, so different from the smell of a school bus. Never mind what Dad said, these Baptists traveled first class.

We hadn't been under way half an hour when we had our first big commotion — somebody slipped a chunk of ice down Eddie Smock's shirt. His piercing shriek got the whole bus laughing, and the uproar increased as he flew up the aisle doing this wild wiggle-watusi-herky-jerky, like a drug-addled puppet.

"Dance, Eddie, dance!" cried Carol Nason to the hoots of the chorus.

"Carol, hush! Did you do this? Ow! Ooo!" Eddie wiggled and shimmied. "Y'aaaaall! Somebody get it out!"

"It's just a piece of ice, Eddie," shouted Matt Smith. His eyes widened when he realized what he'd said. "Look y'all, Eddie's finally got his *first piece of ice!*"

This line flashed through the bus like the funniest joke ever told. You could hear the shrieks of laughter moving row by row to the front. Mrs. Passworth got out of her seat to shoot a killing look at Matt Smith.

"Oooooh, y'aaaaall!" Tim squealed in a flawless imitation of Eddie. "Y'all stop it!"

"Hey kids, tonight is our New Haven out-of-town opening," Eddie said, "only it happens to be Itta Bena and the campus of Harold P. Wayne. They've done loads of publicity, apparently there'll be VIPs and everything. I wouldn't be surprised if the president himself puts in an appearance!"

"President Nixon?" cried Regina Singleton, preparing to be beside herself.

"No, President Frederick — the president of the college," Eddie said. "I'm sure we'll be the biggest thing happening on campus tonight. We're gonna knock their socks off!"

Considering Tim and I got involved as an ironic joke, *Christ!* had really started to matter — to me, anyway. I'd stopped hoping for a hilarious disaster and started thinking, *Hey, maybe we're not that bad.* I wanted Eddie to have a hit because he wanted it so badly. I wanted our Combo not to suck. Mostly I wanted to make Passworth proud of us — the least she deserved after all the hours she spent dodging verbal salvos from Eddie.

"You think Carol Nason is going to take it all off tonight?" Tim said.

"I certainly hope so. I've had enough of her teasing."

Andrea Owens stuck her face between the seats in front of us. "Would you two please stop talking like that? I am trying to read the Bible!"

Now, it was well known that Andrea Owens had touched several members of the chorus of *Christ!* in a personal way — she was one of those extremely pious horny girls who made the hallways and nooks of Full Flower Baptist such a welcoming place.

Tim could not resist. His eyes glittered as he coiled to strike. He said, "Sorry to bother you, Handrea. We'll try to keep it down."

She blinked. "What did you call me?"

"Handrea. Isn't that your name? You know, cause you're so — *handy?* So good at your — *job?*" He illustrated with an up-and-down motion of the wrist.

Andrea flew up from her seat, flapping her wings. "Miz Passworth!"

"My name is Tim," he said evenly, "but you can call me Miz Passworth if you like."

"You shut up!" she cried.

"My apologies, Handrea. I guess I am being a total *jerkoff.*"

Girls squealed. Every boy on that part of the bus burst out laughing. Including me.

Andrea raced up the aisle. In a moment here came Mrs. Passworth on a beeline for Tim. She didn't say a word — simply reached across him, seized me, and dragged me by the arm to the front of the bus. I kicked and dissented.

She plopped me in the window seat, still warm from her own behind, and put herself on the outside to block any attempt at escape.

Andrea Owens gave me a sharp little nod, *So there!* and sauntered back to her seat.

I sat for a minute wondering why Passworth had picked on me. Then I tried to convince her how extremely innocent I was.

"I saw you back there egging him on," she said. "You boys ought not be making sex jokes to a girl. That is not how a Christian gentleman behaves."

"Don't look at me! It was Tim."

"Oh come on, you two are Frick and Frack."

"What?"

"You never heard of Frick and Frack? Couple of old skaters in the Ice Follies. You see Frick, you see Frack. Always together, like you and Tim."

It had never occurred to me that's how Tim and I were seen. Actually I was surprised to think we were seen or noticed at all. Except for the occasional flash of humiliation, I had felt mostly invisible since I came to Minor High.

She patted my arm. "Tim only acts the fool for your benefit, don't you know that? He's only trying to impress you."

"No he's not," I said.

"I don't think it's smart of you to associate with him so much," she said. "Tim's not as clever as he thinks — as *you* seem to think. His shenanigans may have been cute when he was younger, but they're not anymore."

I felt disloyal just for sitting there listening. "Why are you saying this to me?"

"Because you're a good boy, Daniel. I worry for Tim." Her voice softened. "Some of his teachers think he's trouble. He's so changeable — so moody, the way he lashes out at people."

"That's just Tim. He's sick of getting picked on all the time! For a year now we've had Red Martin and all his —"

"I appreciate you sticking up for a friend," she said, "but you can do a whole lot better than Tim Cousins. Do you have a girlfriend yet?"

This was such an outrageously personal question (from a teacher!) that I couldn't wait to rush down the aisle and tell Tim about it. First I felt an overpowering urge to tell Mrs. Passworth the truth — to knock her over with it.

"Yes, I do," I said. "Arnita Beecham."

Her mouth made a tiny O.

I nodded.

She shrank back. "But Daniel, she's . . ." Her lips made a "b," but she couldn't say the rest of it.

I finished it for her: "Black?"

She nodded.

"Well, actually at the moment she's convinced she's white, but — yeah, she is black."

Mrs. Passworth's brow furrowed. "I heard the poor girl has had problems after her accident. Obviously she can't be responsible for her actions. But you! What are you thinking? I thought you were more intelligent than that!"

"I like her. She likes me too. So what if she's black? We're integrated now, remember?"

"So *what?*" she cried. "It's unnatural, that's what! I'm as much for equal rights as the next person, but race mixing is an abomination against the Lord! Don't you know that?"

"No," I said.

"Miscegenation is the worst kind of sin! It's the reason God tore down the Tower of Babel, all the blacks trying to mix with the whites!"

I noticed the bus driver watching us in the overhead mirror. An older black man with a speckled face. He kept glancing at me. I couldn't decide what was simmering behind those cool eyes — resentment of me, or of Passworth — of both of us, probably.

I don't think she had noticed. "No question Arnita is a lovely girl, but this is just as wrong as can be. You need to pray on it, Daniel. Pray real hard."

"I will," I said, hoping to steer her off the subject.

"Do your parents know about this?" she said.

I pictured Arnita stretched out with her feet on our couch. "Yeah."

"And her parents?"

"Yes."

She shook her head. "I find that absolutely incredible. Is it just me or is the whole world going nuts?"

I felt a stab of indignation on Arnita's behalf. "Look, we're not getting married or anything," I said. "But we could if we wanted to. It's a free country."

"Oh no sir, not in Mississippi! Bite your tongue! I keep forgetting you weren't brought up here. We have laws against intermarriage. And even if we didn't — well, it's just wrong! Can you imagine what would happen if Negro men could marry all the white women they wanted?"

The bus driver said, "Nobody want you anyway, lady."

His lips barely moved. He spoke so low and fast that at first I thought it was a trick of my ears.

Mrs. Passworth glanced at me to see if I'd heard. I pretended I hadn't.

"Excuse me, driver?" she said. "Did you say something to me?"

The man's face was grave, his eyes fixed on the road as if he had never glanced away from it a single time in his life.

Mrs. Passworth reached in her satchel for her embroidery project. For the next fifty miles she kept one eye fixed on the driver while she jabbed the needle through the cloth. He never looked at us again.

Trapped there beside her, I was free to let my mind roam over Arnita. How could we possibly be in love when most of the world thought like Mrs. Passworth? How could people be so blind to everything but skin?

A wild whoop a few rows behind us and there went Eddie up out of his seat again, flailing at his shirt.

Mrs. Passworth barely turned her head. "Eddie, take the ice out of your shirt and sit down. It's not funny the second time."

ITTA BENA WAS large enough to have billboards announcing its attractions in advance: Dairy Queen, Itta Bena Ford, State Farm, Skinner Furniture. I pointed out a billboard for the Leflore Motor Court. "That's where we're staying tonight." A silhouette woman in a bathing cap was performing an unlikely dive into a painted swimming pool. The Leflore promised Fine AAA Accommodations, In-Room Telephones, TV, Private Bath, and Electric Heat.

"Oh boy, electric heat," said Tim. "Do you suppose they have parking for horseless carriages?"

I theorized that "electric heat" implied no A/C. "And that means we'll probably die."

"We gonna be roommates, Durwood?"

"Why not? If we get a choice about it." I hadn't spent that many nights away from home. I was interested in all aspects of checking into a motel, sleeping in a strange bed, unwrapping the little pink soap.

"I really don't care," Tim said, "as long as they don't put me in with Eddie." He raised one eyebrow.

I glanced out the window. "Look, we're here."

Tim said, "Itty bitty Itta Bena," a thing that was surely said by many people coming to that town for the first time. We rolled down a street with two blocks of stores on one side. Itta Bena was a plain place, straight lines and blocky buildings, not one bit of decoration on anything.

The Leflore Motor Court was a horizontal strip of rooms with a glassed-in office at one end. The room doors were painted the exact livid green of the algae blooming in the swimming pool.

"All right, kids, shut up and listen up," Eddie called from the front of the bus. "I'll stand by the steps and hand you your room key as you get off. Each room has two beds, two kids to each room, except for me and Miz Passworth and the chaperones."

"Y'all all sleepin' together, Eddie?" called Ted Herring.

"Very funny," said Eddie. "Now, if you don't like your roommate, it's up to you to find somebody to switch with. Do not, I repeat, do NOT come moaning to me about it. Wait — wait —" He had to skip the rest of his welcome speech because the girls mobbed him, snatching keys and hurrying off. They'd been whining for miles about how bad they needed to pee.

As the last ones off the bus, Tim and I were assigned the farthest room from the office, Room 130. The Frick and Frack suite. All down the rank of rooms, kids hollered, ran, and slammed doors. The heavyset manager glowered from the office door, rousing himself to an occasional bark — "Slow down!" "No running!" "You break that, mister, you've bought it!"

When I got to our room Tim was flipping lights on and off,

flushing the toilet, running brownish water in the tub. The room smelled of knotty pine and scratchy blankets. There were two saggy beds, not quite doubles. The TV was an old black-and-white Westinghouse set that received one station, sort of, and the telephone was a kind I hadn't seen in years, a heavy black grandma model with a thick cloth-wrapped cord, like the cord for an electric iron.

Tim danced in from the bathroom, singing, "She wore an Itta Bena teena weena yella polka-dot bikeena . . ."

After all this time he still knew how to crack me up. Along with his song he performed a dance routine complete with high kicks, ending up on his back on the bed, wiggling hands and feet in the air.

"Okay then," I said, "that's your bed since you just messed it up."

He bounded back onto his feet. "Where's the applause, Durwood? Where's the appreciation? Where is the loooove?"

"You are not Roberta Flack. You're not even Donny Hathaway."

He peered out the door. "Hey c'mere, look at Passworth! Man is she unbelievably PO'd about something!"

I looked down to the glass-walled office, where Mrs. Passworth was gesticulating at the phone, raving at whoever was on the other end. We were too far away to hear much.

"Hurry back," Tim said.

Halfway down the rank of rooms, I glanced through an open door and saw Ted Herring making out with Alicia Duchamp. Ted's hands were roaming all over Alicia's bouncy butt. He saw me looking and grinned. I gave a thumbs-up and kept walking.

Eddie Smock was just outside the office listening to Passworth yell into the phone. "Irene, what is wrong?" he kept saying.

"But he can't do that!" she shouted. "He can't just leave us in the middle of nowhere!"

"Would you please tell me what's wrong!" Eddie cried.

"Don't you understand, I have forty-two children with me! I am responsible for all of them! Now your man has left us in the lurch, and I want to know what you're going to do about it! You are the manager, aren't you?"

Eddie tried to get her attention.

Mrs. Passworth waved him away. "But I have told you — the man is lying! *He* made an impertinent remark, and I ignored it. For him to have the nerve to accuse me . . . well it's just beyond belief!"

I pointed across the parking lot to a jumble of stuff — Byron's drums, our Combo gear, the chorus's tambourines, costumes, props. Everything from the bus was heaped on the sidewalk.

"The bus is gone," I said.

"Gone?" said Eddie. "What do you mean gone?"

"Look there. Do you see a bus? I think the driver dumped our stuff and took off."

Eddie said, "Why would he do that?"

"I have no idea." Of course I had an excellent idea, but I wasn't going to be the one to tell Eddie. I remembered the simmering look in the driver's eyes. He must have decided he could not abide one more minute of Passworth.

"But that's absurd, he can't just be *gone*," Eddie was saying. "Maybe he went to get gas."

I shook my head. "He wouldn't dump all our stuff."

I watched as the fear dawned in Eddie that I could be right, this could mean real trouble for *Christ!* "Oh my goodness," he said. "Gosh! What are we gonna do?"

"You better get another bus up here now," Passworth demanded, "and I do mean *now* — or I'm gonna jump through this phone and come down to where you are — are you listening? — I'm coming down there and I'm gonna make you want to crawl back up inside your mama!"

She gave that a moment to sink in.

"And tell whoever's in charge of your company that you will never — ever! — do business with Full Flower Baptist again! Yes? How long? Well, you'd better get him here quicker than that. Goodbye!" She slammed the phone so hard the bell went *ding!*

When she saw us, her face twisted into a smile. "Hello, boys!"

Eddie said, "Irene, what on earth?"

"Oh Eddie, the most ridiculous mix-up. Our bus driver just up and left! Ha! Can you believe it? Took off! Abandoned us! Apparently he thought — well, heavenly days, I don't pretend to know *what* he thought. They're very sorry in Jackson, they're sending another bus, but it won't be here for hours. So for how we're getting over to the college — we're going to have to be creative."

One hour and twenty minutes later we were still dragging our instruments and amps and costumes along the shoulder of the county road — hot, sweaty, bug-eaten, swatting at flies zooming up from the weeds.

I kept thinking how incredibly brave or stupid of that driver, to drive away just because Passworth made him mad. He would lose his job for sure.

"Wouldn't you think they'd have a sign or something?" Ted Herring said. "I mean, most colleges would at least have a sign."

"Eddie," said Passworth, "let's flag down the next car we see, and find out if we're even going the right way."

"You know what we need, people?" Eddie cried.

"A bus!" Matt Smith yelled.

A lot of people agreed with Matt.

"No! We need to sing!"

Sneakers made the sound of trudging on hot asphalt.

"Instead of complaining about it," Eddie said, "we can get warmed up while we walk! Who's with me?"

It was August in Mississippi. We were plenty warmed up.

"Okay, then I'll start." Eddie found the opening note on his harmonica. He sang the first lines of Matt Smith's Act II closing number:

> *I might as well be king of the Jews*
> *As a carpenter I gotta admit I'm really bad news*
> *My cabinets won't open, my drawers all get stuck*
> *I hope when I'm Messiah I'll have better luck*

No one joined in. Eddie's voice trailed off.

There was just enough daylight to make out a hand-stenciled sign in a patch of kudzu:

HAROLD P. WAYNE BIBLE ☞ 100 YD.

"Here we go!" Eddie sang. "Thank you Jesus!"

We gazed with suspicion upon the two-track dirt road leading off into the piney woods.

"Hallelujah," said Mrs. Passworth. "Now can everybody please stop giving me dirty looks?" She got dirty looks just for saying that.

We followed the track and soon came to a clearing with a square red-brick building at the center — churchlike, solid, two stories high, fat white columns on two sides, a wide flight of brick steps. A few beaten-up cars in the yard. Patches of red sand showed through gaps in the grass.

On the steps was a group of black men not much older than we were. College age, I suppose. They wore white short-sleeve shirts, skinny dark ties, black pants. From a distance their skin looked extremely black and shiny. They left off chatting when they saw us coming up the road.

Mrs. Passworth said, "My Lord, what do we have here? Are these workmen? They don't look like workmen."

Eddie said, "Maybe the college is on beyond here. Let me find out."

"Good idea." Passworth held out her arm to keep us back. We gathered behind her while Eddie went to speak with them.

Tim leaned in to my ear. "I'll stay with the Land Rover while Jim wrestles the giant anaconda to the ground," he said. "Good luck, Jim!"

For the first time I noticed how white we were. Full Flower Baptist was an all-white church, always had been — I'd never even noticed. Come to think of it, every church in Mississippi was all white or all black. That's just how it was, even after buses and schools and stores were integrated. I guess the government couldn't make you go to church with anybody you didn't want to.

Here came Eddie to report that this was indeed Harold P. Wayne Bible College, an all-male institution founded fifty years ago to train

Negro circuit preachers for the Mississippi Delta. This building was the campus. They were expecting us.

I thought Mrs. Passworth might faint. "You mean we're supposed to perform for these — oh Eddie, did it not occur to you to ask whether this was a Negro college?"

"No," he said, "honestly, it didn't. I'm sorry. I had no idea. The man sounded white on the phone."

Above us, the double doors burst open — more young black men in white shirts and skinny ties flooded down the steps to greet us, spreading their arms in warm, evangelical hugs. They didn't seem the least surprised by our whiteness. "Welcome, brother! Welcome, sister!" They grabbed our hands, patted our shoulders.

I'd never seen so many brawny young black men in one place. If this crowd had assembled in downtown Jackson, the governor would have called out the National Guard.

Eddie tried to pretend that everything was going just as he'd planned. He kept glancing past the preacher-men to Mrs. Passworth.

Every time one of the black men hugged her, she shrank a little more, until she stood hobbled and bent over like the Wicked Witch melting.

She was helpless to keep the rest of us from being swallowed up in the crowd of men. They moved us up the steps, into the building. The place smelled of old Bibles, floor wax, old air that had never been air-conditioned or even stirred by a ceiling fan. Truly the sweat of black people is spicier and more pungent than white people's sweat. This large room was steamy as a tent revival, fifty years of young men learning to preach in here.

I suppose we were one anxious-looking bunch of white kids.

The sanctuary was two stories high, with pews and a pulpit at one end. The men steered us toward the pulpit. Instead of a piano they led me to an antique pump organ, with foot pedals.

There were lightbulbs dangling from wires overhead, but Mickey and Ben couldn't find a place to plug in their amps. "We thought about putting in some outlets," said the fat man who had hugged me first, "but we figure this old place would burn down in two minutes.

Give me yo plugs, we got extension cords. We'll get you hooked up outside."

Eddie stepped to the pulpit. "Okay, people," he called. "Could I ask our audience members nicely to move back and give us a little breathing room? There'll be plenty of time for us all to meet after the performance, okay? Right now we need to have our preshow confab. All right? Thank you so much!"

"We're here to help, Brother Eddie," called one of the preachers. "Just tell us what you need."

"Well, if you could just give us some breathing room," he said, a little louder. "We didn't realize we were gonna have to walk all the way out here. Frankly we're a little discombobulated."

"Easy, brother." The man was still smiling, but the twinkle in his eye sharpened a little. "We'll give you all the room you need. We are filled with joy to have you-all here tonight."

"Of course you are!" Eddie cried. "Of course! And we're delighted to be here too, let me say! I think you're gonna love our show! You, sir — sorry, what's your name?"

"R. T. Frederick." The man pronounced the initial R as "Arra." "You and I have corresponded, Brother Eddie."

"Oh my gosh — Mr. President!" Eddie cried. "Well hello sir! So sorry, I had no idea that was you! We're very glad to be here, and in just a few minutes we'll be ready to go. Irene Passworth, this is President Frederick!"

"What Eddie is trying to say," said Passworth, "is the sooner you let us get on with it, the sooner we can get it over with and get out of here."

"I understand," said the reverend. He led his students toward the double doors. They milled about on the broad porch, peering back in at us as we formed up a huddle.

Mrs. Passworth said, "Girls, I want you over there in that room. Get changed quick with no fuss. You boys can change in the pews. Move it!"

"I don't know what's your big hurry, Irene," said Eddie. "We can't leave until the bus comes to get us. Or were you planning to make us walk all the way back in the dark?"

Her voice went up five notes on the scale. "I swear, Eddie, don't you push me!"

We members of the Combo put on loud plaid slacks and lime green turtleneck pullovers, neon-colored fringed vests, red-white-and-blue headbands. We were a "musical band of hippies," according to Alicia Duchamp's mother, the costume designer.

This was the first time we'd all seen each other in costume. The effect was disturbing. Some of the girls wore black turtlenecks and white miniskirts, white pantyhose, and black knee-boots. They looked like Beatniks, or Oreo cookies. Others were dressed as flappers from the Roaring Twenties, with sacky dresses and long strands of pearls. Some of the guys were cowboys, with guns and boots and jingling spurs. Some wore Bible-ish clothes, burlap tunics with rope belts. Four or five boys wore dark suits and nerdy black sunglasses, like FBI agents, with angel wings on their backs. Matt Smith as Jesus sported a flowing white robe that looked more like a wedding dress than he realized or he would not be wearing it.

I don't know what Alicia's mother was thinking. Perhaps she was making some kind of statement on modern culture, but how these outfits related to the Jesus story, I could not fathom.

Oh — not to forget Carol Nason! Our Mary Magdalene was definitely a whore, not a prostitute but a real whore, her minidress ripped open halfway to her navel, fishnet stockings, high heels, hair teased and flying in an unruly cloud around her head. She had on so much makeup that she looked plasticized, like a Whore Barbie. It was impossible not to stare at her. I felt a certain tingle. I had heard about whores but this was the first one I'd ever seen in the flesh. It was like seeing a rattlesnake for the first time, or a whale: there's no mistaking it for anything else.

"Carol Nason," snapped Mrs. Passworth, "is that all there is to your costume?"

Carol cringed. "Yes ma'am."

"You're sure there's not some other part to it?"

"Yes ma'am, I'm sure. This is everything Miz Duchamp gave me to wear." Carol looked as if she might either cry or take five bucks for a quick sex act in the back of a car.

"Well go put on something else," said Passworth. "I'm quite sure Mrs. Duchamp didn't intend for you to look like that. Even if she did, you need more clothes."

"I know," Carol said. "I don't think I can . . . I don't think I should . . ."

"You can't, and you shouldn't. What else do you have to wear?"

"Just the T-shirt I wore on the bus. My clothes are back at the motel."

"Go put on the T-shirt. That'll help." Passworth glanced to the doorway, where the men were nudging each other aside for a glimpse of Carol. "Ted, close those doors!"

Ted Herring ran to obey.

"Doesn't everybody look fabulous!" Eddie cried. "Never seen a slicker bunch of performers. You all look very professional!"

"Especially Carol," said Brad Hutchinson to a loud hawhaw from the boys.

"I can't put it into words," Eddie said, "but you look incredible! Alicia, your mother is some kind of genius!"

Alicia was one of our real beauties, a juicy ripe pear of a girl. For her star turn as Mary, her mother had dressed her as a Glamour Virgin, a white satin evening gown with plunging neckline, like one of those soft-focus movie star girls of the Thirties.

And here came Carol with the ripped hem of her skirt hanging down underneath her Go Titans T-shirt. She still had on the wild hair and makeup, the stockings and high heels. Now she looked like a Whore Barbie who's been in an accident and someone has loaned her a T-shirt to get home. That's what I whispered to Tim.

It had been a while since I'd cracked him up. The sound of his laughter made me feel fizzy inside, as if the night suddenly held fresh possibilities.

"Okay folks," Eddie cried, "I just want to give my very special thanks to each and every one of you wonderful kids for being here at the birth of a dream. You're gonna be amazing. The show will be a smash!"

Everybody clapped and said yeah Eddie, woo-hoo! Eddie displayed his desires so nakedly, so proudly. How could you not cheer for him?

Mickey and Ben strapped on their guitars. I sat on a three-legged stool and placed my feet on the pedals of the pump organ. I pumped a few times . . . the high G came out a tremulous wheeze.

Mickey made a face. "That sounds awful."

"Like Grandmaw's emphysema," said Ben.

"It's wild," Mickey said. "Go ahead, play a couple of chords. Listen to this, Byron."

I laid into pumping the pedals. I got the air flowing, and played the syncopated opening chords of the *Christ!* theme song.

I stopped. "What do you think?"

Byron laughed. "It's bizarre. Sounds like '96 Tears.'"

"Combo? You guys set?"

"Right on, Eddie! Ready when you are."

"Okay! Places, everyone!"

The double doors squealed and swelled inward to the river of talking, laughing men. Some flowed upstairs to throng the galleries, jamming into every inch of space, the air warmly heavy with their breathing.

"Ladies and gentlemen," Eddie bellowed. "Full Flower Baptist Church is delighted to bring you the world premiere of an original musical based on the life of our Savior. Ladies and gentlemen, I give you . . . *Christ!*"

He aimed an imaginary pistol at the Combo and fired. And they're off!

The first number was the finger-snappin', toe-tappin' title song. From my place at the organ I saw just a small slice of the audience, but those faces were mesmerized.

> *If you're feeling sad and blue*
> *Who's got real good news for you?*
> *Who died on the cross for you?*
> *Christ!*
> *La la la laaaaaaa!*

The song ended with the boys on one knee, arms spread wide à la Al Jolson, while the girls grinned and twirled their streamer-batons. Byron struck the final cymbal crash.

The answering silence was not long — no more than three seconds, according to Tim — then an explosion of indignation, surprise, outrage, applause.

Some men stormed for the doors. Some of them really liked us, clapping, shouting "Bravo!" Mostly they thought we were hilarious. They roared. They bent over laughing. They slapped each other's backs, wiped tears from their eyes, broke up again reliving their favorite moments.

Eddie had an all-hope-abandoned look in his eyes. You could see him trying to interpret this uproar as good news, but then why were some people shaking fists at him? Those guys laughing so hard they held on to each other? What was so funny?

I glanced at the cue sheet. Sixteen songs to go! The pedals grew heavy under my feet. What made me think this would be fun?

Tim murmured, "Let's get out of here."

I blinked. "What?"

"I can't watch this, Skippy. It makes my stomach hurt."

"We can't run away now."

"Why not?"

I spread my hands, indicating the other guys. "We're part of this. We're the Combo. The Combo is us."

"No no no," he said. "This is pathetic."

"And hilarious," I said. "Isn't it? Just like we hoped it would be."

Eddie waved for us to strike up the next song.

"Hey Mary, guess what?" sang Ted Herring.

> *You're gonna have a bay-beh!*
> *Yeah, ready or not —*
> *I know you don't believe it!*

A commotion arose on the far side of the room — shoving chairs, heated voices. The song limped to a stop.

Reverend R. T. Frederick put his hand on Eddie's shoulder. "I just want to say I am terribly embarrassed," he said, "that some of my brothers will not show you young people the same courtesy we would extend to the least among us."

"That's okay! Really!" said Eddie. "We just want to do our show."

A man called, "But these children are blaspheming! You cannot allow this to go on!"

Reverend Frederick patted Eddie's shoulder. "Your presentation is not quite what we were expecting," he said. "We're accustomed to more traditional representations."

"Wait, you're gonna love the next one," said Eddie, waving madly for us to start.

Byron kicked off a bass beat. Here came Alicia Duchamp sashaying out in her Glamour Virgin gown, belting "Joseph, You've Got to Believe Me."

Alicia's brassy voice went nicely with her pear-shaped bottom. She pranced around on high heels, giving saucy little kicks that quickly distracted the Bible students.

The laughter began to dissipate. I saw appreciation setting in on some of the faces, or maybe something else. Alicia did look fine in that gown. The number ended in a spotlight, on a high note, her head thrown back at a rakish angle — a big round of cheers.

Could this musical be saved?

We jumped into the quick tempo of "Third Manger on the Right," the whole cast onstage, singing and dancing a farcical reenactment of Joseph and Mary's search for a room in Bethlehem. The slapstick and the animal costumes got some nice laughs. I thought I saw Reverend Frederick beginning to relax.

The men who hated us the most had already left. Those who had stayed were either laughing at us or laughing with us, and what difference did it make? They were laughing. The room felt warm through the first act, even warmer in the second. By the time Matt Smith sang "Can I Really Be the Son of God?" it was hot in there, and the audience was on Matt's side.

The stage filled with lepers humming "The Leper's Song," every bit as gloomy as it sounds. I saw Carol Nason at the side of the stage, fiddling with the hem of her Go Titans T-shirt. She looked around to see if anyone was watching, then peeled the T-shirt up over her head and smoothed the skirt of her whore dress.

When the lepers scampered off to dutiful applause, Carol ran on. The spotlight found her. Every man in the room sucked in air.

The Combo played the opening bars, *Duh duh-duh DUM da-DUM!*

"Hello boys!" Carol cried.

Duh duh-duh DUM da-DUM!

"I'm Mary Magdalene — and I'm bad!"

Eddie gaped. That line was not in the script.

Dum duh-duh DUM da-DUM!

Carol strutted down the edge of the stage, dipping coyly, cutting eyes at the men gawking up at her. "Hey fella, whatcha up to tonight? Good to see ya! Hey, handsome!"

Tim said, "What is she doing?"

"I do believe she's stripping."

"Unbelievable. Look at her!"

"She hasn't taken anything off yet, but she sure looks naked."

Reverend Frederick sputtered into Eddie's ear, but Eddie was too busy adoring Carol's performance. His eyes flashed up at her, worshiping her. He'd been trying to get her to sing out since the first rehearsal — and boy was she ever singing out, catwalking all over the stage in her wanton, dressed-but-naked condition.

> *Not that kind of girl, no!*
> *I'm just clay in God's hands to play with*
> *Not that kind of girl, no!*
> *I've only got two hands to pray with*

She was appalling and sexy — a living example of everything the Bible says Thou Shalt Not. The men cheered and wolf-whistled.

Suddenly there was Reverend R. T. Frederick onstage behind her, brandishing a choir robe. He swept her up in it and ushered her off as the students hooted for an encore.

"Let her go! She's not done!" cried a man in front.

"Oh yes she is. Show's over, my friends," he bellowed.

By the time we got through the mob to that side of the room, Passworth was shouting at Reverend Frederick. "I don't care how offended you are, we're not going anywhere until our bus comes to get us! You invited us up here to perform and that's what we were doing!"

"Perhaps you could explain to me," he thundered, "how anyone who calls herself a decent Christian could associate herself with that kind of blatant obscenity!"

Mrs. Passworth put her finger in his face. "Listen, buster, don't tell me what kind of a Christian I am. These children came up here to present their own version of the greatest story ever told. They were singing their hearts out for you. If you're that narrow-minded, well then, it's your loss!"

"Madam," he huffed, "I happen to know the difference between a young lady and a harlot!"

"Mary Magdalene *was* a harlot, you idiot!" she cried. "Read your Bible! It's in there! What kind of a Bible college is this?"

Reverend Frederick ran everyone out of the building, locked the doors, got in his car, and drove off without another word.

A few Bible students were still hanging around outside, with flashlights. They offered to walk us to town.

"Why thank you," said Passworth. "At least there are some gentlemen."

"I thought you all did great," one man offered.

"Yeah, y'all done real good. Too bad some people couldn't appreciate it."

Others chimed in yeah, they liked us too.

"Specially her. What is your name, girl?"

"That's Carol," said Ted Herring. "Isn't she amazing? Carol — you were great."

Carol looked even sexier swaddled in her silky purple choir robe. "Thank you, Ted. I guess some people just can't handle realism."

Passworth said, "I told you to cover up that costume, Carol Ann."

"Yes ma'am. But the T-shirt just looked so silly, you know?"

I felt proud of Passworth, sticking up for us so loudly. That went a long way toward making up for the fact that we were out on the highway again, in the dark, walking back to Itta Bena.

Eddie sagged along at the end of the group, as if most of his helium had been let out. He said he thought the show was playing very well when they stopped it, who knows with a nip here and a tuck there . . . his voice trailed off and he said nothing more.

Walking back didn't feel as long as walking out there, since we knew how far it would be. Chorus members talked in low voices. I followed the skittering flashlight beams.

We topped a rise to a glad sight, the homey yellow lights of the Leflore Motor Court. Parked in front, idling, waiting for us, was a glowing Greyhound bus, lit up cool blue from inside.

Mrs. Passworth said, "I got half a mind to just put us on that thing and go home right this minute."

We groaned. For us, spending the night was the whole point of the trip.

"Oh, I suppose you poor children are exhausted. All right. Go to your rooms now, and shut out the lights. I don't want any trouble, you hear? And listen — y'all did great tonight. Never mind that old man. You made me proud. Give yourselves a nice round of applause."

We clapped politely, but it was not like having other people clap for you.

"Good night, all. Eddie, get some sleep." She slipped into her room and shut the door.

We all watched Eddie fumbling his key in the lock. Finally he got the door open and fell into his room. He slammed the door shut with the key dangling from the outside of the lock.

We watched and waited until he opened the door, snatched the key from the lock, slammed it shut again.

Everyone filtered off to their rooms. Some of the boys wanted to play cards, and there was a rumor that some girls had a bottle of wine.

"Poor Eddie," I said.

Tim sniffed. "Yeah. So what."

The fluorescent light gave our room a ghastly flickering pallor. I turned on the TV — a swimmy black-and-white picture. Miss Kitty's image rippled like gasoline fumes on a hot day.

"Oh please, *Gunsmoke?*" said Tim. "The most boring show in history. What else is on?"

"That's it. One channel. Flip around if you don't believe me." I threw myself across my bed. The mattress had no bounce. "Mm, nice bed."

"You can watch this crap if you want, Skippy. I'm going to sleep." He kicked his shoes off, pulled the covers halfway up his face, and closed his eyes.

"Wait — that's it? You're just going to sleep?"

One eye opened. "Yes."

"You don't need to pee, or anything?"

"No." He snuggled into his blanket.

"Shouldn't you at least brush your teeth?"

"More like my mother every day," Tim said.

I rummaged in my duffel bag for my toothbrush. "Here we are with nobody around to make us go to bed for like the first time ever — and you want to sleep?" I filled my mouth with Crest foam and made burbling gargling sounds.

"Well, Sluggo, if you had brought the whiskey and cards and cee-gars, we could have us a good old-fashioned poker game!"

I bared my rabies-foamed fangs at him. "Yarrrrghhh."

"Lovely." Tim snapped off the lamp, flopped onto his other side.

"Excuse me for living," I said.

He didn't reply.

"Tim?"

"What is it, Durwood?"

"I don't know. Go to sleep."

"With who?" he said.

"Hmm, let me think . . . Carol Nason. But I don't think I can afford it."

"Oh sure you can, she looked like about ten bucks to me. No, but really. That's who you'd want to go to bed with? Of all the people here?"

"I guess so," I said. "Yeah, why not?"

"Okay then. Carol's in Room twelve. You may have to wait, though. There's probably a line at the door." He feigned sleep.

No amount of wheedling could get him to say anything more. He affected a deep, steady sleep.

I pondered Miss Kitty on TV, painted up just like Carol Nason as a grandmother. I wondered if real-life prostitutes had to retire at a certain age, or were there men who paid to have sex with old women? I banished that thought and decided to close my eyes, just for a minute.

I don't know what time it was when Tim got up to turn off the TV, but the sudden silence and darkness woke me a little. I heard him bumping around in the bathroom.

I slid back down into my dream — one of those long exhausting dreams where you're late for every class, you keep missing the bus, the phone keeps ringing, the floor is too slippery to stand, and everyone is mad at you. I woke up in a knot of frustrated tension, let out a big sigh, slumped down in the bed.

I heard voices outside. A dim streetlight glow filtered in through the plastic-lace curtain.

I heard the toilet flush. Tim shuffled in and dropped face-first onto his bed.

Something about those voices made me want to hear what they were saying, way in the middle of the night. Was that somebody laughing, or — crying? Who was speaking in such a low urgent voice?

I padded over to the window. "Tim. Something is weird. Listen."

He said, "Hmm?" but didn't really wake up.

I opened the door to hear better. At once I recognized Passworth's voice. Someone behind her was crying.

I went out. They made a little huddle on the far side of the parking lot. A white police car. They were gathered around a green suitcase. Passworth was there, and the motel manager. One of the chaperone dads. A policeman.

That was not a girl I'd heard crying. That was Eddie.

Every so often he got louder, but not loud enough for me to make out what he was saying.

I glanced down the wall of rooms and saw three or four guys in the doorways, watching this scene: Ted Herring, and two doors down from him Mickey and Ben, and there was Matt Smith.

The manager seemed to be arguing with Passworth. Why would Eddie be crying? My brain tried to make sense of it. Somebody close to Eddie had died, his mother or father. That would account for hysterics in the middle of the night.

I turned back to our room. "Tim, you might want to wake up for this."

He didn't stir.

Eddie pushed Passworth away and started screaming in a high, delirious voice. The policeman wrestled him into the back of his car. The motel manager put the green suitcase in the trunk and closed the lid. The cop got behind the wheel and drove off. The windows were rolled up, but I could hear Eddie's screams trailing off down the road.

Ted Herring went into his room, shut the door.

I walked over to Mickey. "What is it, man? What's going on?"

"Too weird, huh? The son of a bitch woke me up."

"Who did?"

"Eddie. Didn't you get the call?"

"What call?"

"Hell, I thought he called everybody in the whole motel."

"He called you?"

"He woke me up, and he asked if I —" He didn't want to say it. "If I wanted a blow job."

"Eddie said that? No way."

"Yeah, I think he dialed every damn room," said Mickey. "What did he think, we wouldn't recognize his voice? Incredible." He shook his head. "Later, man." He went into his room, closed the door.

The small hairs on my neck prickled up. I felt a cold weight in my stomach.

I drifted back to our room. My first thought: Of course Eddie was queer. Of course! It hit me like water in the face. How could I not have known it before?

I did know it. I knew all along. Tim and I had even joked about it. I just didn't want to think about it as something that might actually be true.

I thought all queers were like that man who kissed me outside the emergency room in Alabama — hasty, lonely, desperate. Twisted men who got pleasure from forcing themselves on boys they found stranded on the roadside.

And maybe that's who Eddie secretly was. But I never thought he was crazy enough to do this. Oh, poor Eddie.

I didn't care how upset he was about his show. It seemed incredibly dangerous to call guys on the phone, guys who knew him, and ask that question, straight out. Someone was bound to recognize his voice and turn him in.

Maybe he had tried it before, and someone had said yes. Maybe he got a thrill just from calling.

I didn't like thinking about it.

Poor Eddie. How could he do something so stupid? Tomorrow, everybody would know.

Poor Eddie.

I went back to bed. Tim was still unaware, sound asleep in his clothes and his shoes. I fell on my bed and crashed down into sleep. I did not have any more dreams.

16

Tim was shocked when I told him. "Wow. Poor Eddie." What else could he say?

We loaded our luggage into the hold of the bus. Most of the boys had these odd, furtive looks, shifty eyes and hands jammed in pockets. The subject of regular sex was unsettling enough, but sex between boys? Unimaginable. I felt sorry for Eddie, but even more disgusted by what he had done. What an appalling way to bring up the subject, calling boys and asking them flat out what they might like. *Hey, want a blow job?* Of course I wanted a blow job, name me one boy on this bus who didn't want a blow job — but the question was, did you want it now? At the Leflore Motor Court? From Eddie Smock?

Everyone slept on the drive home. No one put ice cubes down anyone's back. Passworth sat up front with her eyes on the bus driver, who had the good sense to be white. Tim dozed in the aisle seat. Cool air came up from slots beneath the window, chilling my arm to a pleasant numbness. I pressed my cheek to the glass and watched the green fields go blurring by.

The bus flashed past the Minor exit, the last stretch of I-20 into Jackson. Tim yawned. "Are we there yet?"

"Just passed Minor. Gee thanks, you were great company on the ride."

He stretched. "What did I miss?"

"Not much."

He squinted at me. "You sat there looking out the window the whole way?"

"Yep."

"How come, Durwood?"

"Thinking about Eddie. What do you think made him do that?"

"He's a queer. Does that come as a big surprise to you?"

"No, but — he knew he'd get caught. He had to know. That's what I can't get over."

Tim stared at me for a while. "I guess some people can't help it," he said. "Even if they might get caught."

We left the interstate at Robinson Road. Passworth had the driver turn up the lights, and she stood at the head of the aisle. "Children, I talked it over with Reverend Fain on the phone this morning," she said. "For now we're going to postpone our other performances."

We groaned.

"Postpone?" cried Alicia Duchamp. "What does that mean?"

"We'll just have to wait and see, Alicia. I knew y'all would be disappointed. You all worked so hard. But this is not the first incident with Eddie, they've had all these phone calls at the — well, anyway. Let's try to have some sympathy for him. Sometimes a person doesn't know how to handle his feelings appropriately. Obviously Eddie has some problems. We need to pray for him. All right? Now let's get off this bus in an orderly fashion."

We hissed to a stop in the Full Flower parking lot. Parents leaned against their cars, waiting for us. We stepped down into hot soggy air. I spotted Mom's station wagon, smoke rising from the cigarette she held out the window.

But wait, that wasn't Mom. That arm was hairy.

That was Dad, driving Mom's car. But Dad didn't smoke. "Timmy, I gotta go."

"Don't forget, Sonny and Cher Saturday night. I'll pick you up at six."

"I'm going to Arnita's now. I'll make sure she knows."

"Okay," he said. "Later, gator."

That could not be my father smoking, but yes it was. I threw my duffel in back and got in the passenger side. He made no move to start the car.

He looked exhausted, disheveled. He wore a ratty blue knit shirt, paint-spattered Saturday pants, and flip-flops. First time I'd ever seen him in flip-flops.

"Thanks for coming to get me," I said. "What's going on?"

"What do you think is going on, son?"

"I don't know."

"You've never seen me smoke before, have you?"

"No."

"Well? Were you gonna say something about it? Or just sit there and not say a word?"

I shrugged. "Why are you smoking?"

"I smoke all the time when I'm out of town," he said. "You didn't know that, did you? Maybe I'm different than you think. Maybe I'm not just your mean old daddy. Some people happen to think I'm a lot of fun." He was acting so strange that I wondered if he had taken up drinking too.

He started the car. I glanced across the parking lot. Mrs. Passworth's Nova was already gone. Tim was folding himself into the Pinto.

Dad pulled out onto Van Winkle Road.

"I thought Mom was coming to get me."

"A slight change in plans. I hope you don't mind, I was dispatched to serve as your chauffeur. If that suits your high standards."

"Yes sir. I said thank you."

"How was your little trip, son? What'd you think about that Delta country up there?"

In my entire life, I can say with certainty, Dad had never once sought my opinion on anything. It felt strange to have this chatty, unkempt man smoking a Camel at the wheel of Mom's station wagon.

How could I begin to explain what had happened in Itta Bena? Even if he cared, which he didn't. "It was okay," I said.

"Good." He smiled. "Always want our Daniel to have himself a good time. Don't want anything getting in the way of your fun, no sir."

This new Dad was strange, but not altogether unpleasant. He was only pretending to be nice, but it was better than his usual dark silence. "Hey Dad, would you mind dropping me at Arnita's? I promised I would help with her homework."

"No. I need you to come home with me. Gonna help me with a little project. If that doesn't inconvenience you too much."

"What, the grass? I swear, Dad, this whole weekend I'll do nothing but —"

"Not the grass. More important than the grass." This was indeed something new, for there was nothing more important than the grass.

"Dad, where is your car?"

His eye twitched. "It's not my car. It's a company car. It belongs to the company."

"Is it in the shop or something?"

"We don't need to talk about the car," he said. "See, the thing is . . . TriDex has just been taken over by this German company. Beiden something. I swear to God, we beat the hell out of 'em in the war, and now they're over here buying up the durn country. My line of work — I mean, the job I've been doing . . . they're phasing out our division."

"What does that mean?" I knew what it meant but I wanted to make him say it.

He stared straight ahead. "Means I'm taking some time off while they look for a new assignment for me. I'm first in line for any openings. It's not exactly good times in the petrochemical business, unless you happen to be an A-rab. Everybody's cutting back. I understand their position."

"You got fired?" I said.

He shook his head, gave out a small laugh like, can you even *believe* this level of disrespect? He turned a baleful gaze on me: "Not fired. Laid off. Fired is when you don't perform. There was no problem with my performance. District Salesmanager of the Year, three years in a row. I worked my butt off twenty-four years for those sonofabitches."

Dad was not a natural cusser. It made me feel sorry for him, and that was not a natural feeling.

"Let's talk about you, son. How are you doing? Is your life turning out like you hoped it would?"

That was a facetious question, like *Do you want me to stop this car?* I said, "Sure. I mean — so far, so good."

"Fine, fine," he boomed, as if I were one of his sales prospects on the phone. "Real good, very happy to hear it."

He took the Minor exit. At the top of the ramp I said, "Dad, listen — I can walk to Arnita's from here. I'll get a ride home." I made a move to unlock the door.

He put out his arm to stop me. "Oh no. You're coming with me. I need you today."

"For what?"

"We got a job to do." The tires squealed as we pulled away.

"Where's Mom?"

"At the hospital with Janie. Don't you even remember? Your sister had her tonsils out this morning. While you were off doing your own thing. I guess you were too busy to remember."

Mom had told me that was going to happen, but it had passed straight through my brain without stopping. "Sorry, Dad. How's she doing?"

"She'll live. She's got a hell of a sore throat." He swung the wagon onto Buena Vista Drive. I hadn't mowed the front yard in nearly two weeks. The old Dad, the non–flip-flop-wearing Dad, would have had plenty to say about the white trash who must live in a house with a yard like this. This new Dad pulled into the driveway and switched off the engine. He took the house key off the ring, left the others in the ignition. He told me to leave my overnight bag in the car. "And bring those boxes in the trunk."

I carried a stack of flattened moving cartons to the house. He sent me to the kitchen for strapping tape.

There I found Jacko eating a bowl of cornflakes off his little table, under the supervision of Mrs. Wagner, our neighbor from across the street.

"Oh good, y'all are home!" She got up from her chair. "Well I must say, Jack Otis was no trouble at all. Just as pleasant as he could be."

"Thank you, ma'am," said Dad, escorting her out. "Mighty nice of you to do this on such short notice. My wife will be over to thank you."

"Oh tell her not to bother, Mr. Musgrove, it was no problem at all. Y'all just feel free to call on me anytime! Bye, now!"

Dad went from room to room, closing and locking windows. "Okay now, no questions, just do what I tell you. Make up one box for each of you. Put the stuff you think is most important, the stuff they would really want to keep — Bud's trophies and Janie's dolls, and like that. Do it fast. I want to be out of here in half an hour."

"Where are we going?"

"Son? Just do like I say, and everything will be fine. Now get busy." He didn't look all that grim when he said it. For once, I wasn't what he was mad at. I decided to do myself a favor and not challenge him.

I built the boxes, carried one to the Freak Annex, and gathered clothes, my favorite jacket with the elbow patches, the Crimson Tide sweatshirt from Aunt June. *We're moving again. He's been transferred. But wait. He got fired. They don't transfer you after you're fired. I can't fit everything into one box!*

Maybe we were going ahead to the new place. The other stuff would come later, with the moving van.

I made sure to pack my Converse high-tops and my cowboy boots. A few clothes, some birthday knickknacks: a cut-glass prism, an antique shaving mug and brush. I packed the few mementos that had survived the great moving-van fire of 1972 by riding in the trunk of our Oldsmobile: my Hardy Boys books, my Sir Edmund Hillary book, my one-eyed teddy bear.

I gathered Bud's trophies, his Polaroid Swinger and photo albums, all the Boy Scout junk from his underwear drawer. Bud didn't have much stuff, so I put more of my shirts in his box. In Janie's room I started with the dolls, but then, no, she's too old for dolls, so I loaded in coats and dresses and hats, the horse figurines, the storybooks I used to read to her when she was little and cute. I stuck a few dolls on top.

I taped up the boxes and wrote our names in Magic Marker.

Dad was locking windows, closing off the heating vents. He nodded at the sight of my boxes. "Go put those in the back of the car."

I obeyed. Mrs. Grissom's beagle was loitering at the end of our driveway. Dad came behind me bearing Jacko's footlocker and another couple of boxes. He shoved it up to the wheel well and began arranging my boxes around it.

"Where are we going?"

"We'll discuss it in the car."

"Why can't you just tell me?"

"We're making a change, son," he said. "For once I need you to cooperate."

I felt my unease rising — what change? Why were we suddenly dismantling our normal lives? Mom was at the hospital with Janie, Bud was long gone, it was just Jacko and me and Dad packing our lives into boxes. What about my senior year, my best friend, my beautiful kissing girl? What about the valuable contribution I was making to life at Minor High?

I went to the phone in the family room and dialed a number.

Ella Beecham said, "Hey, Musgrove, how you been?" That was a surprise — I'd expected her to hang up, as she had the last ten times I called.

"Fine, Miz Beecham. Is Arnita there?"

"I told you. I don't want you talking to her."

"Please? Just for a minute. It's important."

"Don't, Musgrove. We're busy. We got a lot going on."

"Miz Beecham, I need to talk to her."

Slam! went the phone.

I tried Tim's number. Patsy Cousins picked up on the second ring, bright and shiny. "Hello!" I hung up.

Okay, well, that's it, I suppose. I'm leaving, and there's no one to tell.

Maybe we're moving someplace nice for a change. California would be good. It looked so beautiful and sunny on TV. I could talk Arnita into coming out to California. She could get a scholarship at some good school out there.

But no, Dad would do the boring, sensible thing: move us to a cheaper house in Minor, find a job selling insurance or cars. He always said a good salesman can sell anything.

He came from the kitchen rolling Jacko on his scooter. "We're going for a ride, Jack Otis," he said. "You want to bring a blanket for your legs?"

"I be all right," Jacko said, "long as it's summertime." He looked feeble today, squinting up at me like Popeye with one blue eye. "What you lookin' at, boy?"

"You, Jacko. You feeling okay?"

"Old as Methuselah, that's all. Ol' devil climb up on me in the bedstead last night."

"Push him off next time," Dad said. "Son, why don't you roll Jacko on out to the car."

"Sure, Dad." My strategy of nonconfrontation was working. Dad hadn't yelled at me since we got home.

I grasped Jacko by the shoulders, easing him over the doorjamb. His scooter rolled smoothly across the garage floor.

There was just enough room behind the boxes in the back of the station wagon for Jacko to sit looking out the back window. "Thankee, Danums."

"You welcome, old man."

"Where we gwine?"

"I don't know, but we gwine somewhere. Watch your fingers!" I slammed the gate. "Dad won't tell me. You're the spooky one, you tell me what's going on."

"We gone have the light shining in our eyes," he said.

"What does that mean?"

"Gone shine in our eyes all night long," he said, coughing.

"That's nice. I think I hear Dad calling me."

I went back inside. Dad yelled from the kitchen for me to grab the sleeping bags.

I fished our green Scout bags from the deep back of Bud's closet, above the slide projector. I put them in the car and went back to find Dad up on the kitchen counter with the stove pushed away from the wall, aiming his flashlight down at something behind it.

"What else?" I said.

"Grab those oranges in the refrigerator. And that roll of paper towels. That bag of pecans and the crackers, and some Vienna sausages. We might need a snack."

I gathered it all in a Jitney Jungle sack.

"The keys are in the ignition," he said. "Go ahead and start the car, give Jacko some A/C. I'll be out in a minute."

I was never allowed to drive. Something was really out of whack. I backed the Country Squire down the driveway, turned it around, and backed to the house so that all Dad had to do was step in and drive off. Maybe he would even want me to drive when he saw how well I'd done it.

It was unsettling how calm, how reasonable, he seemed in his flip-flops. TriDex was his life, the thing he believed in the most. He had always been more devoted to that company than to our family or anyone in it, including Mom. And now they had fired him. Shouldn't he be in a big foaming rage about now?

He seemed preoccupied, as if he was working out some complicated problem in his head.

Here he came in his old red plaid hunting jacket, wearing the straw hat Granny gave him many summers ago. In his arms he cradled a shotgun, a mop, and a broom. "Got her turned around ready to go, I see."

"Yes sir."

"Good job," he said.

Good job.

Dad had never said these words to me. Never.

Who was this stranger inhabiting his body?

I got in the seat beside him. He slid the double-barreled shotgun behind my feet.

I didn't know where we were going, but already it was better. The hardness inside Dad had softened, a little. It was the answer to a prayer I'd been praying my whole life without realizing it.

We sailed out of the driveway. Our house looked peaceful, normal. Mrs. Grissom's beagle stood by the mailbox, watching us go.

If this is goodbye, I thought, it's also good riddance. One forty-four Buena Vista Drive was not an address I would miss. Certainly I would not miss a single blade of that grass. It made me happy to see the seedheads poking up and to think I might never have to cut them again.

Mississippi? When we came here I thought I would hate it. While we lived here I thought I did hate it. To my astonishment, now that we might be leaving, I found that I loved it better than any place we had ever lived. Look at that kudzu running wild, swallowing that house and the telephone poles and the trees! You don't see that kind of stuff in Yankeeland. Old billboards collapsed where they stood, and nobody bothered to pick up the pieces. The heat was stronger than in other places, the ceaseless chanting of bugs in the weeds. The pine trees didn't offer much shade. It was not a place for soft people, but for some reason I felt completely at home here.

Besides, I couldn't leave Mississippi. This was where Arnita lived.

"You all right back there, Jacko?" Dad called.

"Yassuh," he said, "but I has been better."

Dad rolled his eyes at me.

Amazing how fast I had abandoned my usual surly opposition to Dad and begun trying to win his approval, just like when I was younger. I was surprised to find myself still the same anxious kid, trying to keep from upsetting him, eager to please him if at all possible.

A couple of lawn chairs chattered together in the back. "Jacko, can you stop that rattling?" Dad called.

He tried, but couldn't reach that far.

"I'll get it." I launched myself over the second seat and jiggled the chairs apart to stop the noise.

At the intersection with McRaven Road, Dad turned left instead of right, doubling back on County Road 11. I knew this road made a meandering loop to hook up with McRaven again, a mile to the east of our house. "Dad, where are we going?"

"Not too far now," he said. "We're almost there. You'll see."

"What's the big secret?"

"Let me tell you a story, son," he said. "You know I was in the Army Air Corps, right after the war? When I got out in 'forty-nine, I saw this ad in the Montgomery paper. 'Chemicals Are Your Future.' The fastest-growing chemical company in America was interviewing at the Whitley Hotel, and if you were a go-getter who wanted a bright future, come see the man."

Dad never talked about anything in the past but the Depression. I listened.

"I got all shaved and bathed," he said, "got myself all slickered up in my eight-dollar suit and took a bus down to Dexter Avenue. Got off at the fountain, walked over to the Whitley. I had to wait while the man finished up with the fellow in front of me. And then I shook Charlie's hand. Charlie Fabricant. First thing he asked me was, did I want to be a TriDex man for the rest of my life. And I said, yes sir, I did."

"You decided that quick?"

"That's how it worked in those days, if you were lucky. Get a job with a good company, give 'em all you got, they'll look after you the rest of your life."

"So this guy who gave you your first job? He's the one who laid you off?"

"He said how ironic it was, him being the one to deliver the bad news after all these years. They thought it wouldn't hurt as much, coming from him. They were wrong about that." His smile was cold. "Twenty-four years and two months. I'd be vested next May. Charlie says all the big companies are doing it now, any excuse to keep from paying retirement."

"Wait a minute," I said. "They won't pay your retirement?"

"Not unless you're vested. And you can't make 'em. Oh you can sue 'em, maybe force 'em to give you a little something eventually, but whatever you got would get eat up with lawyer fees."

Dad flipped on the blinker and turned onto a two-lane dirt track running east through the woods. We drove the red dirt ribbons up the long spine of a hill, past the fresh stumps of felled trees. It was the early stage of a subdivision, odd piles of brush, scraped-off house sites, lots marked with string. At the top of the hill was a broad grassy meadow on a promontory overlooking the countryside.

Nice panorama up here. Dad drove to the far side of the grassy field. He backed the car up to a bluff with a view of the valley. He went to lower the tailgate.

"Are we gonna build a house up here, Dad?"

"No. Help me get these boxes out." We spread a green plastic tarp on the ground and loaded the boxes from the wagon onto the middle of it. We covered the boxes with a second tarp, tucked it tight around the edges and weighted it with rocks.

Dad set up the folding chairs facing out toward the view. On the tailgate between the chairs, he spread a blanket for Jacko. He brought out a sack containing two cans of Coke. He cracked one open and offered the other to me. "Jack Otis, you want some Co-Cola? Daniel will split his with you."

Jacko shook his head.

We sat in the lawn chairs drinking Coke, looking over the valley. I recognized the little grocery store at the crossroads, the bend in McRaven Road. I followed the road down a line of trees to the intersection with Buena Vista and realized I was looking directly down on our house. Right below us, that very roof showing through a gap in the branches.

So this was the hill that loomed over our street. Of course! Many times on my bike I had gazed up this ridge, forbiddingly wooded and steep. I never imagined you could just drive right up to the top like this. "Hey, Dad, that's our house!"

"Not our house," said Dad. "TriDex owns it. Not us. You knew that, didn't you?"

"I think so."

"It's not a bad deal, long as you're working for them. If they terminate you, they keep your house."

"You mean they can sell it?"

"They will sell it, and keep all the money, even though I paid the taxes and took care of it. They got good ol' Charlie Fabricant to call up and explain it to me." He lifted his Coke can for a toast. "It really wasn't his call to make. Here's to Charlie. Doing their dirty work for them." He banged his can against mine.

"I don't get it, Dad."

"I got robbed, son. They took my retirement. The car. And the house we live in. You know what I get? After twenty-four years and two months?"

"What?"

"Two weeks' base pay, and a sincere thank-you."

"That sucks!"

"Watch your language!" He swatted me.

I was dodging his hand when the first flash caught my eye. I turned toward it by instinct.

The windows lit up luminous orange shimmering to blue. The fireball expanded outward from the center of the house, carrying walls and roof with it, the pieces of our house swelling into a ball of fire rising and rising like a mushroom cloud, rolling up into the sky.

In four seconds the heat wave struck my face. A thunderclap shook the air — a huge boom that jolted me out of my chair and toppled Jacko on his side.

Dad shot his fists in the air. "Hooooeeeee!"

The fireball climbed into the sky on a tower of smoke. After the roar came the sounds of tinkling glass, falling metal, timbers crashing. Trees cracked and fell. A hundred dogs barked from every direction.

The ruins of our house made a hot fire. From above, it looked like a hole in the ground with a huge heap of fire at one end. I saw flickering in the trees — Spanish moss burning in the branches.

I pulled Jacko back up to a sitting position. He looked stricken, as if that big sound had jarred him too hard.

Dad stood with his fists raised in triumph.

"Dad, you blew up our house?"

"Not our house," he crowed. "Their house!"

I'd never seen him so happy.

17

IT WAS CRAZY as hell, a total catastrophe, but still I shared some of Dad's exhilaration when he blew up our house. It was the kind of plot Tim and I might have dreamed up — but Dad was a grown man who had figured out how to actually do it. With no one to stop him, least of all me.

Apparently the idea occurred to him shortly after he slammed the phone down on Charlie Fabricant. We'd always been a TriDex family, moving when TriDex said move, jumping when they said how high, twisting our lives into the shape of that familiar triple-D logo. *TriDex — We Know What Bugs You!* One phone call from Charlie Fabricant brought it all to an end.

By the time he came to pick me up at Full Flower, Dad had calculated the cubic volume of the house, the rate at which natural gas would flow from the pipe behind the stove, how long it would take to fill seven rooms. Once he found out from the *World Book* that natural gas is lighter than air (I told you those books would come in handy), he decided to place Mom's silver candelabra on the floor of the bedroom farthest from the kitchen, so the house would be well loaded with gas by the time the fumes reached the source of ignition.

He wanted a big explosion with no large pieces remaining. He didn't want some insurance inspector finding a candelabra in the bedroom, for instance.

I watched smoke billowing from the hole where our house used to be. I had spent my life being afraid of Dad. For the first time it occurred to me that others should be frightened too.

"Man, that was big!" he exulted. "Heck of a lot bigger than I thought!"

"You blew up our house? All our stuff?"

He dismissed this with a wave of his hand. "We saved out what was important. The rest was just yard-sale junk."

I thought of all the Saturdays we'd spent scouring yard sales for that junk while he sat home watching football. I kicked the lawn chair across the grass. "Where are we supposed to live now?"

"Go pick up that chair," he said.

"But my bike was in there!"

"You can get another bike."

Over the barking of dogs I heard sirens wailing from the direction of Minor.

"We need to get back down there," he said. "I called Mississippi Gas before we left. I told her we smelled gas in the house, a strong odor of gas. She told me to get out, they would send a crew right away. Do you understand?"

"You're saying it was an accident?" I said. "It was a leak or something?"

"That's right. A leak in the kitchen. Probably the stove. We'd been having trouble with that stove, remember?" He watched to see how I received this news. But then he was looking past me. "Jack Otis, what the heck is the matter with you?"

Jacko sat glaring up at us with a peculiar look of outrage. His jaw was working but no sound was coming out. His skin was a nonhuman gray, the color of fireplace ashes.

"The noise knocked him over," I said. "You think it hurt him?"

"Jacko." Dad snapped his fingers in front of his eyes. "Say something."

Nothing.

"He doesn't look so good," I observed.

"You're right. Oh for the love of — we better get somebody to look at him. Grab those chairs, hurry. Get in back with him."

I shoved in the lawn chairs and crawled in beside Jacko. Dad stepped on the gas. The Country Squire bounded off across the pasture on wallowy shocks.

Jacko was barely breathing, a shallow pant.

"What, Jacko?" I patted his hand. "What do you need?"

"Water," he croaked.

"I haven't got any water. Here, drink my Coke."

I poured some in his mouth. I could tell it hurt him to swallow.

"Did he drink it?" Dad called.

"A little. Most of it ran out."

Jacko closed his eyes and slumped against the wheel well. "Jacko?"

"What's he doing?" said Dad.

"Jacko? Come on, wake up." Had I killed him with Coke?

"Don't let him go to sleep," Dad said. "They say if they're having a stroke you're supposed to try and keep 'em awake."

"You think he's having a stroke?"

"Well how should I know? Stop talking to me and watch him!"

We flew down the ramp onto I-20. All those years pulling himself across the floor had given Jacko huge leathery hands with knobby knuckles. I massaged those arthritic knobs until I got him to open his eyes, but he didn't seem able to lift his head. He lay gazing up at me. I didn't see any sign of fear in his eyes.

Up to now, I had thought of Jacko as mostly a nuisance. Now that he was dying, it was like leaving Mississippi — suddenly I realized I would miss him.

We raced around the Robinson Road off-ramp and into the emergency bay of the West Central Mississippi Regional Medical Center. Two guys in white hurried out.

Jacko's eyes widened as they lifted him onto a gurney and whisked him away.

He must have thought he was entering heaven, all those people around him in white. They wheeled him into a stretcher bay, strapped a mask on his face, pulled a curtain.

Dad went to the nurses' station to do the paperwork. I sprawled on a chair in the waiting room, leafing through *Modern Medical Technology*. Whenever I closed my eyes I saw a superbright flash, and Spanish moss burning in the trees.

A young doctor came out to tell us it wasn't a stroke but viral pneumonia, very serious for an elderly man with all of Jacko's infirmities. Probably he would be here a week, minimum.

Dad said, "I've got a daughter in this hospital too. Third floor."

"Why don't y'all go on up to her room? I'll come find you when we get Mr. Bates admitted and settled into a room." I'd forgotten Jacko even had a last name. Of course: Mom was a Bates originally, and Jacko was her mother's brother.

In the elevator I said, "At least he's not dying."

"Yeah, pneumonia is better than a stroke," Dad said. "I thought I'd killed him."

"What are you gonna tell Mom?"

"About what?"

"The house. Don't you think she'll notice it's gone? You're gonna have to tell her."

Dad got this exasperated gleam in his eye. "Why do you have to be such a smart aleck? No, it ain't gonna be easy to tell her, and no she won't like it. But it's done. Nothing she or anybody else can do about it now."

I considered a minute. "You want me to tell her it was an accident?"

He stared as if he could see my bones. "You think you could make her believe you?"

"I think so."

He looked skeptical. "You would lie, to keep me out of Dutch with your mother?"

I was skeptical myself. I felt like a kitten that has wandered into the cage to play with the big tiger. It may seem at first as if everything's going along okay, but you just know it's not going to end well.

The elevator door slid open. Mom was in the third-floor waiting room with her palm pressed to the window, staring out at the interstate. When she saw us she began waving the smoke of her cigarette away with one hand, as if it didn't belong to her. "What are y'all doing here? Who's home with Jacko?"

Dad explained.

"Pneumonia! My Lord! I knew he had a cold, but I had no idea it was that bad!" I could see droplets of guilt condensing on her instantly.

Dad said, "You know how old folks are with pneumonia."

She frowned. "Half the time that's what kills 'em. They get pneumonia, then they die."

"As mean as that old man is, he will live to be a hunnerd," said Dad. "Peg. Something else. There's been a little accident at the house."

Her head jerked around. "Accident."

"Listen to me, now. Try not to get upset. There was a gas leak — a natural gas leak in the house. It must have started in the kitchen." He was looking at me, talking to her. Looking directly into my eyes, as if that way, we were both saying the words, he was binding me to him with his Lie. "The gas company said to get out of the house. We got out in time. But honey . . . the house was destroyed."

She shook her head as if she did not recognize the word. "Destroyed?"

Gravely he nodded. "It was a big explosion. There's nothing left."

Mom took a breath of smoke from the cigarette. "Really."

Dad said, "I know it's hard to believe, that it could happen to us again. And we have to start all over again, for the second time. But this time there's a difference."

She narrowed her eyes. "Insurance?"

He nodded. "Yes ma'am. Entire contents, full policy. Five-hundred-dollar deductible."

Mom's eyes welled. "Oh Lord, Lee, tell me it's not true. Tell me this is April Fool's Day . . . Why does everything bad have to happen to us?"

"I'm sorry, sweetheart. I know it does feel that way sometimes."

"Our poor house," she said. "Oh Daniel, you must have been so scared!"

I nodded. "It made this big noise."

That made her cry harder. Dad and I stood on either side of her. He put his arms around her and let her sob into his shoulder.

"I don't think we were meant to live in Mississippi," she wailed. "God doesn't want us to live here."

I stood still and said nothing while Mom wept. This was the first time I'd ever conspired with Dad against Mom. I didn't like it.

"My pictures of Mama," she wailed, "all those things of Gran Bates, her Sheaf of Grain china, and oh Lord, not her tea service too?"

"I saved that box of old pictures," Dad said. "And your mama's Bible, and your jewelry box."

"Thank God," she said.

"And some of your shoes," he said. "Dadgum fortune in shoes, I wasn't about to let 'em all go. And Daniel packed a box for each of them, didn't you?" He fixed me with a look.

"Wait a minute." Mom sniffled, wiping her eye with a Kleenex. "When did y'all have time to do all this packing?"

"It wasn't that much time," Dad said. "We had to move fast."

"You mean while the house was filling up with gas, you had time to run around packing boxes?"

Dad said, "More like grabbing what we could on our way out."

"Why didn't you open the windows and let the gas out?"

"There wasn't time, sweetheart," Dad said. "I mean the house was *loaded* with fumes. Opening one window was not gonna make any difference. We were lucky to get out of there at all."

"Daniel, you're mighty quiet," said Mom. "You helped your father do this?"

"Yes ma'am. It's just like he said."

Mom frowned. "You're a worse liar than Daddy. Lee, what have you done to our house?"

"What do you mean? I just explained to you what happened." I don't think he could have looked more guilty if he'd been wearing black and white stripes.

Her bitter smile. "You destroyed our home, didn't you? Because they got Charlie Fabricant to fire you. And it belongs to the company, so you thought this would be a good way to get back at them."

He thought about it a moment. "That's about right."

"I know you so well, Lee." Her voice thickened. "How dare you lie to my face! To my *face!* How stupid do you think I am, that I wouldn't see right through you?"

"You didn't." He stuck his thumb out at me. "You saw through him."

I fought an urge to grab his thumb and sink my teeth into it. "I'm going to check on Janie," I said, rushing out before they could stop me.

I went in to face the sight of my sister bleary-eyed, red-faced, nose running, jowls puffed up like Alvin the Chipmunk. You hear about tonsils like it's no big deal, but Janie looked like someone who'd just had her throat cut out.

She was furious at Mom. "She practically kidnapped me," she whisper-croaked. "She said we were going to the doctor. She didn't say a word about tonsils till we got here!"

"Yeah, I thought it was stupid," I said, "but she didn't want you getting all flipped out in advance."

She blinked. "You knew about it too? Thanks, traitor!"

"I was going to tell you, Idjit. Really. I forgot."

"If you knew how much it hurts —"

"Stop talking, then," I said. "You're the only person dumb enough to keep talking even when it hurts."

I told her Jacko was in this very hospital at this moment, breathing through an oxygen mask. I told her Dad blew up our house and everything in it, a fact we had to keep to ourselves so the insurance would pay. Janie didn't seem all that surprised. "Mommy said he lost his job," she croaked. "He was really mad last night."

"He still is," I said. "Although he looked pretty happy when it exploded."

Janie sipped 7-Up through a straw. Mom was a strong believer in the magic healing powers of 7-Up. Janie said, "Does this mean Dad is crazy?"

"No more than usual," I said. We shared a grim humor — the quiet jokes of prisoners sharing a cell for life. "Think how it's gonna be when they try to put him in a straitjacket."

"You think they will?" she whispered, in awe of the idea.

"I wouldn't be surprised. This is big. He blew up our house."

"Does this mean we'll be poor now?" said Janie. "He always said we were driving him to the poorhouse."

I told her to stop talking. For once in her life, she did.

In the waiting room I found Mom and Dad watching the five o'clock news. Kent Williams of Channel 12 stood before our house, the smoking hole in the ground. The camera zoomed in on the blown-out windows of Mrs. Wagner's house across the street.

There was Mrs. Wagner, trembling. "They were the nicest family," she quavered. "I was over there this morning. It's a wonder I wasn't killed too!"

"She thinks we're dead," Mom cried. "Lee, they think we're dead on the news!"

"Well, we're not," he said. "That just goes to show you."

"But you've got to call somebody!"

"Who?"

"I don't know, the TV station, the police! How should I know?" There she went, crying again. "Oh Lee, what have you done?"

Mom asked me to please go find Jacko, since everyone seemed to have forgotten all about him. I navigated the maze of elevators and hallways to the information desk. The lady told me Jacko had been admitted to a ward on the fifth floor. The nurses on five would know the room number.

The nurse at the desk on five was a wide woman with that orange-reddish hair black women get when they bleach it. When I said, "Jack Otis Bates," she stiffened. "Oh, are you connected with him? Cause we been looking for whoever brought that old man in here to tell you, if you can't get him to control that nasty mouth of his, he ain't gonna be able to stay on this flo."

"Ma'am?"

"Yeah, I was the first one got tangled up with him, went in there trying to settle him in, nasty old thang starts to calling me nigger, well I tell you right now I don't care who he is, I ain't putting up with that bullshit! Cause that's all *that* is, racist cracker bullshit. Ain't nothing in my job description says I have to put up with it! I told him to stuff it up his old ass, then another girl went in there, he start up with her too. Say he don't want to be took care of by no niggers, for us to go get him a white nurse."

"Look, I'm sorry, if I could explain," I said.

She made a face. "Yeah, go on. I want to hear you explain."

I swallowed. "Well — Jacko's real old. He's from out in the country. And he says that word, but he doesn't really mean it — not like, you know, if I was to say it."

She lifted her chin. "If you was to say it, I would kick yo white ass down the stairs. And if he wadn't crippled, I'd kick his white ass down there too."

"He's got all these black friends back home," I said. "That's what he used to call them, and they liked it."

"Well, I don't like it. Nobody here like it. Are you tellin' me we supposed to *like* it?"

"No," I said. "Just, he doesn't mean it in a bad way."

"Honey, there ain't no good way you can say nigger."

Another nurse came to join in. "This one related to 503?"

"Yeah, tellin' me how some that old cracker's best friends is black, so that give him the right to say nigger whenever he wants."

"That's not what I meant!"

"What it sound like to me," said the orange-haired nurse.

I raised my hands in surrender. "I'll tell him to shut up."

"Yeah, you tell him," she said. "Five-oh-three."

The door stood wide open. Jacko lay crumpled on his side, his nose and mouth covered by a yellow oxygen mask. Tubes ran under his hospital gown.

I went around the end of the bed. "How you feeling, old man?"

He looked pale, decrepit. He pulled the mask an inch from his face. "Hey Danums. They got nothing in this place but nigger nurses."

"Yeah, I can see that," I said. "But they don't like you calling 'em nigger. If you keep it up, they're gonna kick your white ass down the stairs. That's what they said."

"Take me on home, Danums."

"I can't. Home is gone. Dad blew it up."

"Not there," he said. "I mean *home*."

"Sorry, Jacko. You're sick. Doctor says you gotta stay here."

"Yo daddy didn't blow up no house," Jacko said. "It was Miz Wagna, I done tole you. She come from the devil. She is trying to murder us all."

"Shut up and breathe your oxygen, old man. It wasn't Miz Wagner."

His cackle turned into a coughing fit.

Both nurses kept their eye on me all the way to the elevator lobby. They watched me the whole time I stood waiting for the elevator. The bell went *ding!* and I got on, and they kept watching me until the doors slid shut.

18

I RODE IN the back of the station wagon. Mom yelled. Dad drove. He kept saying "Calm down, now" and "Would you calm yourself?" I tried to say something, but Mom whirled on me and told me to shut my mouth, it was just as much my fault as Daddy's for not lifting one finger to stop him.

"It's one thing when a moving van tumps over in the highway and everything burns," she cried. "That's fate! That's an act of God, and nothing you can do about it. But to do it on purpose, Lee, to set out to destroy our home, all the things we — my God, what am I supposed to wear? I don't have any clothes!"

"You can get new clothes with the insurance money. You can get a mink coat."

"What would I do with a mink coat in Mississippi?" Mom shouted. "I don't want new clothes — I want *my* clothes! I want to go home and get in my bed and pull the covers over my head and forget about you!"

Dad shrugged. "I said I was sorry. What else do you want?"

"Oh please — like one 'sorry' is supposed to make up for this? Forget it! I am not forgiving you this time!" She was really wound up. "I'll tell you who's sorry — I am, that I ever met you! And didn't have the sense to keep from marrying you, like Mary Nell tried to warn me. No, I've stuck it out all these years, and for what? Thinking maybe you'd change, but you never do. Your bad side just gets worse."

Dad said Mom was damn lucky to have him, he could have married any girl in Alabama.

She laughed. "Lucky is not the word. I have just about had it with you. You let your temper run away with you, and now you've done this foolish thing, Lee, this childish, idiotic —"

"Watch out." He darkened.

Mom gave birth to a healthy nine-pound sigh. "This *stupid* thing," she said, "which leaves us with nothing."

"Insurance," he said. "Fifty thousand on the contents, full cash payout."

"All of life is not about insurance!"

"At least you could give me some credit for taking it," he said, "after the hell you gave me for turning it down before."

"Credit?" she shrieked. "You want me to give you credit?"

"Guys, would y'all please shut up?" I said, as nicely as I could.

They left off yelling at each other to turn around in their seats and yell at me. What finally shut them up was the first whiff, at the foot of Buena Vista Drive: a scorchy electrical-fire odor.

"Look at all these cars," Mom said. "What in the world?"

"Bunch of durn rubberneckers," said Dad. "Annabelle Wagner is not gonna like them parking all over her grass."

Mom gasped, "Oh my God!" and fell back in her seat.

The snowlike scattering on the landscape was our disintegrated stuff. The explosion had taken down both of the big oaks. Great heaps of greenery lay all over the yard, as if Hurricane Camille had swept up our street.

Hours after the house blew up, people were still lining up three deep at the yellow rope, snapping pictures, having a look. Around the smoldering hole was a herd of Mississippi Gas trucks, two Minor fire trucks, cop cars, sheriff's cars, a bulldozer.

We had to drive all the way up the hill to find a place to park. Our former house was now a tourist attraction. See The Smoking Hole In The Ground! See The Family Walking Toward The Smoking Hole!

Someone had already nailed plywood over the windows on the near side of the Logues' house and all along the front of the Wagners'. Debris littered every yard on Buena Vista Drive. Dad winced when he saw all this secondary damage. In all his careful calculations, I don't think he had ever stopped to think about the neighbors.

From out of the crowd came Ella Beecham, opening her arms to me. "Musgrove! We thought you was dead — and look at you, live as anybody!" She squeezed me hard about the ribs.

"Miz Beecham! What are you doing here?"

She sniffed. "Hmp. I stopped being mad at you when I thought you was dead," she said. "But now that you ain't, I'm going right back like I was."

Arnita slipped up behind me, put her arms around me, kissed my cheek. "Hey you," she murmured. "I knew you had to be okay."

I was shocked all over again by how beautiful she was in her little white sleeveless T-shirt, cutoff jeans crisp against slender brown legs. There was not a flaw of any kind. What a miracle on earth I was ever permitted to kiss this girl, much less do what we did in my bed in the house that now lay scattered all around us. My heart soared to think she had been worried for me — she made her mother bring her out here to see about me! "I'm so glad you're here," I said.

"We were watching the news, and — oh my God," Arnita said. "They said no sign of survivors, but I knew you couldn't be dead. I would have felt it. I was so scared you got hurt or something. Are you really okay? Is your family okay?"

"Yeah. A little shook up, that's all. Jacko's in the hospital. I thought you might be mad at me because of — well, you left that morning without waking me up. . . ."

"Arnita was a little upset," she said, "but I was okay. I could tell your mom didn't want me to stay."

People I barely knew were coming up to hug and congratulate us for being alive. I'd always thought of Buena Vista Drive as a friendless place, but among the crowd were dozens of neighbors, parents of kids from the school bus, two of Janie's teachers, and the pastor of a Methodist church Mom and Dad had attended once.

I saw Mrs. Beecham talking to Mom, actually patting Mom's arm. I was surprised Mom would let her do that. She didn't normally like to be touched.

Dad stepped over the rope and headed toward the hole. Mom hurried after him.

I said, "I need to go with them."

"Musgrove," said Ella Beecham, "what did you do to your house?"

"I knew you'd blame me. Wait here, I'll be back."

Arnita squeezed my hand. "Go on. We'll be here."

At the edge of the hole was a cluster of firemen, cops, gas company men. One man detached himself from the group and came over to us. He was old — maybe forty — his face craggy from a case of long-ago acne. He was solid, built low to the ground. He wore khaki pants and a white shirt with sleeves rolled up.

"Mr. Musgrove, Miz Musgrove," he said, with a nod for me.

"Do I know you?" said Dad.

He extended his hand. "We talked on the phone. Detective Sergeant Jeff Magill, Hinds County sheriff's office?"

"Oh yeah, surely, right." Dad shook his hand. "Well, as you can see we've lost our home."

"I just need to visit with you a little while, get some information for my report. I'm sure you know all about writing reports, the business you're in. Chemicals, isn't that what you said?"

Dad nodded. "TriDex."

"We know what bugs you," said Magill with his nonhumorous smile.

Dad winced. "That's the one."

The name was familiar. Wasn't there a Sergeant Magill involved in Arnita's accident? I decided to keep my mouth shut.

"Were you storing any chemicals in your house, Mr. Musgrove?"

"I may have had some samples in the carport. Pesticides, mostly."

Mom stirred. "My husband wasn't here when it happened," she announced. "He was at the hospital with our daughter, Jane. Daniel and I are the ones who were here."

This was a bold thrust from Mom — a lie wide enough to drive a battleship through, completely disprovable ten different ways, including the fact that it was Dad who reported the "leak" to Mississippi Gas and Mom who'd never left Janie's side at the hospital. I couldn't imagine what she hoped to gain by telling this whopper.

I focused my gaze on Jeff Magill's scuffed loafers.

He seemed not to have heard Mom's remark. "You sure none of those chemicals was explosive?"

Dad said, "I'm in the ag division. We don't handle those lines."

"Because ordinarily, a gas leak will blow out your windows. Not level a house to the ground."

Mom spoke up: "It was a bad leak. You never smelled so much gas in your life."

He peered at her. "Ma'am? I'll be with you shortly."

Mom didn't care for his tone. "But I told you, Lee wasn't even here. Shouldn't you be asking me the questions?"

"Oh I will," he said politely. "Just as soon as I'm done with Mr. Musgrove."

My heart banged away in my chest. Why was Mom acting so guilty? I wasn't sure whether blowing up your own house was an actual crime, but if she wasn't careful, somebody was going to jail. Maybe she thought she was protecting Dad or the insurance money, but I was certain this lie was a bad idea. I knew better than anybody how a harmless little lie could turn into a Lie, and take over your life.

Dad seemed unable to act. That left it up to me.

I said, "Mom, you weren't here. You were at the hospital. You know Dad was here with me and Jacko. Did you take your medication today?"

Mom glared as if I'd just shown everybody a picture of her in her underwear. "What medication? What are you talking about?"

Jeff Magill's eyebrows went up. "Y'all want me to step aside while you get your stories straightened out?"

"Come on, Mom, you're supposed to tell him the truth. He's the police."

"I know who he is," she said through clenched teeth. "You know perfectly well your father was at the hospital, and you and I were here." Her smile for Magill showed the strain. "The child bumped his head in the explosion. They said he might have a mild concussion."

"Aw now, Peggy Jean, honey, that's not so," Dad said gently. He'd caught on to what I was doing, and decided to help me. "She's been down at that hospital all night with our daughter," he told Magill. "She's worn-out. This thing is a shock. She needs to lie down."

"Stop that! There's nothing wrong with me!" she flared.

"Miz Musgrove, I understand you're upset, I know losing your home must be hard," Magill said. "I just need to get this information for my report."

"The boy and I came in and found the house full of fumes," Dad said. "We got Jack Otis out — that's her uncle, he's crippled — and I called the gas company. They said get out of the house. We did, and it blew. It was so loud, it gave the old man a stroke. We've been at the hospital with him ever since. That's where I was when I called you."

Magill turned to me. "You're Dan?"

"Yes sir. Daniel."

"Is that what happened, Dan?"

"Yes sir," I said. "Sorry, Mom."

"I don't know why I even bother," she muttered.

"Any idea what might have ignited the gas, Mr. Musgrove?" Jeff Magill said casually, as if asking him to guess tomorrow's weather.

"I have no idea," Dad said. "I reckon it wouldn't take more than a spark, huh?"

"I reckon not. You having any kind of financial problems?"

"Nope. I ain't rich, but we get along okay."

"Everything all right with your job, your family, like that?"

"Couldn't be better." It would take only one phone call to find out he'd lost his job, but Dad seemed bent on bluffing his way through this. "Well, of course we — I worry about —"

Mom caught him indicating her with his eyes. "Why would you worry about me?"

A pained smile from Dad. "Not you, sweetheart."

"Stop pretending there's something wrong with me!"

"Nothing wrong with you, Peggy," said Dad. "Everything's fine. Calm down. We can get another house."

"I assume you had insurance," Magill said.

"Actually, this house didn't belong to me," Dad said. "I didn't own it. My company holds the title. It's one of our fringe benefits. I imagine they carried a policy on it."

"But it's not in your name?"

"Nope. Alls I got is a little State Farm policy on the contents." Dad was cool under the steady gaze of Magill.

A spindly red-haired man came over to introduce himself as Bert Hinkle, the fire inspector from Minor. "Folks, I'd have to say y'all are mighty lucky to come out of that alive."

"I agree one hundred percent," said Dad.

Jeff Magill said, "What you thinking, Bert?"

"Obvious there was a break in the line, but I can't say why. Musta been a leak somewheres, I'd guess the kitchen. Mis'sippi Gas says they had normal pressure, and I hadn't seen any other indications. I got no clear source of ignition. Probably a spark from a thermostat, or some appliance. I'd have to say accidental, origin unexplained."

"Well that's what we've got, then," Magill said. "I'll make my report."

Dad kept his poker face. He didn't yell "Bingo!" or allow himself to look relieved.

I searched the ground for some recognizable fragment I could take as a souvenir. It all seemed to be splinters of Sheetrock, bits of foil-backed paper, rubbly brick — not a single object you could look at and say, that's a pencil, that's a fork, that's one spoke off a beloved green Schwinn ten-speed . . .

I walked back to the rope line to find Arnita and Mrs. Wagner shaking their heads over the miracle of our survival. I told Arnita I didn't care if the whole world blew up, I still wanted to take her to Sonny and Cher on Saturday night. Mrs. Beecham, having recently thought I was dead, was forced to give her permission.

I saw Mom waving me to come rescue her from the mob of well-wishers. "We'll pick you up at six-thirty," I told Arnita. "You be ready."

She smiled and said she would.

I waded into the crowd. "Hey Mom, Dad says we need to get going."

"Okay honey, I'm coming." She turned for one last round of hugs. "Bless you, sugar, let me go now, we gotta get back to the hospital. We've got two in there to look after now."

A man in a pickup truck followed us up the hill to our car so he could have our parking spot. It pleased Dad to make him wait, and wait some more, until Dad was good and ready to pull out.

We were halfway to town when Mom said, "I guess that went all right."

"Yep, thanks to Mr. Largemouth Bass taking the bait." Dad stuck his thumb back at me.

"You can say that again." Mom grinned.

I sat up. "What are y'all talking about?"

"We knew you wouldn't be able to keep your mouth shut," said Mom. "You've been contradicting us since you learned to talk. The first word you ever said was 'no.'"

I got that cold awful feeling that comes from discovering your parents are not quite as ignorant as you have always assumed. "Wait. You guys were doing that together?"

"Playing you like a fiddle," said Dad. "See, Peg, kids always think they're the ones that invented getting away with stuff. We were doing it long before you even existed."

Mom smiled. "I knew if I told a flat-out lie, you wouldn't be able to resist correcting me. And that would distract the man from what Daddy did. And sure enough! Thank goodness you're so predictable."

I was flabbergasted. I had bought their act completely, even played my assigned part in it. They had totally faked me out. It was like finding out your parents are secretly Bonnie and Clyde, robbing banks in their spare time. Dad fished a cigarette from his shirt pocket and lit it.

"What are you doing?" cried Mom. "You don't smoke."

"Shows how much you know. You want one?"

"What are those, Camels? Yeah, give me one." She lit it with her own Zippo and blew smoke out the window.

"Can I have one?" I ventured.

"No!" they said in unison.

I coughed and rolled down my window.

Mom said, "Since when do you smoke?"

"Only out of town," said Dad.

"Yeah, I don't even want to think about what-all you do out of town. And you always nagging me to quit. You look so stupid with that thing in your mouth. You don't even know how to smoke it!" She snatched the cigarette from his lips and tossed it out the window.

He grinned, and deftly grabbed her cigarette. "Ha!" He took one drag, blew the smoke in her face, and flung that one out the window too.

Okay, maybe this was love, some weird kind of "love" known only to them.

Dad found us two rooms at the Reid Motel, on Highway 80 on the way into Minor, just north of the Dairy Dog. The outside of the motel was homely and the rooms were even worse: hot, smelly, depressing. Dad said he had negotiated a dirt-cheap rate from the owner, Mr. Rashmi Patel. I said yeah, you get what you pay for. Dad said shut up, it was a fantastic deal. "You never had a pretty Injun lady coming to make up your bed for you at home, did you? You been whining about living too far out in the country. Now is your chance to enjoy city life!"

Mom set to scrubbing the bathtubs and putting out roach traps while Dad and I went to retrieve the boxes from the field on the hilltop above our former house. Down in the valley, we could see people still lining up at the yellow rope. It was strange how fascinated they were by something that wasn't there.

After supper at Dairy Dog, we drove to the hospital. Every one of those glowing windows represented a sick person in bed. I had hated hospitals ever since that day in the emergency room in Pigeon Creek. "Mom, do I have to go in?"

"Don't you want to see your sister? And Jacko?"

"I already know what they look like."

Dad turned. "Am I gonna have a problem with you?"

"No sir." I opened my door and got out. All day I had done a good job of saying "sir" and keeping my mouth shut. (Mostly.) I had passed up plenty of opportunities to say something smart. All I wanted was to get through this evening, get over to Arnita's house somehow, and kiss her. Take her down to our place by the river.

"Don't tell your sister about the house." Mom's heels clicked on the sidewalk. "It'll be too big a shock in her condition."

"I already told her." I shrugged. "Sorry."

"Largemouth Bass," said Dad. "I told you, he can't help opening his mouth."

"Hey, y'all. Who does that look like to you? Over there." I pointed to a concrete porch at the end of the building, where an old man slumped in his wheelchair, swatting at the bugs swarming around his head.

Mom followed the line of my finger. "Is that Jacko?"

"Looks like him," I said.

"What on earth is he doing out here?"

"Good question," said Dad.

We hurried across the grass. Jacko lay with his head on the armrest of the wheelchair. With his free hand he swatted at bugs.

"Jacko, what in the world?" Mom cried. "Who put you out here?"

"That nigger nurse."

Mom was furious. How could anyone take a sick old man off his oxygen and dump him outside? "We're going up there and find out," she declared.

I held the door open while Dad maneuvered Jacko's wheelchair into the elevator. Mom seethed all the way. "Unbelievable! What if we hadn't come back to check on him? Would they have just left him out there all night?"

The elevator doors slid open on five. Mom marched to the reception desk, where the nurse with orange hair sat writing in a chart. She studied the chart for the longest possible time before letting her eyes roll up to admit the sight of us.

"Excuse me, ma'am," Mom said, "can you explain to me why I just found my Uncle Jacko off his oxygen, downstairs, and sitting outside?"

"Who?"

"This man." Mom drummed the handles of Jacko's wheelchair. "Mr. Jack Otis Bates, your patient. Who we just found, sitting outside the hospital, getting eat up by mosquitoes — and he tells me y'all put him out there! It's a wonder he's not dead!"

"He looks all right to me." The nurse placed both hands wide on her desk and hoisted herself upright. "I'll help you put him back in the bed."

"No!" Mom yelped. "No ma'am. That's not what I want! I want to speak to your supervisor!"

The nurse smiled. "Supervisor gone home. Mr. Jack, what you doin' up out of yo bed? Don't you know you need to stay in there in your bed and rest, and get you some oxygen?"

She was good. I was impressed by how jolly she seemed. She chuckled at us like we were silly white folks, making such a fuss over nothing.

"I can't wait to hear what our lawyer is going to say about this," Dad said.

"You got a lawyer?" she said. "How come, y'all been in trouble?"

"No!" said Dad.

"It's a wonder, with that temper." She commandeered Jacko's chair, moving us briskly down the hall. "We done told Mr. Jack we don't want him taking hisself outside, not when he 'posed to be in bed havin' his oxygen! Ain't that right, Mr. Jack?"

"Yassum." Jacko's eyes loomed wide — something like fear.

"Mr. Jack even done learned my name," she said. "Hadn't you, sir? Hadn't you learned the proper way to speak my name?"

"Yassum." He cast down his eyes.

"What is it? What is my name?" she said, at the door to his room. "Tell the folks what my name is."

"Nurse Odum," he said.

"That's right, my name is Nurse Odum, and now if you need anything you know how to call me!" She chuckled deeply — the very picture of good humor. Without warning she hooked her arms through his, lifted him out of his chair, and plopped him on the bed just where he was supposed to be. She snapped out a sheet and tucked it around him.

He blinked in surprise. "You sho does move fast for a big woman."

With one hand she spun the empty wheelchair into the corner. "You bet I do, Mr. Jack. Now then, I'll be back to give you that shot, and I don't want you goin' anywhere till I do. You hear me?"

"Yassum."

"Good!" She strapped the oxygen mask over his nose and mouth and beamed at us. "Folks all right now? Everything all squared away?"

Dad couldn't think of anything to say until she was almost out the door. He said, "But that doesn't explain . . ." to her fast-retreating back.

"Lee," Mom said. "Leave it alone."

19

Four kids in a Starlite Blue Pinto, off to see Sonny and Cher: Tim at the wheel, the ringleader, the class clown. His faithful sidekick Daniel riding shotgun. In the backseat, the beautiful Prom Queen, and beside her Rachel Bostick, the formerly obese and now merely fat girl whom Tim had selected as the most appropriate double date with Arnita. Rachel's jaw had been wired shut for several months, as part of her new liquid diet. Already she'd lost more than sixty pounds. She wore a colorful Mama Cass muumuu that was too big for her now. She had learned to speak very distinctly for someone unable to open her mouth.

Arnita was dressed as a white girl — high heels, pantyhose, short skirt, pink sweater set. She looked a little silly and oh my God yummy. I wished I could take her straight down to the river and remove all her clothing, one item at a time.

Tim wore a black shirt, white satin tie with a piano-key pattern, skinny peg-legged black pants like the Beatles in their Liverpool days. I who never thought about clothes had on my usual dumb plaid shirt, jeans, black Converse high-tops.

Arnita said, "I'm so glad to finally spend some time with you, Tim. Daniel talks about you all the time."

Tim's jaw tightened. "Oh no, you're the one he can't stop talking about — Arnita Arnita Arnita, until we're all blue in the face! But he keeps you hidden away like this big dark secret, no pun intended. I had to practically beg him to invite you tonight."

"You did?" She turned to me. "Daniel?"

"No! It was my idea!" I said. What was he trying to do?

"Actually it was that ticket-seller woman, remember Skippy? That Yankee. She talked you into it."

Arnita touched my shoulder. "Did you tell me this story?"

I opened my mouth but Tim got there first. "See, Daniel was nervous about how well an interracial couple would go over in public, considering where we are."

"Where are we?" said Rachel.

"Mississippi."

"Oh, right."

He adjusted the mirror. "But the lady told him nobody would care. So here you are!"

"We're not an interracial couple." Arnita bopped me on the shoulder. "Why didn't you tell me this?"

"I thought it was no big deal. Tim was the one who said they still hurt people for that kind of stuff down here."

"No two stories are the same," said Tim. "It's like Dealey Plaza."

The great yellow flying saucer of the Coliseum glowed on the floodplain beneath the city. The parking lot streamed with cars. From this distance it looked glamorous — my mind sketched in palm trees, a range of purple Hollywood mountains, searchlights waving in the sky.

"Okay, now I'm getting excited," I said. "Look at all these people! Tim, remember when we were afraid we'd be the only ones here?"

We whipped off the interstate at High Street, into a slow-moving river of Sonny and Cher fans flowing down to the fairgrounds. Tim drove to the farthest edge of the parking lot and parked the Pinto sideways across two parking spaces. "No door dings," he said, getting out.

"Can't be more than thirty miles to the Coliseum," I said. "We can be there by Christmas."

Rachel laughed. "Do y'all always get on each other like this?"

We fell in with a wide stream of people inching past tables stacked with Sonny and Cher T-shirts, posters, fancy souvenir programs. At ten bucks a pop, the program cost more than a ticket to the show — the world was changing in mysterious ways.

The ticket-takers were Shriners, old men in tiny red fezzes and red shorty vests. "Thank you joy the show," they muttered, "thank you joy the show." The lines at the snack bar stretched to the middle of next week. We followed the herd down a ramp into the dim vastness of the largest room in Mississippi.

"I hope we have good seats," said Rachel.

Tim said, "It's general admission."

"Oh no — Timmy, why didn't you say so? We should have been here hours ago! Now we'll have to sit way up there!" She waved her hand at the distant balcony, which did appear to have the only seats without people in them.

Tim gawked. "This place is so huge, I never dreamed it would fill up this fast."

"Are you crazy? Sonny and Cher are the hottest thing in the country. Their show's number one, and they've got like five hits on the radio."

"I thought me and Durwood were the only ones who liked them."

"Who's Durwood?"

"Never mind." He rolled his eyes so only I could see.

"I don't care where we sit," said Arnita. "We'll be fine."

We climbed up and up, and kept going up. I didn't look behind us at the dizzying drop. We found four seats together, near the ceiling. The stage was a little white patch, way way down there.

Rachel and Arnita chattered and gossiped like old pals while Tim and I made disparaging remarks about the people climbing up to sit near us. Tim kept leaning around Rachel to talk to me. Finally Rachel said, "Timmy, am I in your way?" and got up to swap seats with him.

Tim said, "Never mind, I'm gonna go take a look around. I'll be back before it starts." He trotted off down the steps toward the ramp.

He was gone quite a while. I entertained the girls with my imitations of Howard Cosell and Muhammad Ali while keeping one eye out for Tim. From the way the stagehands were scurrying around, it looked like the show might start any minute. "I'll go find him." I slid past the girls' knees. "He's gonna miss the beginning."

"Should I go with you?" Arnita said.

"You stay with Rachel. I'll bring him right back."

I leaned to kiss her — a soft kiss on the forehead, innocent as a kiss could be. My lips were still touching her when my eyes met the eyes of the woman four rows above us.

"Would you look at that?" She made no attempt to keep her voice down. "You'd think they'd have the decency not to do that in public!"

"Don't look if it bothers you," said her husband.

"Don't it bother you?" the wife shot back.

I removed my lips from Arnita's face and straightened up.

Arnita smiled. She'd heard every word. "Kiss me again," she whispered.

"Later."

"Why? It's not against the law."

I wasn't trying to make a public statement. I was used to kissing her without thinking about it first.

"I'll be right back," I said, and fled, scattering feathers in my wake.

I ran into Tim at the foot of the ramp.

"Durwood, you're psychic! I was coming to get you!"

"We better get back to our seats. The thing's about to start."

"Not quite yet, there's some comedian that goes on first. Listen, I went exploring. There's something you need to see."

"What is it?"

"I can't explain. Trust me, it is worth the trip." He disappeared down the tunnel.

I caught up with him two levels below, just past the snack bar. "We're gonna miss the show!"

"Would you trust me for once?" He led me to a door marked PRI-VATE DO NOT ENTER, opened it, and pulled me through.

No alarm sounded. No guard came running.

"Where does this go?"

"Guess," he said.

"Somewhere we're not supposed to go."

"Aw come on — ain't you got just a little of that ol' Skippy spirit left in you? Live a little, son. Take a chance! Come out of your hidey-hole!"

"But Tim —"

"My name is not Butt Tim."

I couldn't help smiling. "Excuse me — Butt Face Tim. The girls are waiting for us, and there was this woman behind us —"

"Go back to the girls, then. Or shut up and come on!" He took off in a hurry and I followed, loping fast down hallways, down stairs, through a corridor that curved along the outer wall of the Coliseum.

Passing a cart piled with coils of electrical extension cord, Tim stopped to hoist one onto his shoulder. "You take one too. So it looks like we belong."

The coil was heavier than it looked. I remarked that I made a much more plausible roadie than Tim in his artistic black clothes and piano tie.

"Next time I'll dress like a slob to be on the safe side," he said.

We came to a wide double door with sounds of people on the other side. "If they catch us," I said, "will they kill us?"

"I don't think so. Just give 'em your name, rank, and serial number." He pushed through the door into another hallway. This was a backstage party featuring large hairy bearded men in motorcycle jackets, their skinny girlfriends, oily guys in suits, a sprinkling of flashy women who were dressed not unlike Carol Nason as Mary Magdalene. There were actual tie-dyed hippies with drawstring pants, sandals, mountain man hippie beards, tiny blue-tinted John Lennon specs.

Friends of Sonny and Cher! We never got to see people like this in Mississippi!

Tim hoisted his bundle of cord, nodding hello as we slowly pushed through the throng. The air was thick with smoke and cologne. I tried not to look like an out-of-place kid who is afraid of being discovered and thrown out. I kept patting my coil of cord as if to say, "This electrical cord is urgently needed at a nearby location."

No one noticed us. I followed Tim straight through the party and out the other side. He opened the first door on the left. He waited for me to go in, then followed me.

He got this loopy satisfied grin on his face. "Do you see where we are?"

I saw a mirror framed in lightbulbs, a low dresser, three colossal flower arrangements, and half a dozen large trunks propped open, exploding with spangles, feathers, sequins, capes, hats.

"Her dressing room," he said. "These are her costumes."

"Oh shit — Tim! What the hell? Let's get out of here! What if she —"

"Shh, sh sh sh shhhhh . . . keep it down, Durwood. I want to meet her."

"Are you crazy? What if somebody came in right now, they'd think we're trying to steal something!"

"But we're not. Oh my God, look at this!" He lifted a bejeweled cap from its wig stand. "She wore this when she sang 'My Funny Valentine.' Remember? The week Joe Namath was the guest star?"

"Vaguely. I don't have all the episodes memorized like you."

The walls of the dressing room were draped in fringed paisley silk. A golden cherub dangled on a ribbon beside a bust of Cleopatra with broken-off nipples. There were snapshots of little Chastity taped around the edge of the mirror, and several framed, badly drawn portraits of Cher, obviously given to her by fans whose love for her exceeded their artistic ability. I thought it was nice of her to carry these homely pictures of herself on the road.

"Look at this one." Tim picked up a satin-padded hanger holding two little sparkly strips of sequins.

"Wow. Big earrings."

"Not earrings. It's a costume."

"No way!" I didn't see how those two little bits could cover any significant part of a person. "I'd love to see her put that on."

"Or take it off?" He jiggled the hanger to make the sequins dance. They were still dancing when Cher came through the door.

She wore a plain white T-shirt, tight hip-hugger bell-bottom jeans. She looked stunning with absolutely no makeup. She looked just like herself on TV only taller and younger — a girl, really. Not too much older than us. Long face, striking cheekbones. The most gorgeous tan in the history of skin.

The sight of Tim jiggling her costume stopped her. "Who gave you permission to play with my G-string?"

"Hey, nobody, sorry," Tim stammered, replacing the hanger on the bar. "How you doing?"

"I'm fine — who the fuck are you?"

"Uhm, Tim."

"Are you one of the new kids?"

"Brand-new," he said with a sheepish grin. "And off to a really embarrassing start. Sorry."

"No kidding," she replied. "If this was Son's dressing room and he caught you fucking around with his stuff he would kill you. What are you, a dancer?"

"We're crew," Tim said. "Jimmy told us to bring these extension cords in here, something about a stereo?" He was always so quick with a convincing tale. I hoped there was a Jimmy.

"The idea is for you to set it up before I get here," said Cher. "So I can fuckin' *use* it. Not have the thrill of watching you guys install it." I was impressed how many times Cher had already said the word "fuck."

"Oh, we're not installing it," Tim said. "We just brought the extension cords."

She threw herself down on the sofa. "Okay, fine. Thanks and get out." We were halfway to the door when she said, "Wait a minute. That accent. Are you guys from here?"

Tim said, "Yeah."

"Where are we again?"

"Uhm . . . you mean . . . ?"

"What city is this? Alabama?"

"No, this is Mississippi," Tim said. "Jackson, Mississippi."

"Oh, that's right. God help us. How bad is it here?"

"How bad is what?"

"Don't they hate black people down here? Half my dancers are black, you know. We never used to tour this far south."

"Some people still do," Tim said. "But the ones that do — they wouldn't come to your show, I don't think."

"Oh good," Cher said. "We don't have many racists in California. I didn't know what to expect. I was so afraid we'd run into Bull Connor all over the place, I wouldn't let anybody bring pot on the bus even."

Tim's face lit up. "You like pot? I've got a joint."

I knew Tim had kept smoking it after that first time in the Full Flower elevator, but I never dreamed he would try smuggling it into a concert.

Cher grinned. "Yeah?"

"You want to smoke it?"

"Well, hell yes," she said.

"Cool!" He fished it from his shirt pocket.

Cool was hardly the word. Cher wanted to smoke a joint with us. Never in my wildest dreams! Now of course I had to smoke it. I didn't have a choice. Cher's eyes were remarkable, brown pools of feline intelligence. Just to be in the presence of someone this famous was causing a shrill whistling sound in my ears. My mind marched in circles on this dumb tootling Disney parade, as I floated up out of my body to picture myself standing there with Cher the real live Cher who was talking to Tim and peering over at me me ME ME! All of us people together in the same room!

Cher twiddled the joint between her long fingers. "Can I keep this for later? Is that terrible of me? If I smoke now, I'll forget all the words to the songs. It's not your last dope, is it?"

"No! No!" Tim said. "Keep it! Smoke it with Sonny. Whatever you want!"

I was thinking how smoothly the superstar had just finagled that joint from Tim. She glanced over at me. "Your friend doesn't say much, huh? Boo!"

I'd been happy to stand there like a lump while Tim did all the talking. But now Cher had called upon me to demonstrate my command of English. "Hi," I ventured. "I love how you sing." Oh what an idiot. I cringed, inside and out. Why couldn't I be cool, like Tim? Why did I have to reveal my true moron nature with my first utterance? This is why I hadn't dared open my mouth.

She took mercy upon me with a smile. "You got a name?"

"Daniel. Musgrove." Idiot idiot idiot, the echo resounded throughout the Coliseum.

"You guys aren't crew, right? You're fans. How'd you get back here?"

Tim shot me a look of bottomless disgust. Dumb ol' Daniel gives away the whole show the first time he opens his mouth. "We just kept going through doors, and nobody stopped us," he confessed.

"Only the best security for Sonny and Cher," she said. "I guess I have to have you thrown out now?"

Tim held up a hand. "No, we'll go. Sorry to bother you. Thanks for being so nice."

"Oh, that's okay. You're sweet," she said as if it pained her to admit it. "Are you guys boyfriends?"

"Uhm — no!" Tim was aghast, sputtering. "We're not — you know — we brought girls to the show! They're up in our seats waiting for us!"

"Hey honey, relax, it's okay either way," she said. "Some of my best friends are faggots. *All* of my best friends, actually. But you don't have to be, if you don't want to."

The door flew open with Sonny Bono behind it. "Where the fuck have you been!"

"Don't come in here yelling at me!" she retorted. "This is my dressing room! Get out!"

Sonny Bono wore full stage makeup and a shimmery Nehru-collared shirt, purple stretch pants, white patent-leather boots with five-inch pimp heels. "I'm standing up there by the band thinking we're about to go on, and you're still sitting here in a T-shirt talking to — who the hell is this, the Hardy Boys?"

"My fans," she said with a little wink for us. At least that's what I heard her say. Tim later claimed she said "my favorite fans," but I think he made that up.

That was one of the most thrilling moments of the whole thrilling thing — when she winked at us, then set into fighting with Sonny, not playfully as in the opening of their show, but in deadly earnest. You never heard so many "fuck"s in three minutes. At first I was delighted that they would rip into each other with the two of us watching, then I was appalled, then I began to get the feeling they were used to fighting in front of people. Maybe even liked it. I guess when you're this famous, you need an audience for everything you do.

"I know you like 'em young," Sonny was saying, "but could you please keep your hands off the fifteen-year-olds? You could get us arrested."

"Me? Me?" she protested in that throaty famous voice. "What was her name, in Aspen? The promoter's little girl? Sydney! She really *was* fifteen!"

"I didn't fuck her," he said.

"Only because I stopped you."

"That's right," he said. "If she'd been eighteen, I would definitely have done it before you got there."

"You'll fuck anybody who lets you, Sonny! That's just a fact. You always have, and you always will."

"Fuck you," he said.

"Oh. I am so sick of this!" she moaned. *"Fuck!"* She burst out in a big belly laugh.

Sonny wasn't amused. "Get dressed and be up on that stage in five, or I'll sue you for breach of contract." He slammed the door going out.

It was obvious they had done a lot of fighting. They were good at it. But I thought that was no way for Sonny Bono to treat a great star like Cher. I didn't care what she might have done to him, he didn't have a right to speak to her without respect. He didn't deserve to be married to her.

Tim said, "Wow! What an asshole."

"Shut up!" Cher leaped from the sofa. "He is not an asshole! — yes he is, but who the hell are you to say that?"

"Sorry," Tim said. "Just — he was so nasty to you, and I —"

"What do you know?" she snapped. "You don't know anything. Get out. Get the fuck *out!*"

We got out. We went straight through that door, through the party, through the double doors. We fell upon each other, laughing. It was the most incredible amazing thing that had ever happened to anyone! The adventure of a lifetime! Who would ever believe us?

Tim stopped laughing. "Oh my God, you're right. We don't have any way to prove it. We didn't get an autograph or anything."

"It's okay. We're both witnesses. We know it happened."

"No, we have to go back, Skippy. We need proof."

"Go back? Are you nuts? She'll have us arrested!"

"What — she took my joint but she's too good to give me her autograph? What did I get from her? Nothing!"

I shook my head. "Man, they sure like to cuss, huh? They really hate each other."

"Yeah, it's kinda disappointing," said Tim. We climbed the stairs toward the exit.

Tim had put his finger on it. Disappointing. When they were hollering at each other it seemed slightly out of control, and a little sad. Not that I held any illusions about the enduring love of Sonny and Cher, but their whole act was built on how much fun they had together, in spite of the fact that she was cool and he was a dork. To discover they actually despised each other — what a letdown!

Faintly above us we heard the clamor of the band starting up. "You build somebody up in your mind, you know," Tim said, "and you think, man, I'd love to be them, their life must be so perfect. But she seems miserable. And I don't care what she says, Sonny is a complete asshole."

"Yeah," I said, "she didn't much like it when you pointed that out."

"That was my big mistake. Otherwise I believe she might have taken us with her on the tour bus. Don't you think she was kind of attracted to me, Dagwood?" He smoothed his hair to emphasize his studly appeal.

"Oh yeah," I said. "Definitely."

"Well, Sonny sure did think so — 'Keep your hands off the fifteen-year-olds.' Who do you think he was talking about? Us!" He snapped his fingers. "Damn, I can't believe we didn't get her autograph!"

Neither one of us mentioned the disconcerting moment when Cher asked if we were boyfriends. I almost brought it up to make a joke of it, then decided against it. Maybe it was the way Tim was dressed, all in black with that white satin piano-key tie. Obviously Cher didn't know that in Mississippi that was a pretty dangerous question to ask somebody. Obviously things were different out there in California, where all her friends were.

20

AT FIRST ARNITA and Rachel refused to believe us, but when I described Cher's paisley wall drapings and feather boas spilling from trunks, they got excited and begged us to take them down to meet her.

Too late! The lights suddenly went out. The crowd sent up a huge roar.

Tim was too excited to stay in his seat, and went wandering off again. I wasn't about to miss the start of the show to go looking for him again.

The spotlights converged on one corner of the stage, making a pool of light into which Sonny and Cher suddenly strode, hand in hand. The roar doubled. Sonny Bono threw his hands up as if the noise startled him. Cher waved one lanky arm, and threaded two fingers through her straight, straight hair, her trademark gesture.

A huge projection of Sonny and Cher shone on a giant screen above their heads. In the time it had taken us to climb up from her dressing room, Cher had transformed herself from a great-looking girl in a T-shirt into a bronze goddess, mostly naked, sprayed with diamonds, hundreds of glittering diamonds clustered artfully around the crucial junctures of her body. Beside her, waving, was Mr. Droopy Mustache in his shiny shirt, which was just as lividly purple at a range of one hundred fifty yards. "Hello Mississippi!" he boomed into his mike. "Or should I say 'Mis'sippi'? How you-all doing tonight?"

The crowd roared hello. I wondered why the hell Tim had gone exploring just when they were taking the stage. And he'd been the most excited to see them! Meeting Cher was too much for him. He had to go outside to calm down.

Even from our altitude, it was obvious that Sonny and Cher were barely occupying the same stage. They didn't touch or look at each other. They sang "All I Ever Need Is You" to separate audiences on either side of the Coliseum. They maintained a buffer zone of about ten feet between them at all times.

Some men follow rainbows, I am told . . .

The moment the song ended, Cher left the stage in a cloud of dazzling light and applause. The spotlights narrowed down to Sonny, who dragged out a wooden stool to sit on while he sang "You Better Sit Down, Kids." His voice was so nasal, so blandly unappealing that I knew the truth, once and for all: there would never be a Sonny without Cher.

"Where the heck is Tim?" Rachel said. She had managed to wedge a soda straw through a space in her teeth, at the side, so she could sip from her cup of Tab.

"I was wondering that too," I said. "Maybe he's trying to get closer."

Sonny Bono finished his song, acknowledged the polite applause, and left the stage as Cher reappeared to a loud grateful roar. Now she wore a black leather harness contraption with many straps, buckles, and sequins. She sang "Gypsies, Tramps, and Thieves," and went off to a massive ovation.

Here came Sonny again, hauling that stool from stage left. He sang a song called "Laugh at Me" that I thought was really asking for it, honestly. By now it was clear that Sonny's main function was to stay onstage long enough to give Cher time to change into her next costume. And here she came, in a slinky red-and-silver extravaganza with a V-scoop back that went all the way down to the crack of her ass.

Arnita said, "Didn't they used to sing together? They're not even on the stage at the same time."

"They can't stand each other, can't you tell?" I felt smug, with all my inside information. "He was yelling at her the minute he came in her dressing room."

"And they act so lovey-dovey on TV," she said. "Let's don't ever do that, okay? If you want to break up with me, just tell me. Don't put on some stupid act."

I reached for her hand in the dark. "Okay. But I don't want to break up. Ever."

She leaned in to kiss my cheek. I squeezed her hand and smiled.

Cher's voice sounded like a lovely French horn playing in a lower register.

I saw a man, and he danced with his wife . . .

I was still smiling when the Coke hit me. A twenty-four-ouncer with lots of slushy ice, a big soft paper cup full. It struck at an angle across my neck and sent a geyser of icy soda slopping over me, Arnita, and the kid sitting directly in front of us.

I turned, half expecting to find somebody in the row behind us embarrassed to death about having accidentally dropped a Coke. But the people behind us were turned around too, craning behind them to see who had launched it.

Up there in the dark, I knew, was a woman who hadn't liked me kissing Arnita.

Arnita was way ahead of me, rising from her seat. "Let's get out of here."

"Good idea." I followed her up.

Rachel cried, "Oh my God, you guys are soaked! What happened?"

"We're leaving," I said.

"Leaving? Why?"

"Come on, Rachel. I'll explain it outside."

A brave man would have marched up four rows to where that woman sat. A brave man would have dragged her and her husband out of their seats and addressed the situation in such a way that they would apologize to Arnita, to me, and to the sopping kid in front of us, who was now glaring at me.

"Look, it's not my fault," I told him. "Somebody up there threw a Coke on us, okay?"

He kept glaring as if to say that a brave man would march right on up there and deliver swift retribution. Obviously I was not that man. I was just as much a boy as he was. I was ashamed of my whole species, ashamed of that stupid woman for being so mean, ashamed of myself for my cowardice and for putting Arnita in this situation.

But brave enough to march up there and straighten them out? No. I'd spent my whole childhood learning the First Law of Dad: at the first sign of conflict, flee. Better to get the hell out of there and stay alive. One day when you're stronger maybe you can come back and make a better fight, and win.

We squished down the ramp to the curving corridor around the perimeter. "I can't believe that," Rachel said. "What gave her the idea you two were even together?"

"I kissed her," I said.

"And I kissed him back," Arnita said. "On the cheek."

Rachel frowned. "That's not illegal."

"Probably is, in Mississippi." I blew out a breath. "God, I hate this place! It's always this huge deal over who's black, who's white, who hates who, what's the significance. I'm so sick of it I could puke."

"You're right, Daniel," Arnita said. "That's the only thing people see. The outside layer. It's ridiculous."

She was only trying to agree with me, but for some reason this rubbed me the wrong way. "Oh, you're one to talk! The way you go around trying to confuse everybody."

She jerked back as if I'd slapped her. "What does that mean?"

"What good does it do for you to go around pretending you're white?" I said. "You're not white, okay? You're black. Just face it. Everybody knows it. Including me. *And* you."

"Daniel —"

"If you're not black, why did that woman throw her Coke on us? Huh? Tell me that."

"You don't have to yell," she said. "What happened is not my fault."

"No, it's my fault, for humoring you." The anger in my own voice surprised me. "I thought I could just pretend along with you, and no one would notice us, and everything would be fine."

"You can't help it if other people are stupid," said Rachel.

"No, but at least you can face the truth about yourself," I said. "Instead of making up some fairy tale to make yourself feel better."

Arnita stopped walking. I hadn't counted on her eyes suddenly brimming with tears. "So what is the truth, Daniel? What is it you want me to face?"

"Look, you know I — you know how I feel about you, okay?" I grasped her shoulders. "But you should be over this white thing by now. It's not doing anybody any good. Least of all you."

Her eyes darkened. She pulled away. "God! I really hate it that you felt like you had to humor me. All this time I thought you believed me."

"Wait, now. Don't change what I said."

"You sure waited long enough to tell me what you really think!" she cried.

Rachel cut in. "Y'all, don't take it out on each other, please! It's nobody's fault."

"Butt out, Rachel," I said.

Tim chose that moment to come rushing up. "Where y'all going? I was coming to get you! I found us four amazing seats right down front, on the side!"

"We're leaving," I said. "Some woman threw a Coke at us."

"What?" He gaped at the brownish damp stains all over us. "Why?"

"Let's just go, okay? I don't want some confrontation." My mind was racing even faster than my pulse. I set off at a determined pace toward the exit doors. Halfway there I realized I was walking alone.

It was a long walk back to where they stood. Rachel was explaining the situation to Tim.

"It was a twenty-four-ouncer, I think," I said. "Had to be. It was full too."

Tim snickered. "That's kind of hilarious."

"No, it's not."

"Maybe not right this minute," he said, "but in about ten minutes it will be."

"You know, Tim," said Arnita, "everything is not funny."

He peered at her oddly, as if she were insisting the sun had just turned into the moon. "Sure it is," he said. "Everything is funny all the time."

That was as plain a statement of the First Law of Tim as you'll ever hear. Everything is funny. As long as it's funny, it doesn't have to matter. As long as you're laughing, you don't have to care. And of course who was the one always laughing up a storm beside him? The other half of the Laff Team?

Tim said, "Y'all can leave if you want. I'm going back in to watch."

"We can't leave," I said. "We came in your car."

He shrugged. "So calm down, come back in, enjoy the show."

"I'm sopping wet, Tim," said Arnita. "I want to go home." I'd never heard that particular chill in her voice.

Tim said, "Well go, then. Nobody's stopping you."

She turned to me. "Will you take me home, please?"

"It's not my car! Timmy, look, we're wet, and we're mad, and the whole thing's kind of ruined anyway. You're not even watching the show. You're out here."

"I'd be in there right now, but I'm standing here talking to you," he said in his most reasonable tone.

Rachel spoke up. "Timmy, they want to go home."

"Oh, you too? Good, y'all can split a taxi three ways! My God, people, you're all overreacting! Whatever happened is over. Nobody's going to lynch you, Arnita. They probably dropped the Coke by accident. God!"

I glanced at Arnita, who was glancing at me. We caught each other thinking the same thing.

She pinned Tim against the concrete block wall while I dug my fingers in his pocket and yanked out his keys. "Come on, girls, I can drive!" I danced back out of his reach.

He lunged at me. I tossed the keys to Rachel, who lobbed them at Arnita. We played keep-away, zigzagging back and forth all over the corridor. Tim got the keys away from Rachel, but I wrestled them from his hand and ran a swift wideout pattern to the exit doors. By the time I made a miraculous Hail Mary pass to Arnita, everybody was laughing but Tim.

"Give 'em back," he said. "Give 'em *here!*"

Rachel cried, "Oh shut up, Timmy!" through locked teeth.

"Fuck off!" he barked. "Don't you tell me to shut up!"

Her smile dissolved. She cast her eyes down.

Tim whirled on Arnita. "Give me those keys!"

She said, "Here," and put them in his hand.

Her surrender caught him completely off guard. I'd never seen him beaten so easily. At once he switched to begging. "Can't we go in for one more song, please please please? Pretty please? One song, then we'll go."

I longed to go in with him. The truth was, we had been looking forward to this show a long time. And now we were here, we'd been chased out of Cher's dressing room by Cher herself — did we have to miss the rest of this historic evening because of one idiotic woman in the audience?

"Maybe one song," I said.

Arnita's eyes registered my change of attitude. "Oh. Now you want to stay?"

"Just for one song. Don't you think that sounds fair?"

"You stay, then," she said. "I'll find a way home."

I took her arm. "No. I'll go with you. I mean, just — tell me what you want me to do."

She didn't say anything. Her eyes stayed on me, waiting for me to decide.

"Rachel, you'll stay with me and watch the show, won't you?" Tim said.

Rachel shrugged. "You're the one with the car." She hadn't looked up from her shoes since he told her to fuck off.

I had stood by all evening watching Tim pretending to be nice to Arnita. All the time I could see through his act. Every glance, every seemingly offhand quip, was a little arrow aimed at her. It was only now that I recognized his master plan for the evening. He wanted me to choose him over Arnita, and he wanted me to make that choice in front of her. He hated Arnita, the space she was taking up in my life. His best friend was not supposed to have other friends, especially not some girl.

I had the fleeting thought that Tim was nowhere near his seat when that woman supposedly threw the Coke at us. It occurred to me that he might even have been the one who threw it — I could believe that. That's how much he hated Arnita.

I didn't care for that smile of satisfaction when he thought he had me talked into staying. I had to wipe that smile off his face. "Enjoy the show, Timmy. Rachel, take care. Arnita, let's go." I took her hand and led her toward the exit.

She dropped my hand. "No, Daniel, why don't you stay, and I'll call Jimmy to come get me in the taxi."

"Oh, we're definitely calling Jimmy, how else are we gonna get home?"

I couldn't resist looking back. Tim and Rachel were watching us. Tim said something to Rachel and they started toward us.

"Look, he's changed his mind," I said. "Now he'll offer to drive us, but it'll be our fault he has to miss the concert."

"Fine with me," she said. "As long as I get home."

Tim came up with his arms folded across his chest. "I guess we can go. It's kind of a dud anyway. Sonny Bono sucks so bad."

We were almost to Minor before Tim announced we were missing the show of a lifetime and it was all my fault.

I was ready for him. "If you hadn't been up walking around, you wouldn't have missed the first half of it, which you did without any help from anybody. So just shut up."

"I didn't miss it. I was right down in front, to the side of the speakers. Where we could be sitting right now."

Rachel was riding shotgun in silence. In the back, Arnita sat beside me just as silent. When I touched her hand, she moved her whole body closer to the door.

It was summer and no air-conditioning, but it was cold in that car.

"Look, Arnita, I told you the truth," I said. "Would you rather have me keep lying to you?"

"No, thank you," she said politely.

When in doubt, I thought, try funny. "Why do I get the feeling this has turned into, like, the worst date of all time?"

"Not even close," Tim put in. "Are you forgetting Prom Night?"

How cavalierly he introduces the subject! What a delicate touch! He picks the thinnest ice in the world and goes skating on out there, doing high jumps and double axels.

"Oh come on, not that," I said.

"Why not?" In the rearview I saw his eyes dancing. "That was Arnita's big night! You've never told her about your encounter with a certain seat belt that shall remain nameless?"

"Leave it alone, Tim," I warned.

Sure enough, he had tickled her interest. "What happened? Tell me, Tim."

"Well first, on the way to the prom, your boyfriend gets a nosebleed and gets himself stuck in the seat belt in the back of my dad's Buick, and he can't get out." Tim's eyes flicked from mirror to road and back to us in the mirror. "We had to cut the belt to get him out. [*We!*] Skippy bleeding like a stuck pig. With a Maxi Pad up his nose. Talk about funny — now *that* was funny."

"Okay, enough," I said.

"No, Daniel, let me hear this," Arnita said. "You always want to talk about what happened to me that night. I've never heard a word about you."

Rachel said, "Timmy, can we just go home now? Let's talk about something else!"

"No, Arnita wants to hear this, and we have to give her everything she wants." He flashed his gregarious smile. "Isn't that the deal?"

He blamed me for making us leave the concert. So now he would have his revenge through Arnita. He would do what he'd wanted to do all along: break us up and get rid of her.

I couldn't think of a single way to stop him other than to grab the wheel, swerve into a telephone pole, and kill us all. I saw right through to the end of what he wanted to do, and there was nothing I could do about it. That's how helpless I was, how strongly in his thrall.

He switched off the radio. "What Arnita wants," he said, "is the truth. The whole truth and nothing but. And really, Skippy, does she deserve anything less?"

I had the sensation my whole life was flash-frozen in place, suddenly brittle, about to shatter into ten million pieces. I fought to keep my voice even. "Do you know what you're doing?"

"Oh, I do." He grinned. "What you used to nag me to do. 'It's the right thing, Timmy, it's the only honest thing.' You want to do the honors? Or you want me to?"

"Tim, don't."

"I guess that means me," he said. "Arnita. We were on Barnett Street on Prom Night. We saw you talking to Red Martin. He was hassling you. You fell off your bike, and he drove off. Left you there on the ground. Daniel and I stopped to help. You didn't want to have anything to do with us, you were kinda drunk. I wanted to drive along with you, make sure you got home. But Skippy here grabbed the wheel, and . . . you hit us. You ran into our bumper. That's when you fell and hit your head."

It was such a simple story. He told it just that fast, and it was over.

Arnita squeezed her eyes shut. "That's not how it was," she said.

"We didn't stop to help you," Tim said. "We drove to a pay phone and called an ambulance. We came back, to see if they showed up. But we didn't stop."

"Why not?" She opened her eyes but she wouldn't look at me.

"We were scared," Tim said. "We thought they would blame us. They had Red, they weren't looking for us. So we just went home."

When I had pictured this confession it was always me doing the confessing, and Tim trying to stop me.

Rachel said, "Y'all, please cut it out."

Arnita turned to face me. "Daniel?"

You cannot imagine how quiet it can be in a Starlite Blue Pinto speeding down I-20.

My voice scraped in my throat. "I was scared too."

"You looked dead," Tim said. "We thought you were dead."

She winced. "So the part I remember — with Red —"

"That was the first time you fell. The second time is when you got hurt."

She looked straight into my eyes. "You were there, and you never told me?"

I felt a desperate urge to make up a new story, try to blow some air back into our old deflated Lie. But what good would that do? In the end it was just me and Arnita, and the truth I had to tell her.

"That's right," I said.

She hugged her own arms. "And you let Ella go on pestering them until they arrested Red Martin."

I rested my face on my hands. "We didn't care about Red," I said. "He's an asshole. We were glad they arrested him. It was justice for what he did to us in school."

"No it wasn't," Tim put in. "That didn't even begin to count as justice. He still has to pay."

Her eyes wouldn't let me go. "Is that why you came to our house? And did all those chores?"

I pictured Ella Beecham shaking her finger at me. *Musgrove!*

"Your mother knew the truth," I said. "She saw right through me. That's why she made me do all those things. It was like a payback."

"That's why you were nice to me? And helped me with my homework and spent all that time, and took me for walks, and . . . ?"

"At first it was." I tried so hard to tell the truth now, as if it might make up for the Lie. "But then it changed. I got to know you. I fell in love with you. You've got to believe me."

"No." Suddenly she was crying. "How can I believe you? You're a liar."

There! Call the devil by his name!

I was hoping she would not cry. When she cried, everything began to fall apart. She didn't love me anymore. How could she? She had trusted me and I had betrayed her from the very first day. It was as if we had come together to build something incredibly complicated, an elaborate model of a city skyline with hundreds of intricate nuts and bolts and connections. And then she started crying. And the tiny parts holding everything together dissolved, and our beautiful city collapsed.

Tim was watching me in the mirror. His eyes looked satisfied.

"Stop the car," said Arnita.

"Keep going," I said.

"Aw, come on," Tim said. "We're almost to Minor."

"Stop it, I said! Let me out of here now!"

"Whatever you say." He applied brakes and swerved onto the shoulder, skidding to a stop in loose gravel. Car horns bent and blared around us.

"Tim, don't stop here," I said.

Arnita said, "Rachel, let me out."

"Please wait," I said. "Give me a chance to explain."

Rachel got out, flipped the seat forward. Arnita launched herself out the door. I scrambled after her.

She tottered down the edge of the highway in her heels, outlined in the Pinto's headlights.

"Arnita, wait!"

"Get back in the car!" she cried. "Don't you come near me!"

Cars whipped past at high speed, flinging up bits of gravel, lashing us with gusts of turbulence. Arnita turned to face the traffic. My God, she was beautiful as she stuck out her thumb.

"Let us take you home!" I cried. "Hitchhiking is dangerous!'

A big white Lincoln flashed its brake lights and pulled to the shoulder. A Continental Mark IV Brougham with the fake spare tire inset in the trunk lid. Arnita took off her shoes and ran lightly across the gravel to meet it.

I chanted the license plate to memorize it: 30L4340. *Thirty L, forty-three forty.*

The driver leaned to open the passenger door. Arnita said something to him, and hopped in the front seat. The car scratched off. She never looked back.

21

I MADE TIM FOLLOW the white Continental all the way to East Minor. We watched Arnita jump out and hurry to the porch. Lincoln Beecham came to open the door. She pushed past him and went in.

Nobody in the car said a word until we had dropped Rachel at her house. Tim backed the Pinto into the street. "Now Durwood, I know what you're going to say, so don't say it."

"What am I going to say?"

"I was horrible, I was reckless, I've put us in danger," he said in a mincing little-girl voice, his imitation of me. "If she goes to the cops now, we both go to jail."

"You don't get it at all," I said. "Arnita won't do that. She's a really good person, unlike you — or me. She'll tell her mother she's not sure anymore. They'll drop the charges against Red."

"That's what you were gonna say?"

"No, Tim. I got nothing to say to you."

"Aw come on, Skippy . . ."

"You don't have to drop me off anywhere. I'll get out at the next corner."

"Aw Skipperino, don't be that way." He reached out as if to tousle my hair.

I knocked his hand away. "Don't touch me."

"You know something, Skippy? Let you in on a little secret. You're better off without her. You really are."

"I didn't realize till tonight how much you hate her."

"I don't hate her," he said. "She's cute. I see why you like her. She sure is wild about you."

"Not now," I said. "You took care of that."

"Nah — she'll get over it. Give her time. Before you know it she'll be sweet on you again, you watch."

"Not a chance. You wanted to kill it, and you did. Did that make you happy?"

Tim chewed his little finger. "What choice did I have? She's in love with you, son. Anybody could see that from ten miles away. All of a sudden I realized, you don't have to put on this act anymore. You've done a great job getting close to her, but it's not necessary now. You've got her so crazy about you she'll never turn us in, not even now when she knows everything. She's in love."

"That's not why you did it."

"I had to do something! Or else what, you keep getting more and more mixed up with her? One of these days she finds out the whole thing anyway — and then look out. Or were you gonna try to keep it a secret forever?"

"That's what you promised. What you made me promise."

He grinned. "Ah, but don't it feel good to get it off your chest?" He thumped his breastbone like Tarzan, to illustrate how good it felt.

We were idling at the Dairy Dog corner in a line of cars, waiting for the light to change. No time like the present when it comes to opening a door and stepping out.

"Skippy, where are you — hey! Get back in the car!"

I dodged a pickup truck and ran across the road. I didn't care whether he followed me or not.

I didn't let myself look back until I was all the way across the parking lot. The Pinto's taillights disappeared up Minor Boulevard.

*   *   *

BAM. I THOUGHT it was Dad's hand smacking the thin wall between our rooms, but no, it was dark, the TV off, Janie curled up on the other twin bed. Someone pounding on the door. I stumbled to answer it.

Barely dawn out. Tim looked alarmed and wide-awake. He still wore his black clothes from the concert. "That is some weird news, huh Skippy. Did you get the call?"

"What call?"

"Eddie Smock killed himself," he said.

"Oh my God. No way."

"Night before last."

"How?"

"He hung himself," Tim said. "Passworth said he was blue when they found him. They tried to revive him, but he died in the ambulance."

I didn't have to ask why Eddie might want to do such a thing.

It must be the worst thing in the world, to feel so low you just want to die.

But I guess there are worse things. Like being suddenly revealed to the world as a queer. The kind who makes desperate phone calls to boys. Eddie decided he would rather die than be known as one of those. So would I. So would any self-respecting boy in Mississippi.

The door to Room 30 flew open. Dad was a fearsome sight in his sagging Fruit of the Looms. "What the hell is this!"

"Oh hey, Mr. Musgrove. Sorry to wake you up."

"Who the hell are you?"

"That's Tim," I said. "You know. My best friend?"

"Sorry to wake y'all up, sir," Tim said. "It's just — this guy from the show we were doing for Full Flower Baptist? He died."

"What you mean, died?"

"He killed himself."

"Well for pity's sake," Dad said, "it's five-thirty in the morning. Can't it wait a couple of hours?"

"No sir, see, the funeral's today, way up in the Delta. And his mother, Miz Smock? She wants us guys from the show to be his pallbearers. We gotta leave in like an hour to make it up there in time."

"Well, come back in an hour, then." Dad moved to close the door.

Tim stopped it with his foot. "No sir, but see, first we have to go to Full Flower to get our costumes. Eddie's mother wants us to wear the costumes from the show."

Dad looked from Tim to me, trying to decide who annoyed him more. He settled on me. "Get your clothes on and go. Don't wake up your sister." He slammed the door.

"Whoa," Tim said. "What's with Mr. Personality?"

"Shh — he can still hear you."

"Sorry," he said. "But I mean, God."

I changed the subject. "What does a pallbearer do?"

"We carry the coffin. I think that's about it."

"She really asked for us?" I said. "We barely even know Eddie."

"Yep. And she insists on the costumes. Passworth was real clear on that. My damn mother promised her I'd pick 'em up, so there's no way we can bail out now."

The costumes! Now I was awake enough to recognize the implications of that. "Oh no. Tim. Oh God, no."

"I know, Skip. It's gonna be bad. But what can we do? It's his mom. Her son is dead."

He was right. If Eddie Smock's mother had asked us to carry his coffin (his *coffin!*) the least I could do was go carry it.

Poor Eddie.

The sun was still trying to rise when we met Alicia Duchamp's mother in the Full Flower parking lot. We transferred eight costumes in dry-cleaning plastic from her trunk to the back of the Pinto. Mrs. Duchamp insisted on giving us a hug (soft, plump, a whiff of baby powder) and five dollars for doughnuts. We took the money straight to Krispy Kreme, ate a dozen glazed in the store, and bought two dozen to go. We inhaled those doughnuts like the weightless sugar-drenched french fries they were. To wash them down we bought huge Cokes — the size of the one that hit me in the neck at Sonny and Cher.

Soon we were buzzing north out of Jackson on a bumpy old two-lane. At first I didn't say much. "Look, about last night," Tim said.

"Don't talk to me about last night." I turned to face him. "I'm here because Eddie is dead and we have to go do this. That's all. If you want to get through this day, just leave it alone."

"Ooh, Skippy," he said, mock-impressed. "You're still royally pissed, huh."

"It's beyond that. You — you're just amazing, Tim. The things you will do. Is there anything you won't do?"

"Not really. If you want something, you have to do what it takes to get it."

"You wanted Arnita to get out on the side of the interstate?"

"That was her choice."

"You wanted her to hate me? You wanted — no. No. Just forget it. We can't talk about her."

"That's probably a good idea," he said.

"But can I ask you one thing?"

"Why not?"

"That night up in Itta Bena. When Eddie made those calls. Why didn't he call our room?"

"I don't know," he said. "Never thought about it. Maybe we weren't his type."

"He called all the other boys, right?"

"I don't know. Did he?"

"I didn't hear our phone ring that night, did you?"

"No. I slept through the whole thing, remember?"

"But then . . . when did you put on your shoes?" I said.

"What?"

It was a small detail. I had not paid much attention when I first noticed it. I put it away and meant to forget it. But it kept nagging at me, like a gnat at the corner of my eye. "When you came back from the bathroom, you had on your shoes. But you took them off before you went to bed."

"Did you see the floor in that bathroom? It was filthy." He watched me carefully. "Why do you ask, oh great Durwood?"

"Just wondering."

"No, tell me. You know the rule: if you think it, you have to say it."

I faked a grin. "I just had to find out if you really are so neurotic you would put on your shoes just to go pee."

He smiled. "Ah, I get it. You think I went out that night? Why would I go out?"

"I don't know. You tell me."

"You think Eddie called our room and I went over to his room? Is that what you're trying to say?"

"No," I lied.

He grinned. "You are so chock full o' shit, Skippy. Is that what you've been doing since we got back? Putting this whole scheme together in your busy little brain? Here's what I did that night, wanna hear? I went to bed. I went to sleep — after you quit talking my head off. When I woke up, you told me they were taking Eddie away for making dirty phone calls. That's it, buddy boy — that right there is the entire extent of my involvement in the conspiracy. Now what kind of a moron does that make you?"

He was an excellent liar. Better than ever.

"You know, if you've got a problem," I said, "there are people you can talk to about it. That's all I'm gonna say."

He winced. "Oh, okay. I'm fucked up. What are you saying, I should see a shrink?"

"You could."

"I went once, okay? The woman was an idiot. She was evil. All she did was ask the same question over and over, how does that make you feel, how does that make you feel. Like killing you, lady! Dammit! We better not talk about this either." He sighed. "Man, I'm telling you. If you live up here, you better like it flat."

He switched on the radio. "Jungle Boogie" jumped out of the speakers, *Get down tonight bay-beh!* It was the right song at the wrong time. He switched it off again and fished a joint from the glove compartment. "Didn't y'all's worldly goods burn up around here somewhere?"

"Not here. Highway 61. Just south of Greenville." I didn't like to think about that day.

Tim took a hit off the joint and offered it to me. I declined. If Cher was not around I wanted no part of his drugs.

"Your family, Dagwood, I don't know," he said. "Talk about weird. First you got all your stuff burned up, then your house explodes, then there's spooky old Jacko, and now you're all living in the Gandhi Motel . . . some people might say that situation's a little crazy too, but I don't hassle you about it. Do I?"

"What are you talking about?"

He was furious. "I don't like you saying I'm fucked up. Okay? I don't like it. I'm fine. My problems are none of your business, okay? There's nothing wrong with my family — it's not like at your house. Sorry. Your *motel room*. Can you imagine if my mother had to spend one night in that place? She'd be up all night with the Lysol and the bleach."

"Okay, Tim, you're fine. If you say so. It's just — I don't like what you did to me."

"I said I was sorry for last night," he said.

"When did you say that? No, you didn't!"

"I say it a lot, but you never listen. I swear to God, Dagwood, I keep no secrets from you. I tell you everything. But all I get from you is these questions, these goddamn ultimatums, all these holy fucking speeches about what an asshole I am. Okay, I can take it. I may even deserve some of it. But give me a break! Fuck! We're going to his funeral, right? I'm driving us up there and paying for the gas! What more do you want?"

"I want you to shut up and drive," I said.

"You shut up."

"Fine! I will!" I folded my arms.

He turned on the radio, cranked the volume, and puffed his joint. I rolled down the window to let the wind suck the smoke out. We kept up our sullen silence through a string of dinky towns. Outside Parchman we passed the gate of the Mississippi State Penitentiary, the prison sprawling beyond a cotton field speckled with black men in white jumpsuits. From a distance they didn't look like people, just white coveralls with black specks for faces, broiling under the sun. I bet every last one of those men was sorry to be where he was.

My own skin was sticking to the vinyl seat. The Pinto had a perfectly good air conditioner, but Tim refused to turn it on because his father told him it put a strain on the engine.

"Of course it puts a strain on it, that's what an engine is for," I said. "To strain, and work hard, and make us cool. That's why they put A/C in cars, by the way. So you can turn it on when it's nine hundred degrees out, and not die."

He sighed. "Let's just bury this son of a bitch and try not to get on each other's nerves, okay? People survived for many years before air-conditioning. You're not going to die."

We drove into the town of Tutwiler, to the Kool 'N' Kreemy drive-in, where we found Passworth and the *Christ!* boys waiting for us — six guys in a parental-brown Ford LTD. They looked about as miserable as I felt. They were Ted, Mark, Evan, Sam, and two Steves I could never quite tell apart. We shook hands and stood around quizzing each other about our prior funeral experience.

Take it from me, any seventeen-year-old boy would rather stick nails in his eyes than go to a funeral. Death is so far from your plans at seventeen that a funeral seems silly, a meaningless ritual, something for old folks to obsess about. Accidents happen. People get old and die. Big deal. A lot of stupid fuss about nothing. Stick 'em in the ground and move on.

Mrs. Passworth was a vision in a shapely black suit, tiny black hat, filmy Jackie Kennedy veil blurring her face. She gripped a Kleenex, and her eyes were shining already — you could tell she was going to be crying a lot today. "Hello, boys, thank you for coming. Eddie's mother will be so grateful."

We mumbled politely, you're welcome and oh God please strike us dead, take us out of here, God, take me first! I expected everything from that point forward to be awful, and mostly it was, but first we got Kool 'N' Kreemy burgers and fries, which turned out to be the best in the world.

Passworth instructed Tim to hand out our costumes. He was busy talking to Sam, and tossed me the keys. I opened the Pinto's hatchback. The boys crowded around, grabbing up hangers.

On the bottom I found our Combo outfits in clear plastic. Lifting them out, my hand snagged a corner of a brown blanket —

A glimpse of polished wood. I tugged back the blanket to find the last thing I ever expected in Tim's car: a double-barreled shotgun, a hunting rifle, and eight or nine boxes of ammunition.

I pulled the blanket back over them before anybody noticed.

Lots of guys in Minor were hunters. I'd gone out with .22s with Bud at Granny's place, shooting at (and mostly missing) squirrels and doves. But I'd never heard Tim mention guns.

I couldn't ask him about it with the other guys crowding around, complaining about the costumes. Two by two, we went into the Kool 'N' Kreemy men's room to change. Tim and I lucked out with the Combo outfits, which looked normal compared to some others.

Tim said, "Get a load of Evan Livingstone." Evan looked terribly hot in his black wool Mafia suit with sunglasses and angel wings sprouting from his back. The other boys looked cooler but no less uncomfortable. Good thing Matt Smith wasn't there — I didn't think I could handle another vision of Jesus in his wedding dress.

We mobbed Passworth, begging her please don't make us do this, please let us wear our own clothes. "This is Eddie's mother's request," she said. "Do you want to disappoint her? On the day she's burying her son?"

We really wouldn't mind that, but no one had the nerve to say so.

"Of course not. You all look adorable." She straightened her hat. "There's no church part, we're meeting at the graveside. You go to a town called Longstreet, go left, and it's supposed to be six point two miles up that road. Just follow me."

Tim asked Evan and Sam to ride with us. Before we could even get back in our cars, Passworth shot off in her Nova. Watching her at the overhead projector day after day, you would never imagine Mrs. Passworth drove like the road was on fire. Her dust was still floating in the air at the crossroads of Longstreet long minutes after she'd passed. By the time we rolled up to the church, she was already out of her car bossing the funeral director around.

This was a pretty little graveyard, in the exact geographical center of nowhere. A falling-down country church, formerly white. Tottery headstones, a rusty iron fence. A green funeral canopy with scalloped edges. A hole and a pile of bright red dirt, which a man was presently concealing with a roll of green felt. Another funeral guy came to greet us, a barrel-chested man in a black suit. "You must be my pallbearer corps."

We said, Yes, we were.

"Thanks for coming, men. And thank you for the service you're doing for your friend today."

He introduced himself as Freeman Gillion. He gave us a quick course in the art of pallbearing. "Lift with your knees, not your back. If you feel yourself losing it, just say 'I'm out' and step out. No one will think any less of you. When you've recovered, you can step in again. It's all a matter of balance. And don't lock your knees. I've seen lots of strong men keel over doing that."

"How heavy is it gonna be?" said Ted Herring.

"Heavier than you think. Mr. Smock only weighs one forty-five, but this casket is the Heavenly Vision — that's three hundred fifty pounds of solid bronze. That's why we needed eight of you — although y'all are big men, six could probably handle it. Never hurts to have a couple extra on a hot day."

Mr. Gillion was that rare grownup who can tell you what to do without making you feel dumb for not knowing. I liked him for calling us "men."

"You should feel proud to be associated with a funeral of this quality," he said. "His family asked for nothing but the best, and brother, they got it — we're talking forty-eight-ounce bronze with a natural brush finish and cream velvet interior. Top of the line. It costs a good deal more, but the thing about bronze is, the casket itself will never erode."

We received this information with the awed silence it deserved. Mr. Gillion thanked us again, and went to check the placement of chairs at the graveside.

"I think I'm dying," Tim said. "Or maybe I died and this is what hell is like."

"Aw, he was okay," I said.

The day had started hot and gotten hotter, and now, at the peak of the afternoon, the sky was bleached white, the sun beating its heavy hammer on us. The Steves were a couple of sweaty cowpokes, and poor Evan was melting in his Mafia suit. It was a relief when the long black hearse came gliding into the churchyard, followed by a fleet of shiny black limousines, one after the other.

I'd never seen so many limousines. Eddie would have loved it. And he would have loved our costumes, and our misery at having to wear them.

Mr. Gillion formed us into lines at the back of the hearse. I peeked at the bronze casket, polished and sleek with rounded corners, like a fat gleaming cigarette lighter.

Dozens of Smocks spilled from the limousines. I recognized Eddie's mother from some of the *Christ!* rehearsals. It is simply being truthful to say that Mrs. Smock was a piggy-looking woman, very plump with a pig nose, pink cheeks, and a flushed pink complexion. Today she was jammed into formidable foundation garments and a black dress. Her plump calves were cinched at both ends, like sausages.

Eddie's father must have been the pale white-haired man clinging to her arm. He appeared to be not so much aging as collapsing.

From the corner of my eye I saw Tim looking at me, barely repressing hilarity. If I made any kind of face at this moment, he would crack up. I frowned and turned away. I'm not sure which part he found funny — the snuffling relatives, the sirenlike wail of Eddie's mother at her first glimpse of the open hole, the eight of us in our preposterous getups, or all of it in combination.

I worked to make my face as sober as the funeral director's. I forced myself to picture Eddie's dead body, embalmed and powdered inside that gleaming box.

Imagine being borne to your grave by an assortment of cowboys, Mafia angels, hippie Combo players, and ancient shepherds from the Holy Land. Some of the mourners looked quizzical, but mostly the women took one look at us and broke down in tears.

They must have thought we were Eddie's closest friends, we mourned his passing so deeply that we wore these costumes in tribute to him.

The whole thing gave me the willies. I prayed for it to be over fast.

We walked Eddie's casket out of the hearse on its rollers, and Christ! the thing was heavier than I thought, heavier even than Mr. Gillion had promised. I saw veins pop out on Ted Herring's neck. Behind me, Tim groaned.

Mr. Gillion's voice was inaudible to everyone but us. "Fellas all right?"

We grunted, desperately scraping our shoes in search of a solid foothold.

Mr. Gillion counted us off and we began to move. See the people get out of our way! Pick up a casket and watch how they open up a path for you!

I stood on the right side, second from the back, with Mark and Ted ahead and Tim behind me on the corner. It felt like I was lifting the thing myself. We lurched across thirty yards of uneven ground, around headstones, toward the tent. Above the sounds of our struggle I heard the insistent *zizz* of insects in the woods.

Suddenly, right in front of me, Ted Herring said, "I'm out," and stepped clear. The load on our side seemed to double. (Mr. Gillion was wrong — immediately I thought less of Ted.) The casket sagged — I braced it against my hip, gripped the slippery rail, and hung on for dear life. I had a clear vision of the box thudding to the ground, the lid popping open, and dead Eddie rolling out into the dirt.

"Steady . . ." Tim strained at the corner.

Freeman Gillion stepped in to help. The casket leveled out. We moved under the tent. It was tricky walking that close to the hole without slipping in. "Right here, hold it," said Gillion. A mechanical whirr as the elevator rose to meet the bottom of the casket. "Excellent job, gentlemen. Thank you."

We were sweating into our costumes now. We formed a line opposite the chairs for Eddie's family. Funeral men moved in with a blanket of roses for the coffin. The other mourners crowded around the tent.

Oh please no, here came Mrs. Smock and her shaky husband, determined to greet each pallbearer personally. All dressed in black, coming down the row, grasping each boy's hand for a word, Mrs. Smock worked the reception line like Queen Elizabeth. Mr. Smock even looked a bit like Prince Philip, pale and gray, receding into the background.

And now she was pressing my hand. "What's your name, child?"

"Daniel Musgrove."

"Daniel, thank you so much for coming, and for being such a good friend to Eddie. He loved you so much."

"Thank you." She didn't mean it that way, but it creeped me out. I wondered if she had any idea of the real story on Eddie.

Mr. Smock put his weightless hand in mine and murmured, "Thank you, son, thank you kindly."

Beside me, Mrs. Smock took Tim's hand. "And your name?"

"Tim Cousins."

"Well, Tim, thank you, it would have meant so much to Eddie," said Mrs. Smock. "I hope you know how much he loved you."

"Thank you," Tim said. "Sorry he died."

Mrs. Smock moved on. I released the breath I'd been holding.

Funeral men handed out hymn sheets still fragrant with mimeograph fluid. A minister with a glistening pompadour came to the head of the coffin and raised his arms. I admired his elaborate robe with all that piping and cording, around his shoulders a stole in immaculate Ole Miss red and white. There was something familiar about him — was he the preacher at that Methodist church Mom dragged me to once?

When he opened his mouth and began to intone, I realized this was Jacko's favorite Sunday-morning TV preacher, the Reverend

Alfred L. Poole, the curdle-voiced pastor of the Faith Holiness Tabernacle in Vicksburg, Mississippi!

I nudged Tim to see if he recognized the man. I froze when I realized I was gazing directly into Mrs. Passworth's eyes. She was gazing at me and crying as bitterly as Eddie's mother.

"The Lowered hath called our dear servant Edwin, Baskin, Smock to his heavenly home," the reverend announced. "O Lowered, we cry out to thee. Why take one so young and full of life, when there are so many who are elderly and infirm? It does not seem fair, dear Gaud! We cry out to thee for a balm in Gilead to heal our souls, which are forever infested with sin."

Mrs. Smock sobbed against her gray husband's shoulder.

"Now let us join together," the preacher advised, "in singing the praise of his name. Hymn 153, 'I Saw One Hanging on a Tree.'"

This brought a fresh burst of weeping from the ladies. I wondered what Reverend Poole was thinking when he selected it, or if he even knew how Eddie died.

> *I saw One hanging on a tree, in agony and blood,*
> *Who fixed His languid eyes on me as near His cross I stood.*

I didn't think it was very comforting, but then, I wasn't the one being comforted. Thank God Reverend Poole was preaching with his back to us, which helped keep me from exploding.

Everything is funny all the time. I swear, Tim must have thought those words at that moment, so clearly did I hear his voice speaking in my head. I turned. His eyes were fixed on some point in the distance — his lip trembling from the effort of holding it in.

"Merciful is our Father, and ever-mysterious his ways," said the Reverend. "Let us join together in all-comforting prayer. Dear heavenly Father, why hast thou called home thy beloved child, Edwin, Baskin, Smock?"

He preached about the unfairness of it all, the youthful innocence and religious zeal that led Edwin, Baskin, Smock to his service in "the creation of theatrical productions for Christian youth, including these fine young people here with us today," he said, sweeping his hand in our direction. He said Eddie had spent his life working tirelessly to improve the conditions of those less fortunate, although he didn't give any examples. He said Eddie was bound for glory, and the good die young. He said God's ways are revealed on the journey down a darkling path of tribulations our natures have yet to subsume, and a bunch more stuff along that line. He said Eddie was a "born Christian, as opposed to a born-again Christian. He didn't need to be born again — Gaud got it right the first time!"

I thought that was laying it on a bit thick.

"Edwin may have had some difficulties with his thought life, as do many young people on the perilous road to maturity," said the reverend, "but his soul was as pure and unmuddied as a crystalline spring."

The reverend mopped his face with a handkerchief and introduced "a dear friend of Edwin's who has requested time to address you about his most cherished personality traits. Mrs. Irene Passworth."

She smiled and tossed her head walking to the front, as if we were applauding. Had to hand it to Passworth, she did look spectacular in black. She wore these huge Italian movie star sunglasses, wider than her face.

She touched her fingertips to her lips as if to blow a kiss, but she didn't. "I just wonder if any of us really knew the truth about Eddie," she said. "Personally I didn't have a clue. Did you? I never guessed what he was. It seems like, my heavens, we were his family and friends. Shouldn't one of us have seen this coming? Don't get me wrong, I'm not blaming anyone more than myself. I spent a lot of time with Eddie lately. Looking back I can see all the signs I missed. How badly I failed him. But not just me. We all failed him. All of us."

I glanced over to see Mrs. Smock drilling holes in Passworth with those beady eyes. Reverend Poole's glazed smile betrayed a trace of unease.

"I haven't been able to sleep since I heard the news," she went on.

"I've been stripping off these layers of old wallpaper in my front room. It's so thick, why, there must be twenty or thirty layers of old paper on there. Then of course when I got the call, I had to leave it like that, a big mess and not even half done. I mean, I just flew to the hospital. Thinking I could help Eddie somehow. But that was silly. It was way too late to help Eddie. I missed my chance. We all missed our chance."

She swept the sunglasses off her face. "When I left the hospital that night, I promised God that if he would let Eddie live, I would get every last layer of that wallpaper off those walls. But he didn't pull through. And yet — I didn't see any reason to stop. So that's what I've been doing ever since. Around the clock, pretty much."

I was growing uneasy myself, remembering how blue jays could suddenly fly out of nowhere to alight in the mind of Mrs. Passworth.

"In one corner where the paper was loose, I was down to probably the second- or third-to-last layer," she said. "And then here they come again. The same lights as before. Only, my goodness! Something's new! And it hits me. It's the same lights, a little brighter than normal — but it's not even dark out. It's the middle of the afternoon."

Tim nudged me. I took a step sideways, out of nudging range.

I was wondering if the August sun over Mississippi is hot enough by itself to drive a person insane. Everyone seemed stunned into silence by the heat, the weight of the air. I remembered that bad day in algebra, when we all sat paralyzed, waiting for Passworth to stop talking. Out here in the graveyard there was not even a bell to save us.

Most of the mourners appeared hopeful that this story was leading on an ingenious roundabout path toward some wise observation about Eddie.

"There's a period of time I can't account for," Passworth said. "I remember being in my kitchen, looking at the clock, it was ten minutes to two. And the next thing I know, I'm out on the front porch with my shoes off. It's dark. And there's this smell, like someone burned the toast."

Reverend Poole's smile had congealed on his face. His eyes darted between Passworth and the thundercloud gathering over Mrs. Smock.

Passworth was oblivious. "They don't give out much information to any one person," she said. "But I think when it all becomes public, it could be bigger than Pearl Harbor and the Beatles put together. Everything will be revealed pretty soon. I'm just sorry Eddie wasn't able to hang on a little longer. Anyway, God bless him. That's all, folks."

She blinked, and hesitated, as if to make sure she was finished. Then she put her wide sunglasses on and went to the back of the crowd.

Mrs. Smock exhaled loudly through her nostrils, a kind of cough that might have been a *hmph*.

Reverend Poole shook himself from his trance. "Dearly beloved, let us raise up our voices in praise to his precious name, Hymn 113."

Wan voices rose up.

> *There is a fountain filled with blood*
> *Drawn from Emmanuel's veins;*
> *And sinners plunged beneath that flood*
> *Lose all their guilty stains.*

I'd like to know who was picking these hymns. That one went on for about six verses. Reverend Poole raised his arm. "Folks, you know you're in trouble when even the *breeze* feels hot. Edwin's brother, Lawrence, will now make a presentation, and we hope he will keep it short, as the heat out here could be fatal to some of the elderly among us. Lawrence?"

A fat boy of twelve shuffled forward from the line of family, cradling a bulky cassette player in his arms. "Uhm, I just want to play one of Eddie's songs," he said, gazing down at the casket. "That's the thing he liked the most, writing all these songs."

His thumb pressed PLAY.

That box produced a nice Elton John–like opening flourish on piano, and Eddie was singing. Eddie always did have a nice voice, a strong clear tenor with almost no vibrato.

I recognized the song, though I'd never heard it sung slow and ballady like that, in a minor key. I had to smile. At last, Eddie had managed to get this song into a show!

> *I'm just a man, and I walk the path of righteousness*
> *But sometimes I stumble and fall*
> *I don't recognize him, as he whispers in my ear*
> *Temptation is the nature of his call*
>
> *Bless the devil —*
> *He shows me the way not to go*
> *Bless the devil —*
> *Without him, how would I know*
> *Bless the devil —*
> *When he puts me to the test*
> *That's how I know*
> *I love Jeeeeee-sus more!*

Lawrence Smock cradled the player, his smile just as comfortable and sweet as if he was holding a baby, not a cassette player emitting the clear tenor of his brother singing about Satan.

The lyrics brought Reverend Poole out of his prayerful reverie. His face turned the same shade of red as Mrs. Smock's.

I saw that Mrs. Passworth had moved away from the crowd. Somehow her hat had got turned around so the veil draped the back of her hair. Her lips were moving, as if there were parts of her speech she still needed to say.

The song ended. Lawrence Smock pressed STOP and went to stand behind his mother.

Tim leaned close to my ear. "Now *that* is a strange-looking girl."

ON THE WAY HOME we got to laughing so hard that Tim had to pull over. We sat there in the dark and just howled.

It scared me so bad, looking into that red hole going down into darkness. There is nothing more final than that hole in the earth. It was so scary I felt like laughing hysterically for whatever years I had left.

After a while we managed to stop laughing. Tim drove on.

"So what's with the guns in the back?" I said.

He didn't blink. "I'm keeping them for my Uncle Bob. They've got kids, his wife doesn't like guns in the house. I'm supposed to hang on to them for him till deer season."

"You ever shoot 'em?"

"Sometimes," Tim said. "We shoot bottles and stuff on his farm."

I'd never heard him mention Uncle Bob or a farm, but I didn't say that. I told him how Bud and I used to shoot squirrels at Granny's place. We drove on in the darkness. We talked about Eddie, and Mrs. Passworth. We laughed at poor Mrs. Smock's pig nose.

"Man, we've got to get busy," Tim said. "We've got a lot to do before school starts."

"Like what?"

"Dumwood, please! Have you forgotten our ol' pal Dudley?"

"Pretty much. I don't like to waste the energy it takes to think about him." I hadn't laid eyes on Red since that day he came to the river to talk to Arnita. That was weeks ago.

"He played his little trick with the garbage again the other night," Tim said. "My mother comes out to get the Sunday paper and finds, like, our soup cans and coffee grinds and shit scattered all over our yard and halfway up the block in the neighbors' yards. I think it's about to give her a nervous breakdown."

"You sure it's not just some dog? That's what it sounds like."

"It's not a dog. For God's sake."

"But you've never actually caught Red doing it, have you?"

"I don't have to, Skippy. I know him. It's just part of his plan. What is it with you? Ever since he eased up on you and started bearing down on me, you act like I'm making it up. Like I'm blowing it out of proportion."

"I told you. If you would just ignore him —"

"Do you realize school starts a week from Monday? Red will go right back to torturing both of us the first day. Do you want to spend your whole senior year as Five Spot and Stinky?"

"No, but what can we do about it?"

"Not there yet, but soon," he said. "Sometimes it's better to plan ahead."

"What are you gonna do, shoot him?" With the guns and ammo in the hatchback, it didn't seem all that far-fetched.

"Who'd be upset if I did?" he said. "Soon all shall be revealed, O great Skippitus Maximus. I think I have figured out a way to convince him to leave us alone. All in good time."

"Fine. Don't tell me. I don't want to know." Tim was always scheming up new ways of revenge upon Red, but he never seemed to follow through on his ideas. I was sure that was just as well.

South of Yazoo City, a sign for REST AREA. Tim switched on the blinker.

"Gotta pee?" I said.

He gave me an unfathomable look, a measure of affection but also something alarming: an accusation, old hurt, as if there was some angry secret between us. "I just need to stop here a second, okay?"

"Fine with me."

On one side of the rest area was a parking lot for eighteen-wheelers, on the other side a smaller lot for cars. Between them was an A-frame building with restrooms, maps, a drinking fountain. Tim drove slowly through the passenger car lot, then backed all the way to the entrance and cruised down the truck side. He parked at the end of the truck lane, in a spot partly screened by some bushes.

"I'm going in for a minute, okay, Skip? You sit here and if anybody comes, like some police-type person, tap the horn a couple times." He demonstrated: tap tap. "Keep your eyes open. I'll be right back." He reached back under the seat for a small paper bag.

"What the hell are you doing?"

"No questions, Skippy."

"Tim. Tell me what you're up to."

"Just — trust me on this one, okay? Please." His urgent voice. He got out of the car and hurried in.

I switched the key to ACC and found the Spinners, "Could It Be I'm Falling in Love" (witcha bay-beh!). And here came cruising a silver car with a map of Mississippi on the door and a full rack of blue lights on the roof.

I bopped the horn lightly — beep beep!

The state trooper glanced over at me as he rolled by. His car hesitated, then kept going toward the on-ramp. Suddenly his blue lights blazed to life and he raced onto the interstate.

With you, with you, wailed the Spinners, *with you, with yoooooooo-hoohoo.*

A minute later Tim hurried out, stuffing whatever it was back into the brown paper bag.

"There was a state trooper, but he's gone," I said when he opened the door.

Tim slid in. "Let's get out of here."

"Hang on a minute." I stepped out of the car. "I gotta pee."

"What?" He was annoyed. "Now?"

"Sorry. Power of suggestion, I guess."

"Well okay. No — Durwood, wait — no, never mind. Just hurry, okay?"

I went to the stall on the end. I smelled fresh paint and saw the shiny blob of white on the wall, the trickle running down. I peed and zipped up.

I checked every stall and found the same blob of fresh paint in each one.

I washed my hands and went back to the Pinto. Getting in, I glanced to the floor well behind Tim's seat, the brown bag containing the can of spray paint.

"Everything come out okay?" Tim said.

I sat silent for a moment. Then I said, "What did you paint over back there?"

"I don't have the faintest idea what you mean." He flashed his fakiest smile.

"Come on, Timmy. This is me. I'm not going to tell on you."

"Nah, sorry. I don't think so."

"The paint was still wet, you know. I could have wiped it off and read it for myself. But I didn't. I decided I would come back and let you tell me."

He sighed. "You'll just think I'm an idiot."

"Like I don't already?" For the first time I had some small power over Tim. The first whiff of it made me feel a little high.

"I thought it would be funny." His voice was quiet. "It didn't turn out that way."

"What did you write on the wall?"

He breathed out.

"Something dirty," I prompted.

"Not what you think."

"What do I think?"

"Probably you think it's something perverted. But it had nothing to do with me. I put Eddie's name up there, okay? And the phone number at the church office. I thought it would be funny if people would call."

"Just his name?"

"Oh, you know — 'for a good time call Eddie,' like that. It was really stupid, I know."

I didn't say anything.

"I told you, I thought it would be funny if people would call."

"Well, it's not," I said. "What did Eddie ever do to you?"

"Just a dumb joke," he said.

"It's worse than that, Tim. It's sick."

"Okay, now you shut up!" he cried. "First you practically force me to tell you, then you give me this holier-than-thou crap? You think I'm sick? I'm a sicko? Well, you should probably get somebody else to drive you around, then. You don't want to be seen with a sicko!"

"Where else did you write Eddie's name?"

"One other place," he said. "We're going there now."

"Another rest area?"

"Maybe."

Why hadn't he just driven me home and come back on his own to run this errand? What part of him wanted me to witness this awful thing he had done?

Maybe this was a test. If we could still remain friends after this, he would know for certain that I would always be his friend, no matter what.

Or maybe he wanted me to stop him before he did something worse.

I didn't know the answer. All I knew was that Tim was headed down a dark road, and he was not going to take me with him.

The radio announcer sounded so excited about Herrin-Gear Chevrolet's unbelievable low low prices.

"I bet nobody even called the damn church," Tim was saying. "Passworth said something about some calls, but she's so crazy, who knows what she's talking about? I thought it would be smart to get rid of the evidence, just in case."

"Yeah," I said. "Smart."

22

I WASN'T SURE I would go through with it until I was already in Jeff Magill's office and talking. So many times I had pictured myself making this confession in a shadowy room under an idly turning ceiling fan, with a spotlight hard in my eyes. In fact the light was greenish and came from buzzing fluorescent tubes overhead. Jeff Magill didn't have an office of his own, just a piled-up desk in the corner of a room he shared with three other detectives. He pulled a chair over from another desk for me. An overworked window-unit air conditioner chugged trying to recirculate the smoky air.

I was sweating from walking the whole twelve miles from the Reid Motel in Minor to the sheriff's office on East Pascagoula Avenue, downtown Jackson. I'd tried sticking my thumb out a few times along the way, but apparently I wasn't the kind of hitchhiker people pick up.

Jeff Magill didn't seem surprised when I showed up at the door of his office.

I told him the truth about everything, starting with Prom Night: How we knocked Arnita down by accident but fled the scene on purpose. The lengths we went to, letting Red Martin take the blame. How easy that was, since Red was fairly drunk and actually knocked her off the bike first, and drove off, and left her. (Even at this late date, I was hoping this would somehow count in our favor.) I told about the months I had spent doing chores for the Beechams, trying to make secret amends. I told how falling in love with Arnita was just as much an accident as knocking her off the bike.

I told him the whole thing was more my fault than Tim's. Tim was driving that night, but it was my hand that grabbed the wheel. I could have forced him to turn around and go back at once, but I didn't. I stood by silently while Red was arrested and charged for what we did.

I knew it was wrong. I was over at the Beechams' every day. I could have told the truth anytime.

Magill jotted down a few things but didn't say much. He was a good listener. I tried to make him understand how Red had tormented us, without sounding too much like a crybaby.

"We were moving to bring a case against him for the girl," Magill said. "The mother nagged us for months. But the minute we booked him, she got cold feet."

"What do you mean?"

"She refused to press charges. She told the DA she had decided someone else was involved, and it wouldn't be fair to charge just the Martin boy."

"That's me she was talking about," I said. "She was always suspicious of me. And she has this way of reading your mind." All this time Mrs. Beecham could have turned me in and didn't. I was grateful.

"Yeah, she's quite a woman," Magill said, with a glance at his watch. "What else you got?"

I needed something to make him take me seriously. "Tim has guns in the back of his car," I said.

Magill thought about it a minute. "Maybe he's going hunting."

"He doesn't hunt."

"What are you saying? You think he might hurt somebody?"

I didn't. Really I didn't. But I wasn't absolutely sure, and that's what I said.

"Are you mad at him or something?" he said. "Y'all fighting over this girl? Seems like you'd like to see him get charged with a crime."

Of course I was mad at Tim for what he did to me and Arnita, but that wasn't why I'd come here. Or was it? "I just thought you might want to talk to him," I said. "And I wanted you to know the truth. We've been lying about this since it happened. I didn't know you dropped the charges against Red. That was the main thing."

"I appreciate that, Dan. I know it took some nerve for you to come here." His chair squealed as he leaned back. "How's the family getting along? Y'all settled into a new place?"

"We're still in a motel."

"It might be a bit of a wait on that insurance. They'll pay it, though, eventually. They'll have to. Fire marshal ruled it an accident."

"Yes sir."

"Was it an accident, Dan?"

"Yes sir," I said firmly. I had practiced this answer many times along the road from Minor. I had toyed with the notion that one word from me could put Dad in jail, but I knew that wouldn't make him any nicer when he got out.

"See, I wasn't sure," said Magill. "I found out your father lied about losing his job. But I never could imagine a man blowing up his own house to collect on a little household policy. He just didn't seem like the type." He kept his eyes steady on me. "I don't suppose you'd ever tell on him, would you?"

"There's nothing to tell," I said. "Aren't you going to arrest me?"

"Any reason I should?"

"Well — I kind of thought you might." In fact I'd expected him to arrest me and Tim both. I thought a trip to jail was the price we'd both have to pay for getting Tim the attention he needed.

Magill scratched his ear. "In our business, we pretty much have to have some evidence of a crime. Otherwise there's not much we can do. You wouldn't go to all this trouble just to volunteer a lie, would you?"

"No sir."

"So if you're not lying, you didn't hit the girl intentionally. You ran off, but you did call an ambulance. You should have gone back to the scene, but I'm not about to try and make a case on that. Writing somebody's name on a toilet wall — that's vandalism, but you said he went back and cleaned it up. He's got guns, long as he's over sixteen and no criminal record, he can have all the guns he wants. Now if he shoots somebody, or threatens a specific person, that's when you need to call me. Here. Let me give you a card."

I took it and thanked him for his time.

"Sure, Dan — thank you." We shook hands. His hand was warm, entirely dry.

I ran my thumb over the raised letters of his name, the seal embossed with the outline of Mississippi. I put the card in my pocket.

I was sure he forgot all about me before I even got out of the lobby.

It was late in the day but the heat was still stupefying. I spotted a cluster of bikes on a rack between the sheriff's department and the Hinds County Courthouse. A white statue presided over the facade of that big white building — it looked to be Moses, from the gleaming marble tablets in his arms.

I was having trouble facing the idea of walking all the way back in this heat. Twelve miles took almost three hours this morning, when I was fresh. Maybe I could find a bus to the Jackson city limits, but Minor was miles beyond that.

I went to the bike rack intending only to check out the bikes and think about what kind of bike I would get if I had the money. My eye happened to fall on one bike, a red Raleigh ten-speed, not particularly new or expensive but it did possess one quality that set it apart from all other bikes on the rack: it was unlocked.

Look at me! said the bike. No one cares about me! Want a ride?

A smart thief would have checked the windows of the buildings all around to see if the owner of the bike happened to be glancing out at that moment. I didn't do that.

I lifted the red Raleigh from the rack. I swung my leg over, saddled up, and rode off.

I got away clean. I stole it in broad daylight from the rack in front of the sheriff's department, and no one ever knew. If that was your Raleigh ten-speed that went missing that hot August day, 1973, I apologize. That bike still had a lot of good miles on it when someone finally stole it from me.

If Jeff Magill no longer cared about the major felonies we had committed, what was one petty larceny? Stealing was easy, and fun! It put extra spring in my legs to be riding stolen property. I whizzed down East Pascagoula in the shadow of Standard Life, the blank eyes of the derelict King James Hotel.

Racing through on a bike, I thought Jackson was much nicer than it seemed from a car. I flew down leafy streets lined with graceful old homes. Then the homes got less graceful, then became just small shacky houses. The pavement broke up. Black kids played in the street. "Hey black boy," one lanky kid yelled as I bumped toward him. "Hey hey hey, black boy!" That's what I thought he was saying until I zoomed past and realized he was saying "bike boy." He made a grab at my leg. I didn't even slow down.

I rode past the last outskirts of Jackson, out into open country. I was thinking about what was lurking behind my conversation with Magill. Some hint of a suggestion he was trying to make, if only I could be subtle enough to pick up on it. *In this business, we need a crime. Now if Tim shoots somebody or threatens a specific person . . .*

At last I came to the Minor sign, which someone had altered again:

WELCOME TO MINOR

TWO

~~ONE~~ OF MISSISSIPPI'S   TOWNS

There were lights coming on in the first subdivisions. I turned onto Bluff Park Drive, sweating and puffing over the hill.

Bluff Park was Minor's ritzier subdivision. The lawns were large and carefully kept. It was not unusual to see three or four cars in one driveway. In front of a gray cedar rambling ranch house, I saw the car I was looking for: a red Mustang Fastback.

Cherry red. GT. Souped up, with flames down the side.

It sat behind two gleaming Cadillacs and a Chevy pickup so new it still wore dealer plates. I wheeled around and went back to check out the gray cedar mailbox with the house number, 3574, and the word MARTIN.

I cycled slowly away, checking out the general area. No close neighbors, lots of trees, thickets of giant azalea between the houses.

I swept down the long hill onto Minor Boulevard. I hadn't intended to go anywhere in particular, but somehow the stolen bike found its way to the bridge over the Yatchee River.

I checked the hiding place behind the bridge stanchion, but there were no rocks. I rode recklessly down the slope where I used to kiss Arnita for hours.

That was the worst part of it. She didn't love me anymore. Our love had evaporated in a flash — the way gasoline burns. I would never get to kiss her again. Thanks, Tim.

I laid the bike on the grass and sat by the log where we used to sit. I breathed the air in the same place, hoping it might bring back some of the feeling. The water in the river moved so slowly it seemed frozen, like deep green glass.

23

ONCE I KNEW what I had to do, I didn't wait. This was the kind of action you don't sit around and ponder too much, or you'll never go through with it.

I bought supplies at TG&Y and rode to the Texaco station on Hood Street. In the piss-smelling Texaco bathroom I dumped all the bleach from a brand-new bottle of Clorox into the toilet. I carried the bottle outside to the pump and filled it with 87 octane — for my chain saw, I told the guy. When he went in to get my change, I stuffed the length of muslin into the bottle. I tightened the cap, stowed the bottle in the TG&Y bag with the big box of matches.

I dropped a quarter in the phone. I dialed the number and closed my eyes. The phone rang three times. "Yello," Tim said.

I hung up.

I put on my black hooded sweatshirt and slung the bag from my handlebars. Pedaling over to Bluff Park I had time to reconsider. What I was doing was well beyond reckless, into dangerous. The craziest most drastic thing I'd ever done. But I believed I had to do it. I couldn't think of any other way to stop Tim. It wasn't enough for me to know that what we did was wrong. Tim had to know it too.

If Jeff Magill needed a crime, I would give him a crime.

Crickets and other night bugs raised a roar in the leafy darkness of Bluff Park. The occasional pool of streetlight was a gathering place for all kinds of swarming fluttery things.

I rode at a leisurely pace past the excellent darkness of the Martin driveway. The setup was ideal, no streetlamp within fifty feet. The light glancing off the cars was indistinct, a soft glow from the house.

I continued on a few yards beyond their property, coasting to a stop beneath a low-hanging live oak. I laid the bike in a patch of deep shadow, pointed in the direction of my getaway.

I was trying to think through all possible outcomes. I carried the Clorox bottle and the box of big-headed matches across a wide stretch of grass, to the driveway.

I placed the bottle on the pavement beneath the Mustang's back bumper, and fished out the gas-soaked muslin. The insect chatter seemed to intensify. I unscrewed Red's gas cap and tucked it in my pocket as a souvenir.

I stuffed one end of the muslin into the mouth of the fuel tank, unrolled it down the bumper, crammed a couple of inches into the bleach bottle, and carried on unrolling as I crept back from the car, across the lawn. I was worried how quickly the gas might evaporate from the muslin, whether there would be enough fuel to carry the flame to the car.

I wiped my fingers on the grass. My hands trembled as I slid out the cardboard drawer. I made a little bouquet of four matches. I struck them all together on the side of the box. The sudden gout of flame startled me. I steadied myself and knelt down, touched the fire to the cloth.

A bright bluish flame raced quick up the slender white trail, over the grass and up to the mouth of the bottle, which exploded with a heavy *woof!* that blew fire into the mouth of the fuel tank. Red's cherry-red 1972 Mustang Fastback GT detonated with such force that the fastback end sailed up in the air and came down in slow motion, a huge crash, burning, sliding sideways into the pickup truck with a metallic groan.

Flames all over the car! Not just flame decals on the sides. Both cars were burning.

This spectacle made me happier than I had imagined. Death to Red! Death to the Mustang! Burn baby burn!

I jumped on the bike and got the hell out of there. I flashed down Bluff Park Drive into Oak Hill, the long way around to stay off the traffic streets.

Here came a wail from the north — a red ladder truck rocketing down Minor Boulevard with lights and sirens blazing, followed by a pumper truck honking and screaming.

I rode fast toward the highway. You have done it now, Musgrove. You have knocked the nest out of the tree. Now let's see where the hornets will go.

Red loved that car. That car was never less than spotless, shiny and red.

That was the greatest part of the plan. Revenge was mine, and it smelled as sweet and flammable as gasoline. *That's for you, Red! A special gift from Five Spot!*

I had the strongest urge to find Tim and tell him.

No. He would find out soon enough. Soon he'd be having his little talk with Jeff Magill. That was liable to get pretty hot — Tim with all the indignation of the wrongly accused, Magill embarrassed and mad at himself for ignoring my warning.

Tim would hate me when he figured out what I'd done. That was okay by me. I was willing to lose him as a friend, in order to stop him. It had taken me a long time to make up my mind about that.

Tim would try to convince Magill it was me who burned Red's car. Magill wouldn't believe him because I had come to him first, with a warning.

And no one would ever have to find out what Tim really meant to do with those guns.

The plan had other benefits. Red's car was hilarious rising up on its cloud of fire like a toy car. Like a great big burning Matchbox car.

I did a good job of blowing it up, a job to make my father proud.

Demonstrating once again the Musgrove talent for demolition. I was tingling with the same excitement Dad must have felt when he blew up our house. All the violence I ever wanted to do to Red was condensed into that bright bloom of gasoline, the car lifting up, the wrenching crash of metal.

Way back in my mind a little bell was ringing, a persistent alarm bell I was not completely able to ignore. What if things don't go exactly the way I planned? What if Tim and Jeff Magill don't react as I expect?

If somebody saw me do it, or I left some stupid clue . . .

I rode off for the Reid Motel. I would have to scrub hard to get the smell of gas off my hands.

24

I JOGGED ACROSS HIGHWAY 80 to the pay phone. I put in fifteen cents. It rang three times before Patsy Cousins picked up.

"Hey Miz Cousins, can I speak to Tim?"

"Daniel, my God! Where are you? Are you okay?"

"Well — yeah, I'm fine. What's wrong?"

"Well, my Lord, they just came and got Tim, and took him down to Jackson. To the police station."

I stayed silent. Did this mean they would come for me next?

"They said they wanted to ask him some questions," she was saying, "but they wouldn't say what it's about. And they wouldn't let me go with them! Do you know what's going on?"

"No ma'am."

"Come on, Daniel. Tim tells you everything."

"They didn't say why they arrested him?"

"They didn't arrest him. They took him for questioning." Her voice tightened. "Why would you say that? Daniel — if you know something, I swear, you tell me right now!"

"Miz Cousins, I haven't even talked to Tim since Eddie's funeral."

"Is this something to do with that colored girl that got hurt after the prom?"

"I don't think so," I said. "How should I know?"

"Is your mother there? Put her on the line."

"I can't."

"Well, your father then. Let me talk to him now, please."

"I'm at a pay phone. We don't have a phone where we're staying right now."

"Daniel. Now listen to me. I am not accustomed to having the police show up at my door and take my son away. Do you hear me?"

"Yes ma'am."

"Is Tim mixed up in something?"

"Not that I know of."

"He's so horrible and moody these days. We're at the end of our rope. We've tried to get him help, but he won't cooperate. You can't get that kind of help if you won't cooperate even a little. He goes off all the time by himself, God knows where, and the times when he is here, he's so unhappy we can hardly breathe. His poor father is just disgusted with him. Now this. You're his friend. Would you please, please tell me what's going on?"

"Well, it all started with — there's this guy at school," I said.

She pounced on that. "Red Martin?"

"Yeah."

"Oh I know all about Red Martin! That boy has caused us more pain — I wish the same thing would happen to his family. Did Tim tell you how he messed up my yard?"

"Yeah, he's pretty bad," I said. "But Tim overreacts. And that makes it worse." Across the road I saw Mom and Dad and Janie climbing into the station wagon.

"Daniel. What can we do to help him?"

"I'm sorry, Mrs. Cousins, I don't know. Tell him I'll see him at school, okay? I've gotta go —"

I hung up and ran to the car.

I thought we were going to the Dairy Dog for supper, but we drove out old Highway 80 past the turnoff for Old Raymond Road, past the campus of Mississippi Baptist College, past the Hungry L

Truck Stop, the school bus shed and the scrap metal yard, and under the interstate bridge to the Twi-Lite Drive-In Theater.

Dad put on his blinker.

"Are we turning around?" I said.

"We're here, Danny," Janie said. "This is it."

The drive-in had been closed for years. The marquee still bore a few letters advertising its last feature:

UN   KAB   E
OLLY   BRO

Dad was watching my reaction in the rearview mirror. Mom gazed across the road as if there was something incredibly interesting about that Spur station over there.

"What are you talking about?" I said.

"Our new house," Janie said. "We're gonna live here."

"At the drive-in?"

"Isn't it crazy? Wait till you see."

"This is *not* our new house," Mom said. "It's just one of the possibilities Daddy and I are considering. We have a lot of talking to do before any decisions are made."

"No we don't," said Dad. "I told you, I signed the contract."

"Well, anything that's signed can be unsigned," she said.

Dad pulled in at the streamlined pink-and-blue Twi-Lite marquee. When he turned his head I noticed the jaunty toothpick in his mouth. "It's a golden opportunity," he said.

We drove past the deserted ticket booth, the flying-saucer snack bar, and the projector hut, onto a wide field studded with speaker-box poles. In front of each pole was a gravelly hillock that raised your front wheels to give your car the right tilt for viewing the enormous screen. That screen was blotched and torn in places, a dim but dazzling whiteness occupying one whole side of the sky.

"Are we camping here?" I ventured.

"It's such a smart idea, how they built it," said Dad. "It's a wonder to me that all the other drive-ins didn't copy it." He steered past the play-park of swing sets and slides at the base of the screen, and continued around back.

The screen was not just a screen, but a house. The house was built into the screen, or the screen had a house clinging to its back — it was a chicken or egg question. Dad said they were built at the same time by a man called Tex Mooney. The house was one room wide, stacked in three stories, connected with long ramps and motel-style stairs. Tex's wife was in a wheelchair from diabetes, Dad explained, and he didn't want to spend all his time running home from the drive-in to check on her. So he built them a house behind the store, so to speak.

I saw the look on Mom's face. She had heard this story before and didn't find it all that charming. She glared up at this odd, tall building with windows poked in it here and there. "Anything's better than that nasty motel. But don't y'all get attached to the idea of staying here."

"Why not?" Dad said. "If you give it a chance, you might like it. Once I get the business up and running, we can make it real nice back here. It's what you always wanted — country living, right here in the city."

Mom scowled. "Daniel, get those groceries out of the car. I'm going up and lay down. I have a terrible headache." She took her purse and left us all there.

"Are you gonna show movies, Dad?"

"Of course we are. The only reason people quit coming is cause old Tex let the place run down so bad. Old fool sitting on a dadgum gold mine and didn't even know it. A little paint, a little of the old spick-and-span, put the right snacks in the snack bar and show the right picture shows — I believe we'll do good. And no fake butter on the popcorn."

"You mean you're gonna do this for your job?" I wouldn't have been more amazed if Dad had signed up to become an astronaut.

"The sign goes up tomorrow, 'Under New Management.' I hope we got enough letters to spell it."

"Okay well, first of all, there haven't been 'picture shows' since about 1930," I said.

"Don't smart-mouth me, mister."

"And if you want anybody to come," I said, "you have to show the right movies."

"Look, Janie, we got an expert right here in the family."

"I told you it was cool, Danny!" Janie clomped up the steps. "You and me get our own rooms all the way at the top!"

My own room? Those were words I never expected to hear.

Dad watched my face. "What you think about that?"

"Oh, Dad, really? Oh my gosh, thank you." I wondered what was the catch.

"Jacko won't be going up any stairs," he said. "So you still have to come down and help him get in and out of bed." Ah, there it was. Not too bad.

"Sure, Dad, anything — wow, this is unbelievable."

"There's two beds in your room," he said. "When Buddy comes home for a visit he can bunk in with you."

"That's fine," I said.

"It's like living in our own motel!" Janie exclaimed.

"I don't want to live in our own motel," Mom announced from the second-floor railing. "Or a drive-in movie, or a hot dog stand, or a windmill, or anything other than a house."

"You won't have to lift a finger," Dad said. "I'll make you a nice garden. You can live back here like it's any other house."

"But it's not, Lee, it's not! Now, damn it! Look at it!" She clattered down the stairs. "Where did you get this idea that drive-in movies are the next big thing? Nobody goes to the drive-in anymore except teenagers."

"That's because they don't show any good . . . movies," said Dad. "They don't show anything a family can go to."

"There's a reason the man has been trying to unload this place. Drive-ins are going out of business all over the country. I read about it in the Sunday supplement."

"Not this one," he said. "This one is going *into* business, and we're gonna make a lot of money. Wait and see."

"Wait and see," she repeated. "Wait and *see*? Oh, I've been waiting. But I haven't been seeing. You don't even like to *go* to the drive-in movie, now you've gone and rented one, and moved us into it!"

"That is almost correct," Dad said.

"What do you mean?"

"Well, did you hear me actually say that I rented it?"

She stared. "You were talking to Mooney, you were going to offer him rent with an option to buy. Isn't that what you said?"

"Not exactly," he said.

"*What* exactly?"

"Well I asked him, but he had no interest in renting the place. The only thing he wanted to do was sell. He's old now, he's not interested in running it —"

"You've said that ten times," Mom snapped. "Don't tell me you bought it."

"Yeah, I did. I sure did."

That straightened her up. "With what?"

"The insurance money."

"It came?"

"Friday," he said. "While you were in Jackson."

"While I was at the doctor, getting a Pap smear? You took that check and cashed it, and you blew it on this out-of-business, worthless piece of — drive-in — ohh!" She burst into tears, buried her face in her hands, and just sobbed.

Dad didn't make a move. None of us did. We let her cry where she was. Poor Mom. I still feel guilty for that.

I followed Janie upstairs to have a look at our rooms. We kept our voices low.

"My room is kind of little but I love it," Janie said. She had already arranged her dolls on the dresser and tacked up a Bo Donaldson & the Heywoods poster. (Their song "You Don't Own Me" was her personal anthem.) "And look, Danny, you can see out through the movie screen." Behind the narrow bed a high, square window provided a panoramic view of the speaker field in a soft, milky light.

My room had two of these translucent windows, as well as two beds, two dressers, and its own bathroom. My suitcase and my box of belongings were on one bed, waiting for me. I could not believe our good fortune. "Hey Idjit, this is the best house we've ever had."

Janie frowned. "You heard Mom. She's not gonna let us stay here."

"She might not have a choice. I think he already bought it."

"Yeah, he's crazy," she said. "But I love it."

We crept to the edge of the balcony. They were mad enough to be fighting with their door open so we could hear.

"I got an unbelievable deal," Dad was saying. "The man was desperate. He had no idea what the business was worth — let alone the land underneath it. He just wanted out. There's no way we can lose at this price, this close to the interstate."

"You didn't even ask me! How could you do that? I'm your wife. Don't you care what I think?"

"I saw a real opportunity," he said, "and I jumped, and here you go tearing me down. Could I for once have a nice word from you, instead of just criticizing?"

Her voice rose. "That money was not yours to spend however you want! It was my money too."

"That's not what it said on the check."

That was a low blow, even for Dad. Janie and I cringed, thinking what might come next.

"Fine. You want to run a drive-in? Run it." The brisk click of her heels down the gallery. "This is the stupidest thing you've ever done, and that's saying something."

Dad said, "Where do you think you're going?"

"It's a good thing I didn't unpack," she said. "I don't care where I go. I'll go to June's house. Or I can stay with Mack and Wanda. They'll be glad to have me."

"What about the kids?"

"That's your problem," she snapped. "They start school Monday, were you even aware of that? You think I'm gonna jerk 'em out of school and take 'em with me to Alabama just to make things easier on you? Forget that. They seem to like it here too. Maybe you'll all be very happy."

Thanks a lot, Mom!

"Now just cool down, Peggy Jean," Dad said. "Give me that suitcase."

"I'm taking the car," she said.

"You ain't going anywhere, honey, just put that down and listen to me."

"Don't you 'honey' me." She marched down the stairs.

"You gonna run off and leave Jack Otis to tend to himself in the hospital?" he said. "Have you lost your mind?"

"I've lost most of it anyway," she said. "The little bit I've got left tells me to get out of here now, or I won't be responsible. I need to go see my mother!" She stalked into the yard.

She was pretty upset. Had she forgotten Granny was dead?

"That bunch over there hasn't lifted the first finger to see about Jacko," she was saying. "Why is it always my job?"

"Now Peg, you know you're not leaving —"

"Don't you dare call me Peg!" she cried. "You know not to call me that when we're fighting! That's what you call me when we're *not* fighting! Now you've ruined it!" She burst into tears.

I know she saw us watching, but she chose not to look up. She heaved the suitcase into the back of the station wagon.

All our lives it had been Mom and us kids on one side, and Dad on the other. I could not believe she would leave us in the hands of the enemy.

She started the car and drove a lurchy circle around the oak tree. She turned on her headlights and drove out of there.

I ran to my room, to the screen-window to watch her go. She knocked down a speaker pole and bumped her rear tires over two hummocks before she found the road.

Dad said no way would Mom drive all the way to Alabama by herself with night coming on. On I-20 she would have to pass the hospital, and she would not be able to drive by without stopping to check on Jacko. That's when she would come to her senses. She would be back by ten o'clock at the latest.

Ten o'clock came and went, with no Mom.

"Sometimes women just need to blow off steam for no reason," Dad said. "Janie, don't you be like that when you grow up."

"Okay, Daddy," Janie said.

That night when I went to bed I kept seeing Red's Mustang exploding, the fire blooming over and over on the insides of my eyes.

25

THE EARLY SUNLIGHT cast a pair of delicate rectangles on the wall. I yawned and stretched and it came to me: last week of August, the first day of school! Remember what a thrill it used to be in Indiana, the first tang of fall in the air, excited hallway chatter, the chalkboards clean and fresh green as they never will be again the whole year?

Twelve years of school will bore that thrill right out of you. By the time you're a senior, sleep is so much better — and I almost slid back down into it too, but then I got to wondering whether Tim was in jail, and then Janie was at the foot of my bed clanging a lid against a saucepan, yelling, "Get up, buttface!"

Buttface, arsonist, big brother — and a senior! This would be my last first day of school, not counting college, and at this rate who knew if I'd survive long enough to think about college. I kicked out at Janie, but she dodged my foot and went on clanging.

"Stop that, dammit! I'm awake!"

"Rise and shine, Danny," she croaked. "First day of school!" She performed a mean imitation of Mom, who used to wake us up for this day singing at the upper end of her range.

School days, school days
Dear old golden rule days
Readin' and 'ritin' and 'rithmetic
Taught to the tune of a hickory stick

In younger years that song brought us bounding out of bed, rushing to crack open our new school boxes as if they contained presents from Santa Claus instead of pencils. Today we dragged ourselves down to the table for Cheerios. Dad didn't bother to get up. He'd been awake till all hours, fiddling with the machines in the projector hut.

I balanced Janie on the handlebars of the stolen red Raleigh, which I had supposedly borrowed from a friend. "You're too big for this, kiddo. Think one of your friends will loan you a bike for a while?"

"I'll make Daddy drive me. He'll have to get another car, won't he?"

"You better get a bike."

"Danny, you think Mom is ever gonna come back?"

"Yeah, I bet she will."

"When?"

"A week? Two weeks? I don't know."

"I'm not so sure," Janie said. "I think she might enjoy not having us around. She must not like us very much if she stays over in Alabama and won't even call us."

"She likes us okay," I said. "She just needed a vacation from Dad."

Traffic on the highway this early was nothing but log trucks — three big ones roared by us before we could turn off for Barnett Street. We bumped over the train tracks. I went the long way around to avoid the spot where Arnita fell.

A few houses before school, I pulled over to let Janie off. We didn't want to show up together at school. Lowly freshmen don't hang out with mighty seniors. "Have a fun day, Danny. Maybe I'll see you in the hall or something."

"If you do, be sure not to speak to me," I said.

"Same here. Thanks for the ride."

"See ya back at the ol' drive-in."

She said, "Will you please ride me home after school?"

"Yeah, okay. Meet me here after. Don't make me wait!"

She stuck out her tongue. I rode on.

Today would be Arnita's first day at school since the accident. What if we had classes together? Maybe she hated me forever, but then again —

If I tried to explain everything, she might give me a chance.

No. She hated me. And why not? Look what I did to her life.

Tim probably hated me too.

Wouldn't it be better not to go to school today? Just drop out. Ride away on my bike and never go back. I could become a bad guy, a hoodlum. I could burn cars and rob liquor stores and snatch old ladies' purses and make amazing getaways on my stolen bike.

The sign said MHS — WELCOME BACK TITANS

A big crowd of kids milled in the courtyard, in front of the library. Standing up on my pedals, I noticed for the first time that the school library was just a larger version of the snack bar at the Twi-Lite — the same streamlined circular shape, the red-tiled landing pad on the roof. Who was this space-minded architect who had landed his flying saucer–shaped buildings all over Minor?

I made up my mind to go in and start my new life as a senior. If anyone asked where my family was living, I would tell them we lived behind the screen at the Twi-Lite Drive-In, and if they thought there was something silly about that, they could go to hell. I was a senior now. I had settled my scores. I would be nobody's Five Spot this year.

I strolled across the courtyard behind the bouncy cheerleaders Mindy Maples, Lisa Simmons, and Molly Manning, my last-year buddies from Canzoneri's government class. When Mindy saw me, she aimed her twinkle at me. "Oh my gosh, poor Daniel, we all heard what happened to your house! Are you okay?"

"Oh my gosh, Daniel," Lisa said, and Molly said it too. They flocked around me cooing Daniel, poor Daniel, plucking at my shirt, patting my shoulder, telling me they'd been thinking of me, praying

I was okay, how shocking it must be to wake up one day and your house is just *gone* and did you hear the other huge news?

We passed a knot of teachers gathered around the principal, Mr. Hamm, who seemed to have grown even fatter over the summer. His face was bright crimson and sweaty, as if the rigors of the first morning had worn him out already.

Some news came in the library line, some in the cafeteria. Teri Cooper lost her summer job as a log flume operator at Disney World, busted for smoking pot in a service tunnel. Gary Brantley, the star quarterback, got such bad grades in summer school that the coach was making him sit out the season opener against Magee. A black tenth-grader called Roland Simpson (whom no one quite remembered) had died in July when his car hit a tree near Yazoo City. Coach Atkins was no longer teaching driver's ed, since someone informed the school board of his habit of buying a six-pack of Miller at the beginning of each driving session and drinking four or five bottles over the next fifty minutes as his students practiced their parallel parking. From now on the coach would teach only Mississippi History, where supposedly he could harm no one.

On the Fourth of July someone spray-painted a swastika on Bernie Waxman's front door. Waxman was calm about it, according to Jeff Lehorn, but it upset Mrs. Waxman.

Marsha Lockner got pregnant by Mike Devoe and won't be coming back to school.

Oh and did you hear somebody burned Red Martin's red Mustang?

No shit.

Swear to God.

When?

Two nights ago. Burned up! Totaled! And his father's brand-new pickup truck too!

Who did it?

Tim Cousins, I heard. Spent a night in jail for it. He's out on bail.

Nobody came right out and told me this news. I overheard Bruce Dean and Johnny Henry in the line outside the gym.

"Fine with me," Dean was saying. "Red is such a jerk."

Chuck Watson said, "I bet Musgrove was in on it too."

"You guys," said Mary Virginia Ward. "He's standing right here listening to everything you say!"

Our part of the line cracked up.

I said, "Did they really put Tim in jail?"

"Like you didn't know?" Johnny said.

"I didn't. Tell me what happened. This is the first I've heard of it," I said. "I wondered why he's not at school."

Bruce said, "Come on, Musgrove. You had to have helped him do it."

"Nah, that stuff is between Tim and Red," I said. "I don't let Red bother me."

Some of the kids murmured their approval. The minute I left, they would all be discussing what a chickenshit I was.

The line inched forward. "I have to tell you guys, I don't think Tim did it," I said, as any loyal friend would.

Bruce Dean said, "Really? You don't think so? What about if he admitted it?"

I gaped. "What?"

"Yeah, you don't know anything," Chuck Watson said. "He admitted the whole thing to the cops."

"You and Cousins don't talk anymore?" said Bruce Dean. "I thought you two were like married."

"Go to hell, Dean. No more than you and Watson!" I play-punched his shoulder, trying to act as if my head was not reeling. What did he mean, Tim admitted it? How could that be?

It had to be wrong.

I burned the Mustang. I know, I was there. What I didn't know was that on the ride downtown, when Jeff Magill asked Tim if he set fire to Red's car, Tim smiled and said, Yes sir, I sure did. When asked if he acted alone, he said, Yes sir, I did. And I'm not sorry, either, he said. I would do it again in a minute.

Why would Tim admit to something he didn't do? I couldn't believe it. That was not in my plan. And I thought I'd been so careful to work out all the angles.

He was supposed to deny everything and put the blame on me. That's why I called his house first, to make sure he was there before I burned the car — so his mother could swear he was right there at home with her. The trail would lead to me, after Jeff Magill put the fear of God into Tim first. Eventually I would pay for what I had done.

That was my plan, anyway. But then he took the blame and screwed it all up.

At the head of the line Coach Barnes thumbed through a box and came up with my schedule for my senior year at Minor High:

Homeroom, Deavers *(old hag)*
English IV, O'Neal *(yes!)*
Algebra II, Passworth *(aieee!)*
Geology/Physics, Robichaux *(help me Jesus)*
Spanish II, B. J. Allen *(nice lady)*
American History, Coach Rainey *(long naps, head on desk)*
Band, Waxman *(of course)*

I had to call Tim and find out what the hell he was up to. I wanted to go to the band hall, say hey to Waxman and look for Arnita. But first I had to go to the auditorium stage to pick up my textbooks.

I walked through the echoey shadows to the back of the stage. I handed one copy of my class sheet to Mrs. Williford, then skulked about finding the right books among all the boxes. Once I had assembled my stack of knowledge, I carried it to Mrs. Williford's table for the sign-out sheet.

Over her shoulder I saw Arnita step from the shadows onto the stage.

My God, look. She stopped the room dead. The lights suddenly brightened, conversation dimmed, all motion stopped for a moment. Her hair was still boyishly short. She wasn't wearing her glasses — was she wearing contacts? The crisp line of white blouse against her brown skin. A short skirt followed by very long legs.

Her glorious smile was aimed at Mrs. Flora, the math teacher, not me. She didn't see me there.

You would never guess this girl had spent any time in a hospital. She radiated health, intelligence, nerve. She was more beautiful than ever.

I was glad for the shadows to hide in. I felt ugly, oafish, and large. My heart filled with hurt. How could I ever think she belonged with me? Suddenly I knew how unworthy I was, how impossible any idea that we could have been together. Arnita had always been way beyond me. I felt as doomed as that dork Arthur Miller must have felt at the moment Marilyn Monroe said yes.

"Here, Daniel." Mrs. Williford handed me a piece of paper. "Your locker assignment. Everybody's packet is in their locker. Fill out the registration forms and have a parent or legal guardian sign the ones with the checkmarks, are you listening to me?"

I turned. Arnita was gone. Had she seen me and fled?

Shouldn't flatter myself. More likely she didn't care about me at all.

In the bottom of locker 318 I found the registration packet with my name Magic Markered on the front. Some papers had fallen out and ended up on top. I gathered them into the folder and joined the herd headed to the auditorium.

26

I TOOK A SEAT on the aisle in the back, in case I saw a chance to sneak out. First-day assembly was supposed to be inspirational and motivational, a way to build school spirit. But it was led by Mr. Hamm, who would have had trouble inspiring mold to grow. First he read a prepared talk on the topic of tornado safety. Then he began reading from a long list of new rules and regulations, many of them dealing with a crisis of chewing gum under the desks.

"It's like urinating in the pool," said Hamm, to cries of "ewwww" from the girls. "Nobody ever admits to doing it, but somehow the pool continues to turn yellow. Now I know everybody takes the chewing gum out of their mouth and sticks it under the desk so the teacher won't catch you chewing it. It's traditional. I did the same thing when I was in school. But what I didn't consider, what I want you boys and girls to consider, is that it took our maintenance man Mr. Beecham one hundred and thirty-four hours this summer to scrape all the gum off the undersides of the desks. We're starting the year off clean. There's not a speck of gum on a single desk in this school. So the next time you take the gum out of your mouth, I want you to stop and think about Mr. Beecham having to scrape your gum off with his own two hands, hour after hour. Would you please do that for me, put your gum in a piece of paper and put it in the trash where it belongs?"

Next he announced that Mr. Waxman and the Mighty Marching Titans would be traveling to Jackson the second week in September to play for President Nixon at the Mississippi Coliseum. (Maybe ten people clapped, about the same number that hissed or booed.) The chess team was going to Columbus to play in a tournament with the Baptist Boys Home. Anyone caught trying to make drugs in the chemistry lab would be not suspended but expelled. And would the young ladies *please* not flush their sanitary napkins down the commodes, use the designated receptacles. (Massive groan from the guys.)

Hamm read the names of seven new teachers, a timid-looking lot who straggled up from their seats to wave at us. We clapped with an excess of courtesy, knowing how swiftly we would bend them to our will.

Mr. Hamm frowned and went on discussing the new policy of random locker searches. "This is for your own protection," he said. "We intend to keep harmful substances out of our school at all costs." A few potheads made oinking pig sounds, raising a big laugh from everyone else. "Okay, settle down," Hamm said.

After the long weird summer it felt good to be back in a mass of laughing people my age.

"Before we get to the nominations for class officers," Hamm called into the din, "we have a special visitor today. We are so pleased to welcome back one of our favorite students, who is making a fine recovery from a very serious injury. I've asked her to speak a few words about how glad she is to be back in school. Would you please welcome —" he glanced at the sheet in his hand "— Arnita Beecham."

God what a round of applause as she walked to the podium. She turned on her megawatt beauty-queen smile and melted the place. Everyone knew she was lucky to be alive, and now look how much more lovely she is! Every school has a superstar, and now, forever, Arnita was ours.

She no longer belonged to me. But God I still loved her. I did.

Even though she hated me. That changed nothing for me, except that seeing her made me want to cry. I felt so lonely. I'd blown it so bad.

She bent to the microphone. "Hey, y'all," she said, and everybody said Hey. "I didn't know I was going to be talking today. I didn't write a speech. But I did get all those cards you sent to Arnita, and the flowers. And I heard you wrote songs. I want you to know I really appreciated all of that. But that's not what I want to talk about."

Uh-oh. I hunkered down in my seat. I heard another stir behind me, and turned to see Red Martin coming in, flanked by two lineman buddies. He made a big disruption by strutting into assembly, just as he had when the cops hauled him out of here, back in the spring. He swaggered like a prizefighter returning to the ring, smacking his gum, savoring all those eyes on him. He plopped in the third row with his friends.

Arnita watched him all the way to his seat. "I know the truth is not really what school is about," she said. "But lately I've decided it's the most important thing there is, telling the truth. So that's what I want to do."

Mr. Hamm came back into view at stage left with his arms folded over his belly.

She smiled. "Don't worry, Mr. Hamm, I'm not gonna talk about school."

Mr. Hamm pantomimed relief.

"The truth is, you've all been making a mistake about me," she said. "I know you think I'm black. Probably thought so the first time you saw me. I may look black to you, but you have to understand that I'm not."

Oh no. Not today. Why, Arnita — the first day of school? Tell the world? Make your life so much harder?

I would have gone up there to stop her, but she wouldn't have listened to me.

"This is something I only realized after my accident," she went on. "It's not that I minded being black. Really, I love black people. They are the kindest, the best people I know. I'm not one of them, that's all. I mean, think about it, who would choose to be black? Why would you choose to be the one everybody looks down on?"

Shanice James stood up. "What the hell are you talking about?"

"Hey, Shanice. I'm just telling the truth — *my* truth, anyway. It's just — something happened to me. Being black turned out to be all in my head. It's just a part of my brain that got hurt. It doesn't have anything to do with who we are. It's a figment of our imagination. I think it may be that way for you too. You think you don't have any choice about it, but you do. I'm not black anymore. And I'm never going to be black again."

"Sit down!" hollered Red's friend Carl. "Down in front!"

Shanice gave him a nasty look and sat down.

"You're only black if you want to be," Arnita said. "I've been a lot happier since I found out."

Mr. Hamm said, "Arnita?"

She ignored him. "It's just so much easier not to be black. You have a nicer house. You have more money. There are oak trees in the yard. The kids have plenty of toys. The dad sits in a recliner with his feet up."

"Thank you, Arnita," said Hamm.

"I'm not done yet," she said evenly. "You asked me to talk, so let me talk."

A few shouts of support, but I could tell that most of the assembly was on Mr. Hamm's side. He shrugged as if he was afraid to stop her. She was pissing off the black kids. The white ones too. There was nothing in what she said to make anyone happy.

I hadn't drawn a real breath since she'd started talking.

"You all should try it," she said. "We could have a week where everybody can be who they're not. If you're black, you can be white. If you're white, you could try being black. Find out how it feels. Wouldn't you like to know?"

"What's wrong with you?" That was Brian Fairchild, on his feet. "Why do you want to be white? Black is beautiful."

"If black is beautiful, Brian, why do they have to force white people to go to school with you? If black is beautiful, why does everyone hate you? Why do people throw Cokes at you when you're just sitting there minding your own business? You can say black is beautiful all day long, but wake up. The only people who think that are black."

"That's society's problem," said Brian. "That's not *my* problem!"

"Oh yes it is," said Arnita. "They want you to be black! That's all. They don't want you to be anything else!"

"For you to stand up there and say you ain't black —"

"They can only make you black if you let them," she said. "If you participate. Don't you get it? There's only one —" Her voice disappeared. Mr. Hamm had unplugged her mike.

"No, Brian's right!" Shanice cried. "Who do you think you are? You're as black as I am."

"Hey!" Red stood up. "She wants to be white. Let her be white if she wants to!"

"Oh shut up, you stupid cracker!" snapped Shanice.

"Don't you tell him to shut up, nigger!"

There it was. From Red's buddy Carl. The word dropped like a bomb, like a great big stink bomb bursting over the heads of the assembly.

Mr. Hamm was paralyzed by the cloud of animosity sweeping the auditorium. I couldn't see who threw the first punch, but soon there were lots of punches. As if on a signal white guys and black guys jumped over their seats and started whaling on each other.

Arnita was saying something into the dead mike. I couldn't hear for the shouting.

There were a dozen boys fighting, six hundred kids stampeding for the doors. I was glad to be in the back corner — four loping steps and I could be out that door. I saw Arnita moving back from the edge of the stage, the trampling herd.

Janie. Where was Janie?

I parked myself inside the main exit and watched the flood of kids thinning out. To my relief I didn't see any broken little-girl bodies littering the aisles. The male teachers waded into the edges of the fistfight and had it mostly broken up by the time the cops arrived — four cops in the first wave, then four more.

I found Arnita by the circuit breaker box behind the curtain, stage left.

She turned to look at me. There was nothing in her eyes for me, one way or the other. She was cold.

"I know you hate me," I said.

She didn't deny it. She didn't say anything.

"Why did you do that?" I said.

"It was important. Listen — keep away from me, Daniel. You're not my friend." She turned and walked off across the hollow stage. Each click of her heel put another hole in me.

Then I saw who was waiting for her at the door. Dudley Ronald Martin smiled and gave me a little salute, an index finger tipped off his eyebrow. He put his arm around Arnita and escorted her out.

27

I PACED BACK and forth, screaming inside my head, How stupid to let yourself fall for her! Look what she turned out to be: a faithless mixed-up troublemaker of a girl, so confused and full of herself as to think she could reinvent black and white and make a whole new category just for herself!

She hated me so much she let Red Martin put his arm around her. How weak of me, to let her hurt me this much — to let myself care about her this much, when I'd known all along how damaged she was.

I should not care for anyone, ever. That's the secret of a happy life: care about nobody, never get hurt.

I called Tim from the pay phone in the courtyard beside the library. I didn't stop to ponder it. Too much had happened for me not to call. He picked up on the second ring.

"Hey," I said.

"Hi Daniel."

"Should I call back? Your folks there?"

"Nope. Sitting here by myself."

"Why'd you call me Daniel?"

"It's still your name, right?"

"But not Skippy, or Dagwood, or —"

"Durwood. When were you going to tell me?"

"Tell you what?"

"What you did to Red's car."

Okay. Here we go. "I thought you did that, Timmy."

"Uh-uh. Not me. That was a hundred percent you, Skip."

"Not me," I lied.

"Sure it was," he said easily. "You did it exactly like I would have. You're the only one who would have done it that way."

I felt a little welling of pleasure at the compliment, though his air of calm was unnerving. I meant to bluff my way through. "I don't know what you're talking about."

"Aw come on, Skip — you think I'd be pissed at you? Forget it. How could you know they would blame it on me? Seriously, don't worry. I'm not gonna tell anybody. I said it was me. I confessed the whole thing. Christ's sake, we're best friends, aren't we?"

"Of course," I said.

"That's what best friends do for each other," he said. "I'm taking the fall on this one."

"Tim, that's nuts."

"You did it, I knew you did." He laughed. "And it's so damn brilliant I wish I *had* done it. Was it as great as I think? Tell me everything. Did it make a big boom?"

"Tim. You confessed because you thought you were covering up for me?"

"Of course. Now quit faking. We're friends, remember? I know the hell out of you. I know you better than you do."

"I don't get it —"

"Oh Skippy! You are lying your ass off. Stop! I forgive you, okay? Jesus, it's not like you set me up on purpose!"

No, not like that at all. "Tim —"

"Because how could you know I'd confess," he said. "You kind of stumbled into committing the perfect crime. Where are you now?"

"School."

"I'll be there in three minutes."

I never imagined Tim's first reaction to my treachery would be this automatic loyalty to me. That he would take the whole crime on himself to keep me out of trouble. God, was he really that naive? Did it never occur to him that I might have set out to betray him? Mr. Paranoia, oblivious to his friend and sidekick Judas. What had I done to deserve such trust?

All I had to do now was go along with him. Let him take the fall, let the consequences work their steadying influence in his life, go on with our friendship as if nothing had happened.

Holy God. I could hardly believe my luck. I began to rejoice. My plan was working better than I imagined.

Here came the Starlite Blue Pinto streaking up Old Raymond Road. Tim popped open the passenger door, a little grin on his face. "Skippo! Where'd you get that bike?"

"Yard sale. Not bad, huh?" We hooked thumbs.

"Let me open the hatchback."

I stowed the bike and got in, riding shotgun. I tucked my registration packet by my foot. Tim slammed in a Joni Mitchell tape and scratched off from the curb — only boy I know that can burn rubber in a Pinto while playing Joni Mitchell. Not that much rubber, but still.

He wore a black leather jacket over a ribbed undershirt that revealed his beanpole torso. He was whiter than pale, never any sun these days except for the occasional funeral. The shock of hair spilled over half of his face to the jawline, a big swoop like David Bowie's hair, jet-black.

I said, "How was jail?"

"Deeeelightful," he said in a nasal honk.

"Don't do Eddie to me," I said.

"Oh man, was that Eddie? Sorry."

I blew out a sigh. "I can get out of this car, as you know."

"Where have you been, Skip? I drove by that hellhole motel fifty zillion times. Y'all's car is never there."

I explained that we'd moved to a slightly less hellish place. I didn't say where. I knew Tim would make horrible fun of the drive-in, and I wasn't ready to hear it.

We turned onto the Old Vicksburg Road, heading west with no destination. Tim described how he'd had to invent some details of his confession to Detective Magill. "They found part of a Clorox bottle. What did you use bleach for? I said to wipe off fingerprints."

"I poured it out," I said. "I just needed the bottle to put the gas in."

"Ah." A sly smile to acknowledge my admission.

"You should have seen it blow," I said. "It was incredible."

"Oh come on, Skippy, tell me everything."

"Tim. This is bad trouble you're in. We've gotta straighten this out."

"I said forget it, okay? You would do the same thing for me, right?"

Yes, I said. Maybe my biggest lie yet.

Tim wasn't faking. He wasn't even angry. He seemed as cheerful, in fact, as I'd seen him in months. A new lightness about him, a carefree tone in his voice. He had replaced the Carpenters sticker on the dashboard with a cutout of Suzi Quatro in a leather corset, but all he wanted to listen to was this mournful album *Blue*.

I told him all the details, the reconnaissance, planning, and execution. I told him about the lengths I went to, to give him an alibi. He listened intently and shrugged it off.

One night in jail seemed to have loosened him up, relaxed him. As if he was finally free of some long-standing worry.

I would never forgive him for Arnita. But what did he really do that was wrong? He just told her the truth — as I should have done, long ago. Getting rid of her that way was mean, but it was also the right thing. He offered me the chance to tell her myself, and I didn't have the courage. Tim was right, Arnita deserved better than a lie.

We zipped over the tops of round hills, a deep goldy end-of-summer green. Tim thought it was hilarious that the band would be playing "Hail to the Chief" for Nixon later in September. He pointed out that he had already done more time in jail than Nixon.

I told him how Arnita's little speech on the subject of her whiteness had sent the assembly into an uproar.

"She always did like an uproar," he said.

And guess who was waiting for her at the stage door?

"Oh no. Oh man, you're kidding. Oh, poor Skippy — Christ, what a kick in the balls! Listen, don't you worry about it. It's all gonna work out. I just know it is."

"How can it work out? Don't be stupid. She hates me."

"And now she thinks she's white? Isn't that what you said?"

"Ever since the accident."

"She always did act kind of white," Tim said. "That's how she got so popular. I bet she has more white friends than black ones."

"That's not what I'm talking about. She's not the same person at all. She's this other girl named Linda. At least some of the time. She's better now."

"Durwood, you need to stay far, far away from this girl, okay? Trust me on this. She is extremely crazy."

"Not crazy. Brain-damaged. We were there, remember?"

Usually when I brought up Prom Night, Tim glared as if he'd like to slug me. Now he just sadly shook his head. "And you're as stuck on her as ever."

"I guess so."

"Jail wasn't as bad as you'd think," he said. "You sit in a little room with bars on the door, what's wrong with that? They bring you books to read, beanie-weenies and potato salad for supper. Better than my mother would've fixed."

He acted cavalier about it, not like someone who had learned any lesson at all.

The hills began to roll higher and deeper, the two-lane swooping down a long descent from the forest into a gathering of gas stations and small motels. A sign pointed the way to Vicksburg National Military Park.

Tim said, You wanna?

I said, Why not. At the visitor center we bought Cokes and paused to admire the diorama of the rat-eating citizens of Vicksburg.

Driving through a columned arch, we crossed onto federal

property — you could tell by the smooth new asphalt and the groomed swales of grass flanking the road. Poor Mississippi couldn't afford such swanky roads.

The hills of the battlefield were studded with monuments to the dead. Around every bend was a grand vista leading to another magnificent obelisk. The monuments of the victorious Yankees were larger and more elaborate than the Southern ones. Illinois had gotten entirely carried away with a full-scale Pantheon in white marble at the head of about five hundred steps.

Every little while along the park drive was a turnout, a clearing with a line of cannon and a historical marker to explain which part of the battle was fought here. We passed row after row of white headstones in the national cemetery, all the dead from the battle and many more besides. Now we could taste the muddy air off the river. The road curved steeply up and around to the highest ground for miles, Fort Hill.

We parked, and walked to the crest of the ridge. Cannon glared out over the wide brown glittering river. This hill commanded the bend in the river for miles. The view stretched on forever to the west.

I pushed the red button set into the annotated map. "With these cannon," a scratchy deep voice intoned, "the Army of Vicksburg under General Pemberton controlled navigation on the mighty Mississippi, and earned this sleepy riverside village the title Fortress of the Confederacy. . . ."

Tim boosted himself up onto the speaker slots, muffling the voice with his butt. "Mm-hm," he said, wiggling. "Keep talking!"

I sighted down the tapering barrel of the cannon to a tiny barge, way down there on the wide muddy river. "Give me powder and a ball, sir," I cried, "and I'll blow that thar Yankee to hay-dees!"

Tim grinned. "I'll give you a ball! You're really into this stuff, huh Durwood. How you know so much about it?"

Earlier he'd made fun of me for trying to explain Grant's flanking movements downriver. "There's these things called books. If you look inside 'em you'll find all these words?"

"But you act like you really care about all this! Aren't you happy the South got the shit kicked out of it?" He raised his invisible rifle and squeezed off a shot. "I'm not sure it really matters. Like the Indians. I know the white man slaughtered 'em all. I know I ought to care. I just don't."

I started telling him how my great-grandpa Otis P. Musgrove walked home from Chickamauga on his shot leg, but he didn't care about that either.

"Would you die for the right to own a slave, Durwood?"

"Heck no. I'm a Yankee. You know that."

"No you're not. If your grandpa's a Reb, you're one of us. You were born in Alabama, dammit. Try to act like it. Would you die for Alabama?"

"No way," I said. "It's just a place. I'm not gonna die for a *place.* Anyway, what would I want with a slave?"

"Well, I think we have learned that would be your type." He waggled his eyebrows.

"Touché, dickhead." I took a swipe at him.

He used his imaginary machine gun to mow down dozens of Yankees charging up the face of Fort Hill. "What would you die for, Skip?"

I'd never thought about it, and I told him so.

"Well, think about it," he said.

"I don't want to. I kinda like the idea of not dying. At least not for a while."

"I'm serious. Is there anything on earth you'd be willing to give up your life for?"

I considered all the immediate possibilities.

"The country?" I ventured. "I mean, if we got attacked. Like Pearl Harbor. And if we all had to fight, I would go. Not with Nixon in charge, though. And not to Vietnam, thank you very much. That looks like no fun at all." I thought of Bud with his lucky bad foot, which had kept him at the base in California so far. His last postcard said he was learning to surf.

"Anything else? What if someone came in and tried to murder your family, like *In Cold Blood.* Would you die to stop 'em?"

"They're gonna murder the whole family, or just some of them? Do I get to choose which ones?"

He boosted himself up to straddle the cannon. "What if it was me? What if somebody was trying to kill me, and you might get killed trying to stop 'em? Would you do it?"

"Yeah," I said.

"You would?"

"Sure. You'd do the same for me, right?"

"Yeah," he said. "All right. That's all I wanted to know."

"Why?"

"No reason." He had a goofy smile, unaccountably happy. "I knew that's what you would say." He peered down at the black cast iron barrel emerging from between his legs. "Here's what you need, Durwood. Here's what that girl really wanted. Look here." He patted it, stroked it.

"Not funny," I said.

Tim hopped off the cannon. He pushed the red button. "With these cannon, the Army of Vicksburg under General Pemberton controlled navigation on the mighty Mississippi . . ."

The Vicksburg Dairy Dog was just like the one back home. We ordered burgers, onion rings, coffee. Evening was falling, but inside the Dog was bright as noon. Dad would kill me for going AWOL from the Twi-Lite. Too bad. I would just have to get killed. Janie and I had spent the whole weekend helping him clean up his damn drive-in, and now I had declared an afternoon off for myself.

Janie! Oh God. I'd promised her a ride home after school, then forgot her completely. I wondered how long she stood there waiting for me, after I'd ordered her not to keep me waiting.

Ah well. She's my sister, she'll just have to get over it.

We got back in the Pinto. "Where to?" I said.

"Anywhere you want." Tim turned to look at me. "You got any ideas?"

"Not really. I guess home. School tomorrow."

"I'm not going tomorrow," he said. "I'll go Friday, I think. I'm pretty sure I won't go before Friday."

I said, "Want to take the interstate back? It's faster."

"Yeah, we could," he said. "Or else, I don't know. What do you feel like?"

That was an innocent question. I don't know why my skin prickled up in gooseflesh. I wasn't quite sure what he meant by it.

Suddenly there wasn't enough air in the car. I rolled down my window and groped for the dashboard and switched on the radio — a crash of loud static. I twisted the dial and landed on a station playing Jackie Wilson, "Say You Will."

I turned it up loud. We rode without talking. If you drive eighty on the interstate, you can get back to Minor in no time.

Finally I said, "I'm having a hard time getting over what you did," I said. "She's pretty special to me."

"I know, Skippy," he said. "And I appreciate you giving me another chance. I'll take you on home, if you want. Where is home these days, anyway?"

"You can drop me at the Jitney Jungle. I'm supposed to buy food for the house. Mom went to Alabama to see her family for a few days."

"I'll take you to the store and then home. I don't mind."

"No, that's okay."

"What's the big secret, Mumwood? How come you don't want me to know where you live?"

"It's kind of a dump. I don't think we'll be staying there long. Did you say you're not coming to school tomorrow?"

"I'm not sure I'm even coming back to school," Tim said.

I stared at him. "What?"

"I'm just not sure." His face looked paler than before.

I switched off the radio. "What are you talking about?"

He put on a tight little smile. "You didn't look in your packet, huh?"

"Packet?"

"Registration."

"What about it? It's right here."

"You found it in your locker, right? Just like every year on the first day of school."

"Yeah."

"But didn't you find a little something extra? In your locker, on top of your packet? A couple of extra pages, stapled together?"

"I thought some of it fell out. I didn't look at it yet. What are you talking about?"

"It's a gift from Red," he said. "His latest project. Apparently he's been busy over at the Xerox place making up a bunch of them. He must have got to school real early this morning. He managed to put a copy in every single locker."

"Tim —" I pulled out two pages, stapled together. He turned on the dome light.

Police Incident Report, Sheriff's Department, Hinds County.

The date at the top was November 23, 1972.

Arrestee: Cousins, Timothy R. Case number 000385-22F-1972.

Offense: Indecent exposure.

Offense: Unnatural intercourse.

Offense: Open and gross lewdness in a public place.

Offense: Sodomy, second degree.

"What is this?" I said.

"It's fairly self-explanatory." Tim kept his eyes on the road. "Or at least Red seemed to think so."

Location of offense: Rest Area #183N, I-55 South.

Suddenly I grasped what Tim was trying to tell me. All over Minor, students were finding copies of this report with their permission slips, sign-up sheets, the fall football schedule.

Tim told me he'd been arrested once before, at Thanksgiving. Reckless driving, he said. Spent a night in jail. They'd suspended his license.

No mention of driving anywhere on this page.

REPORTING OFFICER'S NARRATIVE (Brief narrative
of the facts surrounding the offense and the arrest)

    At 9:20 PM, Reporting Officer (R/O) was conduct-
ing undercover vice operations when he observed

arrestee loitering near the restroom building.
R/O was approached by arrestee, who made overt
sexual advances. R/O declined, returned at 9:45
PM to find arrestee loitering with another subject, engaged in public lewdness and indecent
exposure, specifically masturbating in view of
the officer. Arrestee again made overt sexual
advances. R/O placed subject under arrest and
escorted arrestee to vehicle. Arrestee was handcuffed, informed of his rights, and transported
to HCSD. Transportation proceeded without incident. At 10:52 PM, R/O turned the arrestee over
to HCSD personnel for processing. At all times
while in custody, arrestee appeared coherent. Although uncommunicative, arrestee was coopera-
tive.

DEFENDANT'S VERSION/REMARKS (What did the defendant say about the offense or his/her where-
abouts at the time of offense?)

Arrestee asked why he was being arrested and
then said, "Oh wow. I can't believe this s**t."
Otherwise, arrestee remained silent during transportation to the station and during processing.
Arrestee declined to answer any questions until
an attorney was present. However, arrestee coop-
erated physically and did not resist in any way.

"The whole school is reading this?"

"My mother got a visit from Marjorie Schlatter's mom. Marjorie
opened her packet and voilà. Her mom ran right over to show us.
Wasn't that nice of her?"

"Jesus. Tim."

"Yup. It's Red's copy — see down at the bottom where he had to
sign for it? D. Ronald Martin. Ol' Dudley. His lawyer must have got

it for him. He could've covered up his name before he Xeroxed it. But he wanted everybody to know he put this out."

"Payback," I said. "For burning his car."

"There you go."

"Oh God. Tim. I'm sorry." I shook the pages. "This is true?"

"Well, not exactly. There's a little more to it than that." His skin looked translucent in the dashboard light.

"But they found you guilty of this?"

"Nah, they dropped the charges. I was a juvy. Slap on the wrist. My folks never even found out."

"How could they not find out?"

"I told you — I used you as my excuse. My one phone call was to tell 'em I was spending the night at your house. I was so lucky you didn't call me that night. They let me out the next morning. Remember when I was supposed to be taking those advanced placement classes out at West Hinds? I never went. I used the money to pay a lawyer. He handled the whole thing. The folks never knew. Until today when Marjorie's mother came over. Mom thinks that was the only copy and somehow it got in Marjorie's packet by mistake. She doesn't know about Red and his Xerox machine."

"What did she say?"

"She doesn't believe it. She says it's a case of mistaken identity. Dad wants me out of the house."

"Oh God," I said. "I'm sorry, Tim. This is too much."

"Yeah it is. Finally, too much." That grim smile returned. "I guess all's fair in love and war, isn't that what they say?"

I turned away. I didn't want to know more. What could it mean? Sodomy? Indecent? Lewd? Gross? Unnatural? It sounded like that song on the sound track of *Hair*.

This happened a couple months after we met. Imagine — Tim had gone through this whole indecent unnatural thing, busted for these crimes, and never breathed a word to me. His best friend. Imagine holding that inside, all this time.

This was where all the trouble began. The words on these pages were the awful thing he didn't want me or anyone to know.

That feeling I had gotten from him a few minutes ago? — that was a definite feeling. Oh God. Did that make me one too? Because I'm his friend? Because I could sense that he — that he was asking —

My hand wandered to the back of my head. Each of my fingertips found its way to one of the spots where my hair would not grow.

These words were the reason Tim drove away from Arnita on Prom Night, instead of stopping to help her. The thing that was gnawing at him all along. And now everyone in the world would be reading them.

So why was Tim smiling?

He switched off the dome light. "Today was just a perfect day, don't you think? It was so great just riding around, checking out the stupid monuments. Did you like it?"

"It was okay," I said. He wanted us to be friends again, like before.

"The weather was so perfect too. There was no way you could have made it any better."

What I did to Red was bad enough. Setting fire to his car was every bit as unnecessary as it was satisfying. But what Red turned around and did to Tim — for revenge — well, forgive me if I thought that was the lowest of all. It didn't help that it was all my fault.

Red could get a new car. I could get new friends. But Tim was destroyed. He could never go back to Minor High. He'd have to go somewhere else to graduate. Who could walk down the halls of a school knowing everyone had read what was written on this paper?

Lewd. Unnatural. Open and gross. Fag queeny fairy faggot homo queer, lurking and jerking off and God knows what else (sodomy, second degree!) in a roadside rest stop. He was a dead man.

"Red went to a lot of trouble to do this," I said. "Tell you what, Tim. Call it off. Give up. Let him win. If this is how he fights, it's not worth it."

He brushed the hair from his eyes. "Red is not going to win. I can't let that happen."

"He already won, okay? Read this. It's over. Admit it. It was you against him, and he won."

"What about you?" He raised an eyebrow. "You're not on my side anymore?"

"Not for this fight. I'm done with it. Aren't you done yet?" I shook the stapled pages at him. "Doesn't this feel like enough to you? What do you wanna do now, kill Red? You can't do that. I'll probably go to jail for burning his car, and you can't even go back to school now. It's gone too far, Timmy, you've got to stop."

"Friday I can go back," he said. "That's what I was thinking."

"But everybody will know!" We got out to unload my bike from the hatchback.

"That's the thing. That's why I don't want to go tomorrow. I need some time to get used to the idea." I smelled his cinnamon gum. "Do you hate me?"

"No," I said. "You hate me?"

"Never. I never will, Skippy." He shoved me away. "Go on. I'll see you Friday."

I didn't go into the Jitney Jungle. I watched until the Starlite Blue Pinto was gone, then I pedaled slowly uphill.

Poor Tim. I had loved being his friend. I felt sorry I couldn't be his friend anymore. I didn't hate him for what he was, but I couldn't be around him after this. Could I? I would never forget what had happened to me outside the emergency room the day Granny died. I had to make sure it didn't develop into anything that might resemble a problem. I knew it was not contagious, at least not in the obvious way, but it was better not to take chances. I knew for sure I was not that way because I had made love with a real live beautiful girl. Maybe sometimes I wondered, or let us say I tried to imagine certain things. And it felt like the kind of dark alley you don't wander down alone at night.

28

Debbie Frillinger eyed the empty space beside me at the table. "Hey Daniel, can I sit here?"

"Sure. How's it going, Debbie?"

She slid her lunch tray alongside mine. "Okay. Where's Tim?"

"He didn't come to school today," I said. "He hasn't been here all week." This was Thursday, and I hadn't seen him since he dropped me at the Jitney Jungle Monday night.

"What's wrong, is he sick?"

"Didn't you get those extra pages in your packet?"

"Extra . . . you mean that stuff about when he got arrested? Yeah, I read that. That was awful. That's not why he didn't come to school?"

"I think so. Listen, Debbie, I want you to know, I had no idea —"

"What a horrible thing for Red to do," she said. "What a creep! Everybody hates him now. It's one thing to pick on somebody, but to take something so personal like that and spread it around? That's just cruel. And he went to so much trouble to do it! Disgusting."

She surprised me. I'd assumed everyone would be grateful to Red for exposing the terrible queer in our midst. "You think so?"

"Timmy shouldn't have messed with his car," Debbie said. "Red loved that car."

"Yeah, that was dumb," I agreed.

"But Red drove him to it. He picked on him so bad. When is he coming back?"

"Who, Tim? I don't think he'll be coming back to school," I said. "Not here, anyway."

"Why not?"

"Well — what do you think? He's embarrassed that everybody found out."

"What, that he's a homo? Oh come on, Daniel, don't be ridiculous. Everybody knew that."

My mouth fell open. "They did?"

"Of course! For years."

"Well, not me!"

"Please. *Tim?* He's your best friend — and you had no idea?"

"Nope. I swear."

Debbie sat back. When she spoke, it was softly: "Does that mean you're not?"

"No! Of course not! Why, did you — what did you think?"

"Well, Dianne always swore you weren't. She said you can't be that good a kisser and still be . . ." She grinned. "But Tim was a great kisser too, so that doesn't prove anything."

"My God." A flush of heat rose up my neck. "Why did you ever think that?"

"Well Daniel, I mean, come on. You and Tim are inseparable."

"I never knew about him. Swear to God."

She pursed her lips. "I can't believe you're that innocent."

I RODE OVER to the Spur station to call Tim. For the third night in a row Patsy Cousins said he wasn't home. "I don't know, Daniel, he says he's out practicing his routine."

"What routine?"

"Some new show he's in. I've learned not to push him too hard for details. He tells me what he wants me to know. It seems to work better that way. You know how worried we were."

"Okay, thanks. I guess I'll see him in school tomorrow."

"Wait. Daniel. He doesn't seem quite so down now, does he? I mean, to his father and I, it seems like a big difference just in the last week or two."

Tread with care. She didn't realize that the whole world had already learned about Tim. "Yeah, I guess so," I said. "We went to Vicksburg the other day. He did seem a little happier."

"We think so, too. He's not brooding around the house so much. I'm sure we were making a fuss about absolutely nothing. Thanks for sticking by him, Daniel. You're a good friend."

I said goodbye and went back across the highway. Janie was excited about our first shipment of movies. Friday night was to be the grand opening of the Musgrove-owned-and-operated Twi-Lite Drive-In. I'd begged Dad to let me and Janie help him pick the movies — his idea of a classic was *The Green Berets* — but while I wasn't looking, he'd phoned up a movie distributor. Here came a huge box of red plastic marquee letters, still affixed to their snap-off frames, and a stack of battered green film cans.

I didn't recognize the titles but they were definitely drive-in movies: *Enter the Dragon, Invasion of the Bee Girls, Hitler: The Last Ten Days, Scream, Blacula, Scream!, House of Psychotic Women, Last Tango in Paris, The Young Nurses.*

I examined the rims of the cans. "Any of these any good?"

"Beats the heck out of me," Dad said. "I don't know why they couldn't send one or two a person's ever heard of. The man said he was sending the drive-in rotation for the fall. What is this *Tango in Paris?* Who wants to see some movie about French people dancing?"

I consulted the sheet. "It says Marlon Brando. It might be good."

"How about the Hitler one for the grand opening?" Dad said. "People love stuff about Hitler."

Janie and I groaned.

Dad said, "All right then, the tango one. I really don't care."

I said *House of Psychotic Women* would draw a bigger crowd. Dad said he had lived it, he didn't want to watch a movie about it. Janie said she would rather see *Invasion of the Bee Girls.*

"I'm partial to *The Trouble With Angels*, myself," said Dad. The first four reels of that old Hayley Mills movie were the only celluloid Tex Mooney had left behind in the projection booth. Dad had been watching those reels a lot, late at night, after we were asleep. I would sometimes awaken to see Hayley's eye blown up giant-sized on the wall of my room. "I told the distributor I'd give him top dollar for the last two reels. I would sure love to know how it ends."

"Hayley Mills decides to become a nun," I said. "We saw it when we were little."

Dad's face darkened. "Why did you tell me? Don't you think I wanted to find that out for myself?" His irritation dissolved. "Wait a minute. Hayley Mills does?"

"It's kind of a twist at the end."

"That ain't even believable," he said. "Dang, I wish you hadn't told me that."

Jacko said he sho would like to see a picture with Tom Mix in it. Dad said Tom Mix was a silent movie star and had been dead a long time. Jacko said all the best picture shows had Tom Mix.

I went to help him into bed. Since he got home from the hospital, the old man spent most of his time in his room on the ground floor.

Tomorrow was Friday. I doubted Tim would show up at school. What could he gain by coming? He could only lose, in ways I didn't want to imagine. He needed a fresh start — a county school, maybe, or one of the Council schools. If you're a pariah, you do what you have to. One year as the new guy somewhere, he could go off to college and everything could work its way back toward normal.

I was beginning to get used to the idea of finding my own way without him.

Just got my eyes closed and drifting to sleep when here it came again, the square of light on the wall, the opening credits, the trouble, the angels. Dad was playing the first reel again.

Gonna have the light shining in our eyes, all night long.

Friday when I woke up I didn't want to go to school. Wouldn't it be better just to go on and transfer to the county school with Tim, get a new start for myself while I'm at it?

Forget it. Stick to your plan. Life as a solo.

I had to stop being Tim's sidekick. I had to be nobody's sidekick. I had begun to understand the urge that made Bud hide himself in his room at the start of his senior year, with no friends and no desire to make any. He was planning a clean getaway. That might be a good strategy for me: Spend this year in my room, watching Hayley Mills's eye and plotting my escape from this place. Counting off the days until I could leave. One Mississippi, two Mississippi . . .

I left Janie waiting for the school bus; she had talked our old friend the Hooterville driver into changing his route, just to pick her up. On my Raleigh (I considered it mine now) I had given up Highway 80 for my fine secret cross-country path. In reality it was a maintenance road for a gas pipeline, but I pretended it was a secret roadway built just for me: a cinder-covered path shooting a straight line from a point just east of the drive-in, over the hills to the practice field behind Minor High. Riding it made me think of the days when I rode my Schwinn in from the country to do Mrs. Beecham's chores and be near Arnita.

A fine, coolish morning with a sparkle of dew on the grass, the first hint that summer might not last forever. I loved flying down the inclines and standing up on the pedals to march over the hills. I was thinking Mom should come on back to see how we'd fixed up the Twi-Lite. Dad was even acting a little nicer these days. He'd hardly raised his voice since Mom left.

On the phone Mom said she missed us, but she didn't sound too torn up about it. In her absence Dad and Janie and I were on our best behavior, taking turns looking after Jacko, pretending to get along. We thought it would just have to last until Mom came back. I couldn't imagine the three of us facing the idea of life with . . . just us.

I came over the last rise breathing hard, into view of the sprinklers sending great water-arcs across the practice field. The junior varsity squad was doing jumping jacks just out of reach of the spray. I heard the shrill of the three-minute bell. I rode around Titan Field, up the service road, along the band hall, to the front of the school.

I locked my bike and made a dash for it, across the courtyard and down the hall. Slid into Mrs. Deavers's homeroom an instant before the last bell.

After homeroom I decided to stop by the library, one of my favorite places to while away study hall. The librarian was Mrs. Sidney, thin and delicate as a china teacup, with a refined Delta accent that spoke of magnolias and plantations. Though she was barely forty, she dressed like an old lady — shapeless colorless dresses, spinster glasses, her hair in a bun.

I asked if she knew of any books about Mississippi architects. She said she doubted there was such a book. I asked if she happened to know, then, how to find out who designed Minor High School, and the Twi-Lite Drive-In, and the Mississippi Coliseum. Was it possible the same person could have designed all three?

She steered me to a shelf with a few architecture books, and said she would help me make an interlibrary request to track down the information. "This is for a class project?"

"No ma'am. I'm just curious."

"Hm." A prim smile. "We don't get much of that around here."

I wedged myself on a rolling stool with a stack of large flat books. For the next forty minutes I submerged myself in a sea of Frank Lloyd Wright and Mies van der Rohe, so many long fantastic buildings I forgot why I'd come in here. The bell rang. I closed up the books and began wedging them into the shelves.

I was thinking if I told Tim about my talk with Debbie Frillinger — if he knew that even a Jesusy girl like Debbie didn't hate him for what was on those Xeroxed pages — maybe there was a chance he could come back to school after all. Let a little time go by, let things settle down, and then it might possibly work.

I heard a car backfire. A percussive explosion loud enough to make me jump.

But the sound couldn't be a car, it came from inside the school.

A firecracker. Somebody had set off a firecracker in the hall!

Something in the sound was not a firecracker — a ripping sound, the air being torn in two, lightning striking too close.

Mrs. Sidney put her head out the door, into the hall. Whatever she saw out there brought her scrambling back inside. "Great heavenly days," she cried. "They're shooting a gun!"

The second blast seemed twice as loud. The echoing roar pierced by a girl's scream. Not a Halloween scream. Real fear.

I knew better than to stick my head out that door. Without moving I found that I had entered a different place.

Somebody ran by the doorway, then somebody else. Then a lot of people running. Coach Barnes yelling, "He's got two guns, now get out of here! Go!"

See, I knew. When the coach said that, I knew. My ears had told me that was gunfire, but I could not face the full meaning of who it was until he said that. And then I knew everything.

There was nobody else it could be.

"Oh, Lord," Mrs. Sidney cried, "please don't hurt anybody."

I got calm. Way too calm. My heart stopped beating. All the liquid inside me froze, cracked, burst the vessels, and sent the blood washing back through me with such force that I had to lean against the wall. Mrs. Sidney gripped my arm. "Honey, are you all right?"

I tried to push past her. "I need to go."

"Where?"

"I know who it is. I need to go see."

She clung to my arm with thin fingers. "Who? Who is it?"

"Let me go. I've got to stop him."

"Oh, no. You'll get hurt! Stay in here with me!"

Like an answer, a burst of gunfire down the hall. This was a different gun — a sharp whip-crack sound, four rapid shots — *blam blam blam blam!*

That brought a big scream, many girls screaming at once, as on the Zipper at the carnival.

Through the library's glass wall I saw windows popping open along the row of classrooms in the courtyard. Kids tumbled out and ran for their lives. I heard a thunder of running in the hallway, people shouting and running.

Oh, don't do this. Stop now before you hurt somebody. This is bad enough don't make it worse. That's what I would tell him. But first I had to find him and hope he didn't shoot me before I could speak.

"Miz Sidney." I pried her fingernails from my flesh. "Let me go."

"Young man, you are not going out there!"

I loved her for that — she didn't even know my name and she wanted to save me! Or did she want me to save her? "Get out of the school, go out the back way!" I said, and pushed her away.

I have never been brave. I did not want to start now. The brave people in movies are always the first to die. But I was the only one who knew him. I knew very well that what he started, he would be determined to finish. If anyone in this building could convince him to stop, it was me.

I stepped into the hall and started walking toward the sound, upstream through a panicky rush to the back of the school.

Probably he was too far gone to listen. He might even kill me. But nobody else stood a chance.

The first shot had gotten my attention. The second shot had made it more than an accident.

It seemed to be coming down the hall to the left, from the vicinity of Hamm's office and the main entrance.

Down the hall to the right I heard people banging on a door, guys shouting, hurling chairs against a door. Mrs. Norcom, the biology teacher, ran past, screaming, "Out the windows! Go out the windows! The doors are blocked!"

Blam! Another blast from the left, the principal's office. People slipped to the floor like a crowd in a comedy movie, skidding into pileups. Not much screaming now, just the sound of kids trying to get out of there.

I heard the crash of glass breaking, someone smashing out windows.

For one moment I let myself entertain the idea that Red Martin might have —

No. I knew this anger. I knew whose it was.

Parts of the school were emptying fast, kids spilling out all available windows. The X where the hallways crossed was no-man's-land.

Lisa Simmons skittered down the hall in her bare feet, shrieking, "Don't shoot me don't shoot me!"

A storm of firing — *blam blam blam blam!* He had lots of ammunition. He could have easily killed her. He was showing off now, shooting for fun. Scaring the hell out of everybody. He wasn't going to hurt anybody.

I had to stop him.

Oh God. For the first time I was afraid.

I didn't think he would hurt me. But I didn't know him anymore. If he shot me and killed me, well, that's what I got for being his friend. I hoped I wouldn't be paralyzed, and I thought, If you shoot me please shoot to kill. I do not want to end up like Jacko.

I hoped he would know it was me before he shot. I didn't want to die in a random act, please.

On the east side of the hall some teachers had barricaded themselves in their classrooms. Kids crouched by their desks, the blinds down and shut, as for a nuclear bomb drill. There were only high skinny windows on that side of the school, no way out of those rooms without getting into the line of fire. I think I was the only one in the building not terrified senseless, because I knew who was shooting and why. He'd been shooting for four minutes maybe. It seemed like a week since I was sitting in the library stacks.

On the other side of no-man's-land, to the left beyond the first set of lockers, a door opened in superslow motion. This was the janitor's closet, where Lincoln Beecham kept his dustmops and brooms and cleaning machines. That was Beecham in his navy-blue work shirt and trousers, coming out of his room. In that little room Lincoln Beecham kept his folding chair and a portable radio he played very loud. When he opened the door, the O'Jays were shouting out "Love Train."

Tell all the folks in Egypt — and Is'ral too . . .

Mr. Beecham had it cranked up so high that he had no idea what was going on out in the hall. He had heard neither the shots nor the screams. I could tell that from the untroubled way he raised his hand in greeting and ambled toward me, into the X of hallways.

I put my hand up to stop him, opened my mouth to say *stop*, but a bullet caught him in the side and spun him around. The second one slammed him into the lockers, and put him down on the floor on his back.

"Tim?" My voice sounded hollow. I walked out into the X and looked down the hall.

I blinked. Nobody there. "Tim, it's me. Don't shoot!"

No answer. The hall stretched away, a thousand miles long. Broken glass on the floor by the office, wires dangling from the ceiling.

I turned back to make sure I wasn't dreaming oh please God please let me wake UP!

Lincoln Beecham on his back, his arms flung out, a dark pool spreading from his side over the spotless floor.

I could still hear people screaming running, I could see down the hallways in all four directions. No one in sight.

Faint sirens approaching. I knelt on Beecham's right side because the pool of blood was spreading on the left, and I didn't want to get it on me. I thought of the first aid diagrams in the Boy Scout manual. There were no instructions for how to help someone dying in a pool of blood. There was a smell, kind of a tang to it — oh God. That was blood.

Too much blood on the floor. There was nothing I could do for Mr. Beecham.

Oh now look what you did Timmy her father you killed him it's way beyond serious now you are killing people.

"Hey Skip-ayyyyyyyyy . . ." A voice floating in the air all around.

Out front I heard car doors slamming and the bloop of sirens racing up to the front of the school.

Click click as he keyed the microphone. "Skip Skip Skipperino! Skippetto! Where you be stay at, Skippeh? Come to Papa!"

He clicked off the mike and started shooting again — out the window, I think. God how much ammo did he have?

He was in Mr. Hamm's office. That gave him a clear view of the courtyard, the library, the main entrance. A perfect sniper's nest.

And he wanted me to join him there.

Think now. Be smart. Is that really the only choice?

"Now hear this!" His boisterous echo. "Durwood, this is *fun!* This is just what I always wanted to do! Oh and for all you little people out there — all you very special cowering people — just like to say helloooooo, thank you all, fuck you all very much!" He laughed and tried to sound maniacal, then he switched to monkey noises, hoo-hoo-haa-haa-HAA!

Behind the forced wildness I heard how frightened he was.

He could not turn this into one of his jokes. He was killing people.

My old life was gone. I did not want this new life. I did not want to think of Lincoln Beecham bleeding on the floor.

I placed one foot in front of the other. I remembered Tim describing a book he'd read about that guy in Texas, what was his name, climbed up in the tower and shot all the people. Charles Whitman. Went to the top of the Texas Tower and shot everybody in sight. Once Charles Whitman had killed the first one, Tim said, he was blooded. He had nothing more to lose, so why not just run up the score?

It was one of those things you talk about. We talked about a lot of things.

I must have been in shock remembering that, as my shoes crunched in glass. It felt more like the opposite of shock, a super-awareness, all-encompassing clarity, dreadful calm. It felt like a dream, but awake. I could see a whole chain of cause and effect going back — I did this, so he did this, so I did this, on and on infinitely into the past. I began to understand a lot of little things. Jokes that didn't feel like jokes. Odd statements. *I'll go Friday, I think. I'm pretty sure I won't go before Friday.*

I floated above the hallway looking down on myself as I approached the door of the principal's office. Men shouting outside, more sirens now. Cars screeching to a halt.

Blue haze floated in the air, a strong firecracker smell. The glass wall of the outer office lay in a glittering splash across the floor, the counter, the back-to-back typewriters of Miss Pitts and the other secretary. He had shot up the trophy case, leaving a jumble of blasted trophies at the bottom.

"Tim." I said it loud. "I'm out here in the office. Don't shoot me."

"Who iiiiis it?" His mocking falsetto.

"It's Daniel."

"Are you alooooooone?"

"Yeah. It's just me."

"Hey Skippeh! Come on in! The water's fine!"

"You're not gonna shoot me?"

"Skippy, fuck! Get in here! God, is this far out or what?"

I half expected to come around that corner and see a monster, a horrible creature foaming and raging and swiping at me with its claws. What I found was Tim, standing in a shadow just beyond the blown-out window. Just my old friend Tim wearing a dun-colored hunting vest over a black T-shirt. Black jeans. Black Converse. Knit cap pulled low on his eyes. Smacking gum ninety miles a minute. He looked like a skinny pale commando with that big rifle in his hand. It resembled a hunting rifle except for the magazine stock and the sleek black scope. He had added the scope since I saw it in the back of the Pinto.

He ratcheted out a spent magazine and stuck in a new one. "You might not want to stand there, Durwood. When I shoot this thing, that's right where the casings go."

I moved to the corner farthest from the windows.

The double-barreled shotgun was leaned into the corner beside his left hand. A green canvas duffel on top of Mr. Hamm's desk overflowed with boxes of bullets, shotgun shells, cartridge magazines. Laid out in a row on the desk were an efficient-looking pistol like a German spy might carry, a six-shooter revolver, and a hunting knife with a jagged blade.

"Timmy. Put the gun down and talk to me a minute."

He smiled. "I can't do that, son, sorry. We got some fairly big-time police visitation going out front. I gotta stay on top of things."

"You don't want to die, do you? Stop this now. We can figure this out. I can help you. We'll just wave a white flag. That's all we have to do." All the time thinking, *I'm going to die. Today is my last day.*

"Thanks, Skippy. But I don't want to stop. I'm telling you, this is fun! For the first time in my whole stupid life I am doing what I really want to do. You don't know how good it feels. You oughta try it." He nodded at the table. "Take your pick. You want the shotgun? It's got a kick but I bet you can handle it." He peered at me. "What's the matter, Skip? Aw come on, don't tell me you're fuckin' crying? Jaysus!"

"You killed Mr. Beecham."

"Yeah well, what can you do," he said. "More than just him, actually."

I felt that cold finger slide down my neck.

"Scuse me a sec." He raised the rifle to his shoulder and peered into the sight. The action looked so natural. He fired off a burst.

I grabbed my ears and doubled over. I wasn't ready for how loud it was in that room.

He laughed, screaming out the window, "Dance, motherfucker! Come on back out here! I'll get you!" He glanced at me. "This one's good for distance."

"Who else did you shoot?"

"Oh come on, Durwood, guess! Who do you think I would pick to be number one on the Casey Kasem, American Top For-or-or-teeeeeee?"

I felt a surge of nausea rising. "I am not playing your goddamn games."

"Whoa, whoa now, Skippy gets touch-ay. I decided to do Red first, that way if anybody stopped me, well, hell, at least I got Red, right? I mean, he was always Public Enemy Number One, as far as I'm concerned."

"You killed him?"

"Yeah, and you told me I couldn't! Imagine that. He was easy, the problem was his little lady friend. Now listen Skip, I didn't want to, I swear, but she came at me while I was dealing with him. She tried to get my gun and she almost got it too. She was strong. I had no choice. I'm really sorry. I know how much you used to like her. She was not on my list, I swear."

What?

What did he say?

What little lady friend?

"You don't mean — Arnita —"

"I tried not to, Skip. Now this is not a criticism, okay? But she kinda forced the issue, coming at me like that. A hell of a lot braver than Red, let me tell you. He was down on his knees like a girl. He was crying, man, he was begging like a little girl. You'da loved it. I'd have taken you with me, but I knew I had to get one or two under my belt before you would see I was serious."

"Oh no. You didn't — no." I covered my eyes with my hand. Don't. Don't cry do not think about it now. Put it away for later. He's lying. He's saying this to hurt you. Don't cry little baby you cannot cry now you have to be clear, think straight and stop him. He is saying these things to drive you crazy. He didn't really do it. He's trying to scare you.

Arnita.

I started thinking how to get the rifle out of his hand. In every scenario, though, he just grabbed another gun. He had them laid out before him like surgical instruments.

Something out in the courtyard caught his interest. He leaned forward. "There's somebody in the library. Back in the stacks." He aimed his rifle.

"Wait, that's Mrs. Sidney. She's nice. Leave her alone."

He held his aim steady. "She was never very nice to me."

"You're shooting everybody who wasn't nice to you?"

BLAM!

A crash of falling glass.

He laughed. "Damn, she's quick! Run, woman!" He put down the rifle and picked up the shotgun, broke it open, and stuck in two shells. Clacked it shut. Turned his aim back toward the front of the school. "Don't look now, but somebody's trying to be a hero." I got my hands over my ears before he fired two massive blasts.

One puny-sounding shot came in answer — it sounded like a cap gun, after all of Tim's firepower.

"Haha, coppa, you'll never take me alive!" he cried in a gangster voice. This is the part I cannot explain about Tim. There he stood with a shotgun, trying to kill a cop, and he was *still* cracking jokes, *still* doing funny accents. Trying to entertain me. Trying to crack me up, jolly me along, get me back on his team.

Arnita.

"Tim, goddammit! Stop! This is Skippy here, Tim. You listen to me. Stop this right now."

He cracked the gun, thumbed in two more shells. "In the words of Cornelius and Sister Rose, *It's too late — to turn back now . . .* Come on Durwood, I'm not gonna stop. I'm up to what — four? Lessee —" He ticked them off on his fingers. "Red, her, the coach, the janitor man —"

"You really thought about this, didn't you? You've been planning this for a while."

He stuck his head around the window jamb, and drew back. "Since I first figured out how much I hate everybody."

"But you don't," I said.

"You don't know, son. Just about everybody." He stuck the rifle out the window and fired off a burst without even aiming. Just to keep them rattled outside. I heard indistinct shouts, but they didn't return fire this time.

"Tim. Listen to me. Everybody's turned against Red. Debbie Frillinger says they all think he's a total asshole for putting that report in all the lockers."

"I know." His eyes gleamed. "And everybody will think this whole thing was his fault, too. They'll think that was my motive, because of what he did to me. He'll get the blame for the whole shebang." His eyes gleamed. "There you go, Skip. That's a good revenge. I told you I had a plan, didn't I? Stick with me and we'll get him, that's what I told you. Don't get me wrong, it was great when you burned up his car — I mean that really got him going, didn't it? The way he upped the ante with his Xerox machine? After that I knew I had no choice but to give him the gift that would keep on giving."

"Timmy. That's crazy. You killed him, isn't that what you said? You can't get any more revenge than that."

"Sure you can. His family will find out what he was. They'll have to live with it."

"What do you mean?"

"I wrote 'em a letter. Told 'em every last cruel, horrible thing their beloved Dudley ever did to us. Mailed it this morning. I wrote you one too."

My eye caught a movement outside, his glance followed mine — he raised the shotgun and fired *blam!* It nearly knocked him off his feet.

A canister sailed in from the front of the school on a tail of whitish smoke. It went way wide of our window and landed in the courtyard, clattering across the pavement to a stop beneath the library windows, where it promptly burst in a cloud of white smoke.

"Holy shit, they're shooting tear gas!" Tim's face lit up. "Durwood, this is the big time! You know what this means, don't you?"

"No."

"Remember Kent State. They always shoot the tear gas right before they storm the location. You better take one of these guns and keep an eye on door number two there where the lovely Carol Merrill is standing."

The smoke cloud swelled and blew away from us, through the open windows of the library and into the cafeteria. A few seconds went by — here came a boy coughing staggering into the courtyard, then two girls and three boys, gagging blind groping out into the air, grabbing at their faces.

Tim steadied his wrist with his other hand and braced the revolver against the window frame.

I couldn't let him do this anymore. I leaned over the desk and picked up the German spy pistol by the grip. The cold metal sent a chill throughout my body. I began to shiver.

"Tim, I'm not gonna let you." I tried to sound firm, but the tremor in my voice was fatal.

He turned to see me pointing the pistol at him. His face broke into a goofy grin. "Oh my God, it's Don Knotts! The shakiest gun in the West! Careful there, Barney, you might shoot yourself."

"I'm not kidding. Put the gun down."

"Oh please," Tim said. "Don't make me laugh. You know you're not gonna shoot that thing."

"I will if I have to. You're not killing anybody else."

He was laughing, shaking his head.

I poked the gun into his ribs. "I swear to God. Put it down. It's over."

He pushed it away. "Durwood, I am so disappointed. The other day in Vicksburg, you said you would die for me."

"This is not what I meant!"

"Well, it is what *I* meant. We're in this together now, son. Your prints are all over that gun. You're in here with me. Nobody's gonna know I was the only one shooting."

"Tim. You're not killing anybody else." I wanted to keep him talking. From the corner of my eye I saw people fleeing through the courtyard while I argued with him.

And here came Mrs. Passworth, grabbing the hand of a ninth-grader, yelling, "What are you doing? Don't you know there's somebody shooting out here? Get your heinie back inside that school!"

Tim cut his eyes back at me. "Heinie," he said with a smirk.

Mrs. Passworth put herself between us and the girl — she had the girl by the arm and was dragging her back to the door.

Tim followed their struggle through his telescopic sight.

"Tim. Please don't. Please."

"You'd think somebody out there would have tried to stop me by now," he said. "These cops are such pussies."

Passworth came out into the courtyard again. She walked to the middle of the open space and cupped her hands over her eyes, squinting across the courtyard at us.

At first I had thought she could see us, but she was in bright sun and we were in the shadows of Mr. Hamm's shot-out office. She began edging toward us.

I said, "She's coming over. Don't hurt her."

Tim swung his gun. "Stop where you are!" he yelled. He fired over her head. The sound hammered my ears.

She stopped. "Who is that in there? Is that Tim?"

"Go back in or I'll kill you, I swear!"

"Well I heard you on the PA, but I didn't want to believe it. Would it be all right if I come in there and talk to you? Just for a minute?"

"No! Get out of here! I mean it! I'll do it!" He turned to me. "Get her out of here!"

"Now, Tim," Passworth said, "you know that what happened to Eddie was not your fault. I never told a soul that was you in that room. Eddie was the one who did wrong. You were a child."

His face twisted into a smirk. "She's out of her mind. Listen to her making shit up."

Passworth peered into the mouth of our cave. "Who's in there with you?"

"Daniel," said Tim.

I tightened my grip on the gun. "I'm trying to get him to stop," I called. "Go on out of here before you get hurt!"

"Now, boys, listen to me — both of you —"

"I tell you something, Skippy." Tim put down the revolver and picked up the rifle. "For once, I know a way to shut her up that is one hundred percent effective."

"No — Tim —"

He hefted the gun to his shoulder and looked into the sight. He shot her as if she meant nothing. He squeezed the trigger. *BLAM!* Mrs. Passworth crumpled to the pavement.

I moved forward swiftly, placed the pistol muzzle against the base of his skull. "I'll blow your brains out, Timmy, I swear to God I will.

Put it down. Put the gun down." Ten seconds ago I had been absolutely sure I could never shoot anybody. Now I could do it in an instant.

Tim closed his eyes. He tilted his head toward me. "Okay." A little smile curved up the right side of his mouth. "I'm turning around now. No sudden moves, Skippy." The rifle clattered to the floor.

The turning of his head dragged the mouth of the barrel across his cheek. When it was almost to his nose he seized my wrist with both hands.

His grip was enormously strong. I thought he might break my arm. He managed to get the pistol barrel turned away from his face. He leaned down and kissed me, hard, on the mouth. "I love you," he said. He forced my hand back the other way. I thought he was trying to shoot me, but he got his mouth around the barrel, got his thumb in between my finger and the trigger, and pushed it.

He blew all over the principal's wall.

29

T IM SLUMPED LEFT and thudded to the floor.

I placed the pistol on the desk beside the revolver. My hand and forearm were spattered with blood. I screamed to the police he was dead, somebody please come help me.

All at once cops were everywhere, pouring in the door behind me and the broken windows in front. One of them jumped on me hard, twisting my right arm behind my back as he tackled me.

I felt the bones in my right arm snap in two places, *snap snap.*

I screamed *Oh you broke my arm!* and the guy on top of me said *Shut up shithead I hope I break your goddamn skull too!*

I can't blame him for thinking I was the shooter. He didn't know what Tim looked like. I was the one still alive in Mr. Hamm's office. Naturally he assumed.

He didn't even seem sorry when he finally got off me and stood me up and saw my arm flopping over at that odd angle. He spread-eagled me against the wall and groped me all over without any gentleness, looking for weapons, my arm shrieking hurting so bad I thought I might puke on the wall.

I tried to tell him I wasn't Tim, that's Tim over there he shot himself, Tim Cousins, it was him doing the shooting, not me, for

God's sake you gotta believe me. I was the one who stopped him! I think I was crying. The man kept shouting *Shut up! Shut up!*

"Watch out, Arthur," the second cop said when the first one tried to put my arms behind me. "Look, you did break his arm. Jesus, man, get off him."

The first cop tugged me up by my good arm. "Sonofabitch shoots up the whole school and you want me to wipe his nose for him?"

"I didn't shoot anybody! It was him! I came in here to stop him. He was my friend. Call Jeff Magill, he's a detective — in Jackson, the sheriff's office. I told him about Tim. I swear, please! You gotta believe me."

I kept stammering all the way from Hamm's office through the cluster of cops at the front entrance, into the patrol car, and on to the emergency room. The doctor gave me a shot straight into the arm between the bones that I thought was the worst pain I would ever endure, until a few minutes later he came back in, grabbed my arm with two hands, and twisted the bones back into place. That crunch scraped the edge of my soul.

One deputy stood on each side of me throughout the procedure. When my arm was encased in hardening plaster and the pain was fading to a dull throb, they put me back in their car and drove me downtown.

I was numb. Not from the shot.

Tim said he loved me. He killed all those people. He wanted to die. But he couldn't bring himself to kill himself. He made me do it. I did not want to think about what this could possibly mean.

They took me up from the parking garage in an elevator that smelled of bleach and piss. They put me in a room with two chairs facing across a square table, a mirrored window set into one wall.

My arm barely hurt anymore, but my whole brain was aching. I rested the cast on my knee and lowered my face into the crook of my other arm.

I couldn't make it unhappen.

It began to dawn on me that those minutes in the library stacks, lost in the broad pages of those architecture books, were to be my last peaceful happy minutes for a long time.

A key clicked in the lock. Jeff Magill came in with an unlit cigarette in his hand, his hair slicked to his head. He looked like someone who had just spent the last hour being screamed at. "Hey, Dan. How's your arm?"

"Okay."

"Does it hurt bad?" His voice was hoarse.

"No."

"I'm sorry they broke it," he said. "They didn't have to do that."

"He thought I was Tim."

He nodded. "That's exactly what he thought."

I didn't remember that little gold cross around his neck. Maybe he'd worn it tucked inside his shirt before.

I said, "Can I ask you a question?"

"I'm the one asking questions today," he said, but then, "Go ahead."

"Tim said he shot Red first, and then — Arnita?"

"That's right."

"Are they both dead?"

He watched me closely. "Yes."

All the air went out of me. I sagged back against the chair. I hadn't known how much I was hoping. I whispered the word "fuck" without thinking it. "Did you see her? I mean — are you sure?"

"Yes," Magill said. "He killed her father too. Why would he want to do that?"

I shook my head.

"Daniel. I know you've got answers for me."

"But I don't know why. He didn't say why. He was just shooting. He said it was fun."

"Fun?"

"Yeah."

"Did that fit y'all's usual definition of fun?"

"No."

"Were you there while Tim was shooting people, Dan?"

He asked it casually, but I sensed that was his most important question so far.

"Only Mrs. Passworth," I said. "He shot the others before I got there. She came out of the cafeteria. To get this kid to go back inside. He just grabbed up the rifle and he — shot her. And I loved her. I mean, she was crazy but — well, you had to know her. And it was just for no reason. She was only trying to talk to him. I put the gun by his head. I told him to stop. That's when he . . ." I ran out of breath.

Magill lit the cigarette. "What?"

"He grabbed the gun. And killed himself."

"Just like that, he just —" He pointed a finger at his mouth and pulled the trigger.

I felt my face heating up. I would rather die than tell him what happened. But I couldn't lie anymore. Tim had blasted away any urge I ever had to lie. Lies were what brought me to this place where I found myself, this room with two chairs, a table, Jeff Magill.

"He kissed me," I said. "And he said, um —"

"What?"

"He said he loved me."

Magill gazed at me evenly. "He ever kissed you before?"

"No."

"Had you two ever —"

"*No.*"

He kept his gaze steady on me. "That's the truth? I don't care if you did or not. A lot of boys do things. Just tell me the truth."

"But I'm not like that. I never even knew he was, until like a week ago."

Magill said, "You think he could have been jealous of the Beecham girl?"

"Why would he be jealous?"

"If he had this attraction to you, maybe he was jealous of her, wanted her dead. Maybe that was the real reason for this thing, more than Red Martin."

"Maybe," I said. "But that's not what he said."

Jeff Magill asked questions, hour after hour. The same questions over and over with new ones thrown in to keep me off balance. I told him the story many times. I tried to remember every last detail.

He never asked if I wanted to speak to a lawyer or go to the bathroom or have a drink of water, or if I minded him blowing smoke in my face. He never said I had the right to remain silent, but I had watched enough *Dragnet* to know that.

Behind the one-way mirror I could sense people coming and going. The sound wasn't masked very well and I could hear the murmur of voices in there.

Every so often Magill went out of the room, and I rested my head on my good arm. I felt so weak. If anyone had asked me to stand up and walk out of there I could not have done it.

He returned with a bulky cassette tape recorder in a brown leather case, like the one Eddie Smock's brother played at the funeral. "Here's what I don't understand," he said. "What if every kid who got picked on by some bully decided to do like Tim? What kind of a screwed-up world would it be? I mean, I believe what you're saying, son, but most of this stuff is just so much bullshit. It's just high school — bullies, and grudges, and crushes, and stupid vendettas, and arguments nobody can even remember how they started. There's not one thing you've told me that's anywhere close to enough to make that boy do all this. You don't go shoot five people and yourself because some asshole picked on you. Maybe you go shoot the asshole. But not five people."

"But if the asshole just ruined your life?" I said. "If he put that report in everybody's locker, so everybody would know what you did? That might do it. If you thought you didn't have anything to lose." How could I explain? I didn't half understand it myself. "His mother thought he was getting better," I said. "I did too."

"Yeah, she's here now. That's what she said."

The idea of Patsy Cousins in this building was vaguely alarming. Poor woman, imagine the state she must be in. Tim used to say one glimpse of a cockroach could put her in bed for a week. How would she ever get through this?

"Who else is here?"

"Your folks. And every reporter in town."

"My mother's here?"

"Yeah, and your father, and your sister."

Wow, Mom, that was fast. She had managed to make it all the way back from Alabama before Jeff Magill ran out of questions to ask.

Oh God what I had done to them.

What Dad would do to me.

It would be bad. I knew that. But his reaction just didn't matter that much to me now. He couldn't hurt me. I couldn't be hurt anymore. He might hit me. I would hit him back. He might kick me out of the house. I would gladly go.

I was exhausted and hollow and my mouth was dry, but I could not bring myself to ask Jeff Magill for even a drink of water. I felt so ashamed. I felt like a criminal in my heart. I hadn't done anything to stop Tim, which meant I'd helped him. I felt enough shame for both of us.

I said, "My father is pissed off, I bet."

"That's not how I'd put it," said Magill. "Okay Dan, I want you to focus. Now you're gonna tell me one more time, from the beginning, just exactly everything you can remember. I want every detail. And I'm going to put it on this tape here, so I want this to be just as full and complete a statement as you can possibly make. You understand?"

"You want me to tell the whole thing again?"

"Absolutely. Every word. Don't leave anything out."

We went over my story, around it, behind and under it, we came out the other side of it. The good thing about not lying is, you don't have to think twice before speaking. All you have to tell is the truth.

At last he pushed STOP on the tape recorder and carried the machine out of the room.

When he came back, he brought Dad with him.

"Son."

"Hey Dad."

"How are you, son?" Of course Dad would show fatherly concern in front of the other man. He would wait to get me alone for the punishment.

"I'm okay," I said.

"Come on, then. Let's go home."

I couldn't believe it. I turned to Magill. "I can go?"

"We need to talk more, but yeah, we've both had enough for one night."

"I'm not under arrest?"

"Son," Dad said. "Will you ever learn to quit while you're ahead?"

Jeff Magill almost smiled. He said, "Listen to your father."

That was exactly what I had trained myself not to do. For the sake of getting out of there I said, "Yes sir. I will."

Mom burst into tears at the sight of me. Janie directed a furious stare at the floor. I could tell she didn't like Mom crying in front of all these strangers.

Jeff Magill led us back through the maze of hallways to the piss-smelling elevator. "Don't go out through the lobby. Go to G-3 and tell the officer on duty you want the Pearl Street door."

"Thank you, officer." Dad shook his hand. "We owe you for your kindness."

"Y'all get some sleep," said Magill. "I'll be out there to see you in the morning. Don't be going anywhere, understand?"

"I understand," Dad said.

The elevator doors slid shut. We rode down six floors without a word from anyone. We stepped out into the dim parking garage. The officer on duty pointed to a door that put us out on the street.

I was surprised to find it so dark outside, so late. Dad had his arm around Mom's shoulders. She wasn't crying now. I lagged a few paces behind, and Janie trailed me. I was wondering if my life would always feel this sad from now on.

We walked up to the corner of Pearl and State. Mom's green station wagon was parked just around the corner. Leaned against the hood was Ella Beecham, all in black, with a wide-brimmed black hat.

Mom said, "Aren't you Arnita's mother?"

"Yes," she said. "I saw your car. I was waiting for you."

"Oh my goodness, you poor thing," Mom said, opening her arms and moving to embrace her.

"Better not to touch me." Mrs. Beecham raised her hands. "Don't take offense. Just — I don't want to be touched."

Mom drew back. "Oh, I am sorry. I understand. I feel so awful for you. She was a lovely girl."

"Yes she was," Ella said. "Musgrove, I see you there hiding behind your mama's skirts."

"I'm not hiding. I'm standing right here."

"The police say they can't tell me anything till they're done investigating," she said. "You got to tell me how my baby died."

I took a deep breath. "I didn't see it. I don't know for sure. But it's all my fault, if that's what you're asking."

Dad gave a snort of disgust, as if I'd just given away the whole game. "Son," he said as a warning.

"Sorry, Dad. It's true. He wouldn't have hurt her if it wasn't for me." I turned to Mrs. Beecham. "They were in the gym. Arnita and Red. He shot Red first, and she tried to stop him. To take his gun away from him. He said she almost did, too. She was strong. So he shot her."

"She was trying to defend that worthless boy?"

"That's what Tim said."

"Why weren't you there looking after her, Musgrove? Where were you? You told me you cared about her."

"I do," I said. "But she didn't like me anymore. She hated me. With good reason. I lied to her the whole time, about the accident. It was us she ran into when she hurt her head. Our car, not Red's. We were the ones who drove off and left her. Not Red. Tim was driving, but it was just as much me as him."

"I know all that," Mrs. Beecham said. "She didn't hate you for that."

That stunned me. "She didn't?"

"No," she said. "But I did. I still do. I got no use for you at all."

"I don't blame you," I said.

"What about Beecham? How did he die? They wouldn't tell me that either."

Instantly I saw two possible answers. One was my new friend, the absolute truth. Mr. Beecham blundered out of his closet with the radio too loud. He died crossing the hall to say hello to me.

I found myself telling my first lie since I promised myself not to lie anymore, just a few hours ago. I told her that Lincoln Beecham ran toward the gym at the first sound of gunfire. He died trying to save Arnita.

"I knew it," she said. "I just needed to be sure." She reached out her hand to touch my shoulder, but decided against it and folded her hands. "Musgrove."

"I'm sorry, Mrs. Beecham. It's all my fault."

"Not all," she said. Then turned and walked away.

Minor Boy Kills 4, Self In Assault At School

By Thomas Noyer
Clarion-Ledger Staff Writer

An 18-year-old Minor High senior shot five classmates and teachers at the school Friday before turning his gun on himself.

Four of the victims were pronounced dead at the scene, law enforcement officials said. Minor head football coach Bryan R. Worrell, 42, remains hospitalized with serious injuries.

The gunman was identified as Timothy Wayne Cousins, a senior honor student at the school, son of Mr. and Mrs. Ronald L. Cousins of the Oakview subdivision. Although authorities would not speculate on a motive for the shootings, Cousins was said by some students to have been upset by recent racial incidents at the mostly white school.

Among the dead were a star football player and a Minor High math teacher, Irene Passworth, 43.

The injured Coach Worrell led the Minor High Titans to their fourth Division B championship last season. Hospital officials said Friday night he was in serious condition following surgery for multiple gunshot wounds.

One of Worrell's star players, Dudley Ronald "Red" Martin, 18, was apparently the first student killed.

Cousins entered the gymnasium at 9:32 a.m. carrying a duffel bag containing a 12-gauge shotgun, a 7.65mm semiautomatic rifle, a pistol, and a revolver. After a brief conversation, witnesses said, Cousins pulled out the shotgun and shot Martin.

Arnita Beecham, 17, who was elected the first black prom queen in the school's history last year, was killed as she tried to intercede for Martin, according to students who witnessed the altercation.

The slain girl's father, Lincoln Beecham, 48, the school's janitor, was shot to death in a hallway a short time later, a police spokesman said.

Earlier in the week, Miss Beecham gave a speech on racial issues that incited a disturbance between white and black students at a school assembly. "She was an extremely bright girl with some confused ideas," said Rollo L. Hamm, principal at Minor since 1963. "She was recovering from a serious accident, and had some trouble adjusting after that. This is a terrible tragedy for our school."

It was unclear at press time what connection Miss Beecham's controversial remarks may have had to the shootings.

After the initial assaults, Cousins began roaming the halls of the school, firing randomly at faculty and students of both races. Panic-stricken students were prevented from fleeing because some of the school's exits had been chained and padlocked, apparently to stop the practice of "cutting classes." Many of the students

RELATED STORIES 2A, 4A

escaped through ground-level windows, while others remained in their classrooms throughout the ordeal.

As multiple units of Minor, Jackson, and Hinds County police responded to the scene, Cousins took up a sniper's position in the principal's office and fired dozens of rounds at arriving officers. One teacher reported that Cousins used the public-address system to taunt terrified students still hiding in the school. "This is fun," he was reported to have said. "This is what I have always wanted to do."

At 10:05 a.m. officers stormed the principal's office and found that the gunman had turned his weapon on himself.

A 17-year-old student was taken into custody at the school and questioned at length but will not be charged, according to Hinds County Sgt. Jeffrey Magill. The boy, a friend of the gunman, went unarmed to the principal's office during the shootings in an attempt to stop the assaults. The student was treated and released from West Mississippi Medical Cen-

ter for minor injuries sustained during the assault. His identity was not disclosed due to his age.

"Tim was a bright kid, a nice quiet kid," said Hamm. "He was different than some of the others, a bit of a loner. He had a rather sarcastic attitude, but he was very intelligent. His art teachers liked him. We were expecting great things from him. Certainly nothing of a violent nature."

Police said Cousins had a prior arrest record, stemming from an incident in November 1972. Because he was a juvenile at the time of that offense, authorities would not release details.

Officials expressed surprise that Cousins managed to assemble a collection of firearms that his parents apparently knew nothing about. "He was not the kind of student who enjoys hunting," said Hamm. "If I had to choose a student who I thought might become violent, (Cousins) would have been at the bottom of the list."

Reached by telephone late Friday, the attacker's father, Ronald Cousins, said he and his wife were praying for the victims and their families. He declined further comment.

30

D AD WOULDN'T LET ME go to the funerals. He said I would
only make it worse for the families by reminding them of
things they wanted to forget. For once, I think, he was right.

For eleven days I lived in my room behind the screen at the Twi-
Lite Drive-In. (Grand opening was postponed until further notice.)
I was allowed to read books but no TV or newspapers. It seemed
strange to be grounded as punishment for Tim shooting five people,
but that was Dad's decision and I didn't fight it.

Dad didn't hit me, yell at me, or lecture me. He didn't ask me
about what happened that Friday at school. He didn't want to hear
about it.

Mom tried to listen but then she would burst out crying. Pretty
soon I stopped talking to her.

Janie couldn't stop asking. I told her everything she wanted to
know. It only seemed fair, after all we'd been through together.

Arnita . . .

I couldn't think of anything but her face for a while, then I lost
track of her face and I was left with nothing but her name. I said it
to myself, over and over. I started having dreams where she sneaked
into my room, my old room in the Freak Annex, while I was sleeping. She climbed in bed with me. I could tell she didn't understand

what had happened to her. Those dreams made me afraid to sleep. I got out of the habit of sleeping.

The letter took a week to arrive — postmarked Friday, August 31, 1973, addressed to "Durwood Musgrove, c/o Twi-Lite Drive-In, US Hwy. 80, Minor, Miss. 39904." I have no idea how he found out where we were living. Maybe he'd followed me to the drive-in when I wasn't looking.

Two sheets of paper, folded in thirds. The first was a drawing of a spooky castle poking up through clouds, a sliver of moon in the dark charcoal sky. The second page was a letter in Tim's careful cursive:

Hey Skippy,

I am alive while I am writing this, but when you read it I'll be dead. PSYCH! You can show it to the cops, or burn it. Up to you. I don't care, I'll be dead.

I bet you will say this action is way too drastic & I shouldn't have done it. I won't argue that, but anyways a few things you should know.

1. My fault you got on Dudley's list, sorry. He only went after you because you were/are my friend.

2. When Red put my report in the lockers, I could have told the whole school about him. He knew I would never tell.

3. Don't drive yourself crazy wondering if this is the truth.

4. I am no better than L. H. Oswald or C. Whitman. I want the world to finally pay attention to me. Let's be realistic, this is the only way that will ever happen. Plus, I can take care of everything in one day and it will be worth it.

5. Everyone on earth is lonely or angry or both. But nobody is listening to anybody. How can 1 person be so alone when there are three billion people on the planet? I didn't want three billion people, Skip. Just you.

Love —

T

PS Did you really think we could get through high school without any casualties?

31

J ACKO'S DEATH WAS the dot at the end of the exclamation point. I thought I'd seen every barbed and sharp weapon fate could fling at me, but when I went to lift him out of bed that cold November morning and found him reduced to a little heap on the edge of the mattress, I found out that death is not a thing you get done with. Not ever. It keeps coming at you like a train, it comes on, it won't ever stop, it has all the momentum in the world. First it takes out all the people standing on the tracks in front of you, then you are the only one on the tracks and the train keeps driving toward you, it just keeps coming, it never slows down.

Jacko had pulled the sheet up over his own face. When I pulled it away, he was so unearthly white that I jumped back, off balance, and fell to the floor.

I yelled *Mom!* She came running. Three days later we were standing around a hole in the iron-red Alabama dirt, the graveyard of Mount Zion Methodist outside Pigeon Creek, the plot next to Granny's, as Preacher Bynum recited the Twenty-third Psalm.

When he got to the valley of the shadow of death I heard footsteps in the gravel behind me. I turned to find a man approaching, a big burly Marine in dress uniform, removing his hat as he came. Blocky head. Reddish prickle of hair on his scalp.

My first thought was: Buddy is dead, and this man has come to notify us.

And then I saw that this was Bud.

We hadn't seen him in a year. He'd sent a few postcards since basic training, always some view of a beach in California.

He strode to the graveside and wrapped Mom in a big hug. I thought she might faint with joy. Buddy was her favorite. Her eyes shone with pure admiration for the big muscled soldier the Marines had made of him. Dad straightened up, flushed with pride to have a son who looked this fine.

Bud's arrival caused such a stir that the preacher had to go back to the beginning of the verse and start again.

Afterward we crowded into the fellowship hall to eat ham, pimiento cheese, potato salad, deviled eggs. Buddy was mobbed by old ladies who could not get enough of his uniform, hugging and squeezing and stroking as if he were a big old GI Joe doll.

I fixed a plate and took it off to a corner, by myself. Some old lady came over and tried to talk to me but I didn't talk. Soon she went away.

I looked at the food and decided I didn't want any of it. I threw my whole paper plate full in the garbage. Another old lady told me throwing food away was a sin.

Oh lady, I thought. If you only knew. That is the least of it.

When people are murmuring your name trying not to be heard, you can't help but hear it. Your name hums and bites at you like a mosquito. I heard the general buzz, *Daniel* that's right wasn't he *Daniel* involved with that terrible oh my God *Daniel* how awful they say he's handling it fairly well considering *Daniel* weren't they supposed to be close? Shot five but how many died? I don't know, I'm afraid to ask.

"Well if it ain't the Murderer's Best Friend." Buddy flung his arms around me for a quick, hard hug. "What the hell have you been up to, brother? Wait, don't tell me. I heard."

"Your timing is perfect," I said. "One look at you, and everybody forgot it was a funeral."

"I was late, I'm sorry. Don't give me crap about it, okay? I just traveled ten thousand miles to see about you. Are you okay? Seriously."

"Never been better," I said.

"Don't give me that, Danny. I couldn't get here when it happened. This is as soon as I could come and not go AWOL, all right? I'm sorry."

"It's not like I was expecting you," I said.

"Nobody told me you were in anywhere near that kind of trouble. Or I'd have figured a way to get you the hell out of here. Have you been in school, or what?"

"No, no school." I wanted another subject. "How are you doing, Buddy? How's California?"

"Actually my platoon is in Saigon right now," he said. "We're going up to Dien Bien Phu when I get back. Don't tell Mom. She'd freak out."

"Are you kidding me?"

"No. And shut up about it, okay? I mean it." He gripped my arm. He knew me and my big mouth.

I said, "Do you really have to go back?"

"Oh, yeah. Monday. My CO had to move fuckin' heaven and earth to get me here."

"Jesus, Bud. I didn't know you were — I thought you hurt your foot."

"That's what I told Mom."

"Don't go back, Bud. Stay here."

"Wish I could, brother. I signed the paper. Don't worry about it. Listen, how's Dad?" he said, with a brotherly inflection meaning, How bad has he been lately?

I shrugged. "I guess you heard he went into the movie business."

"Yeah. Everybody down here seems to have flipped out in their own individual way. I bet he nearly killed you when all that happened, huh?"

"Surprisingly not," I said. "He mostly just leaves me alone since then. I think they're kind of afraid of me."

"Mom says you haven't spoken a word to them since it happened."

"What am I supposed to say? You got any suggestions? Really. If I could think of anything."

He clapped his hand on my shoulder. "Damn, Danny. I am so sorry that happened to you. How the hell did you get mixed up with that crazy-ass son of a bitch?"

"That's not how he was," I said. "You had to know him, Buddy, he was a normal guy. He was great, he was funny . . . you would have liked him. He just — he had too much going on inside, I guess. Too many secrets."

"But why'd he flip out? What made him do that?"

"God. That's a long story. I don't think you have time."

"I told you, that's why I'm here."

Dad walked over. "Okay, boys, pack it up and get in the car. We are officially leaving."

Bud frowned. "Dad, I'm only on my second plate."

"Well, fill it up again and put a piece of foil on it. We are hitting the road," Dad said. "*Now.*"

We were too old to leap at the sound of his bark, but we did get up from where we were sitting because he had the keys, he was Dad, and it was easier not to fight him. We said goodbye to cousins, uncles, and aunts. Suddenly everyone was crying again, not for Jacko but for the trouble I was in, the notoriety I had brought down upon us all. At least that's how it felt to me from all the tears and the long squeezing hugs that were meant to console me but only made me want to run and hide.

Janie was still out under the canopy at the graveside, weeping. She was the one who would miss Jacko the most. She had spent hours sitting with him, entertaining him with her magic tricks, listening to his stories of driving around in his goat cart. Now that he was safely in the ground, Dad was jingling keys in his pocket, ready to get the hell out of there.

I'd had enough death to last me the rest of my life. I followed the family down the church steps. Mom complained how rude it was for us to be leaving already, when people had come from all over two states to hug our necks and give us comfort in our time of need. "If you're so almighty anxious to leave, Lee, you should damn well go ride around and come back when we're ready to go," she said. "Remember what you promised on the phone."

Dad ambled toward the car. "How about the kids and I go home, and you stay here with your precious relatives? You seem to like 'em better than us anyway." He glanced at Janie. Her head was trapped in the crook of Buddy's arm, where she was receiving a Dutch rub. "Hey Janie, tell your mother we got along just fine without her."

"Don't be silly, Daddy," she said, breaking free of Bud. "You were a disaster."

"Thank you, Janie," said Mom. "I'm glad someone in this family appreciates me."

"Hey Mom, I do too," said Bud.

"Of course you do, Buddy, you've always been so good to me," Mom said. "And Daniel is sweet as can be."

Oh yes. Thanks for thinking of me.

I opened the tailgate and climbed in the back where the dog of the family rides. Where Jacko used to ride, so he could see out the back window. Everybody else got in front. I stretched out the length of the wheel well and tried to mold myself into the plastic panel, to become part of the car. Maybe you think I was too old to be playacting like that. All I can say is, nobody tried to stop me.

"Turn the radio up, Daddy," called Janie. "They're talking about the flying saucers."

The airwaves of Mississippi had crackled with UFO reports since the October 11 incident at Pascagoula. Two men called Charlie and Calvin were fishing on a riverbank when they said a mysterious blue-glowing spacecraft landed and took them aboard for physical examinations. The two men were so convincingly traumatized that the police believed their story, and within days a full-fledged UFO craze was sweeping the South. Charlie and Calvin had already appeared on *Merv Griffin* and *The Dick Cavett Show*.

I lay back listening to the latest report, aching for Mrs. Passworth. If she had lived another few weeks, she might have been a star.

Dad pulled onto U.S. 80, headed west toward Mississippi. Bud would ride with us to Minor for the weekend, then we'd drive him to the base at Biloxi for his return hop.

Mom turned down the radio and rolled down her window. "I know I shouldn't be happy today, but I can't help it. I've got all my chillun in one car again. I tell you something, Lee, it'll feel good to be home."

"Listen at you, Peg. You swore you'd never set foot in the drive-in again, and here you are calling it home. All I can say is, don't get too attached."

Mom pondered a minute. "What is that supposed to mean?"

"Oh, nothing," Dad said. "Why? Do I seem suspicious to you?"

"All of a sudden you do." She turned her fish-eye on him. "What have you done? Lee? Oh, God, what on earth?"

Bud said, "Y'all. I'm just back for one weekend. Can you please not start up squabbling right this minute?"

Dad ignored him. "I wasn't going to tell you today, what with the sad occasion and all."

"Tell me what," Mom said.

"I've got a little surprise in store for this family."

Oh no. Please, no. The last time Dad said something like that, he blew up the house.

"Is this about your drive-in movie, Dad?" Bud said. "I want you to show me how to run the projector."

"We're not going to be showing any movies," Dad said. "Change of plan."

"What do you mean?" Janie glanced at me, horrified — the hours we'd spent helping Dad fix up that place!

"I looked at one of the movies that man sent over," said Dad. "The one with Marlon Brando? If that's what the pictures are like today, I tell you, I don't want no part of it. I declare, you couldn't eat buttered popcorn and watch a thing like that. So I put the ol' drive-in up for sale. And got me a buyer, like that." He snapped his fingers.

Disappointed groans from Janie and Bud.

"Okay, but your dumb old daddy not only unloaded the place, I got five thousand *more* than I paid. How you like that?"

"Oh happy day," Mom said. "Thank God you didn't have to take less."

"The man wants to build some kind of indoor shopping center right at that interchange," he said. "Turns out your simple-minded old dad landed us on a prime piece of commercial real estate. Can I hear somebody say, 'Way to go, Dad'?"

"Way to go, Dad," said Bud, and Janie said, "Yay, Dad." I didn't say anything.

Dad said, "Not only is your husband a real-estate genius, Peg. I called up old Charlie Fabricant and told him I was halfway thinking of getting back in the chemical business. He practically begged me to come back. It took some sweet-talking, but he finally got me to say yes."

Mom turned full around in her seat. "You didn't!"

"I did! We're a TriDex family again!"

"Oh dear Lord," Mom cried. "Oh Lee, tell me you're not fooling. Did you get your retirement back?"

"Every penny," he said. "Like I never even quit."

He hadn't quit, of course, he'd been fired. And if he'd been re-hired, I know it was not Charlie Fabricant who had done the begging. A few weeks ago I would have had something smart to say about it, but since I had become a molded plastic piece of the wheel well, I chose not to offer an opinion.

"You hate Charlie," Mom said. "You swore you'd never work for him again."

"That's the beauty part," said Dad. "I'm getting a new territory, a whole different district, so I won't have to report to that son of a gun."

"What territory?"

He put on a hopeful smile. "Provo, Utah!"

"*Utah?*" You could have scored glass with her voice.

"There's a booming market for ag chemicals out there," he said.

"They're growing cherries and apricots, and pears, and barley. Climate's supposed to be real nice. Schools are great."

"That's a million miles from anywhere," said Mom, "and anyway, aren't they all Mormons? We're not Mormons."

"Well, that's where we're going," he said. "This new manager Herman Foley seems like more of a straight shooter. At least that's the impression I got on the telephone. Hopefully he's the kind of man that doesn't stab you in the back."

"Dad. Y'all can't move to Utah," said Bud. "I've flown over Utah. It's nothing but rocks."

"They grow alfalfa out there," said Dad. "And they've got a lot of mink farms. Do you know how much malathion it takes to keep down the red ants on a mink farm?"

"There's not even a road across Utah," Bud said. "There's not a blade of grass. I seriously doubt they have cherries."

Mom said, "I hope they have good divorce lawyers out there."

Janie said, "I've never been west of Vicksburg. I think I would love to go to Utah."

"Trust me, you wouldn't," said Bud.

Janie said, "Danny? What do you think?"

Why was she asking me? Did she think I might answer? If she really knew me, she would not be talking to me.

I was thinking about the real reason Dad begged for his job back. If we did move to Utah it would not be for the mink farms or the cherries. It would be for me. For my sake. To get me the hell out of Mississippi.

For the first time in our lives, Dad was putting me ahead of everyone else. He knew I could not keep living in Mississippi, after everything that had happened. Dad was not the kind of man who believed in ghosts, but he knew you don't hang around the graveyard when the funeral is over and the sun is going down.

I would thank him, someday, when I decided to start speaking again.

"Leave him be," Mom was saying. "He'll talk when he's ready. He knows we love him, and nobody blames him for anything that might have happened."

Dad muttered, "Okay, buster, don't flash your dadgum lights at me, I'll move over when I'm good and dang ready." He cut so sharply into the right lane that I slid and banged my head on the wheel well. Sat up rubbing my head as a Starlite Blue Pinto zoomed past our old green station wagon. I hadn't imagined there was more than one Starlite Blue Pinto in the world with those particular pinstripes. There went a shiny one, zooming ahead in the left lane, leaving me in the dust.

ABOUT THE AUTHOR

MARK CHILDRESS was born in Monroeville, Alabama, and grew up in Ohio, Indiana, Mississippi, Louisiana, and Alabama. Childress is the author of five previous novels and three children's books. His articles and reviews have appeared in the *New York Times, Los Angeles Times, Times* of London, *San Francisco Chronicle, Saturday Review, Chicago Tribune, Philadelphia Inquirer, Salon, Travel and Leisure,* and other national and international publications. He lives in New York City.